Refuse
to Sink

Second Chances in
Sapphire Cove

Refuse to Sink

USA Today Bestselling Author

LINDZEE ARMSTRONG

"Happily ever after is not a fairy tale. It's a choice."
—*Fawn Weaver*

CHAPTER One

$\mathcal{M}$eredith rolled to face John's side of the bed, clutching his pillow to her chest in a fierce hug. The faint spice of his aftershave lingered on the fabric, mixed with a pleasantly earthy musk that was uniquely him. She squeezed her eyes shut, feeling her throat tighten in a way that was becoming all too familiar. Her eyes burned like she'd rubbed every grain of Oregon sand into them.

Six days ago, she'd made a simple entry in her calendar for this morning—*Meet plumber @ 9am*. It was yet another bullet point in a long list of problems that were making her photography studio financially underwater, but at least one she knew how to fix. The first year of a new business was never easy, and she had a binder full of ideas to turn it profitable that she was eager to try.

One hour after making that entry, her husband, John, had collapsed in the back room of that photography studio and had never gotten back up.

What she wouldn't give to spend this morning bored and annoyed, waiting for a tardy plumber, instead of holding back sobs at her husband's funeral.

Get out of bed, she commanded herself. She'd been feeling under the weather for a few days before John's collapse—like she had eaten something off, or maybe had a stomach bug—and becoming a widow hadn't improved her health. *Move, Meredith.*

But she couldn't make her muscles obey even the simplest instructions. They remained rigid and stiff, stubbornly clamped around the pillow that still smelled like John.

If she wanted to look her best today—like she was trying and hadn't fallen apart—she needed to get moving. John would want her to put one foot in front of the other. More than once they'd talked about what she should do if he died. When he'd been a Navy SEAL, that threat had always loomed large.

She'd just assumed that, once he left the SEALs, the risk was over.

Who had a brain aneurysm at twenty-nine years old? He'd always been the picture of health. Even after leaving the military almost two years ago, he'd maintained a vigorous physical fitness routine. Had it been the stress of running two businesses—her photography studio and his scuba shop?

If she'd made him go in for that physical six months ago, maybe there would have been warning signs, like sudden high blood pressure. When he'd complained of headaches over the last couple of months, she should have listened instead of teasing him about needing glasses.

A knock sounded at the door, pulling Meredith out of her spiraling thoughts.

Get up, she commanded herself again. What time was it? How much longer did she have to get ready?

Would they start the funeral without the grieving widow?

She pried open her eyes and the blurry green numbers on John's alarm clock came into focus. It was a few minutes after eight. Hopefully, the plumber wasn't on his way to the studio—she couldn't remember if she'd canceled the appointment.

John would have already been up, his perpetual cheeriness driving her crazy. She wasn't a morning person, but his years in the military had trained him to be one. The faint splash of water from the shower would have slowly lulled her into wakefulness, and—if she didn't get out of bed quickly enough—John would have yanked the covers off her with a cackle.

She had always hated that. Would let out a growl of frustration and stick out her tongue. But then he'd hover over her, arm muscles taut as he rained kisses across her face until she was laughing.

What she wouldn't give to have him yank those covers off her one more time. How could he really be gone? Her stomach churned, bile rising in her throat until she jerked upright, a hand pressed to her lips.

Another knock sounded, this one longer and more insistent. "Mer, honey? It's Vanessa. Let me in, okay?"

The sound of her best friend's voice finally convinced Meredith to let go of John's pillow. Her toes curled against the cool tile floor, the early-September air already brisk. She'd inherited this beach bungalow after her grandmother's passing five years ago—about a year before meeting John—and had always hated the tile. The grout lines between the cracked pink ceramic squares always looked dirty, no matter how hard she scrubbed.

John had promised replacing the flooring would be the next stop on their remodel journey. He, Sawyer, and Zach had been trying to find a weekend when they were all free for the job. The three men were more than friends. They were like brothers. Over the past few years, they'd become Meredith's family every bit as much as they were John's.

She padded to the front door and swung it open to reveal Vanessa looking pretty in a simple black dress with a dark coat draped over one arm. The dress was fitted, with three-quarter length sleeves and a hemline that just brushed Vanessa's knees.

Meredith's heart dropped, nausea clawing at her throat once more. She hadn't even thought of a dress. Didn't own a single one in black. There was a dark navy number she sometimes wore to church, but it had bright pink hibiscus flowers embroidered across the skirt—hardly appropriate for a funeral.

What had she worn when burying her grandma? That was the last funeral she'd attended. She had a vague recollection of donating the dress to a church charity sale because she hadn't liked the memories associated with it.

"I thought you might want some help getting ready." Vanessa's lips turned up in a sad smile. She'd pulled her caramel brown hair back into a simple bun at the base of her neck and wore only the barest traces of makeup.

Meredith leaned against the doorframe. She couldn't remember the last time she'd felt this exhausted—not even after the grueling two-hour photo shoot she'd done last month with an extended family of thirty, including five babies. "I couldn't get out of bed."

"I figured. Can I come in?"

Meredith nodded, stepping aside. "How long do we have?"

"Not quite two hours. I didn't want you to have to rush."

Meredith pinched the bridge of her nose and took a deep breath. There was so much to do to get ready. She needed to shower and especially needed to wash her hair—she couldn't remember the last time she'd done that. Probably should curl it. Definitely needed to apply makeup, even if she would cry it all off. And there was still the matter of something to wear.

Did she own a pair of nylon stockings, or would she need to shave her legs? She tried to remember what else she had in her closet. Maybe she could wear that long black skirt with her dark gray top. The top was a little casual for a funeral, the skirt a little boho, but at least she wouldn't have to shave. It was a better option than the dark blue dress with bright pink flowers.

"Come here." Vanessa draped her coat over the edge of the couch, then pulled Meredith to her in a tight hug.

The front door still stood wide open, inviting every fly in Sapphire Cove to take up residence in the tiny bungalow. Meredith didn't care. She pressed her face into Vanessa's shoulder, trying to hold back her tears so they wouldn't mar the fabric. Had it really only been a few years ago that their roles were reversed?

Vanessa's husband had been a military man, too—active-duty Army—and killed in action. After hearing the news, Meredith had hopped the first plane to South Carolina and spent two weeks helping her best friend pick up the pieces of her life.

"I don't know where my iron is," Meredith mumbled. "My skirt is probably wrinkled. And I'm not sure if my gray top is clean."

John had died on laundry day, and her hampers were still overflowing. She also had never made a flyer for the studio's back-to-school sale and still had about ten photos to edit from a lifestyle photo shoot she'd done two weeks ago. Despite having only a handful of photos left to edit, she hadn't been able to so much as open her laptop.

"I brought you a dress." Vanessa held out her arm, revealing a black garment bag draped over it that Meredith hadn't noticed before. "Linda told me to take three sizes, just in case. I'll return the others tomorrow."

Meredith pressed a hand to her lips. "That was really nice of her."

But that was Sapphire Cove. Her fridge currently burst with the generosity of the townspeople. Linda's Boutique was the only clothing shop in town and just three doors down from John's shop, King Trident Scuba Diving.

But it isn't John's shop anymore, Meredith realized with a fresh wave of grief. *It's mine.* Zach and Sawyer owned a percentage, too, but they'd both taken a step back over the past year as they focused on their own ventures, and she knew they wouldn't have put up a fight if John had wanted to sell.

What do I want? The question felt like a plea. Not to be crushed under an ever-increasing mountain of debt would be nice. She kept busy as a photographer during the summer months, when tourists were eager for family photos on the beach. But her studio didn't get near the traffic she'd hoped for and the overhead was higher than she'd expected. John's scuba shop hadn't exactly been a smashing success, either. Few came to coastal Oregon for scuba diving, but John hadn't wanted to give up. Only weeks ago, he'd mentioned branching out to include whale watching tours, something he'd planned to bring up to Sawyer and Zach after he did more research, and at the beginning of the year he'd started taking classes online to work toward his business degree.

Meredith stared at Vanessa, panic making her entire body icy. What would become of both businesses now? The monthly payments on their small business loans weren't cheap. Since they were self-employed, health insurance premiums were astronomical and covered next to nothing. She and John hadn't seen the need for life insurance once he left the Navy, since they were both so young.

"I—" Meredith couldn't get out anything else. *I can't do this. I don't know how to exist without John. I don't want to spend today burying my husband.*

Vanessa handed Meredith the garment bag, her expression understanding. "One thing at a time. Go get ready and I'll make you something to eat, okay?"

"I'm not hungry."

"I know, but I'm going to make you breakfast, anyway."

Meredith ran a thumb over the logo on the garment bag. The last thing she wanted right now was food, but Vanessa was right. Hadn't she woken up early the morning of Vanessa's husband's funeral to make pancakes and feed little Grayson while Vanessa got ready? "Thanks."

Meredith zoned out in the shower, her mind going blessedly blank as the hot water soothed her aching muscles.

But soon the steam made her light-headed, so she turned off the water and reached for a towel.

The thought of blow drying and curling her sun-bleached blonde hair was exhausting, but she made herself do it, anyway. Then she applied a little eyeshadow and blush before getting dressed. Vanessa had chosen well and the conservative black dress hugged Meredith's waist in a flattering way before flaring gently at the hips. Vanessa had even included a pair of pantyhose and low-heeled black pumps, which was a relief because Meredith hadn't been able to work up the energy to shave her legs.

One last touch and she'd be ready. Meredith opened the lid of her jewelry box and stared at the necklace nestled inside. The pendant, a coiled rope twisted around a boat anchor, was about the size of a silver dollar. She ran a thumb over the words etched into the thin bar across the top. *Refuse to sink.*

Three months into dating, John had revealed he was a Navy SEAL. The revelation had pulled the rug right out from under her. She'd already fallen for him hard, but hadn't known if she was cut out for the rigors of military life. How was she supposed to cope knowing that every time he left on a mission, it could be his last? It had been hard enough to spend time apart when she'd thought he was just a run-of-the-mill seaman stationed on a ship somewhere in the middle of the ocean.

Breaking up had seemed like the only option. She'd told John as much, but he said he wasn't giving up on them that easily. Instead, he'd given her this necklace and explained how the anchor represented his job with the SEALs, and how the words represented his faith in her ability to be strong when he was gone.

That was the moment she'd known she would marry him.

Meredith stared at the anchor, then fastened the chain around her neck with trembling fingers.

The smell of warm toast and freshly cooked eggs pulled her toward the dining room. Vanessa stood at the stove in the small kitchen, one of Grandma's vintage aprons protecting her black dress.

"You look beautiful," Vanessa said, her eyes sweeping down Meredith's form. "The dress fits great."

Meredith smoothed down her skirt. "Don't let me forget to thank Linda. I left the other two sizes hanging in the garment bag in my room."

"I'll grab it from you later." Vanessa turned to the fridge, swinging it open wide. "Do you want apricot or peach jam on your toast? Ooh, or plum. Looks like the church ladies are keeping you well-stocked."

Just the thought of food had Meredith's stomach revolting. "I don't know if I can eat."

"At least try. How about peach jam?" Vanessa grabbed another apron. "Here, put this on so you don't get your dress dirty."

Vanessa was in full-on mom mode. Meredith put on the apron and grabbed the butter from the cupboard. It was easier than protesting again. "Is Grayson with your parents?"

Vanessa nodded, popping the lid on the peach jam. Meredith wrinkled her nose at the smell. She'd never been a big fan of homemade jam, preferring more savory options like bagels and cream cheese.

"Dad's going to stay home with him so Mom can come. I didn't want today to bring back any bad memories."

Bad memories of his own father's funeral. Compassion welled within Meredith, along with a whole new empathy for Vanessa's situation. As hard as today was, it could be worse. At least she didn't have to tell her child that his father was dead.

For the first time in more than a year, she was grateful for John's insistence they wait to have a baby. After spending his formative years being bounced from one foster home to another, he'd wanted to wait until their businesses were stable—and, by extension, their finances—before bringing a child into this world.

"Today won't be easy for you, either," Meredith whispered. "Thanks for coming anyway, Ness."

"I would never let you go through this alone." Vanessa busied herself spreading jam on the toast. "We've got about twenty minutes until Sawyer gets here. That should be enough time to eat."

"He'll be early." Meredith took a deep breath, the smell of eggs making her queasy. "Are Zach and Cheyenne at the church?"

"Yes. The funeral home has everything ready, and it looks beautiful."

Meredith accepted the plate of food from Vanessa, gratitude mixing with her grief.

"Cheyenne said there's already a decent crowd gathering," Vanessa continued. "I'm sure half the town will come to offer their condolences."

Meredith nodded again. She'd lived in Sapphire Cove—in this very house—her entire life. Had been raised by grandparents who'd lived here their entire lives, too, after her mother died from an overdose without ever revealing her deadbeat father's name. John had wholeheartedly embraced this town, and they'd embraced him right back.

"Eat." Vanessa motioned to the plate. "Before the eggs get cold."

Meredith obediently took a bite, holding back a grimace. Grief had always affected her appetite. She'd been crushed by each of her grandparents' deaths and for months afterward, eating had been a chore.

Losing John hurt so much more than losing either of her elderly grandparents.

Meredith forced another forkful of eggs down, following it up with a bite of too-sweet toast. How could she do it—walk into that church and keep her composure while everyone told her how much they'd loved John? What a tragedy it was to lose him in the prime of his life?

She knew the truth. For most of the town, life would go on after today. For her, time had stopped with John's last breath.

As the ambulance raced to the hospital while the paramedics worked feverishly, she'd sent Sawyer and Zach a frantic text. Zach and Cheyenne had been shopping an hour away, but Sawyer had rushed to the hospital and been with her when the doctor came into the waiting room, face solemn.

Meredith had collapsed against Sawyer before the doctor even spoke. She didn't need to hear the words. His face had said it all.

I'm sorry, Mrs. Gilbert. We did everything we could.

The memories were too much. Meredith bolted for the bathroom, barely making it to the toilet before she lost the contents of her stomach.

Vanessa was beside her in an instant, holding back her hair and murmuring sympathetic platitudes. Meredith's stomach heaved again while her cheeks burned with humiliation.

She flushed the toilet and grabbed a tissue, wiping her mouth. "Sorry about that."

Vanessa's expression was pained. "Don't apologize. I threw up the morning of Andrew's funeral, too."

Somehow, that eased Meredith's embarrassment. "You did?"

Vanessa nodded. "In the bathroom at the church. No one knew."

The doorbell rang, interrupting their conversation.

"It's probably Sawyer," Vanessa said. "I'll get it while you clean up."

Meredith brushed her teeth and reapplied her lipstick, the deep murmur of Sawyer's voice from the front room calming her anxiety. She carefully removed the apron and looked at herself in the mirror.

Her eyes were ringed by dark circles, her skin even paler than usual. John would have kissed her on the temple, wrapped his arms around her waist, and insisted he still found her beautiful.

She clutched her anchor pendant, rubbing a thumb over the etched words.

Refuse to sink, she commanded herself. She could do this. She had no other choice.

Sawyer stood in the front entryway, his feet shoulder-width apart and hands clasped together as he spoke to Vanessa in a low voice. Meredith paused, the sight of him in full military uniform making her heart twist. As the wife of a Navy SEAL, she'd imagined this moment. Wondered what it would feel like to wear a black dress and attend her husband's funeral, surrounded by men in uniform.

It also reminded her of John on their wedding day. Had that been the last time she'd seen him in his dress uniform?

No. That had been yesterday at the funeral home during the viewing.

Sawyer pulled her to him and she sank into his hug, clinging to his chest the way she had at the hospital. Maybe, if she could just hold on to her friends, she'd make it through today.

"Thanks for coming," Meredith said.

As much as she loved Vanessa—as much as she needed her today—she needed Sawyer, Zach, and Cheyenne even more. Vanessa hadn't known John. Had only met him once at their wedding. But Sawyer and Zach—her family—had fought alongside him. Had saved his life repeatedly, just as he'd saved theirs.

"Of course." A muscle in Sawyer's jaw twitched, as though he were fighting back tears. "Are you ready to go?"

Ready? A panicked laugh bubbled up inside her. She'd only had four years with John—barely longer than a heartbeat. When he'd been a SEAL, she'd accepted that on some level. But in the almost two years since he'd gone civilian, she'd started counting their future together in decades.

"I can't believe this is happening." She blinked rapidly, trying to hold back the choking grief.

"No one's going to rush you, Mer. Take all the time you need."

Time. Like waiting another ten minutes would make burying her husband any easier.

Meredith rubbed a thumb over her pendant. "Let's go."

CHAPTER Two

*C*emeteries shouldn't be so peaceful.

Sawyer stood stiffly, his feet spread shoulder-width apart and hands clasped in front of his buttoned uniform jacket. The September air was warm enough to make the layers uncomfortable, but Sawyer didn't acknowledge that. He was too focused on the sound of chirping birds in nearby pine trees. The almost inaudible crash of waves in the distance.

The shuffle of feet as mourners shifted their weight.

He'd seen more than his fair share of death. Caused a lot of it, too. Death wasn't quiet or calm. It was gunshots and violence and pain. It was adrenaline making the senses sharp and an almost animalistic urge to kill or be killed.

A butterfly flitted near the casket, its wings a vibrant red—the color of freshly spilled blood.

He closed his eyes, taking a steadying breath. When he'd received Meredith's text, it had felt like resurfacing too fast from a dive. He, Zach, and John had always known that chances were high all three of them wouldn't make it to old age. But Sawyer had never once considered that death might come early, even after they left the SEALs.

In fact, that was *why* John had left the Navy. Why Zach had left. Neither of them had wanted to make their wives young widows.

Sawyer's gaze strayed to Meredith. Long blonde hair hung halfway down her back in loose curls and a tasteful black dress lent an elegance to her grief. She stood tall, her back straight and chin raised—a Navy wife to the bitter end. Vanessa and Cheyenne stood on either side of her, their shoulders nearly touching in a silent show of support. Sorrow radiated from Meredith like a tsunami of regret.

He swallowed back his emotions and tried to focus on Pastor Blake's words of comfort.

Watching Meredith marry his best friend had been nothing compared to this pain.

"I have to quit the SEALs," John had told Sawyer. *"The thought of leaving Meredith alone kills me. I won't do that to her."*

Sawyer had understood what John meant. Agreed with him, even. When Zach had decided to leave the SEALs with John, Sawyer had made the only choice he could—to go with his family. Not the blood relatives with substance abuse problems who had used, abused, and abandoned him over the years, but the family he and his friends had formed themselves.

Meredith shifted, distracting Sawyer as her low heels sank into the soft grass. The canopy erected over the few seats surrounding the grave had prevented the morning dew from burning off, keeping the ground soggy with moisture despite the sunny day. Bright rays streaked across the American flag covering the casket and glinted off the exposed dark gray edges.

How could John be dead? Only eight days ago, they'd played basketball together with Zach at the local community center. John had ribbed Sawyer about his latest date, this one with a pharmacy tech he'd met on an online dating site. It hadn't gone well, and John and Zach kept asking Sawyer when he would stop going on first dates and go on a second one.

Sawyer had ignored them, gone home, and set up another first date. No one could measure up to Meredith, but John and Zach didn't know that, and Sawyer was determined to try. He wanted to get married. Wanted someone to come home to at night, like his best friends had. Longed for a good woman to share his life with.

So, Sawyer had arranged to meet a yoga instructor for coffee during lunch today. Now he was at his best friend's funeral instead.

Meredith brushed a hand under her eyes as Pastor Blake droned on. She looked pale—unusual, since her skin typically sported a healthy glow from all the time she spent doing photo shoots outdoors. He thought he saw her sway and almost reached out to steady her. But then Vanessa wrapped an arm around her waist, and Sawyer relaxed.

Today would be hard for Meredith. Hard for all of them. Sawyer would give anything to make this easier for her. Would trade places with John in a heartbeat if he could.

Meredith leaned into Vanessa, their heads nearly touching. On her other side, Cheyenne took Meredith's hand and gave it a gentle squeeze. The uniform cap shaded Zach's eyes, but

Sawyer watched his Adam's apple bob up and down as he fought back the emotions.

Sawyer blinked quickly, clenching his own hands into fists. He wanted to fall to his knees and scream at the sky that this wasn't fair. John had been too young, too healthy, too *vibrant* to die.

He should be here, bombarding Sawyer with texts requesting help with his latest home project. Checking to see if they were still on for their weekly basketball game. Inviting him over for dinner because Meredith had a new recipe she wanted to try.

The five of them had planned to get together for a Labor Day barbecue the night John died. Sawyer had thrown away the apple pie he'd bought at Baylor's Diner without taking a bite.

The pastor finished speaking and seamen stepped forward to lift the flag from the casket. Sawyer braced himself for the rifle volley, heart squeezing with each shot. But when the bugler began playing Taps, he couldn't stop his eyes from filling with tears.

Maybe he shouldn't have left the SEALs. Sawyer had loved being a sailor, in wartimes and in peace. He just loved his family more.

Meredith's shoulders shook as the seaman stepped forward and presented the folded flag to her. She accepted it, head held high as tears streamed down her disconcertingly pale face. Her eyes were ablaze with resolution, her jaw set in a fierce determination not to fall apart.

Sawyer bit the inside of his cheek, fighting to hold back his own tears. John would have been so proud of how she was handling today.

The Navy chaplain read from the Bible, then they all bowed their heads. Sawyer didn't hear a single word of the prayer, but eventually a chorus of amens rose on the breeze.

They'd done it. Survived the funeral and graveside. Now if only he knew how they'd survive the next fifty or sixty years without John.

Throngs of mourners stepped forward to offer Meredith their sympathies. The graveside was nearly as crowded as the church had been. It was heartwarming to see how much John had meant to others, and Sawyer was glad Meredith had so much support.

He stayed close by as she graciously accepted their condolences, his concern growing as her face grew paler with every passing moment. What would John want Sawyer to do for her right now? Years ago, not long after John had proposed, he'd made Sawyer promise he would watch out for Meredith if the worst happened. Sawyer had balked at the request, the idea of his friend dying too horrible to imagine. Now he felt the weight of that promise.

If only he could protect Meredith from this pain.

The minutes ticked by like hours, but eventually, the townspeople left. Vanessa wrapped an arm around Meredith's waist, the two of them clinging to each other. Cheyenne stood in front of Zach, his arms wrapped tightly around her as she leaned into his embrace.

Sawyer stood alone. He swallowed, thinking of his empty apartment. Meredith had been so happy he was leaving the SEALs and moving to Sapphire Cove. She and Cheyenne had insisted on decorating the place for him, but it had never felt like home. He'd hoped dating would change that. A year later, he still hadn't found someone he wanted to spend more than a few hours with.

His gaze strayed again to Meredith, her pallor making his stomach clench. Before he could stop himself, he was at her side, a hand gently placed in the middle of her back.

"Mer, let me take you home," he said, his voice quiet. "You need to eat. To rest."

She shook her head, wiping underneath one eye as she clutched the folded flag to her chest. "How am I supposed to leave him here alone?"

Sawyer blinked, the question tearing through him. *Never leave a man behind.* It had been drilled into him in the military, and yet he was expected to do just that.

"You do it because you have no other choice," Vanessa said, her voice thick with emotion.

Meredith sank to her knees beside the casket, resting her hand on its polished metal surface as her head bowed. Sawyer was beside her in an instant, desperate to offer his silent support.

He wished he could somehow hold the pieces of her together while she fell apart.

Cheyenne dropped to the ground beside Meredith, followed by Zach, then Vanessa.

"How can this be real?" Meredith whispered, her head still bowed.

Sawyer placed an arm gently around her shoulder. She leaned into him, burying her head in his chest as her shoulder shook with sobs that broke his heart in two.

"Please, Mer," he choked out. "Tell me what I can do to help."

He loved her so much. Seeing her pain made his own more acute. It had only been six days since he'd last seen John, and already it felt like a lifetime.

"We'll do anything," Cheyenne added. "We can camp out here all night if that's what you need."

Meredith half-laughed, half-sobbed, the sound rumbling through Sawyer's chest as her cheek pressed against it. "Can you bring John back, please?"

Sawyer looked up at the sky, blinking quickly. "You know I would if I could."

She pulled back, giving him a watery smile. "Me too." She reached out, squeezing each of their hands in turn. "I love you all so much. I can't tell you how grateful I am to have you here with me today."

"We're not going anywhere," Zach said, his tone firm. "Family sticks together."

Sawyer nodded. He'd move to the cemetery if that's what she needed. Build a tiny house for her right here on John's final resting place.

It was another hour before Meredith was ready to leave. Her knees buckled as she walked away from her husband, but her spine remained ramrod straight and she never looked back. Sawyer helped her into the front seat of his truck, then they drove in silence to her bungalow on the edge of town.

How would he help her through this?

How would he get through this himself?

Back at Meredith's, they sat silently in the living room, each holding a cup of warm tea brewed by Vanessa.

Meredith took a sip, eyes hollow. "You know, I almost broke up with John when he told me he was a SEAL. I didn't think I could handle the dangers of his job. Every time the phone rang, I was certain it was his sergeant with bad news."

They stayed silent, letting Meredith talk. Sawyer had only ever heard John's side of this story. He'd had complete faith in Meredith and total confidence in their relationship. *"Just a bump in the road."* That was what John had told them about the almost-breakup.

"How did he survive all those missions with the Navy, only to die in Sapphire Cove, of all places?" Meredith shook her head. "This has got to be the safest place in the world. The police are glorified traffic cops. Nothing bad ever happens here."

An exaggeration perhaps, but Sawyer understood her sentiment. The missions he, Zach, and John had survived flashed through his mind, making him flinch. So many times, he'd been certain their number was up, but they'd somehow made it through relatively unscathed, at least physically speaking.

"It isn't fair," Cheyenne said, her eyes glistening with tears.

Sawyer agreed completely. But he'd learned as a kid hiding from his alcoholic father that life wasn't fair.

Zach and Cheyenne left first, murmuring that they needed to pick up their ten-month-old daughter, Bailey, from the sitter. Vanessa left soon after so she could put Grayson to bed, but promised to return in the morning. Both invited Meredith to sleep at their homes so she wouldn't be alone, but she refused, just as she had every day before.

Sawyer sat on one end of the couch, clutching the cup of lukewarm tea in his hand, while Meredith sat silently on the other end. With the others gone, John's absence loomed larger than ever, bringing with it a fresh wave of grief.

Had he ever been alone with Meredith? Probably not for longer than the time it took John to use the bathroom. It felt wrong to be here, just the two of them. Meredith huddled in the couch's corner, her legs drawn up to her chin and arms wrapped tightly around them. She looked so fragile—a far sight from the vivacious woman he was used to seeing—that it made him want to weep.

Sawyer set his cup of tea on the coffee table, figuring he'd infringed on her grief long enough. She probably wanted to be alone after the trauma of the day. "I should go."

Meredith lurched forward, her hand wrapping around his wrist. "No!"

He froze at the contact, hating himself for the way it made his heart twist. Meredith didn't seem to notice and tucked a strand of hair behind one ear, biting her lip.

"Please don't leave," she said, her voice soft. "I don't want to be alone right now. It's worse when I'm alone."

The vulnerability in her tone fractured his already broken heart even more. Whatever Meredith needed, he would provide. He wouldn't break his promise to John.

"I'll stay as long as you need me to," Sawyer said. "And the second you want to be alone, just tell me and I'm gone."

She nodded, curling back into her corner of the couch. After the funeral, she'd changed into one of John's old Navy sweatshirts. She tucked her legs up inside it now, resting her chin on top. "I can't believe this is my life now."

Sawyer pinched the bridge of his nose, blinking rapidly. "I keep expecting him to walk through the door with a bag of items from the hardware store."

Her laugh ended in a half-sob. "Those projects are my fault more than his, I'm afraid. I shouldn't have given him such long honey-do lists."

"He loved doing those projects for you." And Sawyer had loved assisting him. There was something satisfying about working with his hands that had partially satiated his need to be useful after leaving the SEALs.

Meredith gave him a watery smile. "If we talk about John anymore, I'm going to cry. Want to watch a movie instead?"

Sawyer wasn't much for movies—sitting still for that long always made him antsy—but John had been a major film buff, with a particular love for over-the-top action flicks. "Sure. What do you want to watch?"

Meredith picked up the remote. "*Top Gun.*"

John's favorite movie. Sawyer must have watched it with him at least a dozen times.

"It's perfect," Sawyer said. "Want me to make us some popcorn while you start it?"

"Sure. There should be some microwave popcorn—"

Sawyer rose. "I know where to find it."

"Of course you do." She shook her head with a self-deprecating laugh. "I don't know where my brain is today."

"Hey, none of that." Sawyer patted her shoulder. "I'll be back in a second."

By the time Sawyer had a bag popped, Meredith had found the movie and had it paused on the opening scene. He sat back on his end of the couch while Meredith sat on hers, the bowl of popcorn in the space where John should have been.

Sawyer reached for the popcorn, freezing when his hand brushed Meredith's. She didn't notice, her eyes glued to the screen.

It had been easy to keep a tight rein on his emotions when John was around. Sawyer would have died before he hurt his best friend. But now John was gone, and Meredith needed comfort. How was he supposed to navigate that while keeping his feelings in check?

He forced himself to not think about it and instead focus on the movie. But when the ill-fated training scene began, a sick pit formed in his stomach.

He'd forgotten about Goose. Hadn't even considered that part of the story when Meredith suggested the movie.

She put a hand to her mouth, pushing the popcorn away. Sawyer grabbed the remote and pushed *pause*, his attention instantly shifting to her needs.

"Is it too much?" he asked. "We can watch something else instead. *Monty Python*, maybe." No one died in that, right? It had been another of John's favorites.

Meredith shook her head, eyes brimming but jaw set in determination. "No. I want to finish this."

Sawyer reluctantly pushed *play*. He watched Meredith more than the screen as Goose's death played out, and when the tears started rolling freely down her cheeks, he couldn't stop himself from pushing aside the popcorn bowl and pulling her to him in a hug.

"I'm okay," she whispered, though her hand clutched at the fabric of his shirt. "I can do this."

"Whatever you need," Sawyer repeated. Meredith didn't let go of his shirt, her head resting on his shoulder.

Sawyer closed his eyes, the guilt slamming him almost as hard as the grief. It made him sick that he was even peripherally aware of how she made his heart race. Not that he'd expected the attraction to disappear, but they'd just buried her husband—his best friend.

When Meredith let go of his shirt and returned to her corner of the couch, Sawyer breathed an inward sigh of relief. Soon her tears turned to laughter, and before he knew it, the film was over.

"Are you sure you want to be alone tonight?" he asked as she walked him to the door. "I can drop you off at Cheyenne and Zach's, or at Vanessa's parents' house."

Meredith folded her arms tightly around her middle, John's sweatshirt hanging on her slight frame. The hem reached nearly to her knees while the sleeves completely covered her hands. At some point during the movie, she'd pulled her hair up into a messy bun on the crown of her head, and her bare feet made this moment feel almost intimate.

"I'm sure." Meredith's lips pursed. "It's better if I establish the new normal as soon as possible."

"Mer, come on." Sawyer almost offered to sleep on her couch but stopped himself. No doubt she'd find that suggestion inappropriate. "No one expects you to be strong all the time."

She met his eyes, one hand clutching the pendant around her neck. "I know. I'm fine, really. I want to be home tonight. Alone."

"Okay then." He didn't push, not wanting to make this any harder for her than it already was. "Call me if you need anything."

"I will."

He kept a hand on the door, searching her face for signs of deception. "I'm serious, Mer—anything at all, day or night. Need someone to drive you to the cemetery at two a.m. so you can be with John? Did you forget to grab potatoes at the grocery store? Is the toilet clogged? I'm your guy."

Meredith laughed, shaking her head. "I'm not calling you if my toilet clogs. That would be humiliating."

"You know what I mean."

"I do." She rose on tiptoes, giving him a quick hug. The unexpected contact startled him, and he forced himself not to inhale the fragrant scent of her shampoo.

For four years, he'd loved her in secret while he watched her love John. It had been easy to keep a lid on those emotions then. He'd sooner cut off his own arm than hurt either of them. But now everything had changed. How was he supposed to support Meredith while protecting his heart?

"You're a good friend, Sawyer," Meredith said. "John and I are both lucky to have you in our lives."

Would she feel that way if she knew how hard he had to fight to hide his true feelings? "I'm the lucky one. Trust me. You're sure you're okay here alone?"

"Yes." She rose on tiptoes, pressing her lips to his cheek for the briefest of moments. "I'll talk to you tomorrow."

He recognized her dismissal for what it was and nodded. "I'll call you in the morning."

It was almost as hard to turn his back on Meredith as it had been to leave the cemetery a few hours earlier. Sawyer clenched his hands into fists, feeling the tears burn. The image of Meredith in the doorway, the tips of her fingers peeking out of John's sweatshirt and her toes curled against the cold tile floor, was seared into his brain.

Maybe he'd sleep in his truck tonight, just in case. It wouldn't even make the top ten list of the most uncomfortable places he'd tried to rest. But what if the neighbors saw him in her driveway all night? The last thing he wanted to do was start unfounded gossip around town.

Sawyer climbed into his truck, glancing at Meredith's house once more. The door was closed, the seasonal wreath slightly askew.

"What am I going to do without you, John?" Sawyer whispered as he pressed the ignition key.

He cried silent tears all the way home.

CHAPTER Three

"*A*re you going to be okay when I'm gone?"

Vanessa stood at the kitchen island, her arms braced against the countertop and brows knit together in concern. Had it really only been last winter that Meredith had convinced John to help her repaint that counter with a special epoxy kit to make it look like marble? She dug her nails into her palms, trying to focus on the sting of flesh instead of the lump in her throat.

He'd wanted to replace the countertops entirely, but she'd been worried about the cost and insisted on trying this cheaper alternative. They'd gotten into a silly argument over the proper technique for applying the epoxy. She'd shoved her phone in his face, angrily scrolling through the dozens of DIY videos she'd watched on the process and demanding to know why he always had to be right. Even now, she could feel the whisper of frustration at his stubborn bullheadedness.

John had eventually conceded defeat and apologized, but by that point, she'd been aggravated by his mansplaining and had pouted like a spoiled child.

He could have gotten mad, too. She'd been behaving unreasonably, after all. But that wasn't John. Instead, he'd blasted her favorite playlist and started belly dancing. The sight of his hairy, toned abs swaying offbeat to the music had been too much and by the end of the song she was laughing. They'd ended up slow-dancing in the middle of the kitchen, the argument forgotten.

"Mer?" Vanessa said.

She blinked, forcing a smile through lips that trembled. "I'll be fine."

The key was staying busy. That was what she'd always done when John was on a mission. It had helped to counteract the fear and loneliness, and when it hadn't, well, working herself into exhaustion at least allowed her to sleep without nightmares. Mostly.

Figuring out how to pay the bills while being crushed by the weight of two failing businesses would be a good place to start. Yesterday, when the darkness of night had threatened to swallow her whole, she'd reluctantly grabbed her laptop and made a list of photography studios in nearby Harbor Bay where she could apply.

She had to close the photography studio. As she'd run numbers in her head while staring at the popcorn ceiling in her bedroom, the reality of her situation had been impossible to escape. She needed a steady job with things like a salary and health insurance, maybe even a 401(k)—not a business that was losing money hand over fist. This week she'd look into selling one of their cars, too. Not John's Ford Explorer that still smelled like him, but her own reliable Honda Civic.

Then there was the scuba shop. It hurt more to think about abandoning John's dream than it did her own. It also would be more complicated, since Sawyer and Zach—and, by extension, Cheyenne—each owned a third of the business.

Was she even on the bank accounts for King Trident Scuba Diving?

"I hate leaving you right now." Vanessa frowned, as though trying to figure out a way to stay.

Meredith covered Vanessa's hand with her own. "Stop. Your top priority right now has to be Grayson and finishing school. I'll be okay."

She was supposed to photograph a wedding this weekend. The thought of lugging around all her equipment without John's help made her want to cancel, but she wouldn't do that to the bride and groom. Besides, she needed the money. Dying wasn't cheap, as evidenced by her maxed out credit cards. She'd had no idea a nice coffin could cost as much as a used car.

"I'll call to check on you every day." Vanessa's brow wrinkled with worry. "And I'll be back permanently in just over a year."

A year. Meredith had no idea how she was going to get through the next twelve hours, let alone the next twelve months. "Ness, stop worrying."

"I can't." Vanessa dropped the dish towel onto the counter. "Everyone checks on you in the beginning, but it doesn't take long for most to move on with their lives. I don't want you to be all alone when that happens."

"You were alone," Meredith pointed out. She'd felt every bit as horrible as Vanessa seemed to feel now when she'd boarded that plane and left her best friend alone in South Carolina.

"No, I had Grayson."

"And I've got the team," Meredith countered. "Sawyer, Zach, and Cheyenne are my family."

"I know, and I'm glad. I just wish you had me close, too."

Meredith squeezed Vanessa's hand. "I will—in one year. What can happen in a year?"

Ten minutes later, Meredith stood on the front porch and watched Vanessa drive away as the icy chill of the crumbling concrete steps stung her bare feet. When the taillights disappeared around the bend in the road, loneliness engulfed her.

For one wild moment, she imagined chasing after Vanessa and begging to go with her back to South Carolina. How was she supposed to wake up alone every day in the bed she'd shared with John?

But leaving Sapphire Cove would require leaving the only people in the world who missed John as fiercely as she did. As much as she loved Vanessa, she needed Sawyer, Zach, and Cheyenne even more.

Her hand curled around the anchor pendant. Eight days without John. A lifetime left.

"I can do this," she whispered.

The emptiness of the house made her want to curl under a blanket and never reemerge, so she grabbed her keys and slipped on a jacket, then headed back outside. She wasn't sure what all needed to be done to close the photography studio, but deciding what to keep and what to liquidate was a good place to start.

Rain whispered on the breeze and her shoes grew damp as she traipsed through the mossy grasses that lined the narrow road. She tried to focus on the chill seeping through her soles, and not the many times she and John had traversed this route together. Seagull squawks combined with the crash of waves, and the shrieks of children floated up from the beach. As a child, she'd always been jealous of the kids whose moms built sandcastles with them. Grandma had been too old for that sort of thing, although she'd always been happy to watch.

Meredith craned her neck, wondering who played on the beach today, but all she could see were craggy rocks and a dog playing in the surf.

"Meredith!"

She turned, raising a hand to shade her eyes from the sun. A silver minivan slowly pulled up beside her, the window rolled down.

"Hey, Peggy." Meredith took a step toward the car, recognizing one of the women from church.

"Everything okay?" Peggy's lips turned down in a frown. "Can I give you a ride or something?"

Meredith peered into the backseat, where Peggy's twin boys fought over a toy stegosaurus. One twin hit his brother over the head with the dinosaur, eliciting a loud wail. They were only three or four years old, and their antics had entertained her and John during many a Sunday service.

"I'm okay, thanks." Meredith rocked back on her heels. "I've been meaning to drop off your baking dish. Thanks again for the casserole. It was delicious."

"Oh, don't worry about that. I'll grab it next time I'm in the area." Peggy pushed her sunglasses onto the top of her head and leaned toward the open passenger-side window. "I know we spoke at the funeral, but I wanted to tell you again how sorry I am about John. If there's anything more I can do . . ."

Meredith flinched, then forced a smile. There weren't enough casseroles in the world to heal this hurt, but the good folks of Sapphire Cove were trying their best. "I appreciate the offer. I'll let you know."

She talked to Peggy for a few more minutes before a flying dinosaur from one twin ended the conversation. Meredith folded her arms against the ever-increasing chill as Peggy drove away, debating just going back home and calling it a night. No one would blame her for binge-watching five hours of television before falling asleep, right?

Her phone buzzed in her pocket, and she pulled it out to see a text from Cheyenne on the group chat. **Did Vanessa leave? Are you okay?**

Meredith's heart lifted at the simple concern. Sawyer had texted her too, but it must have been while Vanessa was still there because she hadn't heard the chime.

I'm okay, Meredith quickly texted the group. **Vanessa's gone and I'm on my way to the photography studio. Thanks for checking on me.**

There. Now she would have to be productive instead of wallowing at home on the couch.

She quickened her pace, making fast work of the short walk to the downtown area. With Labor Day behind them, the summer crowds had dispersed, leaving the sidewalks empty and forlorn. Even the flower baskets that hung from the streetlamps looked droopy.

Her knees trembled as she approached her studio. She avoided the window display, not wanting to see the portrait hanging there of John in uniform among the client photos of families and babies. It took her three tries to unlock the door, her hands were shaking so badly. She flipped on the lights with fingers that felt stiff and cold. She could just make out the faint *drip-drip-drip* of the leaky faucet in the bathroom before the heater shuddered on, blasting her with warm air.

John had died in this building. He'd been wheeled through this room on a gurney, an oxygen mask strapped to his face and a paramedic administering CPR straddling his chest.

Dizziness had her reaching blindly for the wall. A picture frame clattered to the ground while her ears buzzed, and dark spots danced across her vision. She squeezed her eyes tightly shut, bracing her hands on her knees. The frantic calls of the paramedics echoed in her memory. She could almost feel Sawyer's arms holding her upright as she collapsed in the hospital waiting room after hearing the news.

Just breathe, she reminded herself. She sank to the floor, the rough exposed brick wall pulling at her hair. She inhaled slowly to the count of three, then exhaled in the same slow, steady rhythm.

It was several minutes before she forced herself to open her eyes. The picture frame lay on the floor, its glass cracked. She leaned over, gently picking it up. The photo was one she'd taken of John at their wedding. His expression was serious, belying the way his eyes sparkled with life.

"I miss you, John," she whispered, brushing her fingers gently across his lips. Carefully, she placed the cracked frame back on the wall, making sure it was secure, then forced herself to walk down the hallway to her office.

She flipped on the lights, illuminating the small space. A sleek L-shaped desk nestled in one corner, the rolling office chair John had given her for their last anniversary tucked neatly under it. They'd spent an entire Saturday purchasing and assembling that desk. The filing cabinet beside it was something John had found at a yard sale and proudly brought home. Even the walls reminded her of him—he'd helped choose the light blue paint color and put up the white wainscoting on the lower half.

She sank into the chair, running her hands along the leather armrests. She'd always thought of the photography studio as her place. Only now did she realize just how much John had invaded every inch of the building.

"Don't think about him," she whispered, reaching for the mail in the wire basket mounted to the side of her desk.

Don't think about John. Don't think about how much work it will be to close the photography studio without his help. Don't think. Instead, she'd do like her grandma had always encouraged and eat the elephant one bite at a time. Maybe, after going through something as easy as the mail, she'd finally be able to edit the last of those photos for her client and get them sent off. The upcoming wedding photo shoot would be so much more overwhelming if she still had that last project hanging over her head.

Meredith took a deep breath and slid a nail underneath the first envelope. Junk mail—a credit card application she tore into quarters and tossed in the trash. But the next envelope held a bill from the water company, and the amount took her breath away. She knew the bathroom pipe had been leaking, but had they really used up that much additional water last month?

"It's fine," she said aloud, as though that would make it true. She always kept a little extra in her business account for unplanned expenses, but this would stretch the limit.

She threw away a flyer from the city's chamber of commerce about an upcoming event and tore up two more applications for credit cards before opening another bill, this one for internet. Included was a reminder that the price was increasing this month by nearly ten percent.

Her heart pounded painfully in her chest as her entire body grew hot. She tossed that bill aside too, opening the next one—an overdraft fee for the bank from when a client paid her late last month.

She had known things were bad. But with John in her corner, it had seemed manageable. He'd always laughed it off and said the first year of a new business was hard, but things would turn around soon. They'd had high hopes that the back-to-school sale would bring in locals, and John had agreed to dress up in a rented Santa suit come December for special mini shoots.

Soon the desk was littered with torn envelopes and unpaid invoices. Fury shot through Meredith, a white-hot rage that felt so much better than the searing pain of loss. She picked up a paperweight and threw it with a yell. It clanged against the side of her filing cabinet, leaving a dent, before falling to the floor.

Bile rose in her throat, and she reached for the garbage can only to dry heave. Icy sweat had her entire body shaking. She laid her head on the desk and covered it with her arms as loud, wracking sobs shook her body.

Refuse to sink, she repeated, clutching at her hair.

But she couldn't lie to herself any longer. Vanessa was back in South Carolina. Sawyer, Zach, and Cheyenne were all at work. John was six feet under. There was no one around to put on a brave face for. She wasn't just sinking—she was full-on drowning, with no end in sight.

A bell chimed—probably a well-meaning neighbor who'd noticed her car out front and wanted to check in. She hadn't locked the front door, but the sign was still flipped to closed. The thought of facing a sympathetic churchgoer with another casserole dish only made her crying intensify.

"Meredith?" a deep voice asked.

Sawyer. Relief flooded her, accompanied by an intense need for a hug. Him she could handle right now. She opened her mouth to answer, but all that came out was a gasp of air. Her vision grew dim while the world swirled around her in a sickening kaleidoscope. She felt nauseous. Dizzy.

Adrift at sea.

Heavy footsteps sounded in the hallway.

"Meredith!" In an instant, Sawyer was crouched beside her. He hesitated, then pulled her to him in a tight hug. "Oh, Mer."

At the pressure of his arms, she collapsed. Meredith inhaled deeply as the tears flowed in earnest.

"What happened?" Sawyer asked.

She gestured helplessly to the pile of bills around her. "I'm just so overwhelmed. All these bills . . . I know I need to close the photography studio and get a job somewhere else, but I don't even know where to start. And then there's the scuba shop, and I put most of John's funeral costs on the credit card." She hiccupped, burying her face in his chest as her shoulders shook.

"Hey." Sawyer pulled away. "You're not alone, okay? Zach and I have the scuba shop covered for now, so don't worry about that. We're not open that many hours during the off season anyway, and that teen we hired over the summer is covering most of them."

Well, that was something, at least.

"And if you want to close the photography studio, I'll help you figure out how to do it. If you want to keep it open, I'll do whatever I can to make that happen." His Adam's apple bobbed up and down. "If you need assistance paying for John's funeral, I'm happy to do what I can. I'm sure Zach will help, too."

Meredith laughed, grabbing a tissue off her desk to wipe her nose. "Geez, can you imagine how embarrassed John would be if I let you help me pay for his funeral?"

"He wasn't *that* proud." Sawyer lips quirked upward in a grin.

"He absolutely was. Stubborn, too. This place was out of my price range, but he badgered the leasing office until they gave me a discount." Her smile dropped. She looked around the office and let out a heavy sigh. "I'm going to miss this place."

"Hey." Sawyer patted her back, the movement stilted. "You don't have to decide now. There's time—"

"No." She glanced at the pile of bills again, her hand curling around her necklace. Waiting wouldn't make it any easier. "The lease on this place is up at the end of November. I want to get rid of it by then."

Sawyer looked like he wanted to protest, but nodded. "Okay then. What should we do first?"

If only she knew. She looked around the office helplessly, trying to land on a starting point. John would have taken charge and known exactly what to do. She'd always wondered whether that was a trait he came by naturally or had developed after years as a SEAL.

"How about we go through your backdrops and props, that kind of thing?" Sawyer suggested. "I bet you can sell most of it, and that'll help you pay off the credit card."

She grasped at the plan like a lifeline. Memories of John weren't tied up in any of those items, and they'd be easy enough to sell in one of the photography groups online. That was how she'd bought most of the items. "Yes, let's do that."

She let Sawyer hoist her to her feet. The world swayed dizzyingly, and she took a moment to steady herself.

Sawyer folded his arms, his brow furrowed and lips turned down. "Maybe we should stop by Baylor's first for lunch."

Her stomach turned over at the thought of food. How could she simultaneously be hungry and nauseous? "Don't you need to get back to work?"

"Nah, I'm mostly done for the day. I can put in a few hours this evening if I need to." He flashed her a grin. "That's the beauty of working from home."

"Okay. Lunch sounds good, then. Maybe just a sandwich or burger to go."

"Whatever you want."

What would she do without Sawyer? She was so lucky that John had become friends with him and Zach. "Thank you."

"Anytime." His expression turned serious. "I know Zach and Cheyenne have their own lives, but I don't have a wife and daughter who need me. I'm on call for you twenty-four seven. John will come down from heaven and kick my butt if I let you figure this out all on your own."

Meredith laughed, letting him lead her toward the front door. "You know what? I think you're right."

"Of course I am. Anything you need, I'm your guy."

She bit her lip. Yes, she could figure it out on her own. But she was so overwhelmed. John would want her to ask for help. He would want her to lean on his friends right now. "Do you think you can help me figure out how to sell my Honda?"

Sawyer's jaw tightened the barest amount, as though he was struggling to hold back some sort of emotion she didn't quite understand. "Of course. I bet we can have it sold in a week or two, if that's what you want."

"It is. Thanks."

"No problem."

Somehow, knowing that Sawyer really meant it—that he was there to help, no matter what, and didn't view it as an inconvenience—gave her a comfort nothing else had since finding John unconscious on the floor.

CHAPTER Four

ONE MONTH LATER

Sawyer pulled into the empty parking lot of Cheyenne's auto shop, worry gnawing a pit in his stomach like a feral cat tearing through garbage bins.

He knew there was no timeline on grief. But it had been a month, and Meredith was worrying him—enough that he wanted to talk to Zach and Cheyenne. Maybe they'd have some insight into what the three of them could do to help.

The sky had been dark for hours, even though it wasn't quite eight o'clock. He'd purposefully arrived later in the evening, hoping Cheyenne would be done working for the day. Luck was on his side for once. Thick metal garage doors shuttered both bays, hiding the 1967 Camaro he knew she was currently restoring for a millionaire in Silicon Valley, and the 1956 Ford F-100 she'd be working on next. John had been a bit of a car enthusiast and had loved checking out her projects. Sawyer was less of a gearhead, but had always been happy to tag along with the rest of the crew.

He hadn't spent much time in the garage since John passed.

Above the auto shop, light spilled out from the windows of Cheyenne and Zach's small apartment. It hadn't made sense to rent a place when they already owned the garage, so the five of them had worked together to turn the top floor into a cozy home. Even Meredith had assisted whenever she could. She'd looked adorable in overalls, though he'd tried hard not to notice, and what she lacked in skill she'd made up for in enthusiasm.

Sawyer took the iron staircase at the back of the building slowly. How would he even start this conversation? He stared at the pumpkin painted with the messy, broad strokes of a one-year-old, wishing he was here to discuss Halloween plans instead. The pumpkin sat next to a witch's hat welcome mat, and a colorful purple-and-orange wreath decorated the front door.

Muffled shrieks came from inside the apartment, followed by the low chuckle of Zach and the higher, more sing-song laugh of Cheyenne. Based on the hour, Sawyer would guess he was interrupting the bedtime routine. Oops.

He swallowed back a twinge of longing. He wanted a wife and baby. Heck, he wanted a front door decorated with holiday wreaths—evidence a happy family lived inside. Since moving to Sapphire Cove, he'd tried to get over Meredith by dating regularly. But there hadn't been time to so much as open the app since John's passing and Sawyer had canceled his subscription a few days ago. Worry for Meredith had mixed with his own grief until just getting out of bed felt like a

Herculean task some days. He was in no place to pursue a new relationship—not when Meredith needed him so much right now. The past month had been spent helping her sell her Honda and list various photography props and backdrops on resell sites. Zach and Cheyenne had helped when they could, but Bailey was an adorable hindrance, so mostly it was just Sawyer and Meredith.

She'd looked so pale that afternoon and kept pressing a hand to her lips as though nauseous. Her hair had been wet from the shower, her eyes rimmed with dark circles. She'd confided that despite putting in a dozen applications at various photography studios in Harbor Bay and Paradise Green, she hadn't gotten so much as an interview. If she didn't have a job by the end of the month, she'd see if she could get hired as a waitress at Baylor's. Sawyer hoped more than anything she'd find a job in photography. She was too talented to give it up.

Another shriek from Bailey interrupted Sawyer's train of thought. He rapped sharply on the door, and a moment later Zach swung it open. His blue T-shirt was damp, and he ran a hand through messy hair, making it stand on end.

"Hey," Zach said, opening the door wide. "Did I forget you were coming over tonight?"

"No, I just dropped in." Sawyer grinned, looking meaningfully at Zach's wet shirt. "Looks like I interrupted bath time."

Zach laughed, shutting the door behind Sawyer. "Yeah, Bailey wouldn't stop splashing. It took both me and Cheyenne to wrestle her out of the tub."

Another shriek came, this one from the direction of what Sawyer knew to be Bailey's nursery. "Sounds like she doesn't want to get her jammies on, either."

Zach shook his head and grinned, then bent down to pick up a sippy cup half-filled with what looked like milk. "Sorry, this place is kind of a wreck. Come in."

What Zach called a wreck, Sawyer wanted more than anything—a living room scattered with toy blocks and board books, a basket of diapers and wipes neatly tucked beside the entertainment center, and the faint smell of freshly baked brownies in the air.

But he wasn't here to talk about his longing for a family.

"What's up?" Zach asked, motioning to the couch.

Sawyer sat down heavily. "Meredith."

Zach's jovial expression instantly turned to one of concern. "Yeah, Chey and I have been worried about her, too."

Another shriek came from the bedroom, then the soft sound of Cheyenne singing. The shrieks faded as the lullaby floated into the living room.

"I was hoping to talk to both of you." Sawyer scratched the back of his head. "Sorry, I wasn't thinking about bedtime— just that you'd both be done working for the day."

"Bailey will be down in a minute. Don't worry about it." Zach grabbed the television remote. "Want to watch the game while we wait?"

"Sure," Sawyer said.

But he couldn't pay attention to the football game. Wasn't even sure who was playing. One ear was tuned into Cheyenne's singing in the other room because he was eager for Bailey to fall asleep.

Meredith had thrown up three times today while he helped her box up props to ship to their new owner. She'd tried to be discreet, but Sawyer had heard the sounds of her retching in the bathroom. It wasn't the first time she'd tried to hide evidence of nausea since the funeral. He'd also caught her nodding off while they were together more than once. The exhaustion might just be because of depression, but he was starting to wonder if it was something else. She was emotional too, crying at the drop of a hat. But that was probably the grief talking.

The first quarter of the game was nearly over when Cheyenne walked into the living room, her dark hair partially covered by the red bandanna she'd tied around it. She wore denim overalls, one pant leg nearly as damp as Zach's shirt. Sawyer couldn't help but grin. He loved Bailey like the niece he considered her, but the girl had a lot of spunk and kept her parents on their toes.

"Hey, Sawyer." Cheyenne flopped onto the couch beside her husband. "Did we know you were coming over?"

"Nah, I just stopped by."

Cheyenne nodded, seeming unsurprised. She set the baby monitor on the coffee table, static mixing with Bailey's faint coos as she jabbered to herself. "Cool. Hopefully Bailey will go to bed easy tonight. Want a brownie? I just made them."

"Of course he wants a brownie." Zach pushed himself to his feet with a groan. "Let's hurry and eat before Bailey realizes we're enjoying food without her."

Sawyer chuckled, following them into the kitchen. He grabbed three bowls from the cupboard while Zach found the ice cream in the freezer and Cheyenne brought over the pan of brownies that had been resting on the stovetop.

She glanced at the bowls, her brow furrowing. "You couldn't talk Meredith into coming over too?"

He hadn't even tried. The dark circles under her eyes had been the worst he'd ever seen them. "I wanted to talk to you guys alone. Besides, she said she was headed to bed as soon as she got home." Sawyer's hands tightened on the bowls. "I'm really worried about her."

Cheyenne glanced at Zach, her lips turned down in a frown. "We've been worried about her, too. She puts on a good act, but I know she's hurting."

"Of course she is," Zach interrupted. "I mean, if I'd just lost you—"

"Don't even talk like that." Cheyenne dished generous servings of brownie into each bowl, her motions quick and jerky. "No one else is allowed to die, okay? I can't even think about life without you."

"Hey." Zach was around the counter in an instant, his arms wrapped tightly around Cheyenne. She leaned into his embrace, their expressions so tender that Sawyer had to look away.

An image of him holding Meredith in a similar fashion made him feel sick. What kind of monster was he? John had barely been gone a month, and Sawyer had no intention of swooping in on his wife.

He heard the soft sound of lips meeting, and then the scrape of a spatula against a pan. He turned back around, figuring that meant the display of affection was over, and found Zach scooping ice cream onto the tops of the brownies Cheyenne had just dished out.

"We'll save her a brownie," Cheyenne decided. "I'll take it to her tomorrow. Unless you want to, Sawyer?"

He sank heavily onto one of the barstools. "It won't matter who brings it to her because she won't eat it."

Cheyenne leaned against the countertop, her bowl in one hand and brow furrowed. "She looked a little thinner when I checked in on her last week. But I've texted her every day, and she hasn't said anything."

"She's grieving," Zach said, his tone dismissive. "I mean, yeah, it's not great that she has no appetite right now. But it's not exactly weird, either."

"I thought it was that, too." Sawyer rubbed both hands down his face. "But now I'm not so sure." He thought of the way her face had tinged green when he took her a burger from Baylor's a few days ago, and how she'd excused herself after only a bite. The way he'd heard her retching three times today.

"What do you mean?" Cheyenne asked.

Sawyer grunted. "She seems . . . nauseated a lot. I bring her food, and she wrinkles her nose like it's making her queasy. And she's so tired all the time, and cries at everything."

"She sounds like someone who just lost their husband," Zach said gently.

Cheyenne tapped the top of her ice cream with a spoon. "Or like someone who's pregnant."

Sawyer dropped his spoon into his bowl with a clatter. Pregnant? He'd considered some lingering virus that was making her sick, a chronic disease that needed to be treated, even something life-threatening like cancer. Mostly, he'd wondered if they needed to get Meredith on antidepressants and to a good therapist. But pregnant?

He pinched the bridge of his nose, trying to erase the image of Meredith and John wrapped in each other's arms.

Pregnant.

"Oh my gosh." Cheyenne put a shaking hand to her forehead. "Guys, she's pregnant. It all makes sense."

Zach puffed out a horrified laugh. "Come on, Chey. Fate wouldn't be that cruel."

Except, of course it would be. Sawyer ran a shaky hand down his face.

"No, listen," Cheyenne said. "When I brought her some of that homemade salsa from the garden last week, she practically turned green. But last summer she couldn't get enough of it. Remember how she came over here so that I could teach her how to make it? But I swear she nearly hurled when she opened the container."

Sawyer didn't know much about pregnancy, but he remembered how sensitive Cheyenne had been to smells in the beginning. She'd had to wear a construction mask when working in the garage so the fumes wouldn't trigger her morning sickness.

"I don't think that's enough to suspect pregnancy," Zach said.

But Sawyer thought of something else—the way he'd had to work harder lately to avoid thinking about how nicely Meredith filled out a shirt. He'd been angry at himself for even noticing such a thing, but had he noticed because she was filling it out more than normal?

"It's not just that, but the constant nausea lately," Cheyenne said. "She's been tired all the time."

"All signs of depression," Zach pointed out.

"She's also been running to the restroom pretty frequently when we're together. Oh, gosh." Cheyenne put both hands to her cheeks, her eyes welling with tears. "A baby. I can't believe it."

"Hold on." Sawyer pushed away his bowl of brownies and ice cream, his appetite gone. "Maybe she's just got a really terrible cold or something. She has sounded a little congested lately."

"That's probably from crying," Zach said.

"Or pregnancy," Cheyenne broke in. "I was so stuffy all nine months."

Silence fell over them. A baby. Could it really be true?

"Do we mention it to her?" Cheyenne asked. "She probably hasn't been keeping track of, you know, her period and whatever since John's death."

"Geez." Zach ran a hand through his hair. "This is so crazy. Were they even trying?"

"I don't think so," Cheyenne said. "Meredith said something once about John wanting the businesses to be more stable first."

Sawyer had avoided talking to John or Meredith about their family planning choices. It brought up too many feelings that were hard to tamp down.

"I vote we say nothing," Zach said. "Let's just, I don't know . . . Keep an eye on the situation, I guess. If she is pregnant, she'll figure it out eventually."

Cheyenne rolled her eyes, taking a bite of her dessert. "You are such a guy. But yeah, let's monitor things. I might be wrong."

They kept talking, batting around different ideas of how they could help Meredith through this difficult time, as well as discussing plausible reasons for her recent behavior that didn't include a baby.

But now that the idea had been planted, Sawyer couldn't get it out of his head.

CHAPTER
Five

Sawyer slept fitfully, hazy dreams of Meredith and John mixing with memories from his days as a SEAL. When he finally woke up early the next morning, Meredith was at the forefront of his mind.

Meredith and her potential pregnancy.

Maybe Cheyenne was wrong. As he made his bed with military precision corners, just like he'd learned in the Navy, he tried to reassure himself that Meredith's symptoms were for another reason. But by the time he'd showered and dressed, he couldn't stop himself from going to the computer and opening a web browser.

He hesitated, fingers poised over the keys. Then he typed *early signs of pregnancy* and pushed search.

By the time he walked into Baylor's Cafe an hour later to pick up two piping hot orders of sausage biscuits, he felt even more uneasy than he had last night. But Zach was right—they should keep an eye on Meredith for the next few weeks and monitor the situation without saying anything.

Frost clung to the clover in Meredith's front yard and his breath escaped in icy puffs as he rapped softly on her front door. The wreath still had a distinctly Fourth of July theme—he'd see if she wanted him to hunt around in the attic today and bring down the fall-themed wreath he remembered from last year.

The door slowly creaked open. Meredith's bare feet peeked out from under a pair of plaid pajama pants, and a threadbare blue robe hung on her shoulders and nearly covered one of John's old Navy T-shirts. Half her hair had fallen out of its ponytail, and dark shadows still rimmed her eyes.

"Sawyer." She rubbed her eyes. Had he woken her up? "Hey. Did I forget something?"

"No, I just thought I'd bring you breakfast." He held up the to-go bag from Baylor's Diner.

"It's Saturday already?" She dropped a hand, motioning him inside. "You don't have to keep feeding me on the weekends, but I appreciate it."

"I don't mind. Better than eating alone."

Her mouth quirked up at the corners. "True."

Sawyer slipped off his shoes and followed Meredith into the kitchen. A few dishes sat on the drying rack, which made him feel a little better—at least she was eating something when he wasn't around. The rhythmic thump of clothes tumbling in the dryer filled the silence. Meredith's laptop sat on the island—it looked like she was applying for another job.

Maybe he was overreacting. It had only been a month since John's passing, and she was already making an effort to return to some semblance of normalcy. It wasn't like she spent all day, every day, crying in bed.

"I brought sausage biscuits and gravy." Sawyer pulled the foam containers out of the bag, faint traces of steam escaping from the corners.

"Good choice. Baylor's biscuits are the best." Meredith pulled her container toward her and flipped it open.

For a moment, Sawyer didn't realize anything was wrong. Not until Meredith bolted from the table, one hand over her mouth.

"Meredith." Sawyer rose in alarm. He heard the bathroom door slam shut, followed by the sound of retching.

She was throwing up. Again.

He ran a shaky hand down his face. People sometimes lost their appetites when grieving. He'd witnessed it first-hand when other soldiers experienced losses. Once, during his first year as a SEAL, they'd lost a member of their team on a mission and all mourned for him deeply. Then a few years later, one of the guys had lost a parent to cancer, and they'd tried to hold him together through his sorrow.

But Sawyer had never heard of someone being consistently and persistently ill because of the death of a loved one. Not for a month straight.

He closed the lid on both his and Meredith's food and stored it in the refrigerator, then opened the kitchen window to air out the smell. She wasn't sick right now because of grief. She was sick because of the scent of the food—something Cheyenne had said she'd experienced when pregnant with Bailey.

The toilet flushed. Sawyer closed his eyes as water rushed through the pipes. How could he "wait and see" for another month while Meredith continued to exhibit signs of pregnancy? That was John's child she might be carrying. Wasn't she supposed to go to the doctor and take vitamins and stuff to make sure the baby was okay?

The bathroom door opened, and Sawyer met Meredith in the living room. She collapsed on the couch, looking pale and wan. Like she might bolt for the restroom again at any moment. "Sorry about that."

Sorry. There were so many things Sawyer was sorry for, and he couldn't fix a single one.

He sat in the chair across from her and leaned forward, hands braced on his knees and fingers steepled. Would Zach and Cheyenne be upset if he broached the subject with Meredith right now? Pregnancy was an embarrassing thing to talk about with your best friend's wife. But last night's conversation kept ricocheting around his brain like a bullet.

"Mer." He took a deep breath, not quite able to meet her eyes. "Are you feeling okay?"

"What do you mean?" She ran a hand through her hair, looking distracted.

Sawyer motioned to the bathroom. "It's just, you seem to be sick a lot lately."

Anger flashed in her eyes. "I'm not sick, Sawyer. I'm sad. John's dead, remember? It would be weird if I wasn't upset about that."

He winced, feeling like a jerk. Yeah, he definitely should have waited for Cheyenne to have this conversation.

Too late now.

"That's not what I mean. Of course no one expects you to act like yourself right now. But I feel like you've been throwing up a lot lately. I know you think you're hiding it, but I've noticed."

Now it was Meredith who wouldn't meet his eyes. Dang, this conversation was hard.

But he'd already started it, so he might as well push forward. For John's sake—and the sake of his maybe baby. "All I'm saying is that perhaps it's time to go to the doctor. You should make sure you don't have a stomach bug or something."

Meredith pulled her legs up to her chest, wrapping her arms tightly around them and resting her chin on top. "What I have is a severe case of being a widow."

Sawyer swallowed. He could back off. Nod and say yeah, she was probably right.

But what would John do if he were here? What would he want Sawyer to do?

"I still don't think throwing up this much is normal." Sawyer hesitated. "You look like you've lost weight, and it's not like you had any to spare."

Her cheeks glowed pink, and she tucked her head into her knees. "I'm just nauseous all the time. I was like this when my grandparents passed, too. Well, not the throwing up. But I never had much of an appetite."

Sawyer took a deep breath, focusing on the white shag rug covering the living room's dark hardwood floors. "I stopped by Cheyenne and Zach's yesterday, and she mentioned she had a lot of the same symptoms when she was pregnant with Bailey."

"What?" Meredith's sharp tone made the tips of his ears burn, but he didn't look up.

He didn't want to think about this. Didn't want to remember that the girl he loved and his best friend were—had been—a married couple. Sawyer rubbed his eyes, pushing the images aside.

For John, he reminded himself. He looked up at Meredith, hoping she couldn't sense his embarrassment. "Cheyenne said it would explain the constant nausea and the way certain smells seem to trigger you, not to mention how tired you've been."

"No!" Meredith shot to her feet, hands up in a *stop* motion. "No freaking way. John and I . . . We were always very careful."

Sawyer's entire face burned with humiliation. He wanted to be anywhere but here, having this conversation with Meredith. Sweating in the jungles of Columbia. Diving one hundred feet into the ocean. Anything.

In that moment, he missed John so much it hurt. John should be here, having this conversation with Meredith. The two of them should be embracing as they cried happy tears.

Sawyer rose as well. "Come on, Mer. You know nothing is one hundred percent effective."

"No. No way." Her hand clutched at the necklace she always wore, and her voice had risen at least an octave. "Pregnant? Are you freaking kidding me?"

"It was just a suggest—"

"I don't have health insurance. I don't have savings." She threw her hands out, as though to include everything in her life. "My photography business is running on fumes, and I haven't been able to find a job anywhere else yet. I have no idea what to do with the scuba shop."

Her eyes were bright with tears, and the tremble of her bottom lip nearly did Sawyer in.

"I can't have a baby. Not now. Not without John." Her voice cracked on the last word.

"Hey." He gathered her close, smoothing back wisps of her blonde hair as she crumpled into his chest. He tried to push away how right she felt in his arms and instead put all his energies into reassuring her. "I didn't mean to upset you."

"I'm not pregnant," she repeated stubbornly.

He wished he could believe her. "Just go to the doctor and get checked out. Please? Maybe you've got a virus or something and need some help shaking it. I'm worried about you, Mer."

"Yeah, maybe." Her face was still pressed into his chest, her voice muffled by his shirt.

"I can call and make an appointment for you if you need me to." He resisted the urge to stroke her hair. What would John want him to do right now? "I can even drive you to it."

Meredith pulled away, and his arms ached with the sudden loss. "I'm a widow, not a toddler. I can make my own doctor appointments."

He chuckled, happy to see even a glimpse of her former spunk. "Okay then."

She smiled, then looked away quickly. "Thanks for breakfast, Sawyer, but I'm exhausted. I think I'll just go back to bed for a few hours and see if I feel better when I wake up."

"Okay." Sawyer didn't want to leave things like this. There was a weird, standoffish vibe between them now that he hated.

Had he done the right thing by planting the idea of pregnancy in her head? Should he have said nothing and just kept an eye on her for a few more weeks?

"I left the food in the fridge, in case you get hungry later. And I opened a window too, so make sure to close and lock it up before you go to sleep."

"I will. Thanks." Meredith gave him another quick hug. "I don't know how I would have gotten through this last month without you."

He'd always been willing to walk through fire for her. He'd just never had to when John was around. "Call me if you want help at the photography studio later."

"I will," Meredith promised.

By the time he climbed into his truck and shut the door, adrenaline had his entire body shaking. He slammed a hand against the steering wheel with a curse.

John should be here.

Everything was all wrong without him.

CHAPTER Six

Meredith didn't make an appointment with the doctor on Monday morning, despite what she'd promised Sawyer. Instead, she crawled out of bed after staring at the ceiling for an hour and tried to convince herself she didn't feel nauseous.

In the kitchen, she pulled out the biscuits and gravy from Baylor's. Her toes curled against the cold tile floor as she waited for the microwave to ding.

She wasn't nauseous. Certain smells weren't making her sick. Saturday had been a fluke, and Sawyer was definitely overreacting.

When the microwave beeped, Meredith pulled the foam container out and flipped it open. Her stomach churned at the smell, but she took a deep breath—through her mouth, not her nose—and sat down at the barstool, anyway.

She loved this meal. Had spent many a happy Sunday at Baylor's sharing it with John after church.

The first bite had her gagging. By the fifth, she was racing to the bathroom.

After rinsing her mouth and brushing her teeth, Meredith braced her arms on the counter and stared at herself in the mirror. How long had it been since her period? She knew for a fact she hadn't had one since John died. Had it been before or after she got that sinus infection in August?

Definitely before. They'd had that bonfire on the beach with everyone. She remembered now, because she hadn't bothered to wear a swimsuit and instead had played in the sand with Bailey while the others swam. That had been at the beginning of August.

She turned to the side, pressing her shirt tight against her stomach and eying her profile in the mirror. Two months since her last period. Not that she'd ever been the kind of girl who could set her watch by her cycle, but she'd never been this late.

Was it her imagination, or was there a slight bulge to her middle that hadn't been there before?

Meredith lowered herself onto the edge of the bathtub, pressing a hand to her mouth. Yesterday, Sawyer's suggestion had seemed ludicrous. Laughable. She and John had always been so careful.

But what if he was right?

An hour later, she was in a drugstore in Harbor Bay. It was nearly forty minutes from Sapphire Cove, so the likelihood of running into anyone she knew was slim. Still, she glanced around furtively before darting down the aisle labeled *family planning*. She felt on edge, like a teenager trying to steal a wine cooler from her parents' alcohol stash.

She'd never bought a pregnancy test before. Had never had a reason to. They'd been meticulous about taking precautions, despite her longing to start a family. John's reasons for waiting had been rooted in some deep trauma, and she hadn't wanted to push.

Except, what about when she'd been taking those antibiotics for her sinus infection? Would those have made her birth control less effective? The doctor hadn't said anything, but maybe that was the type of thing a woman was just supposed to know.

She shoved her hands in her pockets, staring at the multitude of options for home pregnancy tests. There were boxes with everything from one to five tests. Name brands she recognized, and generic alternatives. Some tests showed the result by one or two lines, while others were digital and said the actual word—*pregnant* or *not pregnant.*

Hope fluttered in her stomach. Or was that just the nausea? The idea that John had left behind a tiny piece of himself was too unbelievably incredible and awful all at once.

She'd watched Vanessa raise her son alone. Was that really what she wanted for her child—an existence without a father? It definitely wasn't what John had wanted for his future kids.

But it would be so wonderful to have a part of John to cherish forever. A little boy with his full lips and silky hair. Someone with the same laugh to remind her of the man she would always love.

He would have made such a fantastic father. The hands-on kind, who was always willing to play catch in the yard or put down his phone to watch a movie. If she was pregnant, unplanned or not, he would have been thrilled.

You're not pregnant. She swiped quickly under her eyes, then grabbed one of the name brand boxes containing a single digital test. The only reason she was even buying one was to prove Sawyer wrong.

Because her life was a mess right now. There was no place in it for a baby. She couldn't imagine doing it all alone—the late-night feedings, the first day of school drop-off, the doctor visits with a sick child.

It would be better for everyone involved if she wasn't pregnant. Yes, she desperately wanted a child. But not now. Not like this.

Not without John by her side.

She was only buying the test to prove Sawyer wrong. Never being a mother was just another way her life had changed in the past month. Because she knew she'd never date again. Never get remarried.

John had been her soulmate. If she couldn't have a future with him, she'd simply have to create a new one alone. One that didn't include things like romantic love and raising children.

When she got home, she shoved the test under her sink without opening it.

"That looks beautiful, Jamie. Hold that pose." Meredith shifted from kneeling in the sand to lying on her side. It was a frigid day, but she barely noticed the bite of cold. Her waterproof coat withstood the worst of the breeze and kept the seawater from soaking into her clothes. "Tim, step a little closer to Jamie. Yes, that's great."

She looked through her camera's viewfinder again. Perfect. She'd positioned Jamie with her back to the ocean, and from this angle, the camera perfectly caught the setting sun. The resulting silhouette beautifully highlighted Jamie's third trimester belly bump.

Jamie had booked this maternity photo shoot the week before John died. But Meredith tried not to think about that.

She snapped a few shots before pushing herself into a standing position and brushing off the sand that clung to her clothes. They had maybe twenty minutes of light left, and there were a few more shots she wanted to get on the pier. The Ferris wheel and carousel on the boardwalk always made an eye-catching backdrop, and the playfulness of those locations would work great since this shoot was to celebrate a baby.

The wind shifted, bringing with it the potent smell of fish. Meredith pressed a hand to her mouth. She would not get sick on this photo shoot, especially since it was the last one she had booked for October. Last year she and John had done mini shoots at the studio for parents wanting to capture their children in Halloween costumes, but this year . . .

Well, everything was different. The studio was as good as closed. John was dead. And she might be pregnant.

Stop it, Meredith commanded as she gathered up her gear. She wasn't pregnant. Her period could be late because of stress. The nausea was just a symptom of her grief. Her tight pants and even tighter bra were a coincidence.

On the boardwalk, Meredith tried her best to forget her worries and focus on the last few shots. For a moment, she could almost imagine that John was simply deployed like he had been so often in the early days of their marriage.

How would she feel about a potential baby if he was still here? Nervous, certainly. But excited to take a test and hopeful it was positive.

She definitely wouldn't have left it hidden under her sink for the past week.

"I think that's it," Meredith said, lowering the camera. "We got some fantastic shots, you two. I should have them edited and to you in a couple of weeks."

Jamie clasped her hands under her belly, bouncing on the balls of her feet. "I can't wait. Thanks so much, Meredith."

Tim put a hand around his wife's waist, pulling her close. "Yeah, we really appreciate it, especially since . . ." His ears turned red, and he cleared his throat. "You know."

Meredith looked away. Would she ever get used to the pity in people's eyes when they brought up John? "I'm honored you hired me to capture this special moment in your life. How much longer do you have?"

Jamie rubbed a hand over her belly. "About a month. I'm so ready to meet this little guy."

They exchanged small talk as they walked together to the parking lot. When they got to their car, Jamie held up a hand. "Wait just a second. There's something I want to give you."

Meredith nodded, feeling uneasy. Was it another casserole? The church ladies had brought over so many she'd had to store some of them in Sawyer's nearly empty freezer.

But when Jamie emerged from their newly purchased minivan—it still had the temporary plates—she had a bottle of premium wine in her hands.

"Here. Just a small thank you for the photo shoot."

Meredith took the bottle, touched. "You already gave me a generous tip."

"I know, but if I were in your position . . ." Jamie gave Meredith a sympathetic smile. "I just thought you could really use a glass of wine right now."

Meredith hugged Jamie, the bottle of wine clutched in her hand. She didn't know Jamie well, just from the casual conversations they'd had at church, but this was the most thoughtful gift she'd received so far. "Thank you. This means a lot to me."

Jamie climbed into the minivan with a groan, but didn't shut the door. "Go home and enjoy that tonight, you hear? You deserve it."

"I will. And make sure to send me a text when the baby comes."

Jamie laughed and nodded. Meredith stood in the parking lot, the bottle clutched to her chest, and waved as Jamie and Tim drove away. She didn't drink often, but a glass of wine and reruns of one of her favorite TV shows sounded divine.

Except what if she was pregnant? Then the wine would be a definite no.

She kept glancing over at the bottle as she drove home, and it felt heavy in her hands as she unlocked the front door.

What was she going to do—not take a pregnancy test and wait until her period started to drink a glass of wine?

She dropped her photography equipment in the spare bedroom and set the bottle of wine on the coffee table in the living room. She sank into the couch, staring at the bottle.

This was stupid. Didn't she have enough uncertainty in her future without letting this loom over her? In five minutes, she could know for sure.

But if she wasn't pregnant, it might feel like losing John all over again. She didn't know if she was strong enough for that.

And if she was pregnant . . .

She pushed herself to her feet, marching into the bathroom with determination. The box was right where she'd left it, wrapped in a grocery sack at the back of the cabinet among a half-used bottle of John's body wash and a nearly empty can of shaving cream.

"Just take the stupid test," she said aloud.

This was no big deal. She was just using the restroom.

The instructions seemed straightforward enough. Minutes later, she paced the length of the bathroom, one hand clutched around her necklace and her stomach churning.

She wasn't pregnant. Definitely not pregnant. Once that test proved so, she'd wait for her period to start and call the doctor in a few weeks if she wasn't feeling any better.

John was dead. Her dreams of sharing a family with him were gone, too.

It would be okay if she wasn't pregnant.

The timer she'd set on her cell phone beeped, making her jump. She fumbled with the phone, and it took her four tries to silence the alarm with her shaking hands.

"You should be here, John," she whispered. Her first time taking a pregnancy test shouldn't have been alone.

She inhaled a shaky breath, then took the few steps to the bathroom counter where the test sat.

One word stared up at her.

Pregnant.

No lines to misinterpret. Just eight letters strung together that said their birth control had failed.

She sank to the floor, one hand over her mouth as tears sprang to her eyes.

Pregnant. She was going to have a baby.

John's baby.

A baby without a dad.

Bile rose in her throat, and she barely made it to the toilet before throwing up.

How could God do this to her—give her a baby just as He'd taken John away? Anger flared so unexpectedly that it took her breath away.

A baby. Pregnant. She must be about two months along. Which meant in seven months, she'd have a tiny human to take care of. How was she supposed to do that when she couldn't even get a job interview?

Her hands shook as she brushed her teeth. The pregnancy test stared up at her from its place on the counter, taunting her.

She knew nothing about babies. Bailey was the only one she'd spent any significant amount of time around as an adult. How was she supposed to figure out how to be a mom when she still was figuring out how to be a widow?

John had done this to her—knocked her up and left. It didn't matter that they had been happily married. She didn't care that he hadn't chosen to die.

A string of curses flew from her mouth. She grabbed the test and threw it in the trash, then immediately felt guilty.

One hand drifted to her belly, resting there. A baby. A tiny human, half her and half John. A tangible, permanent reminder of their love for each other.

The loud chime of the doorbell made Meredith's heart jump. Crap. She'd forgotten that Sawyer was dropping by tonight to show her how to change the air filter on her furnace.

She walked to the front door on autopilot and swung it open. Sawyer wore his typical blue jeans and T-shirt, a flannel shirt opened over the top of it. He held up the boxy air filter. "Hey. You ready to learn how to change this thing?"

"No." Meredith ran a hand through her hair, letting out a disbelieving laugh. "You all were right. I'm pregnant."

CHAPTER Seven

$\mathcal{S}$ awyer's face turned the color of a sand dollar that had been bleached in the sun. He stepped inside, shutting the door behind him.

"You went to the doctor?" His voice sounded strained.

"No. I . . . I took a test. Just barely." She couldn't meet his eyes. What kind of twisted universe had she fallen into, where she was telling Sawyer she was pregnant instead of John? It wasn't fair. "I don't think it's a false positive. The internet said those hardly ever happen. And I'm *really* late."

"Wow." Sawyer ran a hand through his hair, making it stand on end. "Congratulations, Mer. You're going to be a fantastic mom."

Her eyes snapped to his and the sincerity there made her furious. "Are you freaking kidding me?"

"Of course not." He folded his arms across his broad chest. "I know the timing isn't great, but a baby is something to celebrate, right? And you *will* be a great mom."

She stomped to the couch, angrily wiping away her tears. A fantastic mom. Something to celebrate.

She'd dreamed of this moment so many times. None of her fantasies had looked like this.

"Mer?" Sawyer asked. "This *is* something to celebrate, right?"

She flopped onto the couch, and he took a seat beside her.

"John should be here celebrating with me." She gritted her teeth, willing more tears not to fall.

"He would have been so excited."

"Excited. Terrified." She laughed, feeling sick. "This is exactly why he left the SEALs. He didn't want me to have to raise our child alone. Didn't want his kid to grow up without a dad like he did."

"I know." Sawyer rested his hands behind his head, letting out a breath. "How do *you* feel about this?"

The concern is his eyes nearly broke her. She didn't know how to quantify her emotions. Wasn't sure what label to give them. "I feel like a million different colors of paint tossed onto one canvas and swirled into an ugly mess."

"Oh, honey." Sawyer scooted closer, wrapping an arm around her shoulders.

She leaned into him, squeezing her eyes tightly shut. If she didn't think too hard about it, she could almost pretend it was John sitting beside her. "I'm so mad at him."

"John?"

She nodded. "I know he didn't choose to die. But how am I going to do this without him?"

It was a rhetorical question, but one she desperately wanted answered. She ran a thumb over her anchor pendant. The other SEAL wives had talked about getting through hard things because that was their only option.

She wished there was another choice.

Sawyer squeezed her shoulder, then dropped his arm. She wished he'd put it back around her. Maybe then she'd feel less alone.

"It might not always be pretty, and it probably won't be easy. But I have faith in you, Mer. You'll get through this. You're brave and strong and capable."

"I don't feel brave and strong and capable." She hated the tremble in her voice. "I feel stupid for being in this situation."

"Hey now. Be nice to yourself."

"It's true." She shifted on the couch to face him better. "I still haven't gotten a single call for a job interview, and I even sent in an application to Baylor's and the grocery store this week." Not that either of those were good options now. Most places in town were family owned and only offered part-time hours, so they didn't have to provide health insurance.

"You'll find something soon."

"Something that lets me afford daycare and still be around when my baby needs me?" She wrapped her arms around her stomach, biting her lip. "We should have gotten some stupid life insurance when he left the Navy."

"None of us could have guessed he'd need it." Sawyer sighed, rubbing a hand over his face. "John would never have left you in this situation if he'd known."

"I know." She squeezed her eyes shut. "I don't know if that makes it better or worse."

They sat in silence, but it was comfortable instead of intrusive. Meredith tried to accept all the ways her life had changed yet again in the last thirty minutes.

She'd thought John was gone forever. Instead, he'd left her one last gift—a piece of himself in their child.

But then she remembered those last few weeks of Cheyenne's pregnancy, when she'd constantly had a pinched look of misery on her face despite never complaining. The way she'd lean forward, her brow furrowed, and Zach would knead her lower back.

Yes, she knew Cheyenne would coach her during labor and delivery if she asked. Vanessa would fly out to help for a week or so after the baby was born. Sawyer and Zach would assemble the crib and help her figure out how to install a car seat.

But it wasn't the same as having a husband by her side to help—a partner in every sense of the word.

John had been right to want to wait to have a baby. She wasn't ready to do this alone.

"This is a lot." She leaned back into the cushions, digging the palms of her hands into her eyes.

"I can only imagine." Sawyer's voice sounded husky. "But you're not alone, Mer. Not for any of it."

She gave him a wan smile. Sawyer meant well, and he'd certainly proved himself to be a true friend this past month.

But this wasn't something that would be over in seven or eight months. A child was a lifetime commitment, and she'd lost the person who'd promised to walk that path with her.

Sawyer propped one foot over his leg, giving her a wry smile. "Did John ever tell you he made me promise to take care of you if anything ever happened to him?"

"Are you serious?" Meredith laughed, her heart warming. That was so like John.

"It was on the day you two got married. He asked Zach, too. And then, when Zach married Cheyenne, same thing. Our jobs were so dangerous . . ."

Meredith sobered, one hand wrapping around her necklace. "I guess the joke's on us. Who knew that the real danger was in his body all along?"

She wasn't surprised that John had asked his two best friends to watch out for her. It almost felt like he was still here, his arms holding her tightly as he promised everything would be okay.

"Pregnant." Sawyer shook his head, that foot bouncing on his leg and a faint smile on his lips. "I guess that means I'm going to be an uncle again."

"This baby will be lucky to have you."

"And I'll keep my promise to John." Sawyer set his foot on the ground, leaning forward. "I'm serious, Mer. I'll take care of both of you."

She rolled her eyes. "I'm not a toddler that someone needs to take custody of. I appreciate so much all you've done to help me the past month, Sawyer. But I also have to learn how to do things on my own."

A muscle twitched in his jaw, but he nodded. "I know. Just don't try to be too independent over the next few months, okay? There's nothing wrong with asking for help when you need it."

"I know." She pressed a hand against her stomach, imagining the little life she carried inside. "This baby might not have a daddy, but he or she is pretty lucky to have an Uncle Sawyer."

Sawyer grinned, and his entire face seemed to lighten at the compliment. "Are you happy about this, Mer? Not the circumstances, obviously. But the baby?"

"Of course." She looked down at her stomach, rubbing a hand across it. "If John was here, everything would be perfect."

"Yeah."

"You really think I can do this alone?"

"Absolutely." The conviction in his voice made her heart swell. "But you won't have to. Me and the rest of the team will be here to help, however you'll let us."

"Sawyer—"

"That baby is a piece of John." His voice broke on the last word. "I know I didn't love John in the same way that you did. But I *do* love him. And I would never forgive myself if I let your stubbornness push me away."

She cocked her head to the side. This was a side of Sawyer she'd rarely seen before. "You think I'm stubborn?"

He grinned. "Absolutely. It's one of the things I like best about you."

She laughed. "Good, because it's not going anywhere."

"And neither am I." He took her hand in his, giving it a squeeze. "That's a promise you can take to the bank."

CHAPTER Eight

A loud ringing had Sawyer sitting straight up in bed, heart racing as he reached for a gun that no longer rested under his pillow.

He could almost smell the sulfur of enemy fire and feel the beads of perspiration running down his back.

The phone rang again, the vibration making it skitter across his end table. He grabbed for it while running one hand roughly over his face, trying to convince himself he was no longer a SEAL in battle.

Not that a middle-of-the-night phone call was any less anxiety-inducing. The phone's display flashed Meredith's name, and the clock in the top corner said it was 2:17 in the morning.

He jumped out of bed, his heart pounding for an entirely different reason. She'd never called him this late. Not the day he brought her home after John died. Not the night of the funeral.

Not a single time in the month since.

What could have changed since her startling confession about the baby only a few hours earlier?

He swiped to answer the call, demanding, "What's wrong?"

"I'm bleeding." The choked sound of her voice had his entire body growing cold. "I woke up to go to the bathroom, and . . ."

Blood. That wasn't normal, right? He bit back a curse. "Don't move. I'm on my way to take you to the hospital."

He grabbed a pair of jeans, trying to hop into them while still holding the phone to his ear.

Meredith had already lost so much. She couldn't lose this baby, too. John's child.

Sawyer closed his eyes, willing himself to calm down. He had to be the rational one right now. Needed to do what he'd promised John and take care of his family.

"It's not much blood. I think that's a good sign, right?"

Not much. Sawyer didn't know how to quantify that, but he was pretty sure that any blood had to be a sign of a bigger problem. "Yeah, that's probably good. I think we should get you checked out anyway, though." Not just by some random emergency room doctor, either, but a baby doctor, whatever those were called. He'd drag one out of bed if he had to.

"I can't lose this baby, John."

He inhaled sharply, that single word hitting him like a bullet to the heart. But Meredith didn't seem to realize she'd called him by her late husband's name. His best friend's name.

John should be the one taking care of Meredith right now.

He couldn't think about that. Once he'd dealt with the problem at hand, then he'd allow himself to process how he felt. That was how he'd always handled tough missions as a

SEAL. "How are you feeling otherwise? Any aches or pains or, I don't know, contractions?"

Could you have contractions when you were only a few months pregnant? He was so far out of his depth here. Sawyer ducked into the small walk-in closet and grabbed the first shirt his hands touched, immediately ramming it over his head.

"I . . . I don't think so. No." Her voice sounded more confident on that last word. "I feel the same as I have for the past month. I wouldn't even have noticed anything was wrong if I hadn't gone to the bathroom."

That seemed like a good sign. He grabbed his keys and wallet. Maybe he was panicking for nothing, but he would never forgive himself if something was seriously wrong and he didn't take her to the hospital. "I'm on my way. Don't move."

He made the eight-minute drive to Meredith's in six, and only a great deal of self-control kept him driving a mere fifteen miles over the speed limit. The blinds flicked apart as he pulled up to her front door, and she was halfway to his car before he jumped out to help her.

"I'm okay," she said through tight lips as he gently took her arm to help support her. "Seriously, Sawyer. I'm sure everything is fine."

"Me too," Sawyer said. But he didn't like how pale and washed-out her face looked in the moonlight, and he didn't relinquish his grip on her arm until she was safely seated in the passenger side of his truck.

Meredith stayed quiet as he raced through the sleepy streets of Sapphire Cove toward the town's small hospital. What if something was seriously wrong with Meredith? He'd push for them to transport her to a level one trauma hospital in Portland if he felt like they weren't taking good enough care of her.

He wasn't about to let Meredith die in the same hospital where they'd lost John.

"I'll drop you at the front door, then park," Sawyer said as they pulled into the parking lot.

"No." Meredith's hand landed on his arm, squeezing with more strength than he'd thought possible. "I don't want to walk in there alone."

Because the last time they'd been at this hospital, John had died.

Sawyer didn't want to walk in there alone, either. He didn't want to walk in there at all.

Luckily, the parking lot was fairly empty, given that it was nearly three in the morning. He whipped into the closest spot and killed the engine.

"Don't move," he demanded.

"I feel fine, Sawyer. Really."

He wanted to believe that. But there was a vice around his heart that made it hard to breathe.

Women died in childbirth all the time. One guy in the SEALs had lost a sister to that very thing. Sawyer couldn't remember the specifics anymore, but he knew she'd been pregnant, and the baby had died, too.

Sawyer pushed that dark thought out of his head, focusing instead on helping Meredith out of his truck. Why had he gotten a lift on the tires? She practically had to jump to get out of the cab.

He wrapped a supportive arm around her waist, trying to focus on the here and now. Meredith would be okay. The baby would be okay.

They would all be okay.

The red *emergency room* sign glowed above the covered entrance to the hospital. Meredith's steps slowed as they approached the door, and he heard the hitch in her breathing.

He tightened his hold on her waist. "It's okay," he murmured in her ear.

"The last time we were here . . ."

He blinked quickly. "I know."

The sliding doors whooshed open, making his own heartbeat accelerate. The smell of antiseptic wafting through those doors made him want to run.

He barely remembered the frantic drive to the hospital. But when he'd seen Meredith in the waiting room, he'd known that John's condition wasn't good. It had taken every ounce of strength not to fall apart at that moment.

Meredith hesitated, her eyes luminescent in the florescent light spilling through the doors.

"Are you okay?" He was torn between rushing her through those doors and whisking her far away from all the bad memories.

One hand went to her stomach, gently caressing it. He could almost see the resolve overtaking her. "Yeah."

He kissed her on the temple. "I'm not going anywhere. It's going to be okay."

The waiting room looked exactly the way it had last month—empty vinyl-covered chairs, low wooden end tables covered with outdated magazines, the television turned low to some cooking show while closed captioning flashed across the screen. It was overly chilly, too, just like it had been when John died. Sawyer even recognized the same nurse sitting at the admission desk, with her limp brown hair pulled back in a ponytail and a tattoo of a butterfly on her collarbone partially obscured by her scrub top.

Meredith hesitated. Had she recognized the nurse, too?

"Why don't you go sit down, and I'll bring you the paperwork," Sawyer said quietly.

Meredith nodded, her lips chalky white.

Sawyer hurried to the admission desk. The nurse pushed aside the crossword puzzle she was working on and looked up, her eyes flickering with recognition.

"How can I help you?" she asked.

Sawyer leaned forward, keeping his voice low. Not that Meredith didn't know why they were here, but hearing him say it might freak her out. "My friend is pregnant and started bleeding tonight."

The nurse glanced across at Meredith, and her eyes widened. "I thought you looked familiar. I remember you from a few weeks ago."

"Then you can understand why she's a little on edge."

The nurse nodded. "I'll get you back as quickly as I can."

Sawyer brought Meredith a clipboard of paperwork, and soon they were led to a small room that was barely big enough for the hospital bed. Sawyer was just glad it wasn't the same room where they'd been taken to see John after he'd passed. That one had been much larger, with soothing light blue walls and a love seat under one window. There'd been a small end table with a Bible, although the pastor had brought his own when he came to comfort Meredith.

"A doctor will be with you in a moment," the nurse said, yanking Sawyer back to the present. She opened a drawer and pulled out a hospital gown. "Change into this, please. I'll be back in a moment to start your IV."

Sawyer cleared his throat, motioning over his shoulder with one thumb. "I'll just wait outside while you change."

In the hallway, he slumped against the wall next to Meredith's door. His knees shook, the adrenaline finally wearing off. He braced his hands against his knees, trying to take slow, even breaths.

Now was not the time to fall apart. He could do that later once he knew Meredith was okay, and he had her safely back home. In the quiet of his own apartment, he'd let himself feel everything, but right now he had to do what he'd promised John and make sure Meredith was okay.

He'd already lost his best friend. He couldn't lose the love of his life, too, even if they'd never be more than friends.

When Meredith called for him to come back in a few minutes later, he was shaken by how small and fragile she looked in that hospital bed, a thin blanket pulled up to her chin and her stockinged feet just peeking out of the bottom. He swallowed, hoping his fear hadn't shown on his face.

He sank into the single chair in the room, which was already wedged beside the bed. Instead of grabbing her hand like he wanted to, he clasped his hands together and rested his elbows on his knees.

This was John's baby. John's wife. He should be the one sitting here, attempting to erase the worry lines from Meredith's forehead. But since he couldn't be, Sawyer would do his best to keep his promise.

"I can't lose this baby," Meredith whispered. "I know the timing is awful, but it's a piece of John. A piece of me." Her hands went to her stomach, which still looked pretty flat to Sawyer. "I already love this tiny person so much."

"I know." Sawyer leaned forward, resting his elbows on the edge of her bed. "I'm sure it's fine. Maybe you'll just have to, you know, do bed rest or whatever for a while."

"Yeah, maybe. Seven months isn't that long in the grand scheme of things. I could find a job doing graphic design online or something."

"Exactly. Everything will be okay."

He licked his lips, hoping he hadn't just lied to her. Meredith couldn't take another loss right now. It would break her—shatter her into a million pieces that no one could put back together. Not that he wouldn't try.

He shifted in his chair, the vinyl squeaking loudly with the movement. What was taking the doctor so long? Being in this hospital made him more jittery than ten cups of coffee.

"What if it's my fault?"

Sawyer stared at her, the anguish in her eyes making his heart ache. "What are you talking about? Of course this isn't your fault."

"I didn't know I was pregnant." She brushed away a lone tear with her free hand. "It's not like I've been eating well—I'm so nauseous all the time. I haven't been sleeping great, and I haven't seen a doctor yet. Should I be taking vitamins or something?"

He was so far out of his depth here. "I'm not sure. We can ask the doctor."

Meredith nodded, balling the blanket into her fists. "I know nothing about pregnancy or babies. My only experience with them is Bailey."

"That doesn't mean that anything is your fault. No matter what happens, you can't blame yourself. You didn't know, Mer."

She hung her head. "But I should have. Mother's intuition or whatever."

A rap at the door ended the conversation. He did his best to stay out of the way while the nurse started an IV and asked Meredith questions.

If John was here, he would've had Meredith and the nurse laughing. He'd been great with people and had a charisma that everyone loved. Sawyer hated that he made such a poor stand-in.

"The doctor will be in soon," the nurse said, then she gathered up her supplies and left.

"We should probably text Zach and Cheyenne," Sawyer said.

Meredith pressed her lips together, shaking her head. "Not yet. I don't want to wake them up in the middle of the night."

"They'll be mad if you don't tell them."

"I know. I just . . . I'll text them once I know more, okay?"

He wanted to argue, but nodded instead.

They found a rerun of some home renovation show on TV, but Sawyer couldn't pay attention. Every minute felt like an hour, and they watched almost an entire episode before the doctor arrived.

He was an older man with stooped shoulders and a bald head. His white coat hung on his frame, and square glasses slid down the bridge of his nose. Sawyer recognized him, but only vaguely, like perhaps they'd stood behind each other in the grocery store checkout line at some point.

"Mrs. Gilbert." The doctor extended his hand to Meredith. "I'm Dr. Mike, the on-call OB/GYN. And who do you have with you tonight?"

Sawyer accepted Dr. Mike's handshake, the firm grip raising his estimation of the man. "Sawyer. I'm a family friend."

If that surprised him, Dr. Mike betrayed nothing with his expression. "Nice to meet you. Now, Mrs. Gilbert, I understand that you're in your first trimester and experiencing some bleeding?"

Meredith nodded, her cheeks glowing pink. Sawyer's own neck felt hot. Should he step out into the hallway? He didn't want to leave her alone, but also didn't feel like he belonged.

"Can you tell me what's going on?" Dr. Mike asked.

Meredith cleared her throat, not looking at Sawyer. "Um, I woke up around two this morning to use the bathroom and realized I was bleeding."

"I see." Dr. Mike began washing his hands in the small sink. His tone was calm and conversational, but Sawyer felt no more at ease. "How much blood was there?"

"Not much. I only noticed it when I wiped."

"And the color?"

Oh gosh. Sawyer definitely should have stepped out of the room. He felt so far out of his depth here. Did Meredith want him to leave?

"Bright red." She twisted the blanket around her fist. "That's bad, isn't it?"

"Not necessarily." Dr. Mike threw away the paper towels and sat on a swivel chair, facing her. "Miscarriage is always a concern, especially when there's first trimester bleeding. But that's only one possible scenario, so let's not worry too much until we take a look. Are you okay with doing an ultrasound tonight?"

Meredith glanced over at Sawyer, then nodded. "Yeah, of course."

"Great. I'll do a quick exam here and we'll collect a urine and blood sample, too." He glanced over at Sawyer. "You might want your friend to step outside for a moment."

"I'll wait in the hallway," Sawyer said quickly. "Are you going to be okay?"

Meredith nodded, but he could see the fear in her eyes. He didn't want to leave her, but he also wasn't her husband. It would be inappropriate to remain during the exam.

The nurse returned, and Sawyer stepped outside once again. He rested his head against the wall, trying to take slow, steady breaths.

Everything would be okay. Meredith would be fine. The baby would be fine.

They'd all be fine.

The door opened, and Sawyer straightened, surprised to see the doctor again.

"You can go back in," he said. "I'll be back in a few minutes with the ultrasound machine."

"How did the exam go?"

"I'm sorry, but Meredith will have to answer that question due to HIPAA laws." The doctor rested a gentle hand on Sawyer's shoulder. "Let's not worry too much just yet."

"Her husband died last month." Sawyer folded his arms, embarrassed at the way his voice had cracked with emotion. "He was my best friend."

Dr. Mike's eyes softened. "I'm sorry to hear that."

But Sawyer wasn't interested in sympathy. He wanted action—some impossible guarantee that everything would be okay. "Please. She can't lose this baby, too."

"I'll do everything I can," Dr. Mike said. "That's a promise."

Meredith gave Sawyer a small smile when he re-entered the room.

"How'd it go?" he asked.

She shrugged. "He didn't find anything concerning."

His shoulders sagged with relief. "That's a good sign."

"Yeah, probably." But the way she worried at her bottom lip with her teeth told him she wasn't convinced.

Sawyer didn't know what he'd been expecting from a portable ultrasound machine, but it wasn't the cart Dr. Mike rolled in with a small, ancient-looking television screen perched on top.

"You estimate you're about eight or nine weeks along?" the doctor asked.

"About that," Meredith agreed.

"Okay then. Let's see if we can find the source of that bleeding."

Meredith reached for his hand, and Sawyer grasped it tightly. He kept his eyes glued to that small screen, and soon a fuzzy mess of black and white images appeared.

Her grip on his hand tightened. Sawyer placed his other hand over hers, praying with everything in him that the baby was okay. He couldn't make sense of the image, but there seemed to be a lot of movement, which he hoped was a good sign.

"Is the baby alive?" Meredith whispered.

"Yes." Dr. Mike grinned, pointing to something on the screen that looked more like a jumping bean than a human. "That's your baby. See how much it's moving? That's an excellent sign."

Meredith's grip on Sawyer's hand relaxed, her relief flowing through him. Sawyer stared up at the ceiling, saying a silent *thank you* to whatever guardian angel was watching over Meredith—probably John.

"I don't see any indications of bleeding . . ." The image disappeared from the screen as the doctor readjusted the wand, then reappeared a moment later. "Hold on . . ."

Meredith's grip was instantly tight again. "What's wrong?"

The image froze on the screen, then a moment later froze again. Sawyer heard a whir and realized the doctor was taking photos.

"You won't believe this." The doctor chuckled, pointing to the screen. Laughing had to be a good sign, right?

Sawyer would deck this doctor if it wasn't.

"See right there?" The doctor pointed to a white bean on the screen that kept bouncing around.

"Yes," Meredith said.

"That's your baby." The doctor moved his finger, pointing to a slightly smaller bouncing bean next to the first one. "And that right there is your baby, too. Congratulations, Meredith. You're having twins."

CHAPTER Nine

"Twins?" Meredith stared at the two bouncing babies on the ultrasound screen, trying to wrap her brain around this new reality. She wasn't just going to be a single mom—she would be a single mom with *children*. Two of them. It was another out-of-body experience, just like on the day John died. Except this time, she felt . . .

Happy.

Worried, certainly. Anxious about the future. Heartbroken that John wasn't here for this.

But so extremely grateful to have these two tiny babies growing inside.

Her free hand went to her necklace while tears pricked at her eyes. She could almost feel John's presence, like he was here, sharing in her joy. Maybe he'd be their babies' guardian angel.

Sawyer squeezed her hand, reminding Meredith that she wasn't alone. She brushed aside her happy tears and smiled at him.

Twins. Two babies. Two permanent reminders of John.

"And they're okay?" she asked.

"Their heartbeats are right on target, which is an excellent sign. One hundred and fifty-eight beats per minute for baby A and one hundred and sixty-two for baby B. Hear for yourself."

A soft whooshing sound filled the air, like the fluttering of bird wings. She wanted to capture that sound and play it on repeat forever. The awe in Sawyer's face perfectly reflected her own feelings.

"So, I'm not miscarrying?" She wasn't leaving until she felt certain of that, but her worries ebbed with each movement on the ultrasound screen. How would those acrobatics feel when she was nine months along?

So many times she'd imagined lying in bed with John, his hand on her distended stomach as he laughed at each tiny kick of their child.

"There's no unusual blood flow from the umbilical cord or placenta, which is another good sign," Dr. Mike said. "But I'm only seeing one placenta."

A new fear gripped her heart, and she reached instinctively for Sawyer's hand. "Is that bad?"

"Not necessarily. But it means the twins are identical, which automatically makes it a higher risk pregnancy."

And she didn't have insurance. Was self-employed with a highly variable income, depending on the month. Right now, deep into the off season, that income was minuscule.

Anger flared, but she bit it back. Yes, the timing of everything was horrendous. But that wasn't the babies' fault.

Babies.

"And identical twins are more dangerous?" Sawyer asked.

His concern made her feel a little less alone. She might not have John here beside her. But she still had a family, unconventional though it might be.

"They can be," Dr. Mike said. He was still taking pictures and measurements on the ultrasound. "Twin to twin transfusion syndrome only occurs in ten to fifteen percent of identical twin pregnancies, but we'll need to do growth scans every four weeks to monitor for it. There's also an increased risk of pre-term labor, gestational diabetes, preeclampsia, and anemia, just to name a few."

Her optimism was waning again, quickly replaced by overwhelm. She squeezed Sawyer's hand, trying to ignore the tightness in her chest. "That's a lot that can go wrong."

"The key is it *can* go wrong. That doesn't mean it will. We've got an advantage of knowing what we're dealing with early, which means we can monitor you closely. Lots of women don't discover they're having twins until their twenty-week ultrasound." Dr. Mike gave her a smile that seemed genuine. "We can go over everything more in-depth at your first appointment. I'd like you to call my office in the morning and schedule that for next week. For now, I don't see any unusual blood flow or fluid on the ultrasound."

"So why am I bleeding?" Meredith asked.

Dr. Mike shrugged. "Sometimes women spot in early pregnancy because of cervical changes."

Oh gosh. Sawyer's hand in hers suddenly felt like hot lava. Could she disappear from embarrassment?

Maybe she should have called Cheyenne to take her to the hospital. But she hadn't wanted to wake up Bailey, and strange as it seemed, she felt closest to Sawyer right now. They'd seen each other nearly every day since John died, and he'd been such a big help this last month.

A knock sounded on the door, then a nurse entered with a tablet she handed to Dr. Mike. "Here are the test results, doctor."

"Thank you," Dr. Mike said, taking the tablet.

This was it—when the other shoe would fall. A twin pregnancy, while terrifying, was also fantastic and amazing. Too good to be true.

She was just waiting for it to be yanked out from under her.

"Ah, this explains your bleeding," Dr. Mike said. "You have a pretty severe urinary tract infection. I'll write you a prescription for antibiotics that will be safe for the babies and that should clear it right up."

A UTI? "But I don't have any symptoms," Meredith said.

Dr. Mike shrugged. "It's uncommon, but it happens. Pregnancy can mask a lot of the symptoms since they can be similar."

Sawyer pushed a hand through his hair, the relief on his face palpable. "Aside from taking the antibiotics, what can we do right now to keep Meredith and the babies safe and healthy?"

Dr. Mike put away the ultrasound wand, and Meredith sat up straighter, adjusting the blanket to make sure she was fully covered.

"The most important thing from now until those babies come will be getting plenty of rest, eating well, and taking things easy. I estimate you're about ten weeks, based on the size of the babies, so we've got a long way to go until we get them here safely."

"So she's on bed rest?" Sawyer asked.

"Not quite that extreme. But avoid any heavy lifting or straining. Try to eliminate as much stress as possible from your life. Once you hit twenty weeks, I don't want you traveling more than an hour from Sapphire Cove in case you go into pre-term labor."

There was a whir from the ultrasound machine. Dr. Mike ripped off three black-and-white images, handing them to Meredith. She stared at them, trying to rein in the stress she was supposed to be avoiding.

How would she work until the babies came? Her entire job involved lifting, stressing, and straining. She remembered the way she'd crawled around in the sand at that maternity shoot she'd done last week, contorting her body into odd positions for the perfect shot.

How was she supposed to work *after* the babies came? She didn't even want to think about how much childcare would cost for two infants, and it wasn't like she had anyone she could rely on for free babysitting. Sawyer, Zach, and Cheyenne all had jobs, too, and Vanessa was on the other side of the country, going to school and taking care of her own son.

"I'll get those discharge papers for you," Dr. Mike said. "And I'll see you in my office next week."

"Thanks, Dr. Mike," Sawyer said.

Meredith rested her head against the pillows, a wave of exhaustion washing over her.

"Mer?" Sawyer asked quietly, his hand brushing her arm. "Are you feeling okay?"

Okay? The word was laughable. She hadn't been okay since John died. This new, unexpected turn was incredible and terrifying.

"I'm just taking it all in," she said, turning her head to smile at Sawyer.

"Yeah. Twins, huh? That's pretty amazing."

"Amazing," she agreed, shutting her eyes again. "Sorry. I'm just . . . So tired."

"You've been through a lot tonight." The blanket brushed her chin as he adjusted it to cover her better. "Close your eyes and rest. I'll wake you up when it's time to go."

Sleep. Yes, that was what she needed right now.

She closed her eyes and was out within moments.

Sunlight streamed through her bedroom curtains, pulling Meredith out of a dreamless slumber. Why did she feel so disoriented? She blinked, reaching for her glasses.

The bracelet from the emergency room slid down her wrist, bringing with it a flood of memories from last night.

Twins.

She grabbed her phone, squinting at the time. Nearly noon. Vague snapshots of signing discharge papers and being wheeled to Sawyer's truck meshed with a memory of his lips on her forehead as he tucked her into bed. Had he gone home after dropping her off, or was he still here?

She sat up slowly, trying to ignore the nausea. But an intense urge to use the bathroom urged her on. Her trip to the restroom confirmed she was still spotting, and the sight of those pink-tinged droplets made her heart race.

Dr. Mike said it's okay, she reminded herself as she washed her hands, then brushed her teeth. As soon as she ate breakfast—well, lunch—and got ready for the day, she'd head to the pharmacy and get that prescription filled. While there, she could grab some prenatal vitamins, then make a call to Dr. Mike's office and schedule a follow-up appointment for next week.

But first, food.

She slipped into John's ratty blue bathrobe, straining to hear any sign of Sawyer's presence. It seemed silent enough in the living room, but she had a feeling he was still here, watching over her.

Just like he'd promised John.

Sure enough, a laptop sat open on her coffee table. She looked around, finally locating Sawyer in the kitchen.

"Hey." He had a dishtowel slung over one shoulder and dark circles under his eyes. Had he slept at all? "How are you feeling?"

"Better." Other than freaking out over the whole pregnant-with-twins thing. Had it really been less than forty-eight hours since she'd taken that pregnancy test?

"Good." Sawyer motioned to his laptop. "Hope it's okay that I stayed here. I didn't think you should be left alone."

Her mind flashed back to insisting she *wanted* to be left alone in those dark days immediately after John's death and funeral. She'd meant it, too. Had wanted to be by herself, in her own home, where she could grieve in solitude.

But just as much as she'd wanted to be alone then, she was glad Sawyer was here now. "I don't mind. Was the couch too uncomfortable?"

His mouth quirked up in a grin. "Compared to the places I've slept as a SEAL, it was five-star luxury."

She smiled, one hand going to her necklace. John had made similar comments—not that she'd ever made him sleep on the couch. Still, there had been a few hard-as-rock beds at budget hotels and the occasional night spent dozing in an airport during a long layover. They hadn't traveled as much as they'd have liked, but there'd been a few memorable trips during their too few years together.

She pulled a yogurt cup out of the fridge, trying to stay focused on the here and now. Strawberry Greek yogurt didn't sound particularly appetizing, but she was motivated to eat in a way she hadn't been before realizing she was pregnant. "I hope I didn't derail your day too much."

"Of course not." Sawyer leaned against the counter, watching her like she was a glass teetering on the edge of the table, in danger of crashing into a million pieces at the slightest movement. "I stopped by my apartment and grabbed my laptop and a few things before bringing you home. You didn't so much as stir."

They'd stopped by his apartment? Meredith covered a yawn. She must have been out of it to not remember a detour on their drive home.

"Can I make you breakfast?" He motioned to the frying pan drying on the rack. "Maybe some eggs and toast? That's what I had for breakfast."

She held up her yogurt cup. "I think I'll stick with this and see how it settles, but thanks."

Sawyer nodded and slid a paper sack with drug information stapled to the front of it over to her. "You should take your prescription, too. The pharmacist said to take it with food or you'll get an upset stomach."

Meredith took the bag and pulled out the small pill bottle, oddly touched. "You picked up my prescription?"

"Yeah, I hope that's okay." He scratched the back of his neck, looking a little embarrassed. "Figured you should take the first dose as soon as you woke up."

"Thank you." She looked down at the bottle, noting the child-proof lid. Before, she'd always seen them as a bit of a nuisance, but with babies on the way, soon they'd be a necessary safety measure. "I had that on my list of things to do as soon as I'm ready for the day."

"I figured." He pulled a glass down from the cupboard and filled it with water, then handed it to her.

She took it gratefully and swallowed the antibiotic, then took a spoonful of her yogurt to help wash it down. "What would I do without you?"

He gave her a sheepish grin, looking boyishly adorable with that dish towel still slung across his shoulder. "You'll never have to find out."

She looked down at her yogurt cup, his words hitting her with a force she hadn't expected.

She *would* have to figure out how to get by without Sawyer's constant, reassuring presence, just like she'd have to learn how to live without John. Sawyer had his own life to live, and she couldn't expect him to put it on hold indefinitely just because she was having twins. He'd had an active social life filled with regular dates until he'd dropped everything to be her rock.

But this wasn't about getting through the next few months, or even the next few years. Being a parent was a lifetime commitment, and she felt wholly inadequate. If John was here, she knew they could tackle any problem together. But alone?

She pushed back from the counter, her entire body warm and chest tight.

"Mer?"

She shook her head, placing both hands over her stomach. Why was it suddenly a million degrees in here? Maybe standing under the fan in the living room would cool her down.

And maybe nothing would ever help again. She raised her face toward the ceiling, trying to focus on the slowly circulating blades of the ceiling fan. But her chest squeezed tightly, and every breath felt like sucking in needles.

"Hey." Sawyer nudged aside the coffee table so he could stand in front of her. The feel of his powerful hands gently gripping both of her arms was oddly soothing. "It's okay, Mer. Breathe."

"Okay?" She pushed his hands aside, feeling somehow unworthy of his comfort. "Nothing is okay, Sawyer. How am I supposed to do this?"

"Mer—"

"No!" She held up a hand, taking a step back. Her heart raced, the blood roaring in her ears and making her temples throb. "I have no health insurance, no stable income, two failing businesses . . . I've got two human beings I have to keep protected, which apparently means becoming a couch potato until they're born. And yet somehow, I'm also supposed to provide for them while simultaneously doing nothing."

The weight of her burdens would drown her. She clutched at her necklace, rubbing her thumb over the engraved words, but all the refusing in the world wouldn't keep her from sinking.

John had been her buoy amid the chaos of life. With him gone, the waves crashed over her until she thought she would drown. Tears stung her eyes and began sliding down her cheeks, despite her efforts to hold them back.

"Meredith." Sawyer's warm, steady hands were on her arms again. "Calm down, honey. You're hyperventilating."

She laughed, the high-pitched sound grating on her frayed nerves. "Calm down? I'm having twins, Sawyer! I'm having two babies, and I'm broke, and I have no job, and my husband's dead. What am I going to do?"

"All of that is true. But you aren't in this alone," Sawyer said quietly. "I'm here for you, remember? And Zach and Cheyenne will help as much as they can, too, I'm sure."

But having help wasn't the same as having a partner to share the load. She wanted someone to smile at across the dinner table when one of the kids mispronounced *spaghetti*, or who could help her decide on the proper consequence when the children hit each other, or who she could cuddle close with late at night as they whispered their hopes for the future.

"It's not the same." She sank onto the couch and closed her eyes, fighting a wave of grief. "I love you all, and I'm so grateful for your help. But it's not the same as having a husband. I miss John. I need John."

"I know." Sawyer sat down and she leaned into him, letting him wrap an arm around her shoulder. His voice was rough with emotion, in sharp contrast to his gentle hug. "I would give anything to bring him back for you."

She pressed her thumb more tightly over her necklace, feeling the grooves of the engraving. "I wasn't supposed to be a single parent. Or single at all. This isn't how I imagined this, and it definitely isn't what John wanted for his children."

"I know." Sawyer squeezed her shoulder. "He used to talk about how he couldn't wait to be the father that he'd never had to his kids."

"Both of us wanted that." She bit her lip, trying to breathe through the pain. Would losing John ever get easier, or would she just get better at dealing with it? "This sucks. After everything he did to make sure he didn't leave behind fatherless children, it comes to this?"

Sawyer pulled his arm away from her, his eyes luminescent and full of an emotion she couldn't quite define. "Maybe you don't have to raise John's children without a father."

Her hand dropped from the pendant, and suddenly her entire body felt like she'd just done the polar bear plunge. "What are you talking about?"

He turned to face her on the couch, their knees almost touching. One hand massaged his jaw. She hadn't noticed the five o'clock shadow there until now. "Maybe you don't have to do this without a husband, either."

She had to be misunderstanding him. "Sawyer—"

He leaned toward her, his gray eyes staring intently. "No, listen. Your babies deserve a father. Someone who will love them and care for them just as much as John would have."

"They need *John*," she insisted, her voice cracking. "And he's not here."

"No, he's not. But I promised John I would take care of his family, and I *am* here. You're going to need help through this, Mer. Someone who can support you financially, and physically, and emotionally. I can do that."

She sprang to her feet, the pounding of her heart almost painful. "What are you saying?"

He rose as well, reaching a hand toward her imploringly. "You could marry me. We could raise the twins together."

"Oh my gosh." She skirted around the couch. "You can't be serious."

"I wouldn't ask if I wasn't."

Images flashed through her mind of what life had been like married to John. The lazy Sunday mornings spent making pancakes in the kitchen. The late night binge-watching sessions of a favorite TV show. Arguing over home improvement projects, and then making up after the fight was over . . .

"No!" She clutched her head in both hands. The very idea of marrying someone else was horrifying. "John has barely been gone a month."

"I know. But a month ago, we didn't know that John not only left behind a wife, but two kids."

She squeezed her eyes tightly shut, as though that could block out his words.

"Let me take care of John's family. I can be here to help with the midnight cravings and late-night diaper changes and all of that. You wouldn't have to worry about money, or health insurance, or finding a job. I would take care of all three of you."

"Marriage is for two people in love." She dropped her hands, staring at him. "That's not us, Sawyer."

He folded his arms, not blinking. "Marriage is also for two people who are committed to each other and working toward the same goals. That *can* be us. I know I'm not John, and I know it wouldn't be a conventional marriage. But I can give those kids the father that John wanted them to have, and I can help and support you just like I promised him I would."

"John didn't ask you to marry me!" She threw up her hands. "He meant, I don't know, fix my leaky faucet and remind me to get the oil changed on my car."

"No." Sawyer shook his head, his jaw clenched. "That isn't what John meant at all. You can hire someone to fix your faucet. You can remember to get the oil changed. Please, Mer. Let me help you raise the babies. Marry me."

She wanted to launch across the couch and slap him. Instead, she pointed a trembling finger toward the front door. "I think you should leave now."

"Mer—"

"Go, Sawyer! Leave me alone."

The silence in the room was deafening following the volume of her scream. Her chest heaved as she watched him slowly pick up his laptop, the sound of his tennis shoes clacking against the tile floor.

At the door, he paused. "Just think about it, okay?"

She didn't look at him. Didn't answer. How could he suggest such a thing? How could he think for even a moment that she'd replace John—the love of her life—so easily?

John wasn't a ripped T-shirt she could toss into the trash, and marriage wasn't a pair of shoes she could change on a whim.

The screen door squeaked open on rusty hinges, and moments later the roar of Sawyer's truck faded into the distance as he drove away.

CHAPTER  Ten

She couldn't believe that Sawyer had proposed. Had he seriously asked her to *marry* him?

John was probably rolling over in his grave.

Meredith didn't remember shutting the front door or wandering into the kitchen, but she found herself standing in front of the refrigerator, staring at the carton of orange juice that Sawyer must have run to the grocery store for that morning while she slept. He'd probably read online that vitamin C was good for the babies or something. She had no doubt that he'd spent at least one of the hours she slept researching the best ways for a healthy twin pregnancy.

She shut the fridge without pulling out the carton and slumped against the door. Why had Sawyer opened his big mouth and changed everything between them? She'd come to rely on him so much this past month, and now he'd ruined everything. All because of some stupid promise John had forced out of him.

Just the thought of marrying someone else—someone who wasn't John—made her want to fall to the floor and cry.

No John, and now no Sawyer, either. Not that she thought he'd abandon her, but things would be awkward between them, and one or both of them would start pulling away. Would it create distance in her relationship with Zach and Cheyenne, too? Sawyer and Zach had fought together in battle. All she'd done was marry their best friend.

She grabbed her cell phone and initiated a video chat with the one member of her found family who wasn't connected to the SEALs—Vanessa. She'd also been a military wife. Had lost a husband and was raising a child alone. If anyone could empathize right now, she could.

Vanessa answered the phone almost immediately, her smiling face filling the screen. "Mer! I've been meaning to call, but it's been a crazy few days of school. How are you doing?"

Meredith laughed darkly, running a hand through her hair. "Oh, just peachy. Yesterday I found out I'm pregnant with twins, and then Sawyer asked me to marry him."

Vanessa's eyes widened, the camera jostling as though she'd almost dropped the phone.

"Yeah," Meredith said, giving a grim smile. "You heard me right."

"Um, I'm going to need you to back up a bit and tell me what's going on," Vanessa said. "Because holy cow, Mer. It's only been like three days since we talked."

So Meredith told Vanessa everything, starting with Sawyer's suggestion that she might be pregnant and ending with his proposal just a few minutes before.

"I mean, he's clearly lost his mind." She rearranged a wedding photo book on the coffee table with shaking hands.

Somewhere in that book was a photo of John with his arms around Sawyer and Zach, his best men. "It's like his latent protective instincts aren't getting a sufficient outlet since leaving the SEALs, and now he's misplaced all those feelings on me. It's crazy, right?"

She waited for Vanessa to agree vehemently. John had only been dead six weeks. Marrying his best friend because she was unexpectedly pregnant with twins was a horrible plan.

"I think you should marry him."

Meredith dropped the phone, smacking herself in the face. She picked it up quickly, trying to process what she'd just heard. "Wait, are you serious?"

"Yes. Accept his proposal."

This had to be a joke. But Vanessa wasn't laughing, and the situation wasn't very amusing.

"You're really telling me to get remarried?"

Vanessa gave an apologetic smile and nodded. "Yeah."

Meredith leaned her head back against the couch cushion and pinched the bridge of her nose. "Where is Grayson? I don't want him to hear his Auntie Meredith yell."

"Grayson's in my bed watching a movie." Vanessa ran a hand through her hair. "Just listen to me, okay?"

Listen. Listen to her best friend encourage her to move on. To forget her husband and ride off into the sunset with a new man and John's babies. "Fine. What insane reason makes you believe I should marry Sawyer?"

"I think you should say yes, because you're just at the start of this whole journey—widowhood, grief, motherhood, all of it."

"And finding a new husband is the answer?" She let out a disbelieving laugh.

"Maybe, crazy as it seems." Vanessa's voice was soft and compassionate, her eyes filled with empathy. "Everyone thinks the days right after the funeral are the hardest, but they're wrong. That first month, you're on everyone's mind. People bring you meals, and call to check up on you, and offer to do your shopping and clean your house."

Meredith glanced at her kitchen, where the freezer still overflowed with casseroles. But no one had dropped by with food in over a week, not that she'd expected them to.

No one but Sawyer. He'd brought her breakfast every Saturday morning. The text messages from concerned church members had trickled to a couple a week, but Sawyer still checked in on her every single day.

"Everyone will forget about you and get back to their regular lives." Vanessa shifted on the couch, the camera tilting to show a glimpse of a messy kitchen. "The help is going to stop. You're going to realize that this isn't all a bad dream—that you really are alone, and John isn't coming home from this mission. It isn't just another deployment. This is permanent."

Meredith looked away, the room turning blurry with tears. She wanted to scream at Vanessa to stop talking. To quit twisting the knife.

"I know what's in your future, and it won't be easy. I've been living it for three years. Being a single mom has been so much harder than I could have imagined—not just for me, but for Grayson. And there's only one of him. You'll have it twice as hard."

"But you've done an amazing job with Grayson." Meredith pulled her knees up toward her chest, hugging them with one arm, her other holding the phone as she pleaded with Vanessa to understand. "I can do an amazing job with my babies, too."

Vanessa smiled. "You *will* do an amazing job, no matter what you decide. But why make it harder on yourself than it has to be?"

"So I should marry Sawyer for, what, convenience?"

"He offered." Vanessa shrugged, her pink scrub top bunching up with the movement. "Do you have any idea how much it will hurt to leave your newborns with a babysitter so you can go to work? How much paying for childcare is going to cost?"

Meredith winced. She had thought of it—nearly worried herself sick at the ER last night.

"You'll have to handle everything, every stage, alone. The shopping and the cleaning and the potty training and first day of school." Vanessa sighed, leaning back on the couch. "Motherhood is the most amazing journey you're ever going to take. But it's exhausting to squeeze in study sessions while making sure Grayson gets to soccer practice on time, and worrying that his friends aren't always the best influences, and stressing that he's falling behind in math. My house is always a wreck and if it weren't for grocery delivery, my fridge would probably always be empty."

The picture Vanessa painted was grim, far from the cheerful Norman Rockwell scene that Meredith and John had always imagined.

Vanessa's voice was so soft that Meredith had to strain to hear her.

"If someone offered to share all the struggles and joys of parenting with me—someone who treated me with the care and respect that Sawyer shows you—I would marry him in a heartbeat. Grayson needs a male role model, and it's the one thing that I haven't been able to provide for him."

"He's John's best friend." Meredith pressed her forehead into her knees, fighting back the tears. "Marrying anyone would feel like betraying John, but Sawyer?"

"I know, sweetie. But maybe the fact that he was John's best friend is what makes him such a perfect match for you now. He'll love and care for those babies every bit as much as John would have."

"John should be here." Meredith let out a sob. "He would have made such a fantastic father."

"I know." Vanessa's voice was choked, her eyes sparkling with tears. "He was a great guy. But he isn't here anymore. Sawyer is right in front of you, and he's offering to help—to provide for you financially, be a dad to the babies, give you some stability and security. If it weren't for the twins, I'd agree that you should turn him down."

Was this what English majors meant when they talked about irony? "If it weren't for the babies, he wouldn't have offered."

"Which proves my point." Vanessa shrugged again. "You can't only consider what's best for you anymore. Think about what's best for your babies. Sawyer might be it."

It seemed impossible that Vanessa could be right. "But I don't love Sawyer—not the way I love John. Sawyer is a dear friend, but John was my everything."

Vanessa nodded, her head cocked to one side. "True, but I don't think Sawyer is under any illusions about your feelings for him. You should talk to him. Ask what a marriage would look like. Explain your feelings. He'll listen to your point of view, and the two of you can discuss this like adults."

Meredith suddenly had the urge to laugh. She bit her lip, swallowing back the bubbling hysteria. "I really thought you were going to tell me this is crazy, and that Sawyer needs professional help."

Vanessa grinned. "Yeah, I can see why you'd assume that. But your life is different now. Maybe a marriage of convenience is exactly what you need to get through the next few years."

"And then, what? We get a divorce?"

"Talk to Sawyer," Vanessa repeated. "And let me know what you decide, okay? I love you, girl. You've got this."

Meredith had never felt less in control of the situation. But Vanessa was right about one thing—she needed to talk to Sawyer. "Love you too. Tell Grayson I miss him."

"I will."

Meredith ended the call and tossed her phone onto the coffee table. If her mind had been reeling before, now it was doing cartwheels down a steep hill.

Marry Sawyer. Insane. What would it be like to have a man in the house again?

What would marriage to Sawyer entail?

She pushed herself to her feet and stuffed her cell phone in one pocket, then she grabbed one of John's hoodies and slipped it on. Dr. Mike had told her to stay down as much as possible, but she needed air and there was a bench overlooking the beach less than a block from her house.

Five minutes later, she sat on the bench, watching the waves crash into the shore in the distance. She clutched her necklace tightly in one hand, holding onto the anchor pendant like it was her literal lifeline.

"This is insane, right?" she whispered.

The cool October breeze played with her hair, making her neck prickle with goosebumps. She nestled deeper into John's hoodie and inhaled, but only the faintest scent of him remained. She'd refused to wash any of his things, but it hadn't mattered—the scent had faded anyway. Even now, she wasn't certain if it was there, or if it was just the memory of him.

She watched as a dog played in the surf on the beach below, barking happily as he danced away from the waves. His owner tossed a stick, and the dog chased after it. Would she and John have gotten a pet eventually? He'd always thought a child should have a dog.

"I don't know what to do," she whispered. "Things weren't supposed to happen like this. Why did you leave?"

A seagull dipped down, coming up a moment later with a struggling fish in its mouth. Meredith closed her eyes, imagining she and John were walking along the beach hand-in-hand. It had been one of their favorite things to do together, especially at dusk.

A memory came back to her—one she'd nearly forgotten. She and John had been engaged. He'd gotten a few days of leave to visit her, and they'd been discussing their plans to open the scuba shop.

"What about kids?" Meredith had asked. "If we start a new business, that means we'll have to wait a while before having a baby. Doctors kind of like it when you have this little thing called medical insurance."

John's brow had furrowed, that adorable dimple in his cheek popping as his mouth quirked to one side. "I want to have kids with you, Mer. Lots of them."

"I know." She'd squeezed his hand. "But you've always wanted your own business. Something where you can set your own hours and be around a lot for your children."

"I never want my kids to feel abandoned, the way I did." John's voice had grown soft and pained, his light brown hair rustling in the breeze.

"You'd never abandon your kids." While John's career had nearly scared her away, his difficult upbringing and messy childhood had never concerned her. She'd known without a doubt that he'd be an excellent husband and father. "You aren't your dad."

"I know." John's smile had made her insides feel like they were glowing. "I just never want them to feel like they don't have a father, you know? I think even newborns can probably sense that kind of thing, and starting a new business takes so much work. So here's what I propose—we get the business up and running by next May so we can capitalize on tourist season. Then, we give it five years. If things aren't going well by then, I'll get a real job so we can start our family."

Meredith squeezed his hand, her smile so wide it made her cheeks hurt. "You've got yourself a deal."

I never want my kids to feel like they don't have a father. The echo of that conversation made her heart twist. She pressed a hand to her stomach, imagining the two tiny lives within.

But it wasn't like John had willingly abandoned them. He'd died, not become a drunk gambling addict who disappeared. It wasn't the same.

He wouldn't want her to marry his best friend just so his kids could have a dad. Right?

A happy squeal pulled her attention back to the beach. A little girl, maybe two years old, ran up the rocky shoreline, her feet moving so fast Meredith feared she'd do a face-plant in the sand. Behind the little girl, a tall man with a beanie covering his hair chased after her with a laugh. He swept the girl into his arms with a growl while she giggled loudly.

The image morphed into one nearly as vivid as the real thing. She could see it so clearly—Sawyer chasing two bubbly little girls with John's square jaw and her blonde hair down the beach while she held her arms out, waiting to catch the girls. It wasn't the image she'd always hoped for, but it was a pleasant one.

She blinked, turning her attention back to the dog and his owner on the opposite end of the beach. Was she seriously considering Sawyer's offer?

If she didn't marry Sawyer, there would be little time for lighthearted games of chase on the beach. Her days would be long, filled with worries about finances and a constant race against the clock. She'd struggle to stay on top of the ever-present housework in between her day job. Would she even be taking photos anymore, or instead be forced to take a boring desk position just to put food on the table?

She stayed at the bench until the sun dipped low in the sky and she started shivering in John's fleece-lined hoodie. Then she headed home, where she closed all the curtains and flipped on every light.

In the kitchen, her eyes zeroed in on the three ultrasound photos held to the fridge with a magnet. One hand went unconsciously to her stomach.

She would walk through fire for these babies. Do anything to provide them with the best possible life.

Even if it meant marrying Sawyer. Even if marrying Sawyer wasn't what John would have wanted.

But was marrying Sawyer the right thing to do? Would John have approved?

She picked up the ultrasound photos, staring at the blurry white images of her babies. They resembled jelly beans more than humans, but she knew that in a few months, that would change. Her stomach would swell, her body would change even more than it already had, and before John had been gone a year, she would be singing two infants to sleep at night.

She gently traced the outline of her babies with one finger. What would John do if their situations were reversed? What would she *want* him to do?

A slow warmth enveloped her body, erasing the chill of her stint outside. Tears pricked at her eyes, and she held the ultrasound photo to her chest, choking back tears.

If she was gone, and John was faced with raising two babies alone, she would want him to marry a nice woman so that he didn't have to do everything alone. So that her children could have a mom.

John would want the same for her. Yes, his first choice would be to live. For them to raise the twins together and live happily ever after. But that wasn't real life, and she was staring down a very long and lonely reality. Sawyer had offered her a light at the end of the tunnel, and Meredith knew John would want her to take it.

She hung her head, tears dripping onto the hoodie. She must be insane to consider this. Was it even fair to Sawyer? What kind of marriage was he expecting?

She swiped her keys off the counter and headed toward the door once more. There was only one way to find out.

CHAPTER Eleven

He'd finally proposed to the woman he loved, and he couldn't regret it more.

Sawyer set his laptop on the empty spot on the couch beside him and ran a hand over his face. It had been a few hours since he left Meredith's, and he'd spent most of that time fighting the urge to go back over there. She'd asked him to leave, and he had to respect that. In a few days, he'd send her a text and see how she responded.

The living room was dark now, but Sawyer hadn't bothered to get up. Closing the blinds, flipping on lights, focusing on work—it all seemed like too much effort.

His offer to marry her had been impulsive but genuine. It made sense on paper. He could help her through a difficult pregnancy and be the father that John would have been. Getting married would solve Meredith's financial problems. He could put her on his health insurance plan, enable her to stay home with the babies so she didn't have to pay for childcare.

Such a stupid, stupid idea.

Sure, he'd been terrified when she called him in the middle of the night after realizing she was bleeding. But it had only taken him fifteen minutes to get dressed and arrive at her home. While being married would ease a lot of her burdens, it wasn't like he couldn't still help as Uncle Sawyer instead of Dad.

His offer had been beyond presumptuous. Would she even let him help her through the pregnancy now?

He'd blown it. Betrayed John twofold—by propositioning his wife and by scaring her away. He couldn't keep his promise to John if Meredith wouldn't let him in the door.

Zach would kill him when he found out what he'd done.

A knock sounded at the door, timid and unsure. He froze, wondering if he'd imagined the sound.

No. He'd spent too many years honing his sense as a Navy SEAL to second-guess them now.

Sawyer bolted to his feet and tripped, his foot catching the edge of the coffee table. He stumbled his way to the front door and flung it open, barely daring to hope.

She'd come.

"Hey," Sawyer said, surprised at how hoarse his voice sounded. He hadn't been crying, although he'd certainly wanted to.

Meredith shifted uncomfortably from foot to foot, her hands buried in the front pocket of one of John's hoodies. She looked just as she had a few hours earlier—hair pulled back in a loose ponytail, face free of makeup, eyes perhaps a little redder than before. Car keys clanked together as she fiddled with them.

"Hi." Meredith took a deep breath, finally meeting his gaze. "Can we talk?"

He couldn't tell if she was here to forgive him for his temporary lapse of insanity, or to tell him she never wanted to see him again. Either way, the pounding of his heart in his chest was almost painful.

If she cut him out of her life, Sawyer would never forgive himself. John would never forgive him, either.

Would he forgive him if Meredith accepted his proposal?

Sawyer stepped aside, holding open the door wider. "Yeah, of course. Come in and sit down."

"Thanks."

She sat on a lounge chair, perched on the edge as though uncertain she'd be here for long. Sawyer took the couch, sitting as far away from her as possible—he didn't want her to get the wrong idea. Yes, he loved Meredith. Had for years. But she didn't know that, and when he'd offered to marry her, all he'd been thinking about was making sure John's family was okay.

"Were you serious about your offer?" She brushed a strand of hair behind one ear, calling his attention to the wedding ring she still wore. "About . . . about marrying me."

He tried to read the room, but his own hope battled with fear until he had no idea what she was thinking. In the end, he decided honesty was the best course of action. "Yes. But I think I may have given you the wrong idea."

Her eyes flitted to meet his, then away again. "When you say marriage, what does that mean? What would a marriage to me look like to you?"

He knew what she was asking, and his ears burned with embarrassment mixed with desire. But this wasn't about how much he loved her—it was about how much she needed him, and about what he'd promised John. This was loyalty to family, not a play for her affections.

He steepled his fingers so he wouldn't be tempted to take her hands in his. "I know you love John—will *always* love John. I'm not trying to replace him in your life, or in the lives of the babies. He will always be a part of our family, whether things stay as they are now or whether you accept my offer."

He hoped so badly that she'd accept his offer. That he could be Dad to John's twins instead of Uncle Sawyer, since John wasn't here to take on the role himself.

As for Meredith, he would keep his feelings hidden unless she showed she wanted something more.

She stared down at her hands, clasped tightly together in her lap. "When you proposed, I thought you were crazy."

He couldn't help but chuckle. "Yeah, I kind of figured."

She looked up from her clasped hands, her expression unreadable. "But then I called Vanessa, and she told me I should accept your offer."

Whoa. He owed Vanessa big-time. Was Meredith really going to marry him? The possibility was almost too much to hope for.

"Are you only doing this because of John?" Meredith asked.

The answer to that one was easy. He tried to swallow back the tears so his voice wouldn't sound choked. "Of course it's because of John. He was my brother, Mer. I loved him so much, and I would never forgive myself if I could have helped his family and didn't."

She nodded. "And so this would, what? Be a marriage in name only?"

"It's not like we're complete strangers." He scratched the back of his head, looking away. "I've always considered you one of my dearest friends. We're family, right?"

She gave him a fleeting smile, nodding. "Yeah. You've always been my favorite surrogate brother-in-law. Just don't tell Zach."

Sawyer chuckled, ignoring the jab of pain her words caused. He wasn't surprised she'd only ever seen him in a brotherly way. If she'd ever viewed him otherwise, she wouldn't be the woman he loved.

He made an x over his chest. "Your secret's safe with me."

She gave him a tremulous smile. "If I agree to marry you, I'd do my best to be a good wife. But John was my soul mate, and I'll love him forever. I wouldn't be prepared to be, you know, a wife in every sense of the word, and I can't promise I'd ever get to that point."

He nodded, understanding the unspoken meaning. "We'd have separate rooms, obviously. I never thought otherwise when I made the suggestion."

Her shoulders relaxed, her relief obvious. "But that doesn't seem fair to you. Don't you want to fall in love with your soul mate?"

He'd already fallen in love with his soul mate—she'd just been his best friend's other half instead of his. After dozens of first dates over the past year or two, he'd finally accepted that no one else would ever measure up. Meredith was it for him. "I want a family, and you'd be giving me that—a place to call home, two kids to raise with a woman I deeply admire and respect."

She began running the anchor pendant back and forth along the necklace chain, although he was pretty sure she didn't realize what she was doing. "I admire and respect you too, Sawyer. But if we get married, I don't want it to be some temporary fix to my current problems. I won't raise my babies to call you *daddy* only for us to get divorced in a few years and leave them heartbroken and confused."

Just the thought of getting any piece of Meredith in his life forever was more than he'd ever dreamed of. He could keep John's memory alive for her and the babies. Make sure they grew up knowing the stories about their father only Sawyer could tell them. "When I asked you to marry me, I meant for the long haul. I'm all in, Mer. I want to be there when they're christened, and for their first day of junior high, and for their weddings. I want us to have the kids and grandkids over for Sunday dinner every month. It might not be a conventional marriage, or a conventional family, but it would be *our* family. We can make it whatever we want."

"And you're really okay with a marriage devoid of romance? Because I don't think—" Her words cut off abruptly while her eyes welled with tears. She shook her head, lips pressed tightly together.

The thought of trying to force a romance with Meredith that she wasn't interested in or ready for was repulsive. He leaned forward and gently took her hands in his, unable to stop himself from touching her.

"Hey," he said gently, waiting until she met his eyes. He gave her hands a squeeze. "It's not about that, Meredith. I will be whatever you need me to be. I will stay as long as you need me to stay."

She laughed, pulling one hand away to wipe away the tears glittering beneath her eyes. "That hardly seems fair to you."

"Isn't that up to me to decide? I asked you to marry me, not the other way around."

"True." She sighed, looking down at their clasped hands. "I just don't want you to resent me one day for taking away your chance at happiness."

"Oh, Mer." He ached to pull her into his arms. To reassure her it would never be an issue. "Who says we won't be happy?"

She pulled her hand from his, placing them both on her flat stomach. "I just want to do right by these babies. John always wanted them to have a father. If it couldn't be him, I know he'd want it to be you."

He swallowed back his emotions. Sawyer knew he wasn't John—wasn't as funny or fun-loving as his best friend. But he would do his best to be an adequate replacement.

"And what if one day you want more than a marriage of convenience to your late husband's best friend?" Sawyer asked. "What if one day I'm no longer enough for you?"

She shook her head, giving him a sad smile. "You know there will never be anyone for me but John."

The words were both a balm and a sword. Even though he'd never have the relationship he wanted with Meredith, he also wouldn't have to watch her fall in love with someone else—again.

"Before I agree to this, it's only fair that I remind you my financial situation is a mess." Meredith lifted her hands helplessly. "There are loans for both businesses, and we took out a small mortgage on the house to do some of the improvement projects."

Sawyer was already shaking his head. Of all her concerns, money was the one he could most help with. He wasn't wealthy, but he'd invested smartly and was well enough off. He'd be able to support Meredith and the twins easily enough. "We'll figure it out."

"What about the town? Everyone will gossip if I marry you only a couple of months after John's passing. They'll think we were together, you know . . ." Her cheeks glowed pink.

"No one who's seen you and John together would ever think there was something illicit going on behind his back." Yes, the townspeople would gossip, but that would die down quickly enough, and he was more than willing to weather some sideways glances and sharply barbed words. "But if it concerns you, we can always move somewhere else."

"No." The word was abrupt. "I don't want to leave Sapphire Cove, or my house."

Sawyer nodded, relieved. He didn't want to leave, either. "The lease on my apartment is up at the end of this month. I was going to renew it, but I can move into the spare room in your house once we're married instead."

"This is crazy." Meredith rested her arms on her knees and buried her face in her hands. "Women raise babies alone all the time. Marriage? It seems so extreme. Cheyenne and Zach will think we've lost our minds."

Their reactions worried him more than that of the entire town of Sapphire Cove. But now that Meredith was considering his offer, he wasn't about to back down. "Once we explain our reasonings, they'll be supportive."

"And if they aren't?"

The thought was too horrible to consider. "They will be. But even if they aren't, this isn't about them. This is about *you*, Mer. What do *you* need? What makes this easier for *you*?"

She gave him an *are you serious?* look. "Well, the first thing that comes to mind is John not being dead."

"I can't give you that, but you know I would if I could."

Meredith gave him a wry grin. "I know. But I wouldn't be the only one in this marriage, and I can't help but feel like I'll be denying you something important if I agree to it. You'd be giving me so much while I gave you almost nothing in return."

He couldn't believe she thought he was the one getting the raw end of the deal. "Are you kidding me? You'd be giving me a family. That's all I've ever wanted. You'd be allowing me to raise John's children."

Meredith gave him a watery smile. "This whole thing just sucks. I'm so mad at John for dying. He really screwed things up this time."

"Yeah, when I get to heaven, I'm going to kick his butt for doing this to you."

She laughed, rising to her feet. "I'm not saying yes, but I'm not saying no, either. Can I think about?"

He couldn't believe she was even considering his impulsive request. How had he gone from friend to possible fiancé so fast?

"Take all the time you need," he said, walking her to the front door.

She laughed, pressing a hand to her stomach. "I don't think the twins will offer me the same courtesy."

"Good point."

She looked up at him, lips turned down in a frown. "If I say no, will I still get to keep you in my life?"

He couldn't stop himself from pulling her into a gentle hug. "Absolutely. I'm here for you, no matter what. I'll be whatever you need me to be, remember?"

She nodded, giving him a smile. "Thanks, Sawyer. I'll talk to you later."

He made sure Meredith got to her car safely and didn't shut the door until her taillights had disappeared. Then he wandered into his bedroom and collapsed, hope warring with crushing guilt.

What would John think of Sawyer's proposal? He hoped his friend would approve, even if he knew the depths of Sawyer's feelings for Meredith.

I will be whatever she needs me to be, Sawyer promised himself silently. And he would do his best to honor John's memory in the process.

CHAPTER Twelve

Meredith sat alone in the waiting room of Dr. Mike's office, her hands buried deep in the front pocket of one of John's hoodies. Across from her, a little boy who couldn't be more than two peered at the fish tank, his hands pressed against it and nose almost touching while his very pregnant mother tried to coax him to stop smudging the glass.

Her hand wandered to her stomach while a deep regret punched her in the chest. She'd never get to watch these twins of hers welcome a younger brother or sister. There would be no more children after these two.

She looked away before the mom could catch her staring, watching the young couple in the corner. They sat close, heads nearly touching and hands resting on her slightly swollen stomach. Maybe waiting to feel the baby kick? She had no idea when that happened—four months along? Five? Nine?

Maybe she should have let Cheyenne come with her to this appointment. She'd stopped by the garage yesterday and told her and Zach the news. They'd been surprised but supportive, and Cheyenne had promised to share all of her pregnancy advice. Meredith knew nothing about childbirth or babies. Had never even changed a diaper until she and John watched Bailey one night while Zach and Cheyenne had a much-needed date.

She swiped her phone awake almost reflexively, wishing she could call John or even send him a text. He would have closed the scuba shop if necessary to come to this appointment with her, no questions asked.

But there was nothing but a text from Sawyer wishing her luck at the appointment.

She leaned her head back against the wall and closed her eyes tightly. It had been a week since his proposal, and though neither of them had brought it up again, she knew he was waiting for her answer. But the idea of being a fiancée felt as foreign and uncomfortable to her as being a widow.

Sawyer had offered to accompany her to the appointment too, even promising to stay in the waiting room if that would make her more comfortable, but she'd declined his offer as well.

"Mrs. Gilbert?"

Meredith grabbed her purse from the floor and rose, following the nurse back to a small room where she took her vitals. Then Meredith was left alone, sitting on the exam table.

Her feet dangled above the floor and she stared down at them, trying to imagine the next seven months of attending doctor's appointments alone. The last week had been hard. She'd tried her best to follow the doctor's orders and rest, but it hadn't been easy. Bills had to be paid with money she somehow needed to earn. The laundry demanded attention whether she was supposed to lift baskets of clothes or not. Her toilet still needed to be scrubbed and the grout on the shower tiles scoured. Sawyer had still checked on her every day, but she'd kept their interactions short and hadn't asked for help with anything around the house.

At least the bleeding had stopped a few days ago, although she'd felt some sharp twinges in her stomach that made her nervous.

If they were married, would she feel awkward asking him to clean the bathroom or start a load of laundry? Would sending him to the store with a grocery list feel like an imposition? She'd never thought twice about asking John for help with some small task.

Meredith rubbed her eyes, the tension in her shoulders making them ache. This stress couldn't be good for the babies. Maybe the fact that she was so undecided about accepting Sawyer's proposal was her answer.

But if she said no, would she and the others become like most families, who only saw each other on holidays and the occasional long weekend? If she didn't marry Sawyer, someday down the line some other lucky woman would. He'd have kids of his own, and hers would only have an uncle.

If Sawyer or Zach ever moved away from Sapphire Cove, they wouldn't even have that. What if Sawyer married some girl from New York and they moved back east to be near her family?

What would John want her to do?

"Knock knock." Dr. Mike entered the room with a nurse, giving her a warm smile. "Good to see you again, Meredith."

"You too," she said.

"How have you been doing on the antibiotics? How's the bleeding been?"

They talked for a few minutes about how she'd felt since her stint in the emergency room. Dr. Mike promised to write her a prescription for an anti-nausea medication that would help with the morning sickness and gave her a few home remedies she could try as well.

"The pain in your stomach is round ligament pain," Dr. Mike said as he squirted goo on her stomach. "It's very common as your uterus expands."

She nodded, relieved it wasn't something more serious. "Doesn't that usually happen later in pregnancy?"

"Yes, but it's very common for it to start this early with twins. Two times the babies mean everything happens twice as early."

"I guess that makes sense." And was also completely terrifying. She'd noticed her pants were a little tight this morning, but figured that was just because she'd been trying to eat more regularly since finding out about the babies. Was her stomach already noticeably growing? Cheyenne hadn't even looked pregnant until she was almost halfway through the pregnancy.

An image popped up on the large television on the wall in front of her, the ultrasound image much clearer than the one had been in the ER. She kept her eyes peeled to the screen, soaking in every movement of her babies. They still resembled jelly beans more than anything else, but she didn't care.

Those movements were happening inside her stomach right now. Those babies were hers and John's.

But would they call Sawyer dad?

"Everything looks great," Dr. Mike said. "They're active little guys."

"They're boys?" Meredith asked, squinting at the image.

"Sorry, I meant to use the term generically. We won't be able to tell for a few more weeks whether you're having boys or girls, but I still only see one placenta and am confident they're identical."

Which meant they were the more high-risk type of twins. She put a hand to her forehead, trying to absorb this information while Dr. Mike repeated what they'd discussed at the hospital—her need for frequent ultrasounds, how she'd have nearly double the number of doctor visits as someone pregnant with only one baby, the high likelihood of needing a c-section and the possibility that the twins would be premature and require time in the neonatal intensive care unit.

Then, probably because he saw the panicked look on her face, he said he'd have the office's financial clerk send her some information on programs that could help with the costs.

By the time she arrived back home, her head was swimming with everything they'd discussed, and she had a folder full of handouts with information.

How could she get these babies here safely without help, much less raise them alone?

Her phone rang, and she answered Vanessa's video call. Today her scrub top was covered in mermaids.

"How did it go at the doctor's?" Vanessa asked.

"Fine. The babies are fine." She squeezed her eyes shut, trying to force back the tears. "Me? I'm a little overwhelmed and wondering if I'll ever be fine again."

Not that she'd have time to worry about being fine between doctor's appointments and worrying about preterm labor and trying to get her house ready for two humans without being too active.

She missed John so much.

"Oh, sweetie." Vanessa heaved a sigh. "You will be fine again someday. I promise."

Meredith bit her lip. "How long did it take you?"

"No two people process grief in the same way." Vanessa brushed a strand of hair behind one ear. "I won't sugarcoat it—the first year was really rough."

And Meredith would get to spend that incredibly difficult first year dealing with the emotional roller coaster of pregnancy and postpartum. Awesome.

"But it gets easier, and you will figure out a way to be happy again," Vanessa continued. "The babies will bring you so much joy. I don't know how I would have survived losing Andrew without Grayson."

But Grayson had been a toddler, not a newborn. And Vanessa hadn't been pregnant.

"I'm so scared to do this alone." She absently traced a heart on her belly, imagining how much it would change over the next few months. "But that seems like a really selfish reason to marry Sawyer."

"So you still haven't decided what to do?"

"No. Marrying him feels so unfair. I can't be the kind of wife he deserves. We won't have that type of marriage."

"But you already told him that, and he still wants to marry you."

"Maybe he doesn't know what he wants."

Vanessa rolled her eyes. "He's a grown man who can make his own choices. If you don't want to get married because you don't think it's the right choice for you and the babies, that's fine. But if your only hesitation is being fair to Sawyer? Well, let him make that choice for himself. You've given him all the facts."

She stared across the room at the wedding photo of her and John that hung beside the front door. If she married Sawyer and he moved in, would she have to take that photograph down? She felt confident Sawyer would never ask her to do that, but it would also feel strange to keep the photo around. Almost as wrong as taking it down would feel.

"What would John say?" Meredith asked. "If I married his best friend less than two months after burying him?"

"Honestly? I think he'd give Sawyer a giant hug and thank him for watching out for his family." Vanessa lifted her shoulders in a shrug. "These aren't normal circumstances. You've got a high-risk pregnancy and two babies on the way. You're going to need a lot of help, for the next few years especially, and Sawyer's offering that."

"Yeah, in the craziest way possible." Meredith glanced again at the wedding photo, imagining replacing it in a few years with a family photo of her, Sawyer, and the twins. She didn't know if she could do it—move on with her life and leave John behind. The last thing she wanted was to erase his memory.

But wouldn't marrying Sawyer help preserve it? He knew John even better than she did, perhaps. Had certainly spent more time with him and known him a lot longer. Sawyer could share stories with the twins of their father's bravery and courage that she didn't know about.

He can share those same stories even if you aren't married, she reminded herself.

"Sometimes blessings come in ways we don't expect," Vanessa said. Meredith had almost forgotten they were still on the video chat. "So reach out and take it."

Grayson's school bus arrived then, and Vanessa hastily ended the call. Meredith slumped onto her bed, curling up in a ball on John's side. She could no longer smell that faint whiff of his aftershave on the patchwork quilt, and it made her heart ache.

She closed her eyes, imagining her future if she turned down Sawyer. No doubt he would still help in whatever way he could. But her babies wouldn't have a dad—they'd have a kind Uncle Sawyer, who'd stopped by twice a week to toss a ball in the front yard, or maybe help with some project around the house that Meredith hadn't been able to do alone. At least until he got married and started his own family.

As for her, she'd have to get a real job. Maybe something in graphic design that would allow her to work from home, at least during the pregnancy. She couldn't be belly-crawling in the sand for the perfect shot when nine months pregnant with twins. Besides, there were no guarantees or stability in photography—her failed studio proved that much. She needed something with regular business hours and benefits.

Maybe she'd go back to school and become an elementary school teacher. That would at least let her be close to the kids while they were young. She'd only gone to college for three semesters and had never declared a major, but if Vanessa could go back to school with a kid, so could she.

Of course, Vanessa's husband had died in the line of duty, so she had widow benefits from the military. Meredith didn't even have health insurance, and she wasn't sure if she'd qualify for government help.

Her babies would get clothes from second-hand stores, generic box meals, and every birthday and Christmas would hinge on how much she could scrimp and save. Not a bad life—she'd experienced some of the same struggles being raised by her grandparents—but a life much more challenging than what she'd wanted for her babies.

But if she married Sawyer . . .

She could stay home with the babies and be the kind of mom who baked cookies and played with them on the beach. They'd get home-cooked meals each night instead of whatever frozen dinner she stuck in the microwave after work before collapsing on the couch.

There would be no need to leave her babies with a stranger while she toiled away at a job that slowly killed her soul. If she had two little girls, they'd have a father to take them to the daddy daughter dance at the elementary school held every year. If she had two little boys, they would have someone to teach them how to fish so they could enter the town's annual competition each spring.

She'd been worrying it was wrong to ask so much of him, but was she selfish to *not* take up Sawyer on his offer? Saying no would mean denying her children a much easier, happier future. One where Meredith could accompany them on every school field trip and where Sawyer coached little league.

Refuse to sink, Mer. Rise up and make the hard choice.

She kept her eyes tightly closed, imagining that John was speaking to her.

This is Sawyer, she silently argued. *Your best friend. And you want me to marry him? Are you insane?*

John had asked Sawyer to take care of her—not to become her husband. John wouldn't really want her to do this, would he?

She could almost imagine him lounging on the couch beside her, one arm stretched out behind her back and a foot resting on his knee.

Come on, Mer. You know what to do.

Her fist closed around the necklace, the metal warm. For a moment, she could almost imagine she was holding John's hand.

"I don't love Sawyer like that," she whispered to the empty room. "I love you."

She closed her eyes, remembering what it had felt like to be wrapped tightly in John's embrace. If he was here right now, he'd kiss her gently on the lips and tell her she could do hard things. *You've got this, Mer. I trust you.* How many times had he told her that when she'd doubt a decision, whether big or small?

She took a deep breath and quickly typed out a text to Sawyer. **Hey, can you come over right now so we can talk?**

Was she crazy? Was she really doing this?

She pushed send.

Less than a minute later, her phone dinged with his reply.

I'm on my way.

CHAPTER Thirteen

Sawyer swiped his keys off the counter with shaking hands. He was pretty sure Meredith had made a decision. If she said no, would things be able to go back to how they'd been before he impulsively asked her to be his wife?

He couldn't bear losing her after losing John. The thought of being relegated to an awkward family friend was more than he could handle.

In his truck, he turned off the radio because the sappy country song grated on his nerves. For years he'd dreamed about the day he'd get married and have a family, but none of those imaginings had looked like this.

He gripped the steering wheel tighter, as though that would temper his emotions. If she turned him down, he would do his best to act unaffected. He'd be there for her, just like he had been for the past almost two months. Maybe if he didn't act like anything had changed, nothing would.

But if she said yes . . .

He pulled into Meredith's front yard and killed the truck engine, feeling more jittery than a SEAL on his first op. She had the front door open before he could knock, and he wondered if she was as anxious as him.

"Hey," Meredith said, motioning him inside. "Thanks for coming."

"Of course." Sawyer resisted the urge to wipe his sweaty palms on his pants. Meredith looked the same as she had every day he'd seen her since John's funeral—hair pulled back in a ponytail, baggy sweatpants and one of John's oversized sweatshirts.

She looked beautiful.

"Can I get you a glass of water or anything?" Meredith asked as he slipped off his shoes.

She'd never been so formal before. Did that mean she was about to turn him down? Sawyer shoved his hands in his pockets, following her into the living room. She'd straightened up since he was here last. The throw pillows were fluffed and artfully placed in the corners of the couch, and a knitted afghan hung over the back. The used cups and half-empty plates had been removed from the coffee table, and the fireplace mantle looked like it had been dusted.

Didn't she know that cleaning didn't equate with taking it easy?

"No, thanks. I'm not thirsty."

"Okay." She motioned awkwardly to the living room. "Um, I guess we can sit down."

She sank into the couch and he took the chair, not wanting to seem too forward. Her back was ramrod straight, like a soldier standing at attention, and her hands were clasped so tightly together that her knuckles were turning white.

If she turned him down, would he still get to be Uncle Sawyer? Being denied the opportunity to watch John's children grow would feel like losing him all over again. Who else could tell them about the time their late father had sneaked a piglet into the girls' locker room? Even Zach hadn't been around for that particular escapade in middle school.

"How was work today?" Meredith asked.

Sawyer raised an eyebrow. Now he really had no idea what her answer would be. Their futures hung in the balance, and she wanted to make small talk?

"Mer, just tell me what you've decided to do." He ran a hand over his jaw, wishing he'd shaved today. If he'd known they'd be having this conversation, he would have. "I can take it."

"Yeah, okay." Her shoulders nearly touched her ears with tension. "I don't know how to do this."

How to turn down a marriage proposal from a man she'd never been on so much as a date with? He swallowed, mentally bracing himself for the worst breakup of his life.

If John were here, he wouldn't have to hear Meredith turn him down. He could've been content with their happiness and kept dating women he met through singles apps until he found someone to love.

He wished John was here to tease him about his latest date. Wished he, Zach, and John were playing basketball and making plans for Thanksgiving in another few weeks. The holidays were going to look very different this year. Empty without John's off-key rendition of *The Little Drummer Boy* in a high falsetto.

"I don't think there's a manual for this kind of thing," Sawyer said.

"Right." Meredith dropped her hands to her knees, her shoulders relaxing. She pulled at her bottom lip, worrying it with her teeth.

He still didn't know what to brace himself for. For years he'd watched Meredith, and he'd thought he'd learned to read her pretty well. But today, he was at a loss.

She was going to turn him down.

He still hoped she'd say yes.

She lifted her chin, her eyes meeting his intently. "I'd like to accept your offer, if you're still willing."

Had she said *accept*? His ears buzzed like he'd been too near a rifle shot without protective gear. Sawyer leaned forward, his heart pounding in his chest. "Are you saying you'll marry me?"

She nodded, her eyes hooded and lips pressed into a thin line. "Yes, if you'll have me."

He'd wanted nothing but to have her since the moment they'd first met. She'd only had eyes for John, but there'd never been anyone else for Sawyer after that moment.

He'd also never so much as hinted at his feelings for Meredith. Would have sooner cut off his own arm than come between her and John.

Happiness warred with guilt as he imagined what his best friend would say if he could see them now. "That's great, Mer."

"I don't know. I still worry that I'm being selfish." Her hand went to the anchor pendant hanging around her neck, a far-off look in her eyes that made his heart ache. "I love John so much. I'm never going to get over him."

Sawyer had loved John in a much different way, but he understood what Meredith was saying. He would never get over losing his best friend, either. Would feel his absence at each holiday gathering and casual weekend barbecue.

"I would never ask you to get over John." He took her free hand gently in his, giving it a squeeze. "I hope you believe me when I say I have no intention of replacing him, in your life or in the twins'. If it weren't for the babies . . ."

She looked down at their clasped hands. "I know. If not for them, I never would have considered this."

"And I wouldn't have asked," Sawyer said quickly. The thought of trying to start a romance with Meredith so soon after her husband's death was horrifying.

Yes, he loved Meredith. But he respected her and John even more.

"I know you wouldn't have." Meredith took a deep breath. "But my babies deserve a mother and a father. John didn't have that option when he was a child, but they do. And I can't think of anyone he'd entrust that role to more. He loved you so much, Sawyer."

If she kept talking like this, he was going to cry. "He was my brother. I would do anything for him."

Her mouth quirked up in a grin. "Even platonically marry his grieving wife and raise his fatherless babies?"

"They won't be fatherless." He gave her hand another squeeze. "They'll have me."

She gave him a watery smile. "Then these babies are pretty darn lucky."

"*I'm* the lucky one." His throat felt thick with emotion, a confusing array of joy mixed with sorrow for what could have been.

For years, he'd tried to find a good woman to fall in love with so he could start his own family and raise his kids alongside those of his best friends. John had always been a part of that picture, one arm around Meredith's waist as they gazed adoringly at each other.

He still wanted that picture, for Meredith and for John. Even if it meant he'd die alone. But Sawyer couldn't control what had happened. All he could do was move forward with the hand they'd been dealt.

Meredith withdrew her hand, looking down at her lap as though embarrassed. "I don't know what you had in mind for the wedding . . ."

"Whatever you want," he blurted. None of that mattered to him—what was important was the commitment they were making to raise John's kids together. "Name the time and place."

"Then let's do it as soon as possible. Just the two of us at the courthouse, I think."

Sawyer nodded, pulling out his phone to make some notes. A celebration with their friends and family would feel beyond inappropriate, given the circumstances, but he could think of two people who might want to attend. "What about Zach and Cheyenne?"

Her face blanched white, and for a moment he worried she was going to throw up.

"I don't know," Meredith said. "How are they going to take all of this?"

Sawyer had no idea. "Well, they were thrilled about the twins."

"Not sure they'll be as thrilled about us getting married, even if it is for the babies."

Yeah, Sawyer was worried about that, too. "I can talk to them alone, if you'd like."

She nodded, some of the color coming back into her cheeks. "Thanks. Maybe just explain to them why we're doing this, and that we just want to elope."

He nodded. It wouldn't be a wedding like John and Meredith's, or Zach and Cheyenne's. But it also wouldn't be a typical marriage, so it fit somehow. "I'll make all the arrangements. You won't have to worry about a thing."

"Thanks." She motioned to an open door. "I'll clear out the spare bedroom and you can move in as soon as things are finalized."

She was avoiding using the word *married*, he could tell. But that was fine. He was just glad he'd be close enough to help as the pregnancy progressed and around for all the firsts with the new babies. "No, Zach and I will clear out the spare bedroom. You will sit on a chair and boss us around, just like the doctor ordered."

She laughed, but nodded. "Deal."

"I'll let my landlord know I won't be renewing the lease on my apartment." There wouldn't be much to pack up, and whatever furniture Meredith didn't want, he would sell. The pieces were mostly discount items he'd bought for comfort instead of style, anyway.

"And I'll figure out how to rearrange my bedroom so I can fit a crib in there," Meredith said. "That'll work at least temporarily."

Sawyer already had ideas about how he could add an addition onto the back of the house to create a few more bedrooms, but that was something he'd bring up with Meredith later. John might have already mentioned it to her—it had been his idea, after all, and he'd asked Sawyer's opinion on the plans.

"We'll take things one day at a time," Sawyer said. "Your only job for the next seven months is to keep those babies happy and healthy. That's why we're getting married, right? So I can be around to help."

"Thanks, Sawyer." She rose, holding her arms out for a hug.

Sawyer willingly accepted her embrace. They stood in the living room, arms wrapped tightly around each other, for a long time.

"I'm scared," Meredith whispered into his shoulder.

He tightened his grip on her. "That's okay. I am, too."

This felt different from any hug he'd shared with Meredith before. It wasn't the desperate hug she'd given him at the hospital when the doctor informed them John had passed. It wasn't the hug of gratitude they'd shared before the funeral, or any of the dozens of reassuring ones they'd shared in the weeks since.

This time, he wasn't hugging his best friend's wife.

He was hugging his own fiancée.

CHAPTER Fourteen

$\mathcal{S}$awyer climbed into his truck on shaking legs, feeling almost giddy with nerves.

She'd said yes.

He was going to marry Meredith.

Never in a million years had he thought she'd be his bride. How many times had he imagined her walking down the aisle toward him in a flowing white dress, a wreath of flowers in her hair, and a soft smile meant only for him?

No, he told himself as he started the truck. There would be no blushing bride at his wedding. Meredith still loved John. Wished it was him she was sharing her life with, not Sawyer.

He would give her up in an instant if it meant that John could live. It hurt in a way nothing else had to know that his friend was going to miss it all—Meredith's pregnancy, the birth, the next eighteen years of raising the twins. A lifetime of firsts.

But if John couldn't do those things, at least Sawyer could do them on his behalf.

"Don't hate me for marrying her," he whispered aloud.

His only answer was the gentle hum of the truck's engine.

It would be harder to keep his feelings hidden once they were living together, but he'd give Meredith all the time she needed. One year. Twenty years. A lifetime. Some of her heart was better than all of anyone else's, and maybe, one day, she'd want more from him than a platonic husband.

He pushed the thought out of his mind. That wasn't why he'd proposed. Sharing her joy as they raised John's babies would have to be enough.

At home, he grabbed his laptop, ignoring the company emails needing his attention, and began researching how to get a marriage license. Meredith had said she wanted to do it as soon as possible, but had she really meant that?

His phone buzzed. Sawyer stared at it, anxiety making him lightheaded.

He wouldn't blame Meredith if she changed her mind. He still couldn't believe she'd agreed in the first place.

She won't change her mind, he tried to reassure himself. Or maybe it was a desperate prayer.

He swiped open the text, heart in his throat.

Are you sure you're okay with telling Zach and Cheyenne on your own? I feel bad putting that on you.

Sawyer pressed a fist to his mouth, his body going limp. So she wasn't backing out. Not yet.

It's okay, really, he texted back. **I can go over there later today so it isn't hanging over our heads.**

Thanks. I really appreciate it. See you tomorrow?

That simple question had him giddier than a teenager on his first date. **Absolutely. I'll bring by dinner after work.**

Let me know how it goes with Zach and Chey.

Will do.

Dread for the upcoming conversation made concentration nearly impossible, so at seven o'clock Sawyer swiped his keys and headed out the door. Cheyenne should have closed the garage by now, and they'd probably be cleaning up dinner and getting Bailey ready for bed.

He heard Bailey's squeals before Zach opened the door, a towel draped over one shoulder and a stuffed dog in one hand.

"Hey," Zach said, his brows lifting in surprise. "Come in."

Another shriek. Bailey toddled down the hallway, wearing only a diaper, her legs moving just as fast as they could go.

"Hey you." Zach swept her up, playfully blowing on her stomach as she shrieked in delight. "Where do you think you're going?"

Sawyer couldn't contain a grin. That would be him in no time at all, chasing after two energetic toddlers who were his entire world.

Zach would understand why he was doing this, right? He knew how much Sawyer wanted a family.

Cheyenne's voice floated down the hallway. "Bailey boo, where did you go?" She appeared a moment later with a pair of pink pajamas with gray elephants in one hand and a bottle of lotion in the other. "You little stinker. I turned my back for one second."

Zach blew kisses on her stomach again. Her chubby hands went to his cheeks while she laughed wildly. "Can you say, 'I'm sorry,' Bailey?"

She shook her head, laughing as she jabbered away.

"Oh, hey, Sawyer." Cheyenne gave him a tired smile. "What brings you over tonight? Is Meredith okay?"

"Yeah, everything's fine." Sawyer wiped his sweating palms across his jeans. "I was hoping I could talk to the two of you."

Zach and Cheyenne exchanged a look—one of those loaded expressions that communicated a conversation Sawyer didn't understand.

Would he and Meredith ever get to that point? He hoped so.

"Sure," Cheyenne said. "Let me just get Bailey dressed and in bed. Give me twenty minutes, if she cooperates."

"No rush," Sawyer said, although he really wanted them to. "You guys do your thing. I can wait."

He felt like he was waiting for a guillotine to drop.

"Be back in a few, then," Zach said, motioning to the couch with his head. "Make yourself at home."

Sawyer took a seat while Zach and Cheyenne disappeared into Bailey's nursery. He pulled out his phone to continue researching wedding options, each of Bailey's laughs making him more eager for what the future would bring.

A husband. A father. It wasn't exactly as he'd always imagined it, but it was with the woman he wanted by his side forever, and that was more than he'd ever dared to hope for.

If John was watching this all play out from heaven, Sawyer prayed he would forgive him for marrying his wife.

Obtaining a marriage license seemed simple enough. He and Meredith just had to show up with their driver's licenses and a copy of John's death certificate. Three days later, they could bring the marriage license to the county courthouse and be wed in front of a judge.

Could he and Meredith really be married in less than a week?

He shot off an email to his landlord, letting him know he wouldn't be renewing his lease and would be out by the end of the month. He'd just begun researching wedding rings when Bailey's giggles finally subsided and the apartment grew quiet.

Zach and Cheyenne walked into the living room, their hands linked together.

"What's up?" Cheyenne asked as she and Zach sat on the couch, still holding hands.

"Yeah, you're kind of freaking us out." Zach gave him a fierce glare. "You better not be here to tell us that you're leaving Sapphire Cove or something."

Cheyenne swatted Zach on the shoulder. "Stop. Sawyer isn't moving. He wouldn't leave with everything going on."

Well, that was as good a segue as any. "I am moving, actually. Before the end of the month."

"What?" Zach said, standing.

"Shhh." Cheyenne tugged him back onto the couch. "You're going to wake Bailey."

"Sorry. Geez, Sawyer." Zach jerked a hand through his hair. "Your timing sucks, what with John dying and Meredith having twins and all."

"Where are you going?" Cheyenne asked, her lips turned down in a frown.

Sawyer rubbed his palms across his jeans again. He wasn't sure if he should brace himself for a punch in the jaw or to be thrown out of their home. He took a deep breath, then met Zach's gaze squarely. "I'm moving into Meredith's house, actually. We're getting married."

Cheyenne inhaled sharply, then started coughing. Zach glanced at his wife in concern, patting her on the back as she struggled to regain her breath.

"This is a joke, right?" Zach shot at Sawyer. "Because let me tell you, it's not funny."

"Good, because I wasn't trying to make anyone laugh," Sawyer shot back. He looked at Cheyenne, who was still coughing. "Are you okay?"

She put a hand to her chest, breathing deeply. "Yeah, just swallowed wrong. I wasn't expecting *that* to come out of your mouth."

"Because it's ridiculous," Zach said. "This is about our promise to John, isn't it? Now that Meredith is pregnant, you feel like you have to marry her so you can take care of his family like we promised."

Sawyer ran a hand over his jaw, remembering those conversations with both John and Zach before their weddings. That pact—to take care of each other's families if the worst occurred—hadn't been mere lip service.

"Of course it's about John. Meredith is having twins. The doctor says it's going to be a difficult, risky pregnancy."

"And we're all here to help her," Zach cut in. "No one needs to get married."

"Except why *wouldn't* I marry her?" Sawyer rose, too agitated to sit still. "You know how much I've wanted a family. These are *John's* babies. He would hate the idea of them growing up without a dad."

"Probably not as much as he'd hate the idea of you marrying his wife," Zach shot back, rising to his feet as well. "He hasn't even been dead for two months."

"Meredith needs more than occasional help," Sawyer said, his voice rising. "You and Chey are great, but you have your own family to worry about. I can help her more as a husband than as a friend. This way I'll be around day or night. If something happens and she needs to go to the ER again, I won't have to race across town to get to her. I can put her on my health insurance, and pay off her debts, and provide for her so she can stay home with the twins, if that's what she wants."

Zach opened his mouth, then shut it again. "This is so messed up. She's John's *wife*."

"You think I don't know that?" Sawyer took a step toward Zach, heat racing down his spine. "I am acutely aware of that fact."

He'd be moving into a house filled with John's things, decorated with photos of him and Meredith together. The ghost of his best friend would surround him at every turn.

"Guys." Cheyenne jumped to her feet, placing both of her hands on Zach's chest. "Let's all calm down."

Zach heaved, his face nearly red with suppressed emotion. "I'll say it again—she's John's wife."

"And she wouldn't marry someone else two months after he's gone unless it was the right thing to do," Cheyenne said, her tone slow and measured. "Right?"

Zach's shoulders slumped, and he nodded. "Yeah, I guess."

"So let's all sit back down and let Sawyer explain."

Zach slowly sat back down, and Sawyer did the same, his body still tensed for a fight. He wouldn't hurt Zach, but he would defend himself if necessary. They might not be active duty anymore, but once a SEAL, always a SEAL, and the instinct to confront an opponent was strong.

"So you're getting married," Cheyenne said, pressing her hands into her knees so that her shoulders nearly touched her ears. "Wow. Is this going to be, um, a traditional marriage?"

Sawyer looked away in disgust. "Of course not. You know me better than that. I'll be staying in the spare room."

"Okay." Cheyenne nodded, looking back and forth between him and Zach as though waiting for another argument. "So, will you get divorced once the twins are older, then?"

"No," Sawyer said more forcefully. "That isn't an option for either of us."

Cheyenne cocked her head to the side, looking at Sawyer as though she'd just realized something. "You're just going to stay married for the rest of your life to someone who's only a roommate?"

Yep, he sounded like a glutton for punishment. But all Sawyer could do was nod. As hard as this conversation was, nothing Cheyenne or Zach were saying made him want to change his mind about the wedding.

Cheyenne gasped, putting a hand to her lips.

"What?" Zach asked, looking at her.

"You love her," Cheyenne said, staring at Sawyer.

His entire body felt warm. He scratched the back of his neck. No one had ever confronted him with the truth before, but he wasn't about to lie to his family.

"I love her enough to never let her know," Sawyer said. "She doesn't need that right now. What she needs is someone to help her and care for her and support her. What those babies need is a dad. My personal feelings are irrelevant."

Zach swore, slapping his knee forcefully. "You're playing with fire, man. I just hope neither of you gets burned."

"What other choice do I have?" Sawyer held out his hands in a pleading gesture. He desperately wanted his friends' support. "If the situations were reversed, and Cheyenne had been married to John, and you found out she was pregnant with his twins, what would you do differently than I'm doing right now?"

Zach hung his head, Cheyenne's hand resting on his back. "I always suspected how you felt about her," he said finally.

That was news to Sawyer. "I thought I hid it well."

"You did." Zach looked up at him, his elbows resting on his knees. "John never suspected anything, I don't think. I always respected you for stepping aside and doing nothing about it, and I saw how hard you were trying to move on with the constant dates. But this feels weird."

"It feels right to me." Sawyer tapped his chest, swallowing back his emotions. "This isn't about how much I love Meredith—it's about making sure John's kids have a father like he would have wanted for them. It's about letting Meredith stay home with the babies, if that's what she wants, and making sure they have enough money for food and clothes and family vacations to Disneyland. Come on, Zach. You know I would never disrespect John's memory by making a play for his wife when she's vulnerable and hurting. This isn't like that. Not for me."

Zach folded his arms across his broad chest, but Sawyer wasn't intimidated. He had two inches and twenty pounds of muscle on his friend. Not that he'd fight back if Zach started swinging punches. Not at first, anyway.

"We know your heart is in the right place," Cheyenne said, squeezing Zach's knee. "Don't we?"

Zach sighed, his posture relaxing. "Of course we do. I just don't want either of you to get hurt. This is a lot to swallow."

"I know, and I'm sorry," Sawyer said. "You know I'd bring back John if I could."

"I know." Zach's eyes were suddenly wet. "I miss him, you know? Yesterday I looked at my phone and realized we should all be playing basketball."

"Yeah." Sawyer pressed a fist to his mouth, trying to hold back his own emotions. "I miss him too. Every freaking day."

"Well, congratulations." Cheyenne rose, leaning down to give Sawyer a tight hug. "It might not be a conventional marriage, but this is still a really big deal. I know you'll treat Meredith well, and we're happy for you both."

Sawyer accepted the one-armed hug from Cheyenne. "Thanks."

Zach rose as well, offering a hand. Sawyer took it and pulled him to him. They patted each other's backs, and the relief he felt at Zach's acceptance was palpable.

"We're here for you two, whatever you need," Zach said. "When's this wedding happening?"

"Soon." Butterflies swarmed in his stomach, but Sawyer tried his best to ignore them. "Meredith doesn't want to wait, so I'm looking into things. I think we can get married sometime in the next week."

"Whoa." Zach ran a hand down his face. "That's fast."

Sawyer lifted his shoulders in a shrug.

"Well, we'd love to attend the wedding to support both of you, if Meredith's okay with it," Cheyenne said.

"I appreciate that. I think she just wants it to be us and the judge. She's already worried about how others are going to react when they find out we're married."

"We'll pay a friendly visit to anyone in town who dares to gossip," Zach said, pounding his fist into one hand.

Sawyer grinned. It was only a joke—not something they'd actually do, although they could—but he appreciated the show of support. "If you could help me get the spare room ready at Meredith's and all of my stuff moved out of the apartment, I'd appreciate it. The doctor wants her resting as much as possible and said no heavy lifting or straining."

"Of course," Zach said. "Just let us know."

"You're a good man, Sawyer." Cheyenne gave him a warm smile. "John was lucky to have a friend like you. Zach and I are just as lucky."

They talked for a while longer, then Sawyer headed home to make plans for the changes in his life. As he inventoried his apartment, he realized just how little he cared for most of the items in it. He'd bring Meredith by tomorrow after dinner to get her opinion, but other than his bedroom furniture, clothes, and a few keepsakes from his time as a SEAL, there wasn't anything he cared to keep.

He pulled out his phone, texting Meredith. It was nearly ten o'clock, and he didn't want to wake her if she'd already gone to bed.

Just came from Zach and Cheyenne's. They were surprised, but they understand, and we have their full support.

When she didn't immediately respond, Sawyer figured his hunch had been right, and she was asleep for the night, so he pulled out his laptop and began making a list of everything he needed to do. He'd just begun to prioritize the tasks by date when his phone buzzed with a text.

He grabbed the phone, unable to hold back the smile when he saw Meredith's name on the screen.

I'm so glad they aren't upset. Thanks for handling it for us. I just couldn't face them for that conversation.

He was glad she hadn't been there to witness the tension. **I understand. I think it was better for me to talk to them alone, anyway.**

Probably. :)

A glance at the clock confirmed it was after eleven. **What are you doing awake? Are you feeling okay?**

Yeah, just woke up to use the bathroom. I was having crazy dreams about John.

Sawyer stared at the text, feeling an ache in his gut. He could imagine the kinds of dreams she was having—ones where John was furious at her for remarrying so quickly. Whether they were true wouldn't matter when she was being tormented in slumber.

Was he pushing Meredith into something she didn't want to do? He'd done his best to not influence her decision. To just present the facts and let her make the choice.

His phone buzzed again, and he quickly picked it up.

I'm falling asleep again, but we're still on for dinner tomorrow, right? I want to hear all about your conversation with Zach and Chey.

Sawyer curled his hands around the phone, unable to stop smiling. **Absolutely. After dinner, I want to bring you by my apartment so you can tell me what to sell.**

CHAPTER

Fifteen

Meredith paused outside King Trident Scuba, looking up at the brightly colored sign featuring a merman in a scuba mask holding a three-pronged spear. Appropriate, since yesterday had been Halloween. She could still see the look of joyful satisfaction on John's face when they'd flipped on the open sign for the first time, officially launching the business.

The other shops on the street boasted windows decorated with witch's cauldrons and bats, while carved pumpkins sat outside their doors. Candy wrappers from yesterday's trick-or-treaters littered the sidewalk. Every year, the city sponsored the downtown costume parade and local businesses passed out treats. She and John had loved taking part in that annual event, but she didn't know if anyone had passed out candy yesterday. Zach and Cheyenne had taken Bailey to all the various festivities, and Sawyer had ended up with a work emergency requiring him to drive the hour to the Portland office.

She needed to have a discussion with Sawyer and Zach about the shop soon, but dealing with her photography studio had seemed so much easier to tackle. With a flip of a switch, light illuminated the small reception area.

It was her first time in the shop since August. She'd stopped by to bring John lunch from Baylor's only a week before he passed. A client had been a no-show at the photography studio, and she'd needed a basket of fries to ease her frustration.

She took a seat at the reception desk she'd seen John occupy so many times, running her hands along the smooth leather armrests. Collecting information, running credit cards, and making sure customers signed waivers hadn't been his favorite part of the job, but he'd done it cheerfully.

She rested her elbows on the desk and massaged her eyes. The last time she'd been here, she was John's wife. Now she was here as Sawyer's fiancée.

The shop looked much the same as it had this summer. Oregon didn't technically have a diving season, but once October hit, business slowed way down until the spring, so they usually only opened the shop a few days a week. John's absence was evident in the messy row of masks and flippers along one wall and the piles of merchandise on the front counter.

Overwhelmed. That was an excellent word for her current mood.

She picked up a T-shirt from one of the piles, smiling at the logo. It had been John's favorite design—an anchor bouncing on the waves with *refuse to sink* written in a cursive script across it. Her necklace had inspired him and he'd thought it was hilarious, considering the entire purpose of diving was to sink beneath the water. Apparently, he wasn't the only one who got the joke because the T-shirt had become one of their most popular items.

A knock sounded at the door, followed by a bell chiming.

"Zach?" Sawyer called.

She poked her head out from behind the piles of T-shirts. "No, it's me."

"Oh." His eyebrows rose in surprise. "I just came by to check on things since I haven't been here in about a week."

"I haven't been here since summer." She dropped the T-shirt back onto the desk. "Is Josiah still helping out?"

"Just on Saturdays for a couple of hours now that school's started again." He placed his hands on his hips and gave a stern glare. "You're supposed to be taking it easy."

"I am. See, I'm sitting." She motioned to the chair. "I just couldn't stay at home anymore. I felt like the walls were closing in on me."

He perched on the edge of the desk, giving her a sympathetic smile. "It can't be easy to hang out alone all day."

"It isn't." She met Sawyer's eyes, then glanced away, suddenly feeling uncomfortable.

She wouldn't be home alone for much longer. Sawyer's job in cyber security was mostly remote, with only the occasional business trip or day spent at the office in Portland.

He motioned to the pile of shirts on the desk. "So, what are we doing here?"

"I don't know. They were like this when I got here. Same with the equipment."

Sawyer glanced over at the wall of gear and frowned. "Josiah's been slacking off."

"Don't be too hard on him. He's only sixteen." Meredith picked up a shirt, absently folding it. "Should we box up this stuff for next season, or try to sell it for cost?"

"Honestly, with John gone, I think we've only had one group come through for a dive. Zach took them."

She picked up another shirt, trying to fold it through her tears. "He was the heart and soul of this place."

"It was his baby," Sawyer agreed.

His baby, and Sawyer and Zach's albatross. She ran a finger over the King Trident Scuba logo on one of the T-shirts.

"Have you and Zach talked about the scuba shop?"

Sawyer picked up a T-shirt, helping her fold. "Yeah, before John died."

"You both wanted to sell the business," Meredith said. It wasn't a question. Although neither of them had said as much to John, he'd mentioned to her more than once that he feared the business was becoming a burden to the others.

"Yes," Sawyer admitted. He set aside the neatly folded T-shirt and picked up another one. "I was willing to stick it out for a while longer, but once Bailey was born, Zach pretty much checked out."

"It makes sense. Cheyenne's garage is in such high demand, and they were both so busy with that even before becoming parents."

Sawyer placed his hand gently on her arm, his eyes holding hers. "We're not going to do anything with this place that you aren't ready for. On that point, Zach and I agree."

Her heart swelled with gratitude and affection. It felt so nice to have a teammate again, someone who was always on her side.

Sawyer cleared his throat, picking up another T-shirt and folding it intently. "So, uh, I made some phone calls this morning and found out what we need to do to get married."

She curled her fingers into the soft fabric of the T-shirt she held, feeling lightheaded. "What did you find out?"

"We both have to go in person to the county courthouse to get a marriage license. All we need to bring are our driver's licenses and . . ." He cleared his throat, looking uncomfortable. "And we need John's death certificate as proof you're no longer married to him."

She placed both hands flat on the desk, trying to steady her breathing.

Refuse to sink. This was her treading water.

"Sounds simple enough," she choked out.

He picked up another T-shirt, the movement deliberately casual. "Once we get the license, there's a three-day waiting period. While we're there, we can schedule a time with the judge for the ceremony if you'd like."

Meredith nodded. She pressed the T-shirt tightly to her chest, but her vision kept blurring.

"Mer, look at me."

Sawyer had come around the desk without her noticing. Now he was crouched down on the floor in front of her, his hands on the armrests of her chair and his eyes so full of emotion she thought she might drown in them.

"We can take this as slow as you want to," he said, his tone calm. "There's no rush."

She laughed, rubbing her hand across her stomach. "Um, there sort of is. Insane medical bills, remember?"

"Don't worry about that. We can look into some of those programs the doctor recommended for single moms and low-income families. I'll help however I can."

She grabbed his hand, resting it on her cheek and leaning into his warmth. "Why are you so good to me, Sawyer?"

He tucked a strand of hair behind her ear. "I told you, Mer—you're my family. You and those babies."

"And Zach and Cheyenne and Bailey."

Sawyer's mouth quirked up in a grin. "Them too. Although I would never marry Zach, no matter how much he begged."

She laughed, releasing his hand and grabbing her purse off the counter. "No, it's better to do this now. Let's skip dinner and go to the courthouse instead to get the marriage license. If we leave now, we'll have plenty of time to get there before they close for the day."

He held out a hand, helping her to her feet. "We can stop by your house on the way out of town to grab the paperwork."

Oh yeah. She'd have to bring the death certificate. She swallowed back the lump in her throat, trying to keep her hands from shaking as she pulled out her wallet to double-check that she had her driver's license. "Great, let's go."

At home, she retrieved John's death certificate from the firebox in their closet, then told Sawyer she just needed a minute to use the restroom and then they could go.

In the bathroom, she braced her arms on the counter and stared at her gaunt reflection. Her cheekbones were hollow, the dark circles beneath her eyes pronounced, but she'd washed her hair today and let it hang loose around her shoulders.

Today she would get a marriage license so she could marry a man she didn't love romantically.

"I still love you, John," she whispered. "This doesn't change anything. But Sawyer's sacrificing a lot for me, and I'm going to be the best wife I can manage for him."

She'd start by putting on a little makeup and changing into something that didn't make her look like a beggar. When they walked into that courthouse, she didn't want him to be embarrassed to be seen with her.

The light glinted off her pendant, and she traced the words with one finger.

"Time to rise, Meredith," she whispered. "You can do hard things. So start doing them."

CHAPTER
Sixteen

This was really happening. They were in his truck, on their way to the courthouse to obtain a marriage license. Yesterday, while in Portland, he'd impulsively purchased simple wedding rings for them. If Meredith didn't like them, he'd exchange them next time he was in the city. They felt like they were burning a hole in his jacket pocket.

Sawyer tried to relax his grip on the steering wheel. He couldn't remember ever feeling this nervous around Meredith.

He'd been surprised when she came out of the bathroom dressed in black slacks and a pretty pink sweater instead of one of John's hoodies. She'd pulled her hair away from her face with a clip and put on some makeup, too. It made him glad that he'd chosen to wear tan slacks and a dark blue button-up shirt in case he had to head into the office again.

"You look beautiful," he'd told her.

She'd blushed and said, "You mean I don't look like a vagrant."

But he'd meant every word. He couldn't believe she'd agreed to marry him. In just a few days, she would be his wife.

An overly twangy country song came on the radio. Did she like country music? He had no idea.

After years of watching her from afar, being intensely aware of her every action, it surprised him that there was something he didn't know about his almost-wife. But they'd rarely driven together in a car, and when they all hung out, they were too busy talking to bother with music.

"You can change the radio if you'd like," he said, gesturing to the stereo.

"No, this is fine." Her voice sounded tense, and when he glanced over, her knuckles were white from clutching her purse.

Sawyer shot her a mock glare. "If we're going to be married, then we need to be honest with each other. Do you like country music or not?"

"Some of the newer stuff is okay, I guess, but that was way too twangy for my tastes." She leaned forward, scanning for a new station, and eventually settled on a pop song. "Is this okay?"

He flashed her a grin. "I like Taylor Swift. She started as a country singer, you know."

Meredith laughed, the sound making his heart swell. "Look at us compromising."

"Yeah." He glanced over at her, then quickly back to the road. "I think we're going to be alright."

"Me too."

The hour drive to the clerk's office passed quickly. As he helped Meredith out of his truck, he asked, "What would you think about trading this in for a minivan?"

She stared up at him, her eyes wide. "You want to get rid of your truck?"

He tried to imagine Meredith struggling to lift two infant carriers into the back seat. Would they even fit? John's Ford Explorer wasn't much better—not as high off the ground, but not that roomy, either. "We could pick something out together. It might be fun."

Meredith pressed a hand to her mouth, looking green.

Great. He'd made her nauseous with the suggestion. "We don't have to talk about it now."

Meredith nodded, gathering her purse. "Definitely something to consider, but we don't need to decide today."

Because today they would get a marriage license, and Sawyer had a sense that it would take all of her willpower to do it. Sometimes, in his excitement over the marriage and babies, he feared he pushed too hard, too fast. She was still a grieving widow. He was the only one in love here.

"We'll talk about it later," he agreed, trying to keep his voice casual. "Do you have your license?"

She nodded, wrapping her fingers around the soft leather of her purse strap. "Yeah. And . . . and John's death certificate."

The reminder was a bucket of cold water to the face. Sawyer hated himself for being excited about today, even for a moment.

Would remembering John ever get easier? They said time healed all wounds, but it was hard to imagine a day where he could think of his best friend without a gaping sense of loss.

A hand slid into his, soft and warm. Meredith squeezed his hand, and he quickly returned the affection.

He didn't know why this had happened, or how they would get through it. But he did know that together, they would survive.

"Ready?" she asked, pausing outside the courthouse doors.

He'd longed for this moment from the moment he'd first spoken to her. Sawyer swallowed back the bitter taste of betrayal in his throat. Had he ever experienced such a discordant mix of happiness and pain? "Yes. Are you?"

"As ready as I'll ever be."

She didn't let go of his hand as they walked into the building. That show of trust meant everything to him.

The directory near the elevator led them to the third floor, where vinyl lettering on a glass door announced they were in the correct place.

Sawyer took a steadying breath, then dared rub his thumb over the back of Meredith's knuckles.

"Are you nervous?" she asked, staring up at him.

"A little," he admitted.

"Good. Me too."

In the office, a woman with spiky gray hair and trendy cat-eye glasses sat behind a computer. She looked to be in her mid-fifties, with fine lines near her eyes and a curvy figure. The placard on the desk said her name was Traci.

"What can I do for you?" she asked with a pleasant smile.

Sawyer cleared his throat, suddenly aware of just how sweaty his hands felt. Had Meredith noticed?

"We're here for a marriage license," Sawyer said.

Traci's smile brightened. She motioned enthusiastically to the two chairs in front of her desk. "Wonderful! I just need your driver's licenses and any divorce decrees for prior marriages. Let me pull up the form."

Sawyer pulled his wallet from his back pocket and slid his license across the table. Meredith perched on one chair, fumbling to pull her license from her own much larger wallet.

"Thank you," Traci said, taking their licenses. "Are the addresses on these correct?"

"Yes," Sawyer said.

Traci nodded, rapidly typing information into the computer.

"I think you'll need this too," Meredith said, her voice trembling.

She pulled the death certificate from a folder, her lips pressed so firmly together that they turned white. Was she trying not to fall apart? Sawyer's heart ached as he watched her scan the certificate, her eyes lingering over specific lines.

How had John's life been reduced to a piece of paper?

"Oh?" Traci said, her fingers still flying across the keyboard and eyes trained on the computer screen.

Meredith placed the paper almost reverently on the desk. "It's my husband's death certificate."

Traci froze, her hands hovering over the keyboard and eyes wide. Sawyer knew what she was thinking—that Meredith was much too young to be a widow.

"I am so sorry, sweetie," Traci said, her voice gently. "Yes, I'll need that, too."

Meredith and Sawyer answered Traci's questions as she typed in the information they provided. She scanned their licenses quickly and handed them back, but took the death certificate into another room to scan.

She returned moments later, her eyes on the death certificate. Sawyer knew the moment Traci registered John's death date. Her eyes widened, then flew up to stare at Sawyer and Meredith.

"It was a brain aneurysm," Meredith said quietly. "He was a former Navy SEAL and in excellent health. We didn't know he had high blood pressure. I guess it had developed in the twenty-two months since he left the military."

"Oh, you poor dear," Traci said softly.

"I didn't find out about the twins until after the funeral." Meredith reached for Sawyer's hand, and he quickly gave it to her, wanting to offer whatever paltry comfort he could. "Sawyer was my husband's best friend. It's going to be a difficult pregnancy and tough raising the twins alone, so we decided the best thing to do would be to get married."

The questions were obvious in Traci's eyes, but so was the compassion. She leaned forward as though sharing a secret. "If I'm out of line, just tell me to shove it. But did you know that for an additional fee, the three-day waiting period can be waived? I know for a fact the judge is playing solitaire in his office right now and has time to perform the marriage. That would save you a trip back here in a few days."

They could get married today. Sawyer's entire body felt tingled with a nervous energy. Did Meredith want to get married right now?

He brought Meredith's hand to his lips, kissing it softly. "It's up to you. I'm willing to do whatever you want."

She bit her lip, her eyes wandering to the death certificate that still sat on the table.

"I don't want to wait." She picked up the death certificate, tucking it carefully away into the folder. "Let's get married today."

He'd had no idea that getting everything he'd dreamed of could hurt so badly.

"Should we call Zach and Cheyenne? I'm sure they'd race up here if we asked them to."

"No." She straightened her purse on her shoulder and rose. "It's better this way."

Twenty minutes and one phone call later, they were heading to the second floor with the marriage license in hand.

Meredith motioned to her pink sweater and black slacks with a rueful grin. "If I'd known we'd be getting married today, I would have at least put on a dress."

He put an arm around her shoulders and gently kissed her on the head. "You look beautiful."

He knew this image would be emblazoned on his mind forever—Meredith's wavy blonde hair pulled back in a clip, her face lightly dusted with makeup and eyes red-rimmed, the sweater hanging loose about her waist and those slacks making her legs look like they went on for miles.

She was the most beautiful woman he'd ever seen, no question about it.

He paused outside the door to the judge's office. "You're absolutely certain this is what you want?"

She pressed her fingers to his lips, sending tendrils of fire down his spine. Sawyer swallowed, forcing back the emotions.

"I'm sure, Sawyer. When you offered to step up and take care of me and the babies . . . I know I didn't react well initially. But now I am just so incredibly grateful to you. I miss John so much it hurts, but I am going to do my best to be a good wife to you. Once these babies are born, I'll cook and clean and do the grocery shopping and make sure your nice work shirts are always ironed. Well, I'll try to do all of that stuff at least seventy percent of the time."

Sawyer chuckled, still feeling the ghost of her skin against his lips. "I'm not worried about that. This isn't 1955."

"I don't care." Her eyes welled with tears. "You deserve all of that and more. I know what a sacrifice you're making, and I don't take that lightly."

A sacrifice? Guilt slammed into Sawyer. This wasn't a sacrifice—this was a dream come true.

She rose on her tiptoes, kissing him on the cheek. "I just wanted you to know that. Now let's do this. Let's go get married."

CHAPTER
Seventeen

$\mathcal{M}$eredith had always imagined a judge's office would look like what she saw on television—dark wood paneling, a magnificent mahogany desk, and tall bookcases lining the walls that were filled to the brim.

But the office of Judge Hernandez was nothing like she'd expected. The drop-tile ceiling was discolored in one corner from water damage. Berber carpet covered the bottom half of the walls. The room's only decorations were the three diplomas directly behind the minimalistic white desk that looked straight from an IKEA catalog. Clustered together in one corner was a leather couch and two armchairs, all in a rich, brown leather. They looked decidedly out of place among the rest of the furniture.

Judge Hernandez rose from behind his desk, giving them a broad smile. He was much younger than she'd expected, probably in his late thirties, and had a shaved head, wire-rimmed glasses, and a trim physique. He also was only an inch or two taller than her.

"You must be Sawyer and Meredith," he said, giving them both a firm handshake.

"That's us," Meredith said.

He clasped his hands together. "I understand you're here for a wedding."

"Yes." Sawyer's hand hovered near the small of her back, not quite touching. The warmth of his skin still seared like a brand.

"Please, take a seat," Judge Hernandez said, motioning to the couch and chairs. "Traci explained to me the situation. I'm so sorry for your loss, Mrs. Gilbert."

Mrs. Gilbert. But only for a few more minutes. She hadn't even considered if she'd change her last name.

What last name would she give the babies?

Her stomach churned as she clutched the pendant on her necklace like a lifeline.

"Thank you," she said to the judge.

He nodded, moving to the door. "Let me grab two of the clerks to act as the witnesses and we can get you on your way."

This was it—her wedding day, her wedding venue. She glanced down at her outfit and stifled a hysterical laugh. Her wedding slacks, with the bleach stain on the hem. Her wedding sweater with a loose thread on one sleeve.

Sawyer sat beside her on the couch, his eyes clear but posture tense.

He deserved so much more than this.

She ran a hand through her hair, hoping it looked okay. "Pretty different from the last wedding, isn't it?"

Sawyer's lips turned up in a sad smile. "Yeah, I guess so."

For John, she'd worn a white dress that took her two months to find—a fitted sheath silhouette with delicate satin fabric and a long-sleeved lace overlay. She'd worn a crown of flowers instead of a veil and comfortable lace sneakers instead of high heels. John had taken her breath away in his full military uniform, and they'd danced the night away underneath the stars.

Judge Hernandez re-entered the office, accompanied by an older woman in a tweed business jacket and a girl who looked barely old enough to vote in a casual dress.

"This is Carol, our county recorder," Judge Hernandez said, pointing to the older woman, "and this is Beth, her intern."

"So nice to meet you," Carol said, giving them both a nod while Beth raised one hand half-heartedly.

This was it. No turning back now.

Meredith's heart thundered in her chest, and she worried the peanut butter crackers she'd eaten during the car ride from Sapphire Cove were going to make a reappearance.

She was getting married to someone else.

John was never coming back.

She reached blindly for Sawyer, feeling the world teeter. His hand enveloped hers, the rough calluses brushing against her much softer skin. She clung to him, that warm hand her only tether to reality.

This is for the babies, she reminded herself. *This is what John would want.*

Judge Hernandez sat down in a chair across from them, his eyes kind. "Do you have the marriage license and your IDs?"

"Right here," Sawyer said, handing them over.

Judge Hernandez carefully looked over the documents, then nodded in approval. "Let's get started."

Meredith's entire body trembled as Sawyer helped her to her feet. She tried to focus on the gentle pressure of his hand in hers. To not think about how she was getting married to someone other than John.

For her first wedding, she'd spent weeks agonizing over every detail. Their wedding had taken place at the church where her grandparents had married in Sapphire Cove, and the guest list had been relatively small—mostly just the guys from the SEAL team and some townsfolk Meredith was friendly with. But she'd wanted everything to be perfect, from the flower arrangements to obsessing over every word of her vows. She'd spent the bulk of their budget on an excellent photographer, wanting every moment of the day captured on film.

Judge Hernandez stood before them, Carol and Beth standing unobtrusively to one side. Instead of a flowered archway, her backdrop for this wedding was a metal filing cabinet topped with a dusty artificial plant.

"Sawyer Grey, do you take Meredith Gilbert to be your lawfully wedded wife, in sickness and in health, for as long as you both shall live?" Judge Hernandez asked.

Sawyer met her eyes, and she saw no hint of uncertainty there—no regret or second guessing. "I do."

Meredith widened her eyes, trying to keep the tears that had flooded them from falling. When she'd married John, his sergeant had performed the ceremony. There had been a gentle lead-in, with beautiful words about love and commitment.

"And do you, Meredith, take Sawyer as your lawfully wedding husband, in sickness and in health, for as long as you both shall live?"

Her hands trembled in Sawyer's, panic making her dizzy.

Could she really do it? Could she speak those two words that would change everything?

I'm sorry, John.

"I do," Meredith said. Her voice was clear and audible, with only the tiniest bit of shake to it. She supposed that was the best she could ask for under the circumstances.

Judge Hernandez gave an approving nod. "Then by the power invested in me by the state of Oregon, I declare you legally and lawfully married."

That was it. Less than five minutes, and she'd changed her entire future.

"Do you have rings you'd like to exchange?" the judge asked.

Meredith's eyes flew to Sawyer's. She hadn't even considered that. "Oh, we don't—"

"We do, actually." Sawyer reached into his pocket, withdrawing two simple silver-colored bands with no adornment, one much daintier than the other.

She took the larger of the two and slipped it onto Sawyer's finger with shaking hands. It slid easily over his knuckle, the white gold a stark contrast to his tanned skin.

Sawyer smiled, reaching for her own hand. She held it out, only to realize her diamond wedding ring from John still rested on her left ring finger.

The diamond glared up at her, a sharp reminder of how recently she'd belonged to another man. When she'd married John, she'd given herself to him, heart and soul.

She should take it off. Wasn't that what a good wife would do? As unconventional as their marriage was, Meredith was committed to Sawyer.

But it would be easier to cut off her own finger.

"Leave it," Sawyer whispered.

He slipped his ring gently onto her finger. It fit perfectly, sliding next to John's diamond-lined band featuring a modest solitaire.

"Beautiful," Judge Hernandez said. "You may now kiss the bride."

A kiss? Meredith's eyes flew up to Sawyer's, panic making her want to run from the room. Marrying Sawyer was one thing. But kissing him would absolutely feel like a betrayal to John.

She hadn't kissed another man in over four years.

Sawyer's eyes held hers, their steady gaze full of understanding. He lifted her left hand with his, gently pressing a kiss on her knuckles, just above the rings that now nestled together—his and John's. Then he pulled her to him in a gentle hug.

Meredith buried her face in his shoulder, clinging to him as her eyes stung with tears. He dropped a kiss onto the crown of her head, and she hugged him tighter.

She'd thought burying John would be the hardest thing she ever had to do. But moving on, even a little, might be harder.

Meredith let go of Sawyer, suddenly aware that they had an audience. What must these three strangers think of their odd marriage? Probably nothing compared to what the town of Sapphire Cove would think when they found out.

"Wonderful," Judge Hernandez said. "If you'll just both sign the marriage certificate, then I'll do the same, and Carol and Beth can sign as the witnesses."

Meredith nodded, accepting the pen from the judge. It was nothing special, just a basic black pen that you'd buy in a pack of ten at the discount store. She took a deep breath, then carefully signed her name on the line indicated—*Meredith Gilbert.*

Was that her last time signing as Meredith Gilbert? She still wasn't sure what she wanted to do about her last name, or that of her babies.

Their babies. Sawyer was their father now, every bit as much as John. It was a decision they'd need to make together.

Sawyer signed his name as well, and the judge and the two witnesses quickly followed.

That was it. They were officially married.

"We'll get this recorded right away," Judge Hernandez said, sliding the certificate into one corner of his desk. "You should receive a copy in the mail within four weeks."

"Thanks," Meredith said faintly.

"Wait!" Beth called.

Meredith looked at the girl, an eyebrow raised. Her cheeks turned pink, and she looked embarrassed, but pressed on.

"Don't you want someone to take a picture with your phone? It's your wedding day, after all."

"That's an excellent idea," Carol said. "You should have something to remember this day by."

Sawyer wrapped an arm protectively around Meredith's waist, his expression creased with concern. "I don't know . . ."

"Yes, we should take a picture." Meredith fumbled for her phone, bringing up the camera app. It wouldn't be as good as what she could get with her Nikon, but it would have to do. "The twins will want to see what we looked like on the day their parents got married."

"They have that evidence," Sawyer said softly, his eyes sad. "I've seen the pictures from your wedding with John. There are entire photo albums filled with them."

He was always thinking about what she needed. But Meredith had a feeling that what Sawyer needed right now was a photo to remember this day by. It wasn't a traditional wedding or marriage, sure. But it was the only one he'd ever had.

"John will always be the babies' dad." Meredith took his hand, gently placing it on her stomach for the briefest of moments. Her nerves tingled with that brief contact, which had felt unexpectedly intimate. "And now so will you, Sawyer."

He looked away, rubbing a hand over his jaw. She had a feeling he was trying to hide the tears glistening in his eyes. "That means a lot to me."

Meredith took a deep breath, then held out her cell phone to Carol. "Would you mind snapping a few so we can make sure to get a good one?"

"Of course." Carol held up the camera. "Ready?"

She wrapped an arm around Sawyer's waist, leaning into him. "Ready."

His arm fell around her shoulders, heavy but also reassuring. Meredith tried to smile while Carol snapped a few photos, then accepted her phone back, quickly checking the results. Sawyer looked unsure while she looked a little fake, but it would have to do.

"Thank you so much," Meredith said.

"It was our pleasure," Judge Hernandez said. "Best of luck to the both of you."

She was quiet on the drive home, her mind swirling with wordless emotions. Sawyer seemed to sense her need for quiet and didn't ask questions. She appreciated that about him. John had been a talker, always happy to share his thoughts and emotions, and had never really understood Meredith's need for silence. He'd tried to, though, and after almost three years of marriage, he'd learned to give her space when she needed it.

"Are you hungry?" Sawyer asked as they approached Sapphire Cove. "We could stop at Baylor's for dinner if you'd like, or maybe get takeout from Al's Burgers and bring it home? What sounds good to you?"

"Al's Burgers is fine," Meredith said. "Let's take it home. I'm really tired."

They opted for the drive-thru and soon were pulling into Meredith's front yard.

Their yard.

"Home sweet home," Sawyer said before his ears glowed pink.

"We still haven't cleaned out the spare bedroom." Meredith unbuckled her seat belt, looking over at Sawyer. "I'm sorry. I didn't realize we'd be able to get married today, but once she mentioned it . . ."

His hand rested softly on hers. "I'm glad we did it today. I've still got a few days before I have to be out of my apartment. We've got time."

Sawyer matched his pace to hers as they trudged up the steps to the front door.

"I don't know what we'll do once the babies are here," she said as she unlocked the front door. She'd need to get Sawyer his own key, soon. "It'll be a tight squeeze."

"I actually have an idea for that." Sawyer set the bag of food on the kitchen counter. "It was John's idea, actually. He talked about adding an addition to the back of the house. I've got some money saved up and I think that's a great way to spend it, if you're willing."

John had mentioned an addition in passing, but they hadn't had the money, so the conversation went nowhere. "I don't want to spend your money . . ."

"It's not my money anymore. It's *our* money now. I'd like to take you to the bank as soon as possible and add you to my accounts."

And she needed to add him to her accounts, too—the ones that practically had a negative balance.

She pulled her burger toward her and took a careful bite. "I think an addition is a great idea."

"Really?"

She nodded. "I want you to feel like this is your home now, too. You've given up so much for me, and it's only fair. Planning an addition together will help us both feel like this is our place together, I think."

"Okay then." Sawyer picked up his own burger, the smile on his lips making Meredith feel as though she'd accomplished something good. "I'll contact Dan Boyd and see about getting a bid. He should have some ideas about what we can realistically put in an addition."

"Great. And we can start cleaning out the second bedroom tonight, unless you need to get home."

He winked. "This is my home now, remember?"

"Right." She took another bite of her burger, realizing she'd be living with Sawyer soon. Would he sleep here tonight, or go home to his apartment?

"I'll bring a comfortable chair into the room and you can boss me around while you sit there and grow a baby or two."

She laughed, pressing her hand against her stomach. It was still unnoticeable to most of the world, but she was definitely feeling the difference.

"Deal."

CHAPTER Eighteen

$\mathcal{S}$awyer watched as Meredith slowly ate her cheeseburger, her eyes drooping. Her hair had fallen from the clip, and she'd pushed up the sleeves of her sweater past her elbows.

She was, in a word, adorable.

He couldn't believe he'd get to spend the rest of his life with her.

Her head bobbed, the cheeseburger nearly falling out of her hands. He took it gently from her, setting it on the table. She looked up at him sleepily, blinking.

"You're exhausted," he said.

"Sorry." She covered a yawn. "These babies seem to drain away all my energy. Dr. Mike said that's normal."

"You're growing two humans. That would definitely take it out of you." He rose, helping her gently to her feet. "Go to bed. I'll clean up here."

"What about clearing out the second room?"

"We can work on that tomorrow."

She folded her arms, biting one lip. "What will you do tonight?"

There was a tentative edge to her tone, one that reminded him they were both walking into uncharted territory.

He wanted to sleep here tonight. The couch hadn't been half bad, and he'd feel better knowing he was close if Meredith needed something. It wasn't the wedding night he'd tried very hard not to imagine, but that was okay.

Did she want him to stay here tonight? Did she care? They'd already agreed to clean out the second bedroom, and he'd told his landlord he wouldn't be renewing his lease.

Everything was so strange and new.

"I'll head to the hardware store before they close and grab some boxes," Sawyer said. "Since I promised my landlord I'd be out by the end of the week, I should start packing."

"I wish I could help. Maybe Chey could bring Bailey over here during nap time. I could listen for her while they help you."

"We can figure it out." Sawyer wasn't about to let her chase around a one-year-old, but he didn't need to tell her that. "There isn't much to move, anyway. Go to sleep. All I want you to worry about is those babies."

Meredith placed a hand on her stomach, smiling faintly. "You'll be here in the morning?"

Something about the way she said it made Sawyer's heart swell with hope. "Yeah, of course."

She headed to the front door, and for a moment, he thought she was walking him out. Instead, she carefully pulled a key chain from the decorative wall hooks. He recognized the eagle and trident pendant hanging off it immediately.

"Here." She held out the key chain. "You'll need a key to the house."

The Navy SEAL symbol seemed to glare at him. How many times had he seen John pull those keys out of his pocket and set them on the side of the court before they played basketball?

"I can't take his keys," Sawyer choked out.

Meredith took his hand, gently settling the keys in his palm.

He would feel more comfortable holding a grenade.

She folded his fingers around the keys, holding her hands over his fist. "I want you to have them."

He lifted his eyes to the ceiling, then pulled Meredith to him in a tight hug. "Thank you."

They could have gone to the hardware store again tomorrow and gotten a copy made, but this meant so much more to him than a simple way to unlock the home he now lived in.

She pressed her cheek against his chest, her arms tight about his waist. Sawyer rested his chin on top of her head, relishing the feel of this embrace but letting her dictate how long it lasted.

This woman might be his wife, but she was also John's widow. He wouldn't forget that.

When she pulled away, her eyes were red, but no tears fell. "I'm sure you'd rather spend the night at your apartment, but know you're welcome to the couch here, too. There are blankets and extra pillows in the linen closet."

This invitation, on top of giving him John's keys, was almost too much for him. He cleared his throat, hoping she couldn't hear the emotion choking it. "Thank you. I'd like that."

"We can work on clearing space for you tomorrow."

"Sounds like a plan. I have my phone if you need anything before I get back."

Sawyer liked this—the togetherness he felt with Meredith. Like they were a team.

"Call Zach and see if he can help you tonight," Meredith instructed, pausing just outside her bedroom door. "Don't lift anything heavy on your own."

She sounded like a worried wife, and he liked it more than he should. "You're okay if I tell them about the wedding?"

She nodded. "It's probably better if it comes from you."

"Okay then. Goodnight."

"Night," Meredith said.

By the time Sawyer had the fast-food bags thrown away and the kitchen counter wiped down, Meredith was already asleep. He peeked in on her and found her facing the side of the bed he assumed had been John's, curled around a pillow that had to be his as well.

The sight made his heart ache for more reasons than he could count. It wasn't fair that his greatest blessing had come at the expense of his best friend's life.

Had Meredith cried herself to sleep tonight, keeping the tears silent so he wouldn't hear them?

Sawyer gently pulled the door shut, then left for the hardware store. Once in the truck, he called Zach on the vehicle's calling system.

"Hey," Zach said. "I was just thinking I should call you and see how things are going with . . . you know, everything."

Sawyer took a deep breath, flexing his hands on the steering wheel. "Good, I guess. We got married today."

There was a long pause. "That was quick."

"I told you it would be, but the exact timing was a last-minute decision."

Another pause. "I'd love to hear the details."

He knew Zach was deliberately being neutral in his responses, and Sawyer appreciated his effort. But he could hear the unspoken disapproval and worry behind Zach's words.

Sawyer couldn't help flashing back to when Zach had been falling for Cheyenne, and he'd been the one cautioning Zach to take things slowly and not get hurt.

"If you're willing to help me pack tonight, I'm willing to share the story," Sawyer said.

"Sure. I'll let Chey know and be over in thirty minutes."

"I'm grabbing some boxes from the store and then I'll meet you there," Sawyer said.

When Sawyer arrived at his apartment complex twenty minutes after the phone call, Zach's truck was already parked in the lot.

"Hey," Zach said, his hands in his pockets and shoulders hunched as he approached.

"Hey." The awkward tension between them was something Sawyer had never really experienced before with Zach. There'd been the tension of battle, the pinch of annoyance as they bickered over something dumb. But not this uncomfortable distance.

Sawyer unhitched the tailgate, and they both reached for a stack of cardboard boxes.

"So, you're a married man now, huh?" Zach said, his voice gruff.

Sawyer flexed his left hand, feeling the ridges of the metal band. It felt right to wear it, like it belonged there. "Yeah, I guess so."

Married to John's wife. Sawyer could remember him and Zach standing up with John at the wedding as his co-best men like it was yesterday.

They walked to the apartment, arms loaded down with boxes and packing tape.

"How's Meredith doing?" Zach asked.

Sawyer sighed, unlocking his front door. "She's a trooper, as always. I know this can't be easy for her, but she's been nothing but gracious and kind. Today was hard for her. She was already asleep when I left the house."

Zach leaned the stack of boxes against the wall and folded his arms, his jaw flexing. "And how are you doing?"

Sawyer rubbed a hand over the back of his head, not meeting Zach's eyes. "Missing John like crazy. Hating seeing Meredith hurt so much. Wishing there was more I could do to help."

Zach sighed loudly, his shoulders relaxing, and all the tension between them was released like air from a balloon.

"I hate this for you," Zach said. "I hate it so much. I mean, I always suspected you had feelings for Meredith, but you did such a good job at hiding it once they were married that I figured you'd moved on."

As if anyone could move on from Meredith. Just like she'd never be able to move on from John.

Not that he wanted her to. Maybe one day their marriage would resemble something closer than acquaintances thrown together by circumstances. But that was the most he'd allow himself to hope for—a deep, abiding friendship forged by mutual respect and common goals.

He had never betrayed John in life, and he refused to do so in death.

"I didn't want John to worry. I never would have come between them." Sawyer thought of how much it had hurt to see them exchange flirty glances while they cooked, or to catch them kissing when they thought no one else was looking.

It had hurt so bad he'd almost stayed with the SEALs, because he hadn't known if he could watch up close as Meredith and John fell deeper in love with every passing year.

Zach shook his head, eyes bright with unshed tears. "This whole thing just sucks, you know? John shouldn't be dead. We survived so many missions together. So many deployments. And then to die from a freaking blood clot? It isn't fair."

"I know." Sawyer rubbed his nose, looking away. "I miss him, too. And even though I love Meredith, I would do anything to bring John back. Even if it meant trading my life for his."

But Zach was already shaking his head, his jaw clenched. "Don't even go there. Do you think that would have been any easier for me and Chey to take?"

Sawyer locked eyes with Zach. "It would have been easier for Meredith."

Zach didn't argue, just sighed deeply. "We can't change the past. But Chey and I are here for you guys, whatever you need."

Sawyer clapped Zach on the back. "Thanks. That means a lot to both of us."

Years in the military had taught Sawyer and Zach how to be efficient packers, and in four hours every box had been neatly filled and taped shut. There was a small pile of items in one corner that Sawyer would check with Meredith before tossing, and a larger pile of items he would donate to a second-hand store. But other than moving the furniture, everything else was done.

How easy it was to pack up this place that had never really been home. It had been a place to work, to eat and sleep. But he would have felt just as at home—or not at home, as the case was—in a hotel room.

They loaded the boxes into the back of Sawyer's truck, then made one last sweep of the empty apartment. His leather couches were in the living room, but he'd never bothered to get a dining room table. The TV he'd put in his bedroom, unless Meredith wanted it elsewhere, and he'd have to wait to move his bedroom furniture until they'd cleared a space for it at Meredith's. He'd ask what she wanted done with the living room furniture but had a feeling leather didn't really match her aesthetic. Unless she had an objection, he'd try to sell them.

"That didn't take long." Zach clapped Sawyer on the back. "How do you feel?"

"Fine," Sawyer said honestly. "This apartment never felt like home. I won't miss it."

"Want me to come and help you unload things at Mer's?"

"No, I've got it. There aren't that many boxes. Go home to Chey."

Zach nodded without protest. "Text me tomorrow and let me know when you need help loading the furniture."

"I will. Thanks, man."

"Anytime," Zach said.

Sawyer drove through the quiet streets of Sapphire Cove, his heart feeling lighter than it had in years.

Back at Meredith's, he carried the boxes in as quietly as possible and stacked them neatly against the back wall. Then he dragged his toiletries into the small second bathroom and took a shower before tracking down the pillow and blanket Meredith had mentioned and crashing on the couch.

For the first time since John's passing, Sawyer slept soundly.

CHAPTER

Nineteen

Sawyer was up before the sun the next morning, despite having gone to bed so late. He wanted to start off the first day of their new marriage on the right foot. Wanted to let Meredith know that he really was here to be her partner. Their marriage might not be a traditional one, but that didn't mean they had to go through life as distant roommates who happened to share children. He wanted them to be teammates. Best friends, even. He knew neither of them could replace John, but they could form a new, different friendship independent of that connection.

After folding and putting away his bedding, Sawyer headed to the local grocery store. Meredith's fridge had been pretty bare last night when he transferred the meager contents of his own fridge into it, and he wanted to make them a big breakfast. Soon he had bacon cooking in the oven, hash browns frying on the stove, and pancakes baking on the griddle.

Hopefully, none of the smells would make Meredith sick and she'd be able to keep some of it down. He'd read online that protein was especially important for women carrying twins.

The quiet smack of slippers against the laminate floor made him look up from the griddle, and his breath caught. Blonde hair stuck up from her head like a rumpled halo. Her pajama bottoms were wrinkled, her hands nearly hidden by the sleeves of one of John's sweatshirts.

She looked breathtaking. He couldn't believe he'd wake up to this sight every day for the rest of his life.

"Hey," Meredith said, giving him an unsure smile. She folded her arms, taking a tentative step toward him. "Something smells good."

"Yeah?" Sawyer flipped the pancakes, unable to stop smiling. "I was worried it might make you nauseous."

"Nope, not this time." Her stomach rumbled, and she laughed, pressing a hand to it. "I think the babies are hungry, too."

"Good." He motioned with the spatula to a barstool. "It's nearly ready. I'll have hot pancakes for you in just a moment."

"Can I set the table, or—"

"Sit. Doctor's orders, remember?"

Meredith gave him a rueful smile and took a seat. "I think the last time I woke up to the smell of breakfast was when I was a teenager, before my grandma died. John wasn't much of a cook . . ." She pressed her lips together, her brows pinching together. "Sorry."

Sawyer raised an eyebrow, giving the hash browns a stir. "About what?"

"You know." She looked down at the countertop, tracing the marbled lines with her fingertip.

Sawyer added some salt to the hash browns and gave them a stir. What was she apologizing for?

Then it hit him. She'd brought up John.

To her new husband.

Sawyer set down the spatula and reached across the counter, placing his hands over hers. He waited until she looked up at him before speaking. On this point, he wanted to be clear.

"I don't want you to stop talking about John just because we're married now. He was a big part of both of our lives."

She bit her lip but didn't look away. "It's just, you've made such an enormous sacrifice for me and the babies. I don't want to seem ungrateful."

His heart twinged at the uncertainty in her expression. "I would never think that, Mer."

"Good." She pulled her hands away, smoothing down her hair.

Sawyer turned back to the pancakes, giving her some space. "John was my best friend. I want to talk about him still, too."

"Really?"

"Absolutely." He slid two pancakes onto a plate for her. "Besides, those little girls need to grow up surrounded by memories of their father."

Meredith cocked her head to the side, smiling. "Girls?"

Sawyer shrugged, pushing the plate toward her. "Or boys. Do you have a preference?"

"No." Her hands traced her stomach, stretching the fabric so that he caught the faintest hint of roundness there. "I just want babies that are healthy."

Sawyer nodded, placing a pancake on his plate and then pouring batter on the griddle for three more. "Me too."

They said grace, then dug into the food. Sawyer watched in immense pleasure as Meredith quickly downed half of her pancakes and two strips of bacon.

He hadn't thought it possible to be more aware of Meredith. But getting married had changed something, as much as he'd thought it wouldn't, and he suddenly felt more of everything. More protective. More unsure. More aware.

More guilty.

"You've been holding out on me," she said, the surprise in her voice almost insulting. "I knew you could grill, but I didn't know you could cook, too."

Sawyer shrugged, the memories of why he could cook making his mouth taste like pennies. "Growing up, I learned pretty quick that if I didn't make food, then I didn't eat."

Meredith's face softened. Zach had grown up with a picture perfect family until his parents passed away, but Sawyer and John had initially bonded over their awful home lives— John as a foster kid, Sawyer as an abused child with an absent mother and alcoholic father.

"John always said he didn't learn to cook because he never really had a kitchen."

More likely because when he'd been seven, John had stuck a fork in the microwave with his ramen and sparked a fire. No one had bothered to tell him you weren't supposed to do that, but his foster family had still made John eat only stale bread crusts for a week. Had he told Meredith that story? Somehow, Sawyer doubted it. He would have wanted to shield his wife from the rougher parts of his past. Sawyer could relate to that.

"Yeah, the barracks were cheap, but you couldn't have so much as a hot plate in them."

Meredith's lips curved up in a soft smile. Was she recalling some tender moment between her and John? Sawyer took another bite, but the pancakes turned to sawdust in his mouth.

"He always said he preferred the mess hall anyway because he didn't have to deal with the cooking or the cleanup," Meredith said.

"That part was nice. But it's nice to have a kitchen, too." He'd make good use of Meredith's, providing healthy meals to keep the twins growing.

Not Meredith's kitchen. Their kitchen, his and hers.

"One time, when we'd been married about six months, John was home on leave and tried to make me breakfast in bed for my birthday." Meredith's gaze grew faraway, and she chuckled. "I woke up to the fire alarm shrieking like crazy and the apartment filling with smoke. He was so mad at himself."

Sawyer blinked, the reminder that this kitchen had once been John's slamming into him. He could well imagine what John would have looked like—brows turned down in a scowl, face glowing red, nostrils flaring. "Probably because he was worried the firetruck would show up and word would somehow get back to the Sarge."

"That's what he said!" Meredith laughed, the sound making Sawyer's entire being feel lighter. "I asked him how on earth the Sarge would hear about it from two states away, but John insisted he would."

"Oh, he would have." Sawyer chuckled, a fierce longing for his days as a SEAL hitting him. There had been a camaraderie and satisfaction that came from serving his country alongside his two best friends that he hadn't been able to equal since going civilian.

Maybe being a husband and a father would come close. He had a feeling it might.

"Well, we hurried and opened all the windows, and I ran next door to tell the neighbors not to call it in. They were cool about things, thank heavens. We ended up going out to Baylor's for breakfast instead. John's French toast looked like charcoal bricks." Her shoulders slumped, and she dragged her tines through the syrup on her plate. "I miss him a lot."

Sawyer stared down at his own plate, the loneliness blanketing him. "Me too. Thursday nights haven't been the same without him."

Meredith rested her hand briefly on his, making his heart skip, then went back to her meal. "Just because John is gone doesn't mean you have to stop playing basketball. You and Zach should keep playing."

"Maybe." Silently, Sawyer thought they'd be lucky to get in one day a month at the court. Both of them were husbands now, and soon he'd join Zach in fatherhood. Their evenings belonged to their families now.

Meredith pushed her plate away. "After the twins are born, I could play with you. I'm not very good, but maybe with some practice, I'll get better."

Sawyer's heart swelled, and he nodded. "I'd like that a lot."

She carried her plate to the dishwasher, motioning with her head to the boxes he'd stacked neatly against the wall. "Looks like you made some good progress last night."

"I did. Zach came over to help, and we got the whole apartment packed up pretty quickly."

Her eyes widened as she took in the stacks. "Wait, that's all of your stuff?"

"More or less."

"But that's only like twelve boxes."

Sawyer shrugged. "I haven't needed much."

"What about your furniture and stuff?"

Her incredulity was adorable. "Once the spare room is ready, Zach will help me bring the bed over. We can sell the living room couches unless you want to put them here. Other than that, it's pretty much just a dresser and an end table for my room."

Meredith frowned. "Do you want to get rid of the couch and chair? They're pretty nice leather furniture."

Nice, but not her style. "I bought them on sale and I'm not attached, but if you'd like to keep that set and sell yours, we can. There's not really space for both."

She chewed on her lip, looking uncertain, but he could see that she didn't want to swap out the sets. "If you're sure about selling them."

"Absolutely." Sawyer pulled out his phone, making a note. "I'll list them online today."

She folded her arms tightly across her chest. "I guess we'd better make room for your bed in that spare room, then."

The tremor in her voice nearly did him in. As much as he didn't want to sleep on the couch indefinitely, he wanted to hurt Meredith even less.

"We don't have to do this right now if you aren't ready, Mer. I can sleep on the couch until we can get that addition added on." He'd reach out to Dan at Boyd Construction today for a bid.

"That'll take months."

And sleeping on the couch definitely wasn't ideal, but Sawyer wouldn't push her before she was ready. The last thing he wanted was for her to resent him for making her move on before she was ready.

"I've slept in worse conditions." Sawyer nudged her foot with his. "Seriously, Mer. If we're moving too fast—"

"No." Meredith straightened, forcing a smile. "That isn't fair to you. Let's clean out the room today."

Sawyer nodded, wishing he could make this ache go away for her. "I'll call Zach and see if he can help."

The rest of the day was a whirlwind. Sawyer had emailed late last night, telling work he'd eloped and was taking a personal day. He'd also put in a request to human resources for guidance on how to get Meredith added to his health insurance plans—medical, dental, and vision—as soon as possible, then looked into life insurance. He certainly didn't anticipate dying anytime soon, but neither had John, and Sawyer wanted to make sure that if anything happened to him, Meredith and the twins would be taken care of financially.

By the end of the day, he'd sold the couch and chair, moved the rest of his furniture, cleaned the apartment, and turned in his keys at the front office.

As he drove up to Meredith's, it sunk in that it wasn't her place anymore—it was theirs.

Sawyer dragged a rocking chair into his room for Meredith to sit in, and she watched quietly while he unpacked and put things away. They talked about trivial things, but mostly just enjoyed the silence together. At least Sawyer was enjoying it, this sense of companionship with a woman he'd never really experienced.

But as he crawled into bed that night, the reality hit that he was living in John's house, married to John's wife, preparing to raise John's babies.

And while he didn't regret his choices—not in the slightest—he had a feeling living with the guilt would be harder than he'd expected.

CHAPTER
Twenty

$\mathcal{H}$aving a man in the house again felt strange but oddly comforting, and it didn't take long for her and Sawyer to fall into an easy routine.

She woke up most mornings to the lingering nausea and smell of breakfast. Meredith had told Sawyer, after that first morning, that she didn't expect him to cook for her. But he persisted, and she found she enjoyed the ritual of sitting down to a hearty meal and discussing the upcoming day together. John had been more of a protein shake before his run kind of guy, and she'd never been a morning person. He was usually up and ready for the day before she'd even cracked open her eyes.

After breakfast, Meredith would shoo Sawyer into his bedroom to work while she cleaned up the kitchen, which mostly involved washing dishes while sitting on a stool. The clack of his keyboard, accompanied by the occasional soft hum of his raspy voice as he talked on the phone to clients, had become almost like a lullaby to her. She loved to lie on the couch and listen to the symphony as she drifted to sleep. Naps were almost a daily occurrence, and whether that was because of the twins or the mental exhaustion of missing John, she wasn't sure and didn't bother to examine too closely.

They'd been married just over a week when she woke up early for a doctor's appointment. She'd meant to tell Sawyer about it, but he'd gotten a call during dinner last night and she'd fallen asleep before he finished.

When she wandered into the kitchen, fully dressed, Sawyer looked up in surprise. She put a hand to her mouth, trying to stifle her giggle. She hadn't realized he'd been donning one of her grandmother's flowery pink aprons when cooking. He was so tall it barely brushed the tops of his thighs, the apron strings just under his armpits.

He looked adorable.

"What?" Sawyer put a hand on his hip, striking a pose that made her laugh even harder. "Real men wear pink."

She put a hand on the counter, trying to control her giggles. "Yes, it's very dashing. Definitely suits you."

"You don't mind that I borrowed it?"

"Not in the least." She motioned to the bowl he was whisking. "Can I help?"

"Want to stick some bread in the toaster? I thought we'd keep it simple this morning and just scramble some eggs."

"Perfect." She was nearing the end of the first trimester—almost thirteen weeks along—and her morning sickness was finally abating, replaced by a near-constant hunger.

They worked in companionable silence, the sizzle of eggs mixing with the scrape of butter against toast.

"I've got a doctor's appointment in an hour," Meredith said as Sawyer plated the eggs. "Just a checkup."

"Oh." He hesitated, then resumed scraping the scrambled eggs onto the plates. "You'll let me know how it goes?"

"Yeah, of course." She bit her lip, slowly spreading jam onto a piece of toast.

If John was here, she would have assumed he'd go to the appointment with her. Would have wanted him to be there for every step of the pregnancy.

Maybe Sawyer wasn't the kind of husband she shared a bed with. But how did she want their marriage to play out? Decades stretched out before them.

If she started keeping him out now, where would she draw the line?

You married this man so that your babies would have a father, she reminded herself. That meant allowing him to be there for them every step of the way—even when it made her uncomfortable.

Sawyer was too much of a gentleman to ask to attend the appointment. If she wanted him there, she'd have to take the first step.

"You can come with me, if you want," Meredith said, keeping her tone deliberately casual. "I know it's late notice, and I totally understand if you have work—"

"I'd love to come," Sawyer said, his entire countenance brightening. "What time do we need to leave?"

She glanced at the cheerful teal-colored clock shaped like a coffee cup on the kitchen wall. John had teased her for replacing their perfectly serviceable—but ugly—five dollar clock she'd bought on clearance at a big box store. But she'd wanted this house to be a home and had loved decorating it.

"We should leave in about thirty-five minutes, so we aren't late," Meredith said. "It's not far, just Dr. Mike's office downtown."

"Okay then." Sawyer took a bite of his eggs. "I appreciate you inviting me, Mer. I don't want to overstep my bounds, but I want to be as involved as you're comfortable with, not only in the twins' lives, but in yours."

Meredith took a small bite of her eggs, her stomach churning. "I want that, too. It's just . . . hard for me."

Sawyer nodded, that muscle twitching in his jaw again. "I get that. But when I said I'd be whatever you need me to be, I meant it."

But can I be what you need? She blinked quickly, trying to ignore the twinge of guilt.

He'd known what kind of marriage they'd have, and he'd said yes anyway. She shouldn't feel bad for giving him exactly what she'd promised—a platonic friendship and the title of dad.

The doctor's office was half-filled with women in various stages of pregnancy, just like it had been the first time she visited. Meredith checked in at the front desk, her purse strap clutched tightly in one hand, then sat silently beside Sawyer.

It felt more intimate than she'd expected to sit beside Sawyer in this office—even more than when they'd found out she was having twins at the hospital. That had been a stress-filled night of worry, but this . . .

He was her husband. These babies would call him dad.

"Nervous?" Sawyer asked, his leg bouncing up and down as he tapped his foot against the floor.

His own nerves—something she'd never seen him display before—made her own more apparent. "I shouldn't be. It's just a checkup."

He reached over, taking her hand in his and giving it a squeeze. "I'm a little anxious, too."

She smiled at him, the admission making her heart warm.

It wasn't long before they were called back into the ultrasound room, the same one she'd been in before. Had that really been less than two weeks ago?

"Dr. Mike will be in shortly," the nurse said, offering them a smile.

Meredith shifted on the exam table, the paper crinkling beneath her legs. Even fully clothed, she felt exposed. There was a poster on one wall showing how big the cervix would dilate during labor. Awkward.

If John was here, she wouldn't even have noticed the poster. They'd probably have been discussing names for the babies and predicting whether they'd be boys or girls. Maybe making plans for how to decorate the nursery.

Their marriage hadn't been perfect, and it hadn't been easy, especially when John was gone for months at a time with the SEALs. But it had always been familiar. She missed that easy closeness so much.

How had she ended up pregnant and married to a man she had never even kissed?

She blinked, determined not to cry. They hadn't planned on having a baby just yet, and the news of twins would've thrown John for a loop—he'd always worried about having kids before they were financially secure. But despite everything, she knew that he would have been thrilled when she showed him that positive pregnancy test.

A knock sounded at the door, and Dr. Mike entered.

"How's my favorite patient?" he asked.

Meredith shifted, the paper crinkling again. "I think things are going better."

"Your dip test shows the urinary tract infection is gone, so that's a positive. Has your bleeding stopped fully?"

Her cheeks burned. She couldn't look at Sawyer. "I still have a little spotting when I overdo it, but no cramps or anything."

Sawyer grunted from his corner. Great—now he'd let her do even less than she had been doing.

"You need to listen to your body." Dr. Mike sank onto the rolling stool. "Twin pregnancies shouldn't be taken lightly. Even simple tasks can put a strain on your body, so listen when it tells you to slow down."

"I'll make sure she listens," Sawyer said, giving Meredith a stern glare. "We'll do whatever's necessary to keep those babies safe and healthy."

She knew he was right, but it was hard to surrender her independence to a man she sometimes felt like she barely knew.

"I'm glad you have a strong support system right now," Dr. Mike said, pushing a button on the ultrasound machine. "You'll need friends in your corner."

Friends. Right. She glanced over at Sawyer, and he lifted a shoulder as though to say, *It's your call.*

Meredith cleared her throat. "Um, actually, Sawyer and I got married last week."

It was the first time she'd said the words aloud. The first person who knew, other than Zach and Cheyenne.

The shock and disapproval on Dr. Mike's face was brief but unmistakable. He busied himself with the ultrasound machine, and Meredith's heart squeezed.

"Congratulations," Dr. Mike said.

She knew they didn't owe anyone an explanation, but she couldn't help feeling unexpectedly defensive of her new husband. "Sawyer's been an answer to my prayers. Not many men would willingly take on an instant family."

Dr. Mike's expression softened. "I'll admit you caught me off guard, but this really is the best possible thing for the babies. There's a good chance you'll be on partial bed rest for most of the pregnancy, and that isn't easy to do when you live alone."

Meredith swallowed, looking down at her hands clutched tightly together in her lap. Would she be able to work at all during this pregnancy, or entirely reliant on Sawyer's financial support?

She hated feeling like a burden. Being a military wife had taught her the value of independence, and relying on someone else was harder than she'd expected.

Would she have minded so much if John was the husband here with her? Would she have felt like a burden to him, too?

"I'm just grateful that Meredith is allowing me to help her through this," Sawyer said.

The doctor nodded, picking up the ultrasound wand. "Should we take a look at how those babies are doing?"

Meredith leaned back on the exam table, her cheeks burning as she lifted her shirt. Sure, she'd worn a bikini on beach days with the whole group, but this felt infinitely more exposed. But Sawyer stayed near the head of the table, his attention riveted to the television screen as though it were the most interesting thing in the world.

Meredith hid a smile. She appreciated his attempts to grant her as much modesty as possible.

"There are the babies," Dr. Mike said, pointing to the screen.

Her heart leaped right along with her little jumping beans. They looked bigger than last week, even. She idly played with the chain of her necklace, smiling wider with each movement.

She would swallow her pride and let Sawyer help as much as he was willing if that kept her babies healthy and safe. One glance at the rapt look on his face reassured her he wouldn't mind.

"How are they doing?" Meredith asked.

"Measuring right on target for thirteen weeks and within the acceptable range of each other, so no red flags, at least today." Dr. Mike continued to look at the ultrasound, taking measurements and screenshotting certain images. "Good blood flow on both umbilical cords and the amniotic fluid is right where it should be. But I still want you taking things easy."

"Should she still be staying down as much as possible?" Sawyer asked.

Dr. Mike nodded. "No lifting, no straining, and as little stress as possible. Drink lots of water and make sure you're getting enough sleep and eating well. How's the nausea?"

"Better. I think the prescription you gave me is helping." She glanced over at Sawyer, who grinned back at her, his eyes bright. "Sawyer is an excellent cook and has been taking good care of us."

"Good man," Dr. Mike said. "Make sure she keeps following my instructions."

"I will," Sawyer said, and there was a fervor in his voice that made Meredith shiver.

On the drive home, Sawyer said, "Thanks for letting me come today. It means a lot to me that you included me."

"You're going to be the babies' father." Meredith rested her hands on her stomach, cradling the two lives inside. "I want you there for everything. Just make sure you stay by my head during the birth."

Sawyer laughed, the rich sound reverberating through the cab of his truck. She loved that she'd been the one to cause it.

"You've got yourself a deal," he said.

CHAPTER
Twenty-One

The tension in his shoulders dissipated as he passed the sign for Sapphire Cove's city limits. Sawyer relaxed his grip on the steering wheel and eased his foot off the gas as the speed limit changed.

Almost home. He didn't have to make the hour-long drive to the office in Portland very often, but there'd been a meeting he needed to attend in-person today. It had been his first time leaving Meredith in town alone since their wedding two weeks ago, and he'd been surprised at how anxious being away from her had made him. Since falling in love with her, he'd spent months away at a time as a SEAL. But somehow that piece of paper binding them together as man and wife made him feel even more protective of her. Or maybe it was just the pregnancy.

At Meredith's front door, he raised his hand to knock before remembering he no longer needed to.

"I'm home," he called, shutting the door behind him. "Mer?"

"Back here," she called.

Sawyer paused, raising an eyebrow. It sounded like she was in her bedroom. Other than the night he brought her home from the hospital, he'd never been in there.

"Everything okay?" he asked, cautiously walking toward the open door.

"Yeah, just watching some TV."

He leaned against the doorframe, folding his arms. The TV was certainly on, but a gigantic pile of laundry took up most of the bed, too. Meredith sat cross-legged in the middle of it, folding a pair of his jeans.

"You're supposed to be resting," he chided gently.

She set aside his pair of jeans, picking up a pair of her pajama pants to fold next. The sight of their clothes mingled together like that had his entire body warming.

"I *am* resting." She set aside her now-folded pajama pants and picked up a pair of his. "Look, I'm sitting down and everything."

Sawyer swallowed, trying not to get distracted by her slender hands adeptly folding his pajamas. "Does that mean you were good today while I was gone? Didn't overdo it or anything?"

She patted her stomach, which had rounded ever so slightly in the past few days—unnoticeable to most, but something he was acutely aware of. "Me and the babies have been fine. I did some work on my laptop this morning, then Cheyenne and Bailey came over during lunch and we discussed Thanksgiving plans. After that I took a nap, and since waking up I've mostly been watching TV while folding laundry."

It was all so perfectly normal and mundane. Sawyer walked over to the bed and picked up a pair of her socks, balling them together, then reached for a pair of his.

"You had a good day, then?"

"Yeah, pretty good." She blew out a breath. "Actually, there's something I wanted to talk to you about."

"Oh?" He tried to keep his tone casual, but his stomach was roiling with nerves.

"Yeah. I think . . . I think we should talk to Zach and Cheyenne and see how they'd feel about closing the scuba shop. Permanently."

Sawyer looked up in surprise. He didn't know what he'd been expecting, but that wasn't it.

"Wow. Are you sure?"

"Aren't you?" Meredith leaned back against her pillows, letting out a sigh. "That place was John's dream. It was never yours or Zach's."

She was right, and Sawyer didn't insult her by trying to deny it. He'd never thought scuba diving off the Oregon coast would take off. The water was frigid even in July, and the rocky terrain made it a harder dive for beginners. The tropical fish and sea turtle sightings so popular in warmer dive sites were also noticeably absent.

"I wanted to keep working with my two best friends," Sawyer said finally. "Besides, John was a hard man to say no to."

Meredith blinked quickly, looking away. "He was always so optimistic and enthusiastic. But I've been looking at the books this week, and the shop is barely treading water. It makes more sense to liquidate before we're further in the hole."

From a business perspective, she was right. But Sawyer felt a twinge of regret at the thought of telling Josiah that they had to let him go.

Closing the shop would feel like a more permanent goodbye than watching the funeral director close the lid of the casket. If it felt like that to him, what must it feel like to Meredith?

"We're only open on the weekends until at least April," Sawyer said gently. "Are you sure about this? We could keep it open for a few more months before making a final decision."

Meredith's hand went to her stomach. "By April, the babies might be here. It's better to get everything ready for them now."

"Okay." Sawyer ached to hold Meredith close and absorb some of her pain, but it felt too forward, especially in the bedroom she'd shared with John. "We can talk to Zach and Cheyenne at Thanksgiving next week and see what they're thinking."

"That's a good idea. If we can close everything out by the end of the year, it probably would make things easier come tax time."

He hated that she was worried about things like taxes when her life had been so horrifically upended.

Their hands reached for the same shirt, fingers just brushing. Sawyer jerked his hand back, feeling branded by her touch, but she barely seemed to notice.

"Oh, I forgot to tell you. Dan sent me a text and said he could drop by this afternoon to discuss the addition. In fact," —she picked up her phone, glancing at the screen— "he'll probably be here any minute now."

"Good. We can talk about our options. Have you thought any more about what you want in the addition?"

"Not really." She pushed a hand through her hair, looking stressed. "Are you sure we have money for this? I'm sure the babies can squeeze into my room for at least a year or two."

"I'm sure." They'd gone to the bank last week so he could add her to his accounts, though she hadn't made a single purchase yet with her new card. She'd added him to her accounts as well, and her finances had been as he'd expected— no major surprises. It would take some budgeting to pay off the debts, but selling the scuba shop would help and Sawyer was confident they could afford the addition and still have enough to put a little in savings each month. Their only other option was selling the bungalow and buying something bigger, but he knew that would devastate Meredith.

"Okay." She blew out a breath. "I guess it doesn't hurt to at least talk to Dan."

The doorbell rang just then, interrupting the conversation. Meredith followed him into the living room.

"Oh good, Aspen is with him," Meredith said, swinging open the door. "Hey, guys. Thanks for coming by."

Aspen smiled, leaning forward to give Meredith a hug. She wore a fancy blouse, and her hair was curled, while Dan wore a leather jacket and button-up shirt.

"I hope you don't mind. I brought Aspen with me," Dan said as they stepped inside. "Her parents are watching the baby, so we're heading to Harbor Bay for dinner and a movie after this."

"Of course not," Meredith said. "It's nice to see you. It's been a while."

"Yes, thanks so much for coming," Sawyer said. Aspen had been Cheyenne's college roommate, and Sawyer and Zach had stayed at the inn run by Aspen's parents the first time they visited Sapphire Cove, so he knew the couple fairly well.

"Of course." Aspen's eyes turned pained. "How are you doing?"

"I'm doing okay." Meredith's hands lowered to her stomach. "Um, I guess we should tell you since it's kind of why we need the addition . . . I found out a couple of weeks ago that I'm having twins."

The look of shock on Dan and Aspen's faces told Sawyer that Cheyenne hadn't let the cat out of the bag, not that he'd expected her to.

"Wow." Aspen shook her head, then hugged Meredith. "That's . . . Wow. Congratulations."

"There's more." Meredith's eyes flicked to his, and Sawyer gave her a nod of encouragement. She took a deep breath, then faced Dan and Aspen again. "I'm sure word will get out soon enough, so . . . Sawyer and I got married, too. These babies deserve a father, and so when Sawyer offered to be that, I accepted. It felt like what John would have wanted."

It wasn't an enthusiastic announcement of their new life together, but just hearing Meredith say those words—*Sawyer and I got married*—made his entire body tingle.

Now Aspen and Dan looked like a forklift had run them over.

"Huh." Aspen's head bobbed up and down, while Dan's eyes were wide. "That's . . . That's great news. Congratulations, both of you."

Meredith bit her lip, her eyes liquid with tears. Sawyer couldn't resist putting an arm around her shoulder, though he knew how that would look, and she leaned into him.

"I'm so grateful to Sawyer," Meredith choked out, one hand half-covered her mouth. "He's giving up everything to help me through this."

"Well." Aspen blinked quickly, her cheerful tone still a little forced. "That's great. I'm happy for you guys."

Meredith pulled away from Sawyer, and he let her. "Uh, so should we talk about the addition? Sawyer and I have some ideas."

CHAPTER
Twenty-Two

"*M*er? Are you ready to go?"

"Coming!" Meredith glanced at herself in the bathroom mirror one last time, smoothing down the *refuse to sink* T-shirt with the King Trident Scuba logo over her growing belly. After today, there would be no hiding her condition. Maybe that was a good thing, since she was almost halfway through her pregnancy. At least she'd woken up early enough to curl her hair and put on makeup today. Might as well look nice while dismantling John's dream.

Two weeks ago, with the turkey and mashed potatoes from Thanksgiving dinner still heavy in their bellies, she and Sawyer had broached the topic of closing the scuba shop. Cheyenne and Zach had readily agreed, and over three different pies, they'd come up with a game plan.

It had taken months of planning to start King Trident Scuba. Funny that it had only taken hours to figure out how to close it.

Sawyer waited at the front door, keys loosely jangling from one hand. His eyes trailed over her figure, lingering on her stomach.

"I know. No hiding it anymore." She tucked a strand of hair behind one ear, suddenly feeling very self-conscious. "Do I look okay?"

"You look beautiful, as always." His words had her cheeks burning. "I really like that color on you."

Meredith glanced down at the royal blue shirt. It had been one of John's favorite colors on her, too. He'd said it made her tanned skin glow golden—his own personal ray of sunshine. "Thanks."

Sawyer spun the key chain around his finger, the anchor pendant glinting in the light. A memory of John doing the same thing with those same keys flashed into her mind.

"Are you sure you feel up to going? Everyone will understand if you stay home."

Meredith cut him with a glare. "I'm not the only one who misses John, and I'm not the only one selling a business today. We do this together."

He straightened, his eyes glowing with something she couldn't quite define. Pride, maybe? "Okay then. Let's do this."

The red brick exterior of King Trident's Scuba glistened in the weak winter sun, a testament to Sawyer's efforts yesterday with the power washer. Meredith could still remember how the shop had looked when they'd leased it, the red brick turned a dull gray from the thick film of sea salt coating it. It had taken them a week just to clean the building, and there had been many late nights where the five of them ate pizza on the floor of the shop, surrounded by cleaning supplies and buckets of paint.

She pressed a hand to her stomach, taking in the window display she'd helped Cheyenne arrange. The large sign she'd designed to advertise their going-out-of-business sale sat prominently on an easel she hadn't sold yet from her photography studio.

Sawyer's arm landed around her shoulder, reassuring and warm. She leaned into him, readily accepting his silent show of support.

"Let's go inside before we freeze," he said, his warm breath tickling her cheek.

She nodded, unlocking the front door for the last time.

The store looked almost as it had on opening day. Scuba equipment neatly lined one wall, each item carefully cleaned and sanitized. A rack of wet suits stood alongside a smaller rack of T-shirts and zippered sweatshirts. A small shelf held typical tourist trinkets, everything from snow globes to bottle openers. On the reception desk, a row of tablets charged in a neat stack, ready for customers that would never again sign waivers before embarking on a dive. The only noticeable difference was the large sign overhead advertising that everything must go. Meredith had spent every spare moment during the past two weeks finding and posting in various scuba diving groups on social media in the hopes the slashed prices would lure them to the sale.

She rubbed a thumb over her necklace, her breathing ragged.

With a little luck, this place would be empty by tonight. Everything was for sale, from the equipment to the furniture. She hoped her efforts to advertise the sale would prove fruitful.

Zach and Cheyenne arrived a few minutes later, and the next hour was a flurry of activity. Meredith hated sitting back and watching while everyone else worked, but she did her best to assist while still following the doctor's orders.

"It's nine fifty-eight," Cheyenne said, glancing at her phone. "Looks like there are a few customers waiting in their cars. Should I unlock the door?"

Meredith looked around at the shop, trying to commit every detail to memory. She and John had spent so many early mornings and late nights here. They'd laughed, they'd joked, and they'd fought.

Would she ever be able to think of him without a bone-deep ache? Missing him hurt more than she'd thought possible.

"Yeah, let's unlock the doors," Meredith said, smoothing a hand over her stomach.

By lunchtime, the store was crowded with customers, which made it easy to push aside her feelings and focus on the task at hand. Meredith said a silent prayer of gratitude for small mercies.

A fair number of townspeople dropped by. They weren't interested in more than offering sympathetic platitudes, but that was okay. There were enough unfamiliar shoppers buying the dive equipment that Meredith knew her efforts of the past two weeks had paid off.

She rang up purchase after purchase, too busy to feel more than a fleeting sense of sorrow mixed with satisfaction. John would have loved seeing the shop this busy, even if it would have been impossible to organize such a large dive.

By the time seven o'clock rolled around, all that was left were half a dozen T-shirts, a small pile of items to drop off at the church charity bin, and a slightly bigger pile to take to the city dump.

Meredith sat on the barstool Sawyer had brought from their home, looking around at the now empty shop. The desk was gone, purchased by a woman from church for her husband's home office. A college student into diving had purchased the computer. Even the clothing racks were gone, bought by Linda from the dress shop three doors down.

"It looks so weird," Cheyenne said from her spot on the floor, her voice strangely loud in the now-empty space.

"Yeah. I'm going to miss it." Zach ran a hand over his face, looking pained. "I wish I hadn't been so absent from the shop the past year. I should have made more of an effort to pull my weight with the shop."

"Don't think like that," Meredith said quickly. "John knew you had other things pulling your focus. Really, he wasn't upset."

They sat in silence, Meredith on her barstool and Sawyer near her feet, his shoulder brushing her leg every time he moved. Cheyenne sat up, reaching across for Zach's hand.

"I still can't believe he's gone," Meredith whispered. She motioned to the shop, her voice choked. "It still feels like a dream."

Sawyer rested his hand on her foot, the touch comforting and warm. "I'd wake you up if I could."

Soon it became impossible to ignore the ache in her back and the exhaustion making her entire body feel heavy.

"I should get you home," Sawyer said, hopping to his feet.

"We should go as well," Cheyenne said, letting Zach pull her up from the floor. "Bailey has been at Aspen's long enough, and we need to get her to bed."

"Wait!" A desperate need to remember this place, this brief moment when John had lived out his dreams, had her scrambling for her cell phone. "We should take a picture before we leave."

Sawyer's eyes softened. "That's a great idea."

Cheyenne and Zach murmured their agreement. They all huddled close, and Meredith held out her arm and snapped a few quick shots.

She checked that the images had turned out okay, then slipped her phone back into her pocket.

"Thanks," she mumbled.

Cheyenne pulled them all in for a hug. "Let's not think about this as the end of an era, but the beginning of a new chapter."

Sawyer's arm tightened around Meredith. "I like that."

They bundled up in coats and said their goodbyes before leaving. Meredith stared out the truck window, letting her tears fall as the building disappeared from view. Sawyer would return in the morning to remove the sign and load up the donations for the church, then Zach and Cheyenne would stop by after the garage closed to load up the trash and do a quick clean of the building before they dropped off the keys at the landlord's. But Meredith wouldn't return for either of those tasks.

"You did good today, Mer," Sawyer said, one hand resting on the steering wheel. "I know it can't have been easy for you."

She grabbed a tissue and dabbed under her eyes so she wouldn't smear her makeup everywhere. "I just want to move forward and focus on the babies. Closing the scuba shop was the right move for everyone involved, including them."

Back at home, Meredith got ready for bed. She'd expected to feel exhausted, but instead she felt keyed up, her body buzzing with a nervous energy. What she really wanted was to curl up on the couch with a bowl of ice cream and a movie marathon.

She peeked out her bedroom door, feeling strangely shy. Sawyer sat in a corner of the couch, one foot propped on his knee and his laptop balanced atop his lap.

He looked so focused, and she'd taken up so much of his time and attention lately. What if he was working, and she interrupted him? She could forgo the ice cream and watch TV in bed.

She moved to close the door, swallowing back the loneliness. But a hinge squeaked and Sawyer looked up.

"Hey." He set aside his laptop, his brow knitting in concern. "Everything okay?"

"Uh-huh." She bit her lip. They'd been married a month, but they hadn't spent a single evening hanging out together since the wedding. Most nights, she barely stayed awake through dinner.

Sawyer's brow was still furrowed. "I thought you'd be asleep already."

"Me too, but I'm not tired." She rubbed her hands over her belly, nearly hidden beneath a sweatshirt. "I . . . I thought I might watch some TV. Maybe eat some ice cream. But I can go watch in my bedroom if—"

"No, that's silly. If you want to watch TV out here, you should. I can go work at my desk if you want to be alone."

Was that what he wanted? He was so hard to read sometimes—fiercely loyal and protective, but she never quite knew if it was purely out of duty. "You can stay in here if you'd like. I mean, if the TV distracts you—"

"No," Sawyer said quickly. "I was just looking at some plans Dan sent for the addition, but we can go over those later. Watching TV sounds nice."

"I wouldn't mind looking at the plans first."

"Sure." Sawyer grabbed his laptop from the coffee table, grinning. "Dan gave us a few different options. They're all rough drawings, just to give an idea of what we can fit into the space. Once we pick a design, he'll do more detailed plans."

Meredith sat down on the couch next to Sawyer, leaning over his shoulder to look at the laptop screen.

"This is the one that makes the best use of the space, I think," Sawyer said. "It'll give you a brand-new owner's suite and two additional bedrooms in case the babies don't want to share when they get older. The twins' bedrooms would be a little on the small side, but we could turn my current bedroom into a den or playroom."

"And then we'd each have our own en suite." She liked that idea—Sawyer deserved a nice new bedroom with a spacious walk-in closet and a large shower. "But I think I'd want the babies to be closer to me. I'd probably have them share your bedroom."

Sawyer turned to face her, and she inhaled sharply. She hadn't realized how close they were sitting. His Adam's apple bobbed, and she found herself mesmerized by the movement.

"But the two new bedrooms would be closer to your new bedroom," he said.

"My bedroom?" She shook her head. "Oh no, you're the one paying for everything, so you should have the new bedroom."

"With that enormous closet I'll never fill?" Sawyer laughed. "That closet and that bathroom have *woman* written all over them."

"Sawyer—"

He set the laptop back on the coffee table with a grin. "We can argue about this tomorrow. You wanted ice cream, right? Why don't you pick something to watch while I dish us up some."

"I don't know what kind of TV shows you like." She picked up the remote while Sawyer headed to the kitchen. "John liked comedies or competition game shows. I saw an ad for a new medical drama that seems kind of interesting . . ."

He poked his head out from behind the open freezer door. "Harmony Hospital?"

Meredith nodded, surprised. "Yeah. You've heard of it?"

Sawyer nodded eagerly. "Yeah, I've been wanting to watch it, too. I've always liked medical shows."

Meredith grinned, queuing it up. "Me too. John used to tease me about how much I loved drama."

"You mean prime-time soap operas?" Sawyer grinned, setting two bowls on the kitchen island. "That's what he used to call the police procedurals I'd watch."

She laughed, that phrase triggering a memory of John saying that exact same thing when he walked in while she watched a reality dating show. "He never liked anything too intense. Said he got enough of that in the SEALs."

"Yeah." Sawyer scooped the ice cream, and she could see the tension in his arms even from across the room. "I think John and Zach were both more burned out on the military than me."

John had been beyond ready to leave the SEALs, although he'd felt a lot of guilt at his job change. He'd loved his country deeply and felt a strong sense of loyalty to the Navy. He'd just loved her more.

Meredith had been excited, too. In their first year of marriage, they'd spend less than two months together total because of deployments.

But Sawyer had always struck her as a born soldier, and she'd never once heard him express dissatisfaction with his career. John had suspected that if Zach hadn't met Cheyenne, he and Sawyer would have both stayed with the SEALs. But when both his brothers left, Sawyer hadn't wanted to stay behind.

"Do you miss it?" Meredith asked.

Sawyer shook his head, and his smile seemed genuine. "Not anymore. It was a hard adjustment at first, but I'm happy with my choices."

"I'm glad." Meredith accepted the bowl of ice cream he handed her. "It meant a lot to John to have you and Zach so close."

"It means a lot to me, too."

Sawyer hesitated, then sat down beside her on the couch. Meredith realized she hadn't moved from her spot in the center after leaning over Sawyer's shoulder to look at the addition plans.

They usually hugged opposite sides of the couch, like two teenagers on a first date.

She pushed play, and the show's opening scene began—a group of medical interns starting their first day at the hospital.

When was the last time she'd sat this close to a man other than John? She'd dated before him, but never for long and never seriously.

In the show, the main intern was running late and stole a cab from a handsome man, only to show up at work and realize he was her new boss. Sawyer slung an arm across the back of the couch, one foot propped on his knee and nearly brushing her leg.

She'd loved watching TV with John. Would cuddle up against his side, her head resting on his chest while his arms held her close. He'd tuck the blanket up under her chin to make sure she wouldn't get cold. Every time he'd laugh at something on the screen, she'd felt the reverberations in his chest. Sometimes she'd focus on the sound of his heartbeat and imagine hers was in sync with it.

The intern's attending was berating her now for stealing his cab, which had made him late for an important surgery. But there was an undertone of flirting, and Meredith knew they'd get together at some point in the series. It was inevitable.

Sawyer shifted, his arm nearly brushing her leg as he set his empty bowl of ice cream on the coffee table. She took a bite of her own ice cream, her back aching from a day spent on a barstool at the scuba shop. Had that really only been a few hours ago?

It would feel so nice to lean against John right now. To ask him to knead the knots out of her lower back.

She took her last bite of ice cream and leaned forward to set the bowl on the coffee table. Her back twinged, and she inhaled sharply at the brief shot of pain.

Sawyer straightened, instantly alert. "What's wrong?"

"Nothing." She waved him away, leaning back against the couch cushions gingerly. "Just tired and sore. I don't know why since all I did was sit all day. You were the one running around and helping customers."

"That's because I'm not currently growing two entire humans. Here." He grabbed a throw pillow from where he'd tossed it on the floor and rested it on his lap. "Stretch out and lay your head down."

Meredith stared at the pillow, her eyelids drooping. She should probably just crawl into bed and go to sleep, but she wasn't ready to be alone again just yet.

If she accepted his offer, would it be overstepping some invisible boundary in their relationship? She didn't want to give him mixed signals. It looked so inviting, and her eyelids were growing heavy. "Are you sure?"

"Why not?" He patted the pillow. "You'll be more comfortable."

The pillow did look inviting, and her back ached something fierce. She hesitantly stretched out, resting her head on his lap.

Her entire body sighed in relief as her muscles stretched. Sawyer grabbed a blanket, gently placing it over her.

On the TV show, the intern was getting yelled at by an attending for mixing up two patients' charts. Meredith tried to focus on the scene, but all she could think about was how warm Sawyer felt. He smelled nice, too, like sandalwood and cedar. She'd never noticed that before.

The attending made a snarky comment to the intern, and she snapped right back at him. Sawyer chuckled, his warm breath stirring strands of her hair and making her shiver.

The ache in her back dulled from a throb to a faint pulse. Her eyes drooped, muscles relaxing as she nestled against Sawyer. It felt oddly comforting to have his firm stomach pressed against the back of her head.

She was glad she'd married him, as unconventional as their marriage was. It was so nice not to be alone.

Sawyer's fingers gently threaded through her hair, a comforting caress that had her body relaxing even more. When was the last time she'd felt this comfortable? This relaxed?

"Is this okay?" Sawyer asked quietly, his hands lingering at the back of her neck before moving through the strands.

It was more than okay—it felt absolutely wonderful. "Yeah."

He continued to play with her hair, sending pleasant shivers down her spine. Her tired mind wandered, no longer able to focus on the show.

The last thing she thought before falling asleep was how nice it was to no longer feel alone.

CHAPTER Twenty-Three

Meredith stared at the ultrasound screen, holding her breath. Sawyer gripped her hand tightly, and she squeezed it right back.

She was nearly seventeen weeks pregnant. Hopefully, today they'd find out the gender of the babies.

"They're wiggly today," Dr. Mike said with a chuckle. "It's going to be hard to get measurements today. We might be here a while if they don't cooperate."

"That's okay," Sawyer said, his deep voice making her shiver. "We've got nowhere else to be."

She knew that wasn't true—he'd taken the day off work to be here for the appointment, and later this afternoon Dan was coming over so they could finalize the plans for the addition. But she loved that Sawyer didn't care about any of that. His number one priority was her and the babies.

"Think we'll be able to find out what we're having?" Meredith asked.

"Let's hope so," Dr. Mike said. He smiled at them. "Either of you hoping for something specific?"

Meredith glanced over at Sawyer, who gave her a warm smile.

"Yes," she said. "Two healthy babies."

Dr. Mike nodded approvingly. "Well, their heartbeats are still right where they should be, which is great. Good blood flow through the umbilical cords—nothing there that concerns me. I still want to get good measurements to make sure they're growing equally, though . . ."

She watched the screen eagerly, loving each movement of the babies. She hadn't felt them kick yet, but hoped she would soon. Cheyenne said it was around this point she'd first felt Bailey, and Vanessa had said the same.

"Ah, there's the money shot," Dr. Mike said.

Sawyer's grip tightened on her hand. "You can tell if they're boys or girls?"

"I can indeed," Dr. Mike said. He took a screenshot of the video, then pointed an arrow at something that looked more like squiggles than a baby to Meredith and began labeling.

G-i-r-l.

She let out a happy laugh as he finished spelling out the word.

"It's a girl," Sawyer said, and the excitement on his face made her heart swell with pride.

"Two healthy baby girls," Dr. Mike agreed, taking another screenshot. "They're growing right on target. Everything looks great, Meredith. My only concern is that you're already having Braxton-Hicks contractions. Make sure you're continuing to take things easy and resting as much as possible."

"I'll make sure of it," Sawyer said, his smile radiant.

The rest of the appointment was uneventful. Two girls. Daughters. John would have been such a fantastic girl dad—overprotective and doting, the kind of dad who let them paint his nails a sparkly pink and met their boyfriends at the front door with a menacing glare.

What kind of dad would Sawyer be? She knew he'd be protective and kind, but had a hard time picturing him with glitter nail polish and blue eyeshadow.

Sawyer held open the truck door for her and she climbed in with a grunt. It was getting harder and harder to haul herself into the cab.

"Yeah, we should talk about selling this and buying something else," Sawyer said with a wry smile. "Maybe a minivan."

"A minivan?" She put a hand to her chest in mock horror. "I thought a Navy SEAL would sooner give up his trident pin than drive such a soccer mom car."

Sawyer laughed, shutting the door and jogging around to the driver's side. He started the car, and Meredith leaned forward to turn on the heated seats. Christmas was only two weeks away, and the temperatures had turned frigid.

"This truck isn't practical for carting around two babies," Sawyer said.

"But it's your truck. Wouldn't you miss it?"

"Are you kidding me?" Sawyer's smile was radiant. "I'm getting two little girls. I couldn't care less about this truck."

His words did funny things to her stomach. She curled her hands around her purse strap, trying not to think about just how attractive Sawyer looked wearing sunglasses, his hands resting loosely on the steering wheel.

"Girls. I can't believe it." Meredith rested her hands on her stomach. "I guess we can start preparing for their arrival now. Start buying car seats and cribs and stuff."

"Are you excited they're girls? You never really said if you had a preference."

"I don't think I had one." She traced lines on her stomach, wondering how John would have reacted to the news. She didn't think he would have cared one way or the other. "I guess it's still sinking in."

Two baby girls. It suddenly felt more real than ever before. Little girls who would want to take dance classes and play with dolls. Would they have John's eyes? Her nose?

Would they feel like their lives were lacking because they would never know their biological dad?

She was so grateful they'd at least have Sawyer.

"We should set up the Christmas tree today," she said.

Sawyer glanced over at her. "Are you sure?"

"Yeah." She rubbed her stomach. "These little girls deserve to celebrate the holiday, even if they're still in my tummy. I want them to have everything, you know? Holiday traditions and family gatherings and . . ." Her voice choked, and she swallowed quickly. "They've already lost so much. They shouldn't lose Christmas, too."

"They won't know this year." Sawyer's voice was soft and kind. "If it's too much for you, we can skip all of that."

"No. John would want us to celebrate Christmas."

"Okay." Sawyer pulled into their front yard. "After Dan leaves, I'll pull out the tree and we can decorate it."

"Sounds like a plan."

CHAPTER Twenty-Four

Christmas day. Sawyer lay in his bed, hands behind his head as he stared up at the ceiling fan as it slowly turned. A year ago, he'd been alone in his apartment, watching Christmas movies while eating cereal on the couch. Not that his friends had forgotten him—later that afternoon, he'd joined the rest of the group at Cheyenne and Zach's. They'd eaten snacks and played games while Bailey, who was only a few weeks old, slept in a bassinet.

Next Christmas, he and Meredith would have their own babies. He could almost see them in red footie pajamas, gleefully playing with the wrapping paper on their presents.

He didn't know what to expect from today. Yesterday they'd gone over to Zach and Cheyenne's for brunch, and tonight they would come by Meredith's to play games and maybe watch a Christmas movie. But what would he and Meredith do until then?

The scent of orange rolls and bacon drifted into his room, and Sawyer glanced at his phone, surprised to see it was barely eight o'clock. He hadn't expected Meredith to be up so early.

Sawyer tugged a graphic T-shirt with penguins in Santa hats over his head, cursing silently. He'd wanted to get up and make breakfast for Meredith today, but she'd beaten him to the punch.

He had a feeling today would once again be a hard day for her—yet another first without John.

But for Sawyer, it was a different kind of first—his first Christmas with his wife. With the babies she carried and his newly formed family. Guilt had his stomach clenching. He hated that he was excited to spend the day with his best friend's wife.

I'm sorry, John, he said silently. *Sorry I'm living the life that should have been yours. Sorry you aren't here to enjoy it for yourself.*

He didn't know if he ever would have fallen in love with someone else, but he'd been trying.

Sawyer slipped into the bathroom to brush his teeth, feeling strangely giddy. Which only intensified his guilt. Maybe Meredith was his wife now, but her heart still belonged to John, and it was hard not to feel like he was betraying his best friend.

He'd thought he could keep a lid on his feelings, but the more time he spent with Meredith, the harder it became.

She looked up as he entered the kitchen, smiling widely. A snowman apron made her baby bump more obvious than usual, and her bare feet just stuck out from the bottoms of her green pajama pants. But her eyes were red-rimmed and bloodshot. Had she been crying?

"Merry Christmas," Meredith said, turning off the hand mixer.

"I was going to get up and make us breakfast," Sawyer said, dipping a finger into the bowl of icing she'd been mixing.

"Hey!" She swatted his hand, and the playful gesture made his heart leap.

"Sorry," he said as he licked his finger, not at all repentant. "That is amazing. You shouldn't be doing so much, though."

"It's just orange rolls and bacon. I was waiting until you were up to scramble the eggs."

"I'll do that." He pointed to the barstool. "You sit and watch. I'll let you frost the orange rolls when they're out of the oven."

She did as he asked without protest, and he quickly took over preparing their meal.

"I thought making breakfast would make it feel more like Christmas." There was a wistful tone in her voice that made his heart twist.

Sawyer looked up from the bowl where he was beating eggs with a fork. "And has it?"

"No." Her shoulders slumped. "I guess I shouldn't expect it to, though. Everything is different this year. Maybe next year, when the babies are here, it'll feel magical again."

"I think it will." The timer buzzed, and Sawyer pulled the orange rolls from the oven. They looked perfect.

"They'll probably be seven or eight months old if they don't come too early." She rubbed her stomach.

"They'll probably be more interested in the boxes the presents come in than the presents themselves."

She laughed, nodding. "Yeah, probably. Do you think they'll be crawling yet?"

"I don't know." Would they be the kind of babies who were always busy and getting into things, or would they be content to sit quietly while observing everything? He couldn't wait to find out.

Meredith put on some Christmas music while Sawyer flipped the bacon, and soon they were sitting down to eat. Sawyer purposefully kept the conversation light, sensing Meredith's emotions were close to the surface today.

Sawyer pushed back his plate, his stomach pleasantly full. The orange rolls had been so delicious he'd eaten three. "That meal was incredible, Mer."

Her cheeks pinked, but she seemed pleased. "You're always way too complimentary about my cooking."

"Trust me, it's not empty flattery. Your meals always hit the spot." He stood, gathering their plates. "Now, you stay right there and watch while I clean up."

"At least bring me some containers for the leftovers. I can put them away while sitting right here."

He nodded, and they worked with Christmas music as their accompaniment.

"Zach and Cheyenne won't be here until three or four," Sawyer said as he finished wiping down the counters. "What do you want to do until then?"

She motioned shyly to the Christmas tree. "We could open presents. I bought a few things for the babies."

"Me too," he said, smiling at her. "Once we knew they were girls, I couldn't resist."

"Same. I can't wait to see what you got them."

They settled in the living room, the twinkling white lights of the Christmas tree giving the space a warm glow. A small pile of gifts sat under the tree. Sawyer had put his out after she went to bed last night, and she must have added hers before he woke up this morning.

"Here." Meredith picked up a small package, handing it to him. "Open it."

Sawyer eagerly tore off the wrapping paper and opened the box, lifting out a pink dress that seemed impossibly small. It said *daddy's little girl* in a swirling font across the front, and he swallowed back a lump in his throat. Beneath it was a matching dress, but in purple.

"Do you like it?" Meredith asked, her tone shy.

He dropped the dresses back into the box and pulled her to him, dropping a soft kiss on her forehead. "I love them. This means a lot to me, Mer."

"And you are going to mean a lot to them." She pulled away, motioning to the small pile of gifts. "Open something else."

He opened a small package of newborn size diapers and a large box that ended up being a baby bathtub before handing Meredith one of his own packages to open. He'd found the onesies while in Portland for work last week and hadn't been able to resist.

She pulled out the shirts, laughing when she saw the ladybug on the onesie with the words *mama's little shutter bug.* "It's perfect," she said, giving him a quick hug. "Thanks, Sawyer."

"Of course." He sat back on the couch, satisfied with her obvious excitement at the gift.

They opened a few more gifts—pink swaddle blankets from Meredith, a pajama set covered in tiny mermaids from

Sawyer, and a few more outfits from both of them. It didn't take long to get through the small stack of gifts, but he enjoyed every second.

Eventually there were only two gifts left—a slim square package from Meredith, and a triangle-shaped one he'd paid the store to wrap from him.

"Here." Meredith bit her lip, handing him the package. "I've been working on it for the last few weeks when you're at work. I hope you like it."

Sawyer took the package, his curiosity piqued. He carefully tore away the thick silver wrapping paper covered in glittery snowflakes, revealing a box. Sawyer lifted the lid and inhaled sharply.

An image stared back at him from the cover of a book. It was a photograph of him, Zach, and John in basic training, their faces not yet lined by the stress of military life. The image was black and white, and a lot clearer than he remembered it being.

"I feel like the last few months have been all about me and my grief," Meredith said quietly. "I thought it was about time someone acknowledged that you lost a best friend, too."

Tears filled his eyes, and he wiped them away with the back of his hand, embarrassed. He carefully flipped open the cover of the book, revealing another photo, this one of the three of them at high school graduation.

"Mer, this is incredible." He flipped to the next page and realized it was a photo journey of his friendship with John. Zach was in many of the photos as well, and later sometimes Cheyenne or Meredith were present, too. But every image had one thing in common—John.

"I tried my best to enhance the pictures wherever possible," she said.

He flipped the page again, landing on a picture Zach had taken of Sawyer and John at John's bachelor party. It hadn't been a wild affair—just an hour at the shooting range, a late night dive off the coast, and then drinks at the bar before heading home. But Sawyer had savored every second of that night, knowing that the next day—the day of John and Meredith's wedding—things would change in their friend group forever.

"This is incredible." He set the album aside, pulling her to him in a fierce hug. Meredith wrapped her arms around his shoulders, her cheek pressed against his chest as she clung to him.

"I know you miss him, too," she whispered.

He pressed a kiss into her hair, blinking rapidly. "Here, I got you something, too."

She took the triangle-shaped package from him, her eyebrows raised in confusion. Sawyer steepled his fingers, watching intently as she tore away the wrapping paper.

He'd agonized for weeks over what to get her before finally settling on this gift, then had second guessed his decision ever since.

She dropped the wrapping paper to the ground, revealing the display case he'd had custom made for the flag that had draped John's coffin. The frame was a deep walnut color, with a rope design carved into the wood and a gold name plate with John's information at the bottom. A trident had been carved into the wood on one side of the placard, and an anchor similar to the one on Meredith's necklace on the other.

Meredith ran her fingers over the name with fingers that trembled. "I love it," she breathed. "This is perfect, Sawyer."

"I thought we could put it on the fireplace mantle, so the babies can see it every day," he said.

She clutched the frame to her chest, nodding. "Yes. That's a great idea. Will you help me put the flag in it?"

"Of course."

Meredith set the frame aside and rose, returning from her room a moment later with the carefully folded flag. Memories of the funeral had Sawyer's throat clogged with tears, but he held them back as he helped Meredith clean and dry the glass in the display case before carefully placing the flag inside.

She set it on the fireplace mantle and stepped back. Sawyer wrapped an arm around her waist, and she leaned her head on his shoulder. They stood that way for at least a minute, staring quietly at the flag. *I hope I'm doing right by you, John,* Sawyer said silently. *I'm trying my best to do right by Mer and the babies.*

Meredith placed a hand on her stomach, letting out a surprised, "Oh!"

Sawyer glanced down at her, concerned. "What's wrong?"

"Nothing. I . . . I think I felt one of the babies move."

"Are you serious?"

She laughed, nodding. "Yeah. There it is again. Kind of a fluttery feeling."

He ached to place his hands on her stomach, even though he knew it was too early to feel it for himself. Instead, he pulled her to him in a tight hug.

"I guess they wanted to give us a Christmas present, too," Sawyer said.

Meredith laughed into his chest. "Yeah, I guess so."

CHAPTER Twenty-Five

The loud banging of mallets against chisels filled her small home, making Meredith's ears ring. She sat cross-legged on the couch, making silly faces for Bailey while bouncing the stuffed dog up and down like it was dancing.

Bailey laughed, lunging for the stuffed animal.

"Whoa." Meredith threw out her arms, just saving Bailey from a tumble to the floor. She tickled the one-year-old's stomach, eliciting excited squeals.

Cheyenne popped her head out from behind the kitchen island, wiping away a sheen of sweat with the back of a gloved hand. "How's it going over here?"

"We're doing great." Meredith pulled a face, making Bailey laugh. She glanced over the top of Bailey's head, surveying the kitchen. Broken tiles were piled every few feet, revealing the subfloor underneath. "You guys are making good time."

"Good thing, since we've got to have it done this weekend," Zach said wryly.

Sawyer grinned. "I can't wait to see what it'll look like when it's done."

"Same," Meredith said.

It was the beginning of February, and Dan and his crew had made good progress in the last month on the addition. The new walls were painted, and flooring would go in next week. Sawyer had convinced her they should replace the flooring in the entire house at the same time to match. He'd known it had been the next project she and John planned to tackle, but Meredith still felt guilty about spending Sawyer's money.

At least she'd convinced him the new owner's suite should be his. He'd been completely against the idea, wanting her to have the newer, nicer bedroom, until she admitted she didn't want to move out of the room she'd shared with John.

Bailey crawled into Meredith's lap, and she cuddled the little girl close, dropping a kiss on the crown of her head. She smelled like baby shampoo and diaper rash cream, and Meredith's heart gave a happy leap.

She was nearly in the third trimester, and her stomach had grown significantly. Most of January she'd spent researching all things baby—tips and tricks for tandem nursing, the best stroller on the market, whether she should have the girls co-sleep at least initially. Sawyer had sold his truck, and they'd replaced it with a minivan.

She couldn't wait to hold these babies in her arms. To finally know her girls—John's daughters—were safe and secure. The pregnancy continued to progress as smoothly as could be expected, but she'd started having contractions anytime she did something other than sit on the couch, and she grew more uncomfortable physically with each passing day.

Sawyer had been supportive and helpful through it all.

Bailey laid her head on Meredith's shoulder, two fingers in her mouth and eyes heavy. Meredith patted the one-year-old's back, holding her close.

Sawyer rose, reaching for a sledgehammer. Meredith bit her lip, watching the muscles in his arms and shoulders strain against the T-shirt as he brought the hammer over his head and down on the tile in rhythmic motions. He hadn't shaved this morning, and his scruffy beard highlighted the sharp angles of his face.

She'd always known Sawyer was attractive, of course. Any woman who didn't was blind. But knowing he was attractive, and *noticing* his attractiveness, were two very different things. And lately she was noticing more and more.

Stupid pregnancy hormones.

John had always said one of Sawyer's best traits was loyalty. He hadn't been wrong. She still couldn't believe he'd given up any chance at love to help her raise John's twins.

Soft puffs of air blew against Meredith's neck, signaling that Bailey had fallen asleep. Meredith shifted to a more comfortable position on the couch, drawing Bailey closer as she watched Sawyer work. The edge of his T-shirt lifted, exposing a slice of the tanned skin on his back. She bit her lip, her heart quickening.

"Phew." Cheyenne rose and stretched her back, letting out a satisfied sigh when it cracked loudly. She pulled off her work gloves and grabbed her water bottle, taking a long swig. Her lips turned up in a soft smile as she caught sight of Bailey. "Awww. I can't believe she fell asleep with all this noise."

"She's such a cutie." Meredith tightened her grip on the baby, snuggling her close. "And such a good little girl, too. She's just been content to sit here and play together."

"Yeah, she's pretty good, as long as she's got someone's undivided attention." Cheyenne grinned, the love on her face unmistakable. "Let me just wash up, and then I'll lay her down, if you don't mind. I've got her pack 'n play in the car."

She didn't want to relinquish Bailey, but knew she'd probably sleep better in her portable crib than on Meredith's shoulder.

"You can set it up in my room," Meredith suggested. "It's probably quietest in there."

Bailey didn't stir when Cheyenne lifted her from Meredith's arms a few minutes later after setting up the portable crib. She pushed aside the ache in her arms at the loss. Just a few more months, and she'd have more baby snuggles than she'd know what to do with.

Cheyenne returned a few moments later, the baby monitor clipped to her shirt collar.

"It's almost one o'clock. Should I make lunch?" Meredith asked, struggling to her feet. "Sawyer bought stuff for sandwiches yesterday."

"Yeah, I think the guys are getting hungry," Cheyenne said, raising her voice to be heard over the sounds of breaking tiles in the kitchen. "I know I am. But you stay put. I can make lunch."

"No, I can help." Meredith followed Cheyenne into the kitchen. Sawyer looked up, giving her a grin that had her stomach flipping. Orange earplugs stuck out of his ears, the bright green string connecting them resting against the back of his neck.

Cheyenne motioned to the barstools. "At least sit down while you help. Sawyer will have my hide if I let you do too much."

Meredith laughed, pressing a hand to her stomach. "Yeah, he's pretty overprotective of the babies these days."

Cheyenne raised an eyebrow, setting a loaf of bread on the counter. "I don't think they're the only people he's worried about."

Meredith traced lines on her stomach, her face growing warm. She hoped Sawyer could feel the babies kick soon. It was such an amazing feeling, and she wanted to share it with him.

"John always said loyalty was one of Sawyer's strongest traits." Meredith accepted the jar of mayonnaise Cheyenne slid toward her and started spreading it on the first slice of bread. "I know he feels like it owes it to John to take care of his family, now that he's gone."

It felt odd to have this conversation with the men so close, but between the sledgehammers and earplugs, she knew they couldn't hear a thing.

Cheyenne paused, the head of lettuce she'd been unwrapping still in her hands. "I don't think it's just loyalty that makes Sawyer look out for you. He cares for you, Meredith."

"I know." She looked down, swallowing the emotions she couldn't quite name. "He's a good man, and I'm not sure I deserve him."

"Sure you do. I think he's been good for you. You've seemed happier the last few times we've seen each other."

Meredith cocked her head to the side, considering Cheyenne's words. The ache of John's absence hadn't receded, but it had dulled to more manageable proportions. And Sawyer had helped keep some of the loneliness at bay.

"I miss John so much." Meredith dipped her knife in the jar of mayonnaise, suddenly feeling very heavy. "But I don't miss him quite as much when Sawyer's around."

By Sunday evening, all the tile had been removed, and on Monday, Dan and his crew came in to start installing the new floors throughout the entire house. Meredith spent a lot of time at Cheyenne and Zach's, avoiding the dust and noise, while Sawyer oversaw everything at home. But by Thursday evening, the floors had been installed, and Sawyer had mopped the new light gray laminate until it shined.

"What do you think?" Sawyer asked, plopping beside her on the couch.

Meredith shook her head in awe. "It's stunning, Sawyer. I couldn't love it more if I tried."

"Yeah?" He stretched an arm across the back of the couch, taking in the flooring. "I love it, too. Good choice to go with the gray. I think it'll hide the twins' messes pretty well."

She tucked her legs up beneath her, hands resting on her stomach as she imagined the new floor covered in spilled cereal and toys. "Makes the house feel so much warmer. Brighter somehow, too. John would have loved it."

"I think so, too."

"He would have hated that he loved it." Meredith laughed, a dozen conversations playing through her mind. "He always claimed the tile was perfectly fine and replacing it should be low on our priority list, but if he could see it now, he would finally admit that I was right."

"He used to claim you were wrong?" Sawyer made a face. "I thought he was smarter than that."

Meredith giggled, leaning her head on his chest while Sawyer wrapped an arm around her shoulder. She could just picture the laughter in John's eyes as he admitted defeat and conceded that she knew best when it came to home decor.

Dan said the addition should be complete by the end of next week. Now that the floors were in, there were just a few finishing touches left.

Her stomach jolted, and she sat up with a gasp.

"What?" Sawyer asked, the alarm in his tone clear. "What's wrong?"

Another jolt went through Meredith's stomach, and she laughed, placing her hands on it.

"That was the strongest kick I've felt yet."

Sawyer's eyes widened, his face alight with awe. "Really?"

Meredith nodded, grabbing his muscular hand and placing it on her stomach. His touch was light as a feather, the warmth of his hand seeping through her shirt.

She'd hugged Sawyer dozens of times. Fallen asleep with her head on his lap while they watched TV. Held his hand during ultrasounds. But nothing could have prepared her for the feel of his hand cradling her stomach.

A baby kicked again. "There! Did you feel it?"

"Yes!" He placed his other hand on her stomach as well, the joy on his face unmistakable.

Another kick. Meredith laughed, while Sawyer's smile widened.

"I think they like you," Meredith said.

"This is crazy. There are really two little girls in there, kicking away."

"No kidding." Meredith laughed as they kicked yet again. "They're trying to say hi to you, I think. They know the sound of your voice."

Sawyer rested his forehead against hers, hands still splayed across her stomach. "I hope so. I love them so much already."

She cradled his face in her hands, the rough scruff of his beard rubbing against the sensitive skin on her palms. Sawyer's eyes darkened, his breathing quickening.

"Thank you," she whispered. "For everything."

He reached out hesitantly, brushing a strand of her hair behind one ear. "I will do anything for my three girls. Anything."

Her eyes dipped to his lips. What would it feel like to kiss Sawyer? To really, truly be his wife?

She rose abruptly, pressing her hands to her warm cheeks. Her legs felt shaky, her entire body somehow hot and cold simultaneously.

"Well, I'm exhausted. I think I'll head to bed."

Sawyer rose, shoving his hands in his pockets. "Yeah, of course. You should rest. Night, Mer."

"Night."

She hurried from the room without a backward glance.

CHAPTER
Twenty-Six

$\mathcal{S}$awyer dreamed about kissing Meredith all night long. But then John was in the dreams, an AK-47 pointed at Sawyer as he ordered him to stay away from his wife. The gun turned into a crying baby and John threw it in the air. Sawyer lunged forward, catching the infant just before it hit the floor.

Then the baby split into two babies, and they were both crying while Meredith demanded Sawyer feed them. He searched frantically through empty cupboards, but there were no bottles or formula anywhere, and Meredith was saying he never should have made her sell King Trident's Scuba, because the babies had never been hungry there.

He awoke with a renewed determination to push last night out of his mind. Resting his hands on Meredith's swollen stomach and feeling the babies kick inside had been incredible. And yes, there had been a moment when she'd looked at him and there had been a palpable tension between them.

But Meredith had meant nothing by it. She was in a vulnerable situation right now, between her grief over John and her pregnancy hormones, and he wouldn't take advantage of that.

He refused.

It had only been five months since John's passing. That wasn't long enough to even consider—

It wasn't long enough.

He rolled out of bed, determined to keep things as normal as possible between them. In the three months since their wedding, they'd established a routine, and he was going to stick to it.

Nothing had happened last night.

He was just assembling their breakfast burritos when Meredith wandered out of her room.

"Hey," Sawyer said. "Breakfast is ready. How did you sleep?"

"Great." Meredith gave him a perfectly normal smile. Good. It seemed he was the only one who'd spent last night tormented by crazy dreams that were obviously a result of conflicted feelings. "How about you?"

"Fine," he lied. "Just thought I'd get breakfast going so we can leave as soon as we're done."

They were heading to Harbor Bay today to do some shopping for the babies. Meredith still needed to take things easy, but her last appointment had gone well, and the doctor had cleared her for a day trip, as long as she didn't walk too much.

Two hours later, Sawyer had his hands shoved in his pockets. He felt intensely out of place in an aisle of frilly pink baby bedding and crocheted blankets.

"I don't know." Meredith chewed on her lip, her hands on her hips and stomach protruding adorably. "I love the idea of using anchors as a focal point in the nursery, but it doesn't really go with the pink and gray color pallet that I love. Anchors always make me think of navy blue, and there's no bedding that goes with the theme."

"Uh." Sawyer scratched the back of his neck, not sure how to reply. Was he supposed to have an opinion on this kind of thing?

Right now, he'd just be happy if she'd agree to move into the newly finished owner's suite next week when Dan finished the final touches. But she was still insisting he take that room, while she stayed in hers and John's and the babies moved into his current room.

"Maybe anchors are more masculine, and that's why?" She picked up a swaddling blanket, brushing her hand over the fabric. "I mean, how cute are these baby elephants? And there are so many ideas online for gray elephants and a dusty pink color scheme. But I can't seem to give up on the idea of anchors and a beach vibe."

"Uh-huh," Sawyer said. He had no idea what dusty pink looked like, and how it differed from regular pink. And he wasn't sure how baby elephants were appropriate for a girl's nursery, but anchors weren't. Or was she saying anchors were appropriate, but the color blue wasn't?

Somehow, he'd never imagined these moments when he'd dreamed of marriage to Meredith. Not that he was complaining. Just spending time with her was a privilege.

One John didn't get anymore.

Had he really considered kissing her last night?

"I should go with what I love, right?" Meredith said, interrupting his thoughts.

He blinked, trying to focus on the conversation. What were they talking about again? "Right."

"I mean, the twins will be my only babies. I just want everything to be perfect."

The unexpected words had him inhaling sharply. Luckily, Meredith didn't seem to notice.

How had he let himself begin to hope? Because of course these would be their only children. Their marriage wasn't like that, no matter his personal feelings. He'd promised himself to give Meredith the space and time she needed.

If she wanted something different . . .

But she didn't. And he couldn't go down that road.

He should have encouraged Meredith to go shopping with Cheyenne, or to video-chat with Vanessa during this trip to the store. But he'd been so excited to be included in another part of the process. To have her ask him to accompany her to the fancy baby boutique in Harbor Bay.

"Look at this." Meredith picked up a bag of crib bedding. The fabric was a light pink color—was that what she meant by dusty pink?—and gray cartoon elephants with pink bows in their ears dotted the fabric, along with the word *baby* in a swirling cursive script.

"It's nice," Sawyer said.

She frowned, turning the bag over and reading the back. "Nice?"

He was so bad at this. Was nice an insult or something? He had no idea how to talk girl. "It's cute."

This made her lips purse, and he had a feeling he'd said something wrong yet again. "Cuter than anchors?"

He'd spent a lot of time around anchors, and very little around elephants, but couldn't say he'd ever thought of either of them as *cute*. The back of his neck grew uncomfortably hot. It took a lot of restraint not to tug at the collar of his T-shirt. "Whatever you want is great."

Meredith pinned him with a glare. "Don't you care what the room looks like?"

The words felt like a trap, one Sawyer wasn't sure how to escape.

"I just want you to be happy?" He wished it hadn't sounded like a question, but these were uncharted waters. He'd never dated the same woman for more than a few months, much less married someone pregnant with another man's twins.

Coming with her had been a mistake. That moment in the living room last night had been a mistake.

Meredith sighed, putting the bag of bedding back on the shelf. "I wish I knew what would make me happy. I have no idea what I want."

Sawyer bit back a growl of frustration. It was just bedding, and the twins wouldn't care one way or the other what Meredith picked. But this seemed important to her—about more than elephants versus anchors—and so he'd try to be supportive.

Sometimes he wished she could see how hard he was trying.

"You seem really set on anchors," Sawyer said, trying his best to keep his tone gentle. "So let's keep looking for that. We've got time."

"Do we?" She put her hands on her stomach. "They'll be here in two months, max, and that seems like no time at all."

No time at all, and yet he couldn't wait for the babies to be here. Maybe, once they were born, Meredith would start thinking of them as a real family. As her husband in every sense of the word, not just a poor stand-in for John.

But that was unfair to put on her.

He'd promised her. He'd promised John.

"The babies can come without the nursery being finished, but we do need car seats to bring them home from the hospital," Sawyer said. "How about we go look at those?"

"Okay." She rubbed a hand across her stomach. "We can look at cribs, too. And a changing table would be nice."

Sawyer nodded, feeling more confident as they moved away from the frilly pink blankets and toward the car seats. This he had researched extensively, and he went immediately to a model that had received high safety reviews online from multiple consumer reports.

"What do you think of this one?" Sawyer asked.

Meredith glanced at the price tag, then wrinkled her nose. "It's almost twice as much as the other car seats."

"Don't worry about the price tag." Sawyer grit his teeth, pointing to the car seat. When would she stop thinking of the money as *his* and start thinking of it as *theirs*? "I've been reading consumer reports for a few weeks now, and this one gets the highest ratings by far."

"Really?" The worried furrow between her brow disappeared, and she stepped closer, examining the car seat. "What did the reports say?"

He gave her a rundown of what he'd learned, pointing out various features as she examined the car seat. It was one of those kinds for really young babies that looked like a bucket and could unsnap from the base in the car and be carried around.

"What stroller does it connect to?" Meredith asked. She looked around, her eyes landing on a black side-by-side stroller that was the same brand. "Ah. But can you connect both car seats to it?"

"From reading online, we need a frame-looking thing to snap both car seats into. That stroller is for later, when they're not in their car seats so much. I think."

She raised her eyebrows, giving him a smile that had his heart jumping. "Someone's been doing their research. Very impressive, Mr. Grey."

"Here." He pulled the stroller off the shelf, her praise making him uncomfortable. "Take it for a spin and see what you think."

Meredith nodded, giving the stroller a push. It had bigger wheels than what Sawyer was used to seeing—two at the back, but only one at the front. The women in the mommy message boards online called this style a jogger, and all of them talked about how much easier it was to steer than the traditional version.

Meredith did a tight turn with the stroller at the end of the aisle, heading back toward him.

"I like it," Meredith said. "It steers nicely. You want to give it a try?"

Sawyer's eyebrows raised in surprise, but he quickly nodded. Of course he'd be pushing the stroller—hopefully a lot. "Sure."

Meredith walked beside him as he pushed the stroller down the aisle. "Do you think it will be easy to push on the beach?"

"As long as the sand isn't too soft," Sawyer said. "But I don't know if any stroller would easily make it through really loose sand."

"I like it," Meredith said. "But it's so expensive—"

"Safety first," Sawyer interrupted.

Meredith smiled up at him, then nodded. "Yeah, okay. Let's get it, plus the frame one we can stick the car seats on."

In the end, they got not only the strollers and car seats, but two cribs, a changing table, and a dresser. Meredith's eyes had gone huge at the total, but Sawyer had placed a reassuring hand on her back and handed over his card. He'd known today would be expensive, but it was unavoidable. Exciting, even.

Maybe he had no idea what color dusty pink was, or whether elephants or anchors were better nursery decor. But he couldn't wait for the furniture to be delivered and was excited to assemble everything.

It was becoming so real. These babies really were coming, and soon.

As they drove home, she rubbed a hand over her stomach, staring out the window. "Do you think John would have liked what we chose today?"

Sawyer swallowed, the ache in his heart giving a painful throb. "Yeah. I do."

When he'd asked Meredith to marry him, he'd thought he'd known just how painful loving her but not truly having her as his wife would be.

He'd been wrong. So very, very wrong.

CHAPTER Twenty-Seven

$\mathcal{S}$hopping for the nursery with Meredith had flipped a switch in Sawyer. Or maybe it was her offhand remark that these would be her only children.

That meant they would be his only children, too. And while he still had no regrets—would make the exact same decision, given the same circumstances—it was dawning on him just how long a lifetime of platonic marriage would feel like.

He'd thought it was impossibly hard to watch his best friend and the love of his life with each other. But being with Meredith without having her heart hurt even more.

Dan finished the addition. Sawyer had offered the new owner's suite to Meredith one last time, but she'd insisted on staying in the room she'd shared with John. He hadn't pushed the issue.

Work kept him busy for the next couple of weeks. Meredith spent most of her time looking at baby items online, but she seemed to sense his mood and didn't ask him for input too often.

He hated the distance between them, but wasn't sure what to do to fix things. How could he continue being there for her in every way without letting his feelings show?

How would she react if she knew how he really felt?

In mid-February, he had to head into the Portland office. All day, he was a bundle of nerves. Meredith was thirty-three weeks pregnant, and he hated leaving her alone with her due date so close.

When he pulled into the front yard, the sight of Cheyenne's minivan surprised him almost as much as the sound of laughter when he opened the front door. It filled the home, like chimes on a bell. Sawyer quietly shut the front door, the joyful notes sliding over him with the comfort of a warm blanket.

He'd almost forgotten the sound of Meredith's laugh. Her voice had an almost musical quality to it, though she was only an average singer.

"I'm home," Sawyer called.

"Don't come back here!" Meredith said, then laughed again. "It's not ready."

"What are you talking about?" Sawyer asked, amused.

The door to his old room—soon to be the nursery—opened a crack and Meredith slipped out, her large stomach brushing against the door.

"It's so close to done," Meredith said. "Not yet though. Maybe another hour. Don't come back here, okay? I want it to be a surprise when it's all finished."

He loved this side of Meredith—the lighthearted woman who wasn't afraid to be happy. But it also filled him with hope that things could be different between them, and that was a dangerous thing.

"Okay," Sawyer said, loosening his tie. "I'll just watch TV then in the living room, if that's okay." It was early to start dinner, and after a day of meetings, he couldn't face the thought of making phone calls or answering emails for work.

"Great." Meredith gave him a wide smile that took his breath away, then disappeared back inside the nursery.

Sawyer half-focused on the television show he'd found, a reality series about flipping houses. But mostly he just listened to the murmurs coming from the nursery, punctuated by occasional laughter.

It was just over an hour later when the door finally opened again. This time, both Meredith and Cheyenne emerged.

"Hey, Sawyer," Cheyenne said, giving him a bright smile. "How were the meetings?"

"Not too bad," Sawyer said. "How long have you ladies been hanging out?"

"Oh, since I put Bailey down for her nap right after lunch," Cheyenne said. "Zach said he could listen for her."

"Well, thanks for helping Mer," Sawyer said. If he'd known Cheyenne was here, he wouldn't have worried so much while he was at work.

Meredith put an arm around Cheyenne, giving her a side-hug. "Yes, thank you so much for giving up your afternoon to decorate with me. I know Sawyer would have helped, but some things you just need a woman's opinion for."

"I'm honored to be included," Cheyenne said, returning Meredith's hug. She hugged Sawyer next, giving him a wink.

"You're going to love how it turned out. You two have fun. Let's get together for a game night soon, okay? I'll talk to Zach and see what our schedule's like."

They waved goodbye to Cheyenne, then Sawyer turned to Meredith. Her enthusiasm had his interest piqued. "So, the nursery's that good, huh?"

She nodded enthusiastically, grabbing his hand. A jolt of fire shot up his arm, but the touch seemed to have no effect on her. Not that he'd expected it to.

"Come on, I want to show you everything," she said.

He laughed, willingly following her. She paused in front of the door, hand resting on the knob. Sawyer drank in her appearance, wanting this moment etched into his memory. She'd done her hair today, the soft blonde waves curling around her shoulders, and even put on a little eyeliner and lipstick. She wore a high-waisted blue maternity shirt that drew attention to the basketball she seemed to be hiding in her stomach. Her cheeks were flushed with excitement, and there was a glow about her he'd missed since John's passing.

She'd never looked more beautiful.

"Okay. Here it is," Meredith said, swinging the door open. "Ta-da!"

Sawyer had no idea what to expect when he entered the nursery. Just last weekend the furniture had been delivered, and he'd assembled everything while Meredith sat in a chair and told him about some scandal with a celebrity couple. Surely the nursery couldn't look that much different than it had then.

But Sawyer sucked in a breath, his eyes widening in awe at the room. It had been entirely transformed.

"What do you think?" Meredith asked. Her face was open and earnest, and there was a shyness in her tone that was endearing.

The white cribs were side-by-side against the wall he'd painted with pink-and-gray stripes. A pink baby blanket with gold anchors hung over the front rail of each crib. He remembered how excited she'd been when finding the bedding set after an entire day of online shopping.

His eyes moved up, taking in the gold vinyl decal of an anchor with *refuse to sink* in a pink cursive script. The anchor glittered, centered right between the two cribs. A white microfiber glider sat in the corner and floating shelves above it held children's books supported by seashell bookends.

"Oh, Mer." He wrapped an arm around her shoulders. She curled into his side, sending his pulse racing. "It's beautiful. I had no idea there was so much work left to do in here."

The changing table sat on another wall. Beside it, a wicker basket held impossibly tiny diapers and a container of wipes. Above the table hung floofy pom-pom looking things that seemed made of delicate pink and gold paper, but somehow it worked.

"Do you like it?" she asked.

"I love it." He pointed to a few empty frames on the walls. "Are these for pictures of the babies?"

"Yeah, and Cheyenne knows a place where I can get subway art made with the babies' birth stats."

Sawyer wasn't sure what subway art was, but he assumed by birth stats she meant things like how much the babies weighed.

"It's perfect," Sawyer repeated. "I absolutely love it."

Her smile radiated genuine happiness—a glimpse of the woman he loved, one swimming through an ocean of grief but getting closer to the shore.

"Look at these cute pillows that were delivered yesterday." She pointed to the identical clusters in the corner of each crib. "Once the twins are sleeping in here, I'll move them to a basket on the floor or something, but I thought they looked cute for now."

Sawyer nodded, pretending to examine the pillows for Meredith's sake. Each crib had a plush stuffed pillow—he'd take Meredith's word that it was not a stuffed animal—of a mermaid with a bright pink tail, and another turquoise one shaped like a clam.

But it was the middle pillow in each crib that caught his attention. It was square, with a thick gold-colored rope lining the edges. In the middle, a pink anchor with a gold rope running through it was embroidered onto the plush fabric. Above the anchor were the words *daddy's little girl*.

Below the anchor were two lines, one on top of the other, each a series of numbers.

The top number was John's military ID. Sawyer would never forget it—not after all the times he'd heard John rattle it off when calling in something over the radio.

And the bottom number was his.

He couldn't have spoken even if he wanted to. Sawyer pressed a fist to his mouth, emotion welling up within him.

"I wanted them each to be able to hug something that represented both of their fathers," Meredith said quietly. "The two men who love these baby girls more than any others."

Sawyer still couldn't speak. He wrapped an arm around Meredith's shoulders, blinking quickly. She clung to him—not a desperate hug like they'd shared so many times before, but one of comfort and understanding. He inhaled deeply, the scent of her sea breeze shampoo reminding him of freshly laundered fabric and diving with his two best friends.

Her enormous stomach pressed against his as she laid her head on his chest. Her hands caressed his back in slow, comforting circles.

"This is the nicest thing anyone has ever done for me," Sawyer choked out, his voice rough with unshed tears.

Her hold on his waist tightened. "You are going to be these babies' father just as much as John is. I know our situation is . . . unusual. But these girls will never doubt that you are their father, and that you love them every bit as much as John would have."

"I do love them," Sawyer said. "So incredibly much. I think of them as my children already."

He wanted to say more—that he loved Meredith and longed for them to one day be a traditional family, one where the mom and dad shared a bedroom and made their kids groan when they danced in the kitchen.

But he wouldn't risk their marriage by admitting to something as dangerous as romantic love.

A sharp jab hit him in the stomach, and Sawyer froze. He knew it was crazy, but part of him wondered if the babies could read his thoughts and were warning him away from their mother.

Meredith laughed, taking his hand and resting it gently on top of her stomach. "I think they're trying to say hello."

Slowly, Sawyer spread his fingers wider, splaying his palm over Meredith's stomach. He hadn't known if she'd let him feel them kick again.

Another jab. It was one of the best feelings in the world.

"There's actually a person in there," Sawyer said.

Meredith laughed, and the motion made her stomach bounce up and down. The baby seemed to like that and kicked again.

"Two people, actually. It's still hard to believe."

Slowly, giving Meredith plenty of time to protest, Sawyer spread his other hand over her stomach. She grew still, but didn't pull away, and one of the babies rewarded him with another kick.

"I think they like you," Meredith whispered, resting her hand over his.

A few moments later, they moved away and went back to discussing the nursery, but the tension still lingered in the air.

Sawyer couldn't help but wonder . . . Did she feel the way things were changing between them? The chemistry that he felt every time they were together?

Or was it all in his head?

CHAPTER

Twenty-Eight

M eredith stared at the digital numbers on her phone, one hand protectively on her belly as she watched the clock flip from 8:48 a.m. to 8:49.

She dropped the phone on her bed, cradling her stomach as she curled around the babies. Her hips ached and her entire body felt heavy, but the pain of remembering eclipsed the physical discomforts of pregnancy.

Six months ago, at this exact moment, John had still been alive. She'd had no idea she was pregnant. No idea her husband was minutes away from death.

Hadn't known in just a few short weeks she'd be married to John's best friend.

She'd been in the back office, working on updating her website, and John had been in the small storage room where she kept the seasonal props and backdrops. He'd volunteered to inventory what they could use for the Halloween mini sessions she was planning.

The loud clatter as John fell against the metal shelf holding small chairs and couches for children—a deduction made by paramedics based on the small gash on his shoulder—followed by a thump as his unconscious body hit the floor had made her jump.

She flicked on her phone screen. 8:50.

Meredith closed her eyes, the tears already pooling. She knew the exact moment, because her phone had buzzed a reminder to pay the water bill for the photography studio. Meredith had picked up her phone, dismissed the notification, and just turned back to her computer when the crash came.

She hugged John's pillow to her chest, like she had so many times before, and let the aching sense of loss wash over her once again. The pillow no longer smelled like him. She hated that she'd grown used to his side of the bed being empty and cold. Had even considered emptying their small closet of his clothes, because with her maternity wear it was bursting at the seams.

But even as she cried, she was aware of Sawyer moving about the house. Water rushed through the pipes as he started a load of laundry, followed by the faint clatter of dishes as he unloaded the dishwasher. There was the smell of bleach and she guessed he'd moved on to scrubbing out the kitchen sink.

Sawyer was such a good husband. He deserved more than a broken wife who couldn't give him her heart.

One of the babies moved, as though reminding her she wasn't alone—that part of John remained in this world.

Suddenly, she knew where she wanted to spend her day. The cemetery would be cold this early in March, but she didn't care. Today, she needed to spend time with John.

She took a quick shower, not bothering to wash her hair, and hurried to finish getting ready. When had she gone to the cemetery last—two months ago, maybe? She'd only visited a few times since the funeral, and suddenly that seemed like a grievous oversight.

The moment she emerged from her bedroom, John's gray hoodie straining against her ever-growing stomach, Sawyer was at her side.

"Hey," he said, pulling her to him in a gentle hug. "How are you doing today?"

She angrily swiped away her tears, hating that she couldn't seem to make them stop. "Will you take me to the cemetery?"

"Yeah, of course." His Adam's apple bobbed as he swallowed convulsively. "When would you like to go?"

"Right now, if that's okay." Driving through her tears probably wasn't the smartest idea, and besides, she didn't want to make the ten-minute trip to the other side of town alone.

"Sure. Can I make you breakfast first?"

The thought of eating had her stomach churning in a way it hadn't since the first trimester. "I'm not hungry."

"Here." He disappeared into the kitchen, emerging a few moments later with a banana and granola bar. "At least eat this in the car."

If not for the babies, she would have refused.

If not for the babies, Sawyer wouldn't be her husband.

He stayed silent on the short drive, seeming to sense her need for quiet. As their brand-new minivan passed through the open iron gates of the cemetery, Meredith was catapulted back to six months ago.

Sawyer had stayed by her side faithfully from the moment he'd arrived at the hospital. He'd rushed through the emergency room doors, his face hollow and eyes tortured.

"How is he?" he'd demanded, running a hand over his closely cropped hair.

Meredith hadn't been able to get out a word. She'd wrapped her arms tightly around herself and shook her head. The doctors were still in the room with John, but she knew it wasn't good.

Sawyer's entire face had crumpled, the grief immediate and raw. Then he'd crushed her to him in a hug, and together they'd sobbed like babies. Only moments later, a doctor in green scrubs and a white lab coat had solemnly broken the news she'd known was coming.

She stared out the minivan window, watching as John's grave came into view.

"I brought a camp chair for you to sit on and a blanket in case you get cold," Sawyer said softly. "Would you like me to stay with you or maybe wait in the van?"

Meredith tucked her chin into John's hoodie, imagining his scent still lingered. "Can I just call you when I'm ready to go home?"

"Yeah, of course." Had she imagined the catch in his voice? "Let me carry the chair over for you."

She followed silently behind Sawyer, the blanket clutched to her chest and her shoes growing wet in the mossy grass. He quickly slid the camp chair out of its carrying case and set it up for her, then shoved his hands in his pockets.

"I'll keep my phone right by me," Sawyer said at last. His eyes looked pained, his posture hunched. "You'll call me if you need anything?"

She nodded, resting her hand briefly on his arm. What she really wanted was to hug him, but it seemed wrong somehow today.

"Thanks, Sawyer."

"Of course." He gave her hand a squeeze, then headed toward the car. "Will you text me every so often so that I know you're okay?"

His obvious concern almost had her asking him to stay, but she didn't. Couldn't. "Yeah, of course."

She watched the minivan pull out of the cemetery gates, then carefully took her seat in the camp chair. She hadn't thought of where she'd sit while she visited John's grave—at nearly thirty-five weeks pregnant, with the twins due any day, she wouldn't have been able to sit for long on the ground. Probably wouldn't have been able to get up without help, either.

Once again, Sawyer was looking out for her and the babies.

She spread the blanket over her lap, clutching the top of it in her hands. The granite headstone still had that shiny look of being brand new, and John's name stood out starkly on the stone.

"Well, John," she said aloud. "It's been six months since I last held you. What are you up to these days?"

A bird chirped in a nearby tree. Meredith inhaled deeply.

"I'm mostly just growing our babies," she said. "And missing you, of course."

One of the babies gave a hard kick, making her wince. She'd never realized how strong such a tiny thing could be. But that was good. Her babies would need to be strong to grow up without a father.

Except they wouldn't be without one. Not really. Sawyer had stepped up when she needed him the most.

"Our little girls are pretty lucky." She spread her hands over her taut belly. "How many kids can say they have two daddies who love them more than anything? Sawyer really is amazing, John. I always knew that, but I didn't really see it in action until the last six months. I finally understand what you meant about how he's the most loyal person you ever met. Sawyer has done whatever I asked of him and been there for me every single day since you left."

The wind whistled through the trees, and Meredith pulled the blanket under her chin. March was always cold, but today was especially chilly and she could feel the cold seeping into her bones. It didn't matter, though. At least she felt close to John here.

"I miss you so much," Meredith said. "So, so much. Sawyer does, too. We talk about you a lot, actually."

She continued to talk, catching John up on all the addition to the house and other various home projects Sawyer was working on. She told John all about the nursery, and how she'd watched the emotions play across Sawyer's face when she showed him the pillows she'd had custom-made.

"He's really excited about the twins," Meredith said. "Did I tell you about all the research he did on minivans to make sure we bought the safest one? Car seats, too. I was worried about the cost, but he said the babies' safety didn't have a price tag. He's going to be such a good father."

The wind blew harder, and Meredith dipped her nose into the blanket. Her cheeks stung with the cold, and her fingers were growing numb even beneath the blanket.

She wasn't sure what else to say to John. It wasn't so easy, speaking to a gravestone. They didn't speak back.

Sawyer did, though. He not only listened to her endless ramblings, but he responded.

She peeked at the time on her phone. Had she really only been here forty minutes? It felt like a lot longer.

Meredith's thumb hovered over Sawyer's phone number. Six months without John. Shouldn't she want to spend all day here, as close to her husband as possible?

Forty minutes at the cemetery, and she was already eager to go back home. Forty minutes she'd spent telling John about how wonderful Sawyer was.

She missed John with a ferocity that still woke her up at night at least once a week. But Sawyer had eased that ache in a way she hadn't expected.

No, he wasn't John. But comparing the two would be like measuring a 35mm film camera against a DSLR. One wasn't better than the other, and they both produced beautiful images. They were just different.

The wind howled louder through the trees, making her shiver. She dialed Sawyer's numbers with stiff fingers and Sawyer picked up on the first ring.

"I'm ready to come home," she said, and the word felt like a prayer.

"I'll be right there," Sawyer said. "See you in ten minutes."

After saying goodbye, she pushed herself from the camp chair with a groan. Her walk more closely resembled a waddle, but she kissed her fingers and gently pressed them over the cold stone of John's name. The rivets of each letter pressed against her hand while her heart ached with emptiness.

Missing John was like breathing—something she would do as long as she lived. But for the first time, she wondered if missing him was enough. Could she live the next fifty or sixty years on memories alone?

Four years. That's all they'd gotten together.

The dark gray minivan pulled through the cemetery gates, making her heart lift for the first time all day. She slowly made her way to the road, the camp chair slung over one shoulder and the blanket in her arms.

Sawyer was at her side in a moment.

"You should have waited for me," he chided gently. "I would have carried everything to the car."

She knew he would have. If she'd ask him to drive to Illinois because she was craving Chicago-style pizza, he probably would have done that, too.

The minivan was a welcoming hug after the chill of the cemetery. Sawyer had already turned on her seat warmer, and she held her icy fingers up to the air vents.

"Did you have a good visit?" Sawyer asked as he pulled out of the cemetery.

"Yeah," Meredith said.

Leaving the cemetery should break her heart. So why did she feel like she was taking her first full breath of the day?

"Thanks for taking me," Meredith said. "I know I could have driven myself, but . . ."

He reached over, gently squeezing her hand before returning his to the steering wheel. "I know today's hard for you."

What in her life wasn't hard right now? She shifted in the seat, her hips aching from the weight of the babies. "I thought visiting the cemetery would make me feel better."

He glanced over at her. "But it didn't?"

"Not really. It just reminded me he's really gone." She curled her hands into the sleeves of John's hoodie. What had he sounded like when he laughed? She was already forgetting. "You know what I mean, right?"

"Yeah, I do." His hands flexed on the steering wheel, his voice thick with emotion. "Sometimes I pick up the phone to call him before remembering I can't anymore."

Knowing Sawyer missed John nearly as much as she did made it easy to talk about him. "I bet if he's watching us right now, he'd be glad we have each other. I know I am."

Sawyer gave her a warm smile. "And I thank God every day for that."

She did too—thanked Him for sending Sawyer into her life. When he'd asked her to marry him, she'd agreed because of the babies. But now she was grateful to be his wife for herself. When Sawyer was around, she didn't feel so overwhelmed and lonely. She felt like she could do as she'd promised John and refuse to sink.

"I missed you," Meredith said.

The steering wheel jerked to the left. Sawyer quickly corrected, glancing over at her with a bewildered look on his face she didn't know how to interpret.

"Sorry," he muttered. "A cat ran across the road."

Was he clenching his jaw? "I didn't see a cat."

"He was really fast."

There it was again—an almost imperceptible tightening of his jaw. Was he upset she'd said she missed him? But that didn't make any sense. Nothing in their interactions said he disliked being her husband. In fact, sometimes she wondered . . .

But she was probably imaging things.

"I missed you too," Sawyer said, his mouth quirking up at the corner. "I wasn't sure what to do with myself at home alone."

The admission flooded her body, warming up her frozen fingers and toes.

John might be gone. But Sawyer was here, willing to build a life together. He was who she'd lean on when sending the girls to their first day of preschool. Sawyer would be the one to help with middle-of-the-night illnesses. They'd decide together when the girls were old enough for their first cell phone.

"I don't want to spend today sad," Meredith decided. "Let's call Zach and Cheyenne and see if they want to come over tonight. They can bring Bailey, and we'll order a pizza or something."

"Are you sure?"

Meredith nodded, warming up to the idea. "Yeah. And I want to go out this weekend and do something fun. I know we can't do anything too crazy because of the babies, but dinner and a movie, maybe?"

"That sounds good. You make the plans and just tell me when to be ready."

"You've got a deal."

But as Sawyer pulled into their front yard, something niggled at the back of Meredith's mind. It wasn't until they were playing games with Zach and Cheyenne that evening while Bailey did her best to interrupt that Meredith finally realized what their weekend plans for dinner and a movie felt like.

They felt a lot like a date.

CHAPTER Twenty-Nine

$\mathcal{A}$ s a soldier, Sawyer had never been prone to nerves like the other men on his team. When preparing for a mission, a steely sense of calm had always cleared his mind and sharpened his senses. In the SEALs, he'd been in his element.

But the prospect of a night out with Meredith had his palms sweating and mind racing with nerves. He stared at the bathroom mirror, giving his hair one last, careful brush with hands that weren't quite steady.

"Get it together," he muttered under his breath.

This wasn't a first date with a random woman from a dating app—this was Meredith, the woman he'd lived with for the past four months. She'd seen him in his pajama bottoms in the middle of the night, for heaven's sake. They'd been watching television together every evening and shopping for baby furniture on the weekends.

Maybe this felt different because Meredith had been the one who asked to go out, and it felt an awful lot like a date.

It doesn't mean anything, he reminded himself as he flipped off the bathroom light. Well, it probably meant that Meredith was bored. She'd been stuck home a lot over the past few months and that had to be grating.

The faint sound of a blow dryer told him she was still getting ready, so he sank onto the couch and started reading through the backlog of work emails on his phone. But it was impossible to concentrate.

He'd sat on this couch so many times waiting for Meredith to finish getting ready, but John had always been on the other end of the sofa, waiting right along with him. Emotion unexpectedly welled in Sawyer's chest. He pinched the bridge of his nose and blinked rapidly. What he wouldn't give for even a one-minute conversation with John. One last game of basketball. One last text asking for help on a home project.

The hum of the blow dryer cut off abruptly. That odd, unfamiliar sensation of butterflies was back in his stomach—a mixture of nausea and anticipation. Was this what Meredith had felt like when struggling with morning sickness?

Yeah, probably not.

The door clicked open, and Sawyer's breath caught at the sight of her. Her honey-blonde hair hung around her shoulders in soft waves, and makeup nearly hid the light dusting of freckles across her nose and cheeks. She hadn't purchased much in the way of maternity clothes, and as her stomach had blossomed, she'd taken to wearing John's sweatpants and T-shirts more and more.

But tonight, she'd slipped into a soft cotton dress he recognized from a barbecue at Zach and Cheyenne's last summer, only a couple of months before John's death. The dress was white with brightly colored hibiscus flowers, and it had a naturally high waistline and flowing skirt that accommodated her growing stomach. He'd miss seeing her like this when the babies were born. Pregnancy had only enhanced her beauty.

He rose, shoving his hands in his pockets and feeling more nervous than a kid headed to prom. He hadn't been sure what to wear, and in the end had opted for a nice pair of denim jeans and a dressier button-up shirt with the collar open. Meredith's dress paired with his choice perfectly.

"You look beautiful," he said, his voice a husky rasp.

Was that a blush? She smoothed her hands over the roundness of her stomach. "The dress doesn't look too tight? I realized I don't have much that fits and is appropriate for a night out."

Sawyer swallowed, curling his hands into fists so he wouldn't be tempted to pull her to him. "Definitely not too tight. You look great."

She grabbed her purse off the coffee table, giving him a sly smile. "You don't clean up so bad yourself."

What would it feel like to kiss Meredith? To hold hands on their date and come home to the bedroom they shared.

His new owner's suite bathroom had double sinks. They could brush their teeth side-by-side. They'd been married four months, but he still didn't know what her nighttime routine looked like. When they came home tonight, would she remove her makeup or sleep in it?

Would she ever see him as more than the man who'd saved her from raising two babies alone?

"Ready to go?" Meredith asked, grabbing her coat from the rack near the door.

"Ready," Sawyer agreed.

They headed into Harbor Bay, where Meredith picked a nice Italian restaurant with a chicken Parmesan that was out of this world. As they sat across from each other, Sawyer felt electrified and terrified all at once.

Did Meredith think of this as a date? Or was she just getting cabin fever from so much time spent at home?

Meredith took a bite of her cheese ravioli in a creamy mushroom sauce, her eyes fluttered closed in appreciation. Sometimes she did that with food he had prepared, and it was adorable.

"I've been thinking about names for the babies," Meredith said.

He paused, a forkful of food halfway to his mouth. Baby names. He'd been thinking of them as *the girls* but hadn't come up with any names of his own. That felt like something Meredith should have complete say over.

"What have you come up with?" he asked.

She took a bite of a breadstick, chewing thoughtfully. "Well, at first I thought about naming one baby Adelaide, after my grandmother. I've always thought Addie is a cute nickname."

"It's a good name," Sawyer said. *Adelaide.* The name sounded feminine and delicate, just like the baby's mother.

Meredith nodded, tears welling in her eyes.

Oh no. He'd tried to ride out the mood swings Zach had assured him were typical in pregnancy, but they always left him feeling helpless. What about the name had upset her?

Meredith brushed away a tear from one cheek, taking a deep breath. "But then I thought that what I really want is for my babies to be named for the two men who've saved me."

Sawyer's own throat felt a little tight. "Oh?"

"Yeah. What do you think of Savannah Jo and Josie Saige? They both have the first two letters of your name and the first two letters of John's."

Savannah and Josie. The names flowed over him like the warm waters of the Caribbean.

They were perfect. Absolutely perfect.

He put a fist to his mouth, trying to rein in his emotions. "They're beautiful. But are you sure?"

She rubbed a hand over her stomach, her lips turned up in a soft smile. "Yeah, I'm sure. I don't want these little girls to ever forget the two great men who love them."

It wasn't just the twins that Sawyer loved. Did Meredith have any idea how he felt about her?

Would she ever feel the same?

He reached across the table, and she clutched at his hand.

"Josie Saige and Savannah Jo." Sawyer gave her hand a squeeze. "I think they're perfect."

Meredith looked away, a shyness in her eyes that he didn't understand. "Me too."

They talked about their schedules for the upcoming week—Sawyer had a few meetings, and Meredith two doctor appointments—and then moved on to discussing a book they'd been reading together in the evenings when they didn't feel like watching television. It was a slightly different version of the same conversation they'd had over dinner every night since getting married, but there was a shift between them that made it all feel new.

He didn't know what to make of it. Wasn't sure what felt different. Had Meredith sensed the electricity between them lately?

Maybe he loved her so much that his mind was imagining feelings that were very one-sided.

After dinner, they headed to a nearby movie theater for the latest superhero flick. Meredith had picked the film, but he was excited to see it, too.

"John couldn't wait for this one to come out," Meredith whispered as the previews rolled. "Didn't we see the first one all together?"

"Yeah, I think we did." Zach and Cheyenne had come too, and Sawyer had made sure to not sit by Meredith. He was always aware of her, but sitting beside her in the dark while she held hands with John would have been pure torture.

He'd never once resented John for his relationship with Meredith. But that hadn't made witnessing it any less painful.

Now he'd get to enjoy an entire movie with her by his side, while John was six feet under. It wasn't fair.

The lights dimmed completely as the movie opened on a femme fatale tied to a chair in the middle of a dark room with only a single bare light bulb overhead. Minutes later, she'd broken free from her bonds and was easily defeating the Russian operatives who held her captive.

Meredith's hand brushed against his, sending a zing of electricity through Sawyer's body. An accident. She grabbed a handful of buttery popcorn, her eyes glued to the screen.

He let out a slow breath. Told himself to stop making mountains out of molehills. When he'd asked Meredith to marry him, he'd promised her nothing more than a platonic marriage of convenience.

And he always kept his promises.

On the screen, the heroine reunited with the rest of the team, including her sometimes boyfriend, who angrily yelled at her for putting her life on the line yet again. The two were passionately kissing when Meredith's hand brushed Sawyer's again.

His pulse raced, the urge to kiss her just like the couple on the screen nearly overwhelming. But her eyes remained fixed on the movie, like she hadn't even noticed she'd touched him.

She didn't reach for the popcorn. Instead, her hand brushed his a third time. Did she even realize it was happening?

His attention was completely wrecked, his entire body taut with emotions he didn't know how to examine. It was just three accidental hand touches in a darkened theater. He shouldn't read too much into it.

The heroine and her team of superhero companions were in another firefight now. When had the villains found them? All Sawyer could focus on was the heat radiating from the woman sitting beside him.

The entire length of her arm brushed against his as she shifted, sending tendrils of fire to every one of his nerve endings. When her hand brushed his again a few minutes later, he nearly leaped out of his seat.

Was she doing this on purpose?

He could barely hear the concussive on-screen gunfire over the blood roaring in his hands. Slowly, doing his best to make the motion casual, Sawyer flipped his hand over on the armrest so that it rested palm up and fingers splayed.

She probably wouldn't notice. He seriously doubted she was touching him on purpose—

Her hand landed on top of his and she laced their fingers together, then gave his hand a squeeze. She hadn't looked away from the movie screen, but that action had been intentional.

He couldn't think. Couldn't breathe. The witty banter between the heroine and her love interest was completely lost to him over the roar of blood in his ears.

Meredith was holding his hand.

Meredith. Was holding. His hand! Not for comfort, but for companionship.

And she'd been the one to initiate it.

They sat there for the rest of the movie, her warm and delicate hand in his much larger, rougher one. She kept her gaze on the movie screen and Sawyer did his best to do the same.

But his mind was racing, his heart taking flight and coming up with impossible explanations for this slice of heaven he'd been granted.

Were Meredith's feelings toward him changing? John had only been gone six months—barely any time at all. Of course she was still grieving.

But maybe she was also lonely, just like him. Maybe she also craved the emotional connection of a more intimate relationship.

Maybe—impossibly—he had a chance.

Maybe Meredith could love him, too.

As the final credits rolled, she eased her hand from his. Sawyer felt the loss but did his best to tamp back the disappointment. Something had shifted in their relationship tonight, under the protective darkness of that movie theater. And the change felt real. Permanent.

Important.

"What did you think?" Meredith asked as the theater lights flicked back on.

"It was good." Probably. He had no idea what had happened in the movie, but holding hands with Meredith made it his new favorite film.

"I liked it too." She bit her lip, not quite meeting his eyes. "There was, um, a lot to unpack."

Was there a double meaning in her words?

"We'll definitely have to buy it when it comes out on digital and watch it again," he said.

"Yeah, that would be fun. We can add it to the collection. Maybe have Zach and Cheyenne over to watch it one night." Her hands rested on her stomach. "The babies were kicking like crazy the entire time. I think because of how loud it was."

He was definitely reading too much into things.

On the drive home, they talked about what still needed to be done before the babies came. But there was an electricity in the air that was new and exciting.

It's only been six months, Sawyer reminded himself. Six months in which she'd been through a lot, and he wasn't about to take advantage of her vulnerability.

But what if Meredith wanted a real marriage? And wouldn't that be best for the babies?

At home, Meredith dropped her purse on the coffee table, stifling a yawn.

"You're exhausted," Sawyer said. He should've suggested a movie at home, but she'd wanted to go to the theater.

Meredith covered another yawn. "It's barely ten o'clock."

"Yeah, so it's like an hour past your bedtime."

She laughed again, placing both hands on her hips. "Hey now. I'll get back to an adult bedtime once Savannah and Josie are born."

He loved the sound of those names on her lips—the names she'd chosen as a homage to him and John. Would John be as honored to have his daughters share their names as Sawyer felt? He hoped so.

"Your only job is to grow those babies," he reminded her.

Meredith smiled, giving a nod. Then she rose on her tiptoes and wrapped her arms around his neck.

He was powerless at her touch. Sawyer wrapped his arms around her waist, feeling a nudge as the babies kicked against him.

Meredith held on. He wasn't about to be the first to let go.

The scent of her washed over him and he inhaled deeply, wishing he could bottle the smell in more than his memory. Her body felt so right in his arms, her curves soft and unfamiliar, but oh so welcome.

"Thank you for tonight," Meredith whispered, her hot breath against his cheek making him shiver. Still, she clung to him. It took all of his self-control not to slide his hands from her back to her hips. He wanted to explore every curve of her body. To know her better than he knew himself.

Did she have any idea what she did to him?

"Thanks for suggesting we go out." Her hair brushed against his nose, making it tickle. Still, he didn't move. "I'm sorry I didn't think of taking you out sooner. It was a lot of fun."

"We should do it more often," Meredith agreed. "I really enjoyed hanging out together, I mean, other than at home or when shopping for the twins. It felt . . . nice. Normal."

"Yeah," Sawyer agreed.

It felt like winning the lottery.

When Meredith pulled away, he felt the loss like an amputated limb. Tonight had given him a taste of what a real relationship would feel like, and he already wanted more.

"I'm heading to bed." Meredith brushed back a strand of hair, her face illuminated by the soft light of the living room lamp. "Thanks again, Sawyer. I don't know what I'd do without you."

She rose on tiptoes, brushing a kiss across the stubble of his cheek. Moments later she'd disappeared into her bedroom, but Sawyer stood there for a long time, one hand to where her lips had touched.

It would be impossible to sleep tonight without dreaming about a future in which Meredith was truly his.

CHAPTER Thirty

Meredith laughed, Sawyer's arms wrapped tightly around her as they cuddled on the couch. Her silky pink pajamas slid easily against the soft cotton of his own pajama pants and T-shirt as she burrowed closer into his side.

They were watching one of the medical dramas they both loved. Sawyer laughed at the witty banter during one of the cafeteria scenes, and Meredith angled her face up to his.

"I love you," Meredith said.

The sharp planes of his face softened as one of his rough hands gently cupped her cheek. "I love you too, Meredith," he said.

His head lowered toward hers and she arched into his kiss, welcoming the press of his soft lips against her warm mouth. His kiss was confident and commanding and sure.

She eagerly returned the kiss, letting her hands tangle in Sawyer's hair as he pulled her onto his lap. His hands trailed over her flat stomach, coming to rest low on her hips while she pressed herself closer.

A firm hand landed on her shoulder and wrenched her away. She stumbled backward, staring in horror at Sawyer's wide eyes.

John whirled her to face him, his expression a mass of pain and confusion.

"How can you forget me so easily?" he demanded. "You promised to love me forever and now you're falling in love with my best friend."

"You left me." She pressed a hand to her chest, clutching her necklace as she fought for breath between sobs. "I'm lonely, okay? I just want to be happy again. Sawyer makes me happy."

John jabbed a finger toward her stomach, which was suddenly swollen once more with pregnancy. "So you're going to kiss my best friend while pregnant with my babies?"

John's face grew fuzzy, like she was staring at his reflection in a pond. Meredith dropped her head into her hands, tears obscuring her vision.

"You're not here anymore." She hurled the words like a dagger. "If you were, I'd never look at Sawyer twice. But you aren't, and I don't want to spend the rest of my life alone."

"But you promised." John folded his arms across his chest, making his biceps bulge. "If you fall in love with Sawyer, how do you expect me to forgive you?"

"We're married." She wrapped her arms around her belly, struggling to speak through her tears. "He's going to help me raise the twins."

"Fine. But that doesn't mean you have to love him. Not like that."

Meredith startled awake, her heart pounding furiously. She brushed a hand across her pillow and realized it was soaked in her tears.

Just a dream, she told herself silently. *It was just a dream.*

A dream that felt all too real.

She pushed a hand into her hair and squeezed her eyes tightly shut, guilt making it hard to breathe.

What was she doing? John hadn't even been in the ground a year. Was she really going to let her devotion wander so quickly?

Sawyer was an amazing guy. She would forever be in his debt for stepping up to give Savannah and Josie a father.

But he wasn't John. She couldn't forget that.

Guilt kept Meredith buried in her covers long after she typically would have been up and ready for the day. Her stomach rolled with hunger while the babies moved within her, but today even their gentle nudges weren't a comfort.

One fun evening with Sawyer and she'd almost tossed John to the curb.

I'm sorry, she told John, the words a mantra running on a never-ending loop. *I'm sorry, I'm sorry, I'm sorry . . .*

It was nearly eleven o'clock when she heard a soft knock at her bedroom door. Meredith didn't move except to pull John's pillow more tightly against her chest.

Hinges squeaked as the door cracked open.

"Mer?" Sawyer asked, his voice a whisper. "Are you awake?"

She said nothing, keeping her back to the door. The worry in Sawyer's voice battled with the memory of Dream John's anger.

Sawyer's footfalls were impossibly light against the laminate floor as he tip-toed to her side of the bed. Still, she didn't move.

He paused, surprise flickering across his face. "You *are* awake."

She turned her head away, unable to meet his eyes. "Go away, Sawyer."

Her voice sounded wrong. Like it belonged to someone else.

"Hey." He crouched down, resting his arms on the edge of the mattress as he met her at eye level. "What's wrong? Are you sick?"

"No."

"Should I call Dr. Mike and schedule an appointment?"

"No," she said more forcefully. "I'm not sick, okay? The babies are fine."

That was why he'd married her, after all. To raise John's babies. It hadn't been about wanting a relationship with her.

That's a good thing, she reminded herself. She shouldn't want a relationship with him, either.

"Okay." Sawyer pushed himself to his feet, the confusion obvious in his voice. "Can I make you something for breakfast? Pancakes or—"

"I don't want pancakes!" Meredith struggled to sit up, rage flowing through her with an intensity that took her breath away.

She didn't want Sawyer standing in her room, being so considerate and tender. Didn't want John rotting away in a cemetery just a few miles from where she was falling for his best friend.

"Whoa." Sawyer held up his hands, backing away. "I'm just trying to help."

She wanted to fall into his arms and hug away the pain she was causing him. But it would feel like another way to betray John.

Tears obscured her vision as she curled more tightly around John's pillow, guilt making her stomach churn. "I'm sorry, Sawyer. I . . . I just need to be left alone right now, okay?"

"Okay." The hurt in his voice made her heart crack open. "If you need anything, I'll be in my room working."

She nodded, not turning around to watch him leave. When the bedroom door clicked shut a few minutes later, a sob tore through her body.

What was she doing?

Her mood didn't improve over the next week. Sawyer was as attentive as ever, taking care of most of the cooking and cleaning while making sure she didn't overdo it. For her part, she folded his laundry along with hers while watching TV and kept the bank accounts balanced and bills paid.

But guilt brewed in her stomach like a virus she couldn't shake. She missed the easy conversation and casual closeness they'd cultivated.

She missed Sawyer. It wasn't the desperate ache that made her dizzy when she thought too much about John. Missing Sawyer felt different in a way she couldn't identify.

As the week stretched into the weekend, she did her best to stay polite but distant toward Sawyer. He seemed perplexed by her sudden change in attitude. She knew he wondered why she spent so much time alone in her room, but he'd stopped asking if she felt okay after her uneventful appointment with Dr. Mike.

She wasn't being fair to Sawyer. But every time she thought of curling up next to him on the couch while they watched television, or chopping carrots at the kitchen counter while he peeled potatoes and talked about his day at work, John's angry face reappeared in her mind along with the guilt.

How could she be loyal to John while also moving on without him?

On Friday, Sawyer knocked softly on her bedroom door. "Come in," she said.

He peeked his head in, giving her a wary smile. "Want to go to Baylor's for dinner tonight? I thought it might be nice to get out of the house, especially since it's finally sunny for a change."

An evening out with Sawyer sounded so nice. They could sit across from each other at a table—her belly had probably outgrown a booth by this point—and clear the air from the past week. Maybe even share a chocolate milkshake.

There was a small used bookstore near Baylor's. If she didn't have Braxton-Hicks contractions too bad after dinner, they could browse there for a while. Find a book to read together after they finished the current one.

Her dream came rushing back. John's lips turned down in a scowl and his arms crossed defensively. *"You promised to love me forever."*

"Let's just make something at home," she said.

Sawyer folded his arms and leaned against the doorframe, reminding her harshly of John. "I haven't had time to go shopping this week and the cupboards are pretty bare. Getting out of the house will be good for you."

They could hold hands at the bookstore. Maybe, after holding hands for a while, they'd even kiss.

She pressed the heels of her hands into her eyes, wishing she could scrub the image from her mind as easily as she could block out the light. "I'm thirty-five weeks pregnant, Sawyer. Do you really think I want to cram my swollen feet into shoes just so I can eat dinner in a crowded diner, where everyone will give me pitying glances and ask me how I'm feeling?"

He ran his hands over his face, eyes flashing with a steel she'd never seen before. "What do you want, Meredith? Because I've been busting my hide trying to make you happy the last few days, and nothing seems good enough."

Hot shame started at the top of her head and spread to her toes. She wrapped her arms around her stomach, as though that would protect her from his words.

She deserved every barb.

"I'm not made of stone." He rubbed his jaw, then shifted from one foot to the other. "I know you're going through an impossibly hard time, but you're not the only one who lost John. I have feelings, too. And you're kind of walking all over them."

The childish urge to hide under the blankets nearly overwhelmed her. She'd felt awful in a lot of different ways over the past six months. But never like this. Never because of her own actions.

"I think I'm going to head out for a while." Sawyer pulled his cell phone from his pocket, maybe checking the battery or the time. "I'll keep my phone on if you need anything. There's one serving of lasagna left in the fridge if you get hungry."

He didn't slam her door closed, but the click as it closed might as well have been a blast. She hid her head under the covers then, burying her face in John's pillow. One of the babies kicked, and she winced.

Her first fight with Sawyer. It had absolutely been her fault.

She squeezed her eyes tightly shut. If John was here now, she knew what he'd say—*"I can't believe you're treating Sawyer like this. He's my best friend, Mer. He's given up everything for you."*

For an hour she laid in bed, her thoughts swirling. Eventually, the babies forced her out of bed, and after a trip to the bathroom, she heated up the last piece of lasagna. It tasted like sawdust, and after only a few bites, she pushed it away.

She couldn't stop Sawyer's parting shot from echoing in her head. *"I'm not made of stone, Mer. I have feelings, too."*

Had she been treating him like a statue, there merely to serve her own purposes?

For six months, he'd told her he would be whatever she needed him to be. At the hospital, he'd been a shoulder to cry on. At the funeral, he'd been a silent support. He'd brought her meals, helped her clean out the photography studio, encouraged her to watch a movie with him and laugh. And then, when she'd found out about the babies, he'd given up everything to marry a woman who still loved someone else.

Sawyer deserved so much more than what she'd given him. And while one day wouldn't fix everything, she could at least start.

After debating what to do, she pulled out the ingredients for chocolate chip cookies. Sawyer always raved over them when she brought them to parties. Chocolate might not fix everything, but it certainly helped. The babies kicked at her ribs while she dumped ingredients in a bowl, making her wince with each movement. But she was determined to do something nice for Sawyer, however small.

By the time she pulled the last cookie sheet out of the oven, Sawyer still hadn't returned home. She took a break and rested on the couch for a while, then cleaned up the kitchen. By the time she'd washed the last pot, Sawyer still hadn't returned, but the contractions reminded her to take things easy and not overdo it.

She laid down on the couch and flipped on the television, trying not to worry. What if something had happened to Sawyer—a car accident, perhaps?

What if she became a widow twice in one year?

Stop it, she commanded. He'd said he didn't know when he'd be back.

Darkness fell, and the cookies grew cold on the counter. She slipped them into a plastic bag and zipped it closed so they wouldn't dry out. Should she text Sawyer and make sure he was okay?

What if he came home and said he couldn't do this anymore—couldn't be in a loveless marriage with a hormonal basket case who took out her frustrations on him?

She gripped the counter, her breath catching at the very thought.

No. Sawyer was loyal and kind and couldn't. He wouldn't leave her because of one fight.

Headlights flashed across the front window. Meredith hurried to peek out the curtains and let out a sigh when she saw their minivan back in the driveway.

She headed back to the kitchen and pulled out a plate, setting a few chocolate chip cookies on them. Fifteen seconds in the microwave and they'd be almost as good as just out of the oven.

The click of the front door opening had her hands trembling as she pulled the cookies from the microwave. She'd never had a fight with Sawyer and had no idea what to expect. She heard a rustle as Sawyer hung up his jacket and keys.

I'm sorry. How many times and she had John said that to each other? They'd never gotten into big fights, but there'd definitely been a handful of smaller ones over mostly stupid things. Those fights had usually ended with kissing and—

Her cheeks burned. That would not be how the evening ended with Sawyer. The best she could hope for was sharing this plate of cookies without the tension of the last week between them.

Sawyer looked up as she walked into the front room, his eyes zeroing in on the cookies. She held them toward him, biting her lip.

Cookies had been a stupid idea, but they were all she had.

"I know they don't make up for how awful I've been to you the past week, but it was all I could think of as a peace offering," she said.

His expression softened. "You shouldn't have done that. The babies—"

"—are fine," she cut in, holding out the plate again. "Here, take them. They're even warm."

"They smell divine." He took the entire plate and bit into a cookie. His eyes rolled into the back of his head, making her smile with pride. "Just as good as I remember."

"Good." She wrapped her arms around herself, feeling exposed. "Sawyer, I'm so sorry for how incredibly selfish I've been, especially for the last few days. I've taken the brunt of it out on you, and you don't deserve that."

"No, I'm the one who's sorry." He pulled her to the couch and set the plate of cookies on the coffee table. "I should have been more understanding that you're going through something right now. It felt like you were shutting me out, and I didn't know how to handle that."

She bit her lip, not quite meeting his eyes. "Do you forgive me?"

"Oh, Mer. Of course I do." He tucked her against his side in a one-armed hug. She buried her face in his chest, inhaling sharply. His warm scent brought the guilt flooding back, but she was determined not to make Sawyer suffer for her conflicting emotions.

John might not want her to fall for his best friend, but he wouldn't want her to shut Sawyer out, either.

It's just the pregnancy hormones, she told herself as she hugged him. That and it felt so good to be in his arms.

"What happened this week?" Sawyer asked, his chin resting on top of her head as they continued to embrace. "I've been racking my brain, trying to figure out what changed."

"Just a hard week." She couldn't tell him the truth—that she was wracked with guilt because she couldn't stop thinking about kissing him.

She was nothing but a friend to Sawyer. Maybe even a bit of an obligation. Endangering their marriage for something as absurd as feelings would be beyond stupid, especially with the babies nearly here.

"John would want you to be happy." Sawyer pressed a gentle kiss to the top of her head, making her entire body tingle. "You know you can talk to me about anything, right?"

Somehow, she doubted she could talk to him about this. What would he say if she told him she might want more from their marriage than two roommates co-parenting together?

"I know." She grabbed a cookie from the plate and handed it to him. "Here, have another one."

She would bury her growing feelings deep inside. If she didn't tell Sawyer, then she couldn't betray John.

CHAPTER Thirty-One

Meredith threw open her front door, barely able to contain her excitement as her best friend got out of the car.

"Oh, I've missed you so much!" Meredith said, waddling down the stairs. She was thirty-five weeks pregnant and even simple tasks like breathing were difficult these days. Sawyer picked up the slack as much as possible, but today he was in Portland for work meetings.

Vanessa met Meredith with a giant hug. "You look so cute!"

Meredith rolled her eyes. "You mean I look like a whale?"

"Hardly." Vanessa placed a hand on her belly and cooed in a high-pitched voice, "Hi, baby Savannah and baby Josie. I can't wait to meet you."

The back door of the car flew open and Grayson popped out of the back seat, grinning.

"Hey, buddy." Meredith pulled him in for a hug. "I've missed you. Are you excited about visiting Grandma and Grandpa this week?"

"Mom says only a year until we can move home." Grayson gave Meredith a wide grin, showcasing his missing two front teeth.

She tousled his hair and tried to sound impressed. "Looks like the Tooth Fairy visited someone since I saw you last."

Grayson nodded enthusiastically and pointed to his mouth. "I got one dollar for this one, but then I got five dollars for this one! The Tooth Fairy was busy and had to come a day late. Mom said the extra money must be because of a big mess."

"Interest," Vanessa corrected, rolling her eyes. "Guess that Tooth Fairy has been pretty busy lately."

Meredith winked at her friend over the top of Grayson's head. "Yeah, I would say so. Come inside so I can hear all about it."

She spent a wonderful morning catching up with Vanessa while Grayson watched a movie on her couch. After lunch, Vanessa dropped Grayson off at her parents' house before returning to visit some more—without the curious ears of a seven-year-old listening in.

"It looks like you're almost ready for the babies," Vanessa observed as she admired the nursery.

"Yeah, I think so." One of the babies kicked, and Meredith massaged the spot with a wince. "I still need to wash the newborn size clothes and pack a hospital bag."

"Yeah, thirty-five weeks is getting close, especially with twins. They could come any day now."

"I hope I've got another couple of weeks. Since they're identical, Dr. Mike said he'll induce me if they're not here by the time I'm thirty-seven weeks." Meredith smoothed her hands over her stomach again. "I want to meet these little girls so badly, but I'm also nervous about doing this whole parenting thing without John."

"You won't be alone, though," Vanessa said. "You'll have Sawyer here to help."

Just the sound of his name made her smile. Last night she'd caught him watching a video online about how to properly swaddle a baby and nearly keeled over from cuteness. "Thank heavens for that. He's going to be such a great dad."

Vanessa nudged her shoulder. "Aren't you glad I talked you into marrying him?"

That made her throw back her head and laugh. "Yeah, I guess I have you to thank for that."

"Come on." Vanessa motioned to the living room. "I want you to sit on the couch while I get that laundry done for the babies. I'll spill the beans on what I wish I'd packed for the hospital but didn't while it's in the wash."

They were nearly done with the laundry when Sawyer arrived home from work. The creak of the screen door as he pushed it open made her heart leap in anticipation and she hurried to greet him.

"Hey." She clasped her hands together so she wouldn't be tempted to hug him. Would he mind if she did? Sure, they'd hugged before, but always as a form of comfort, not greeting. "How was work?"

"Great." Sawyer gave her an amiable smile as he hung up his jacket and nodded in Vanessa's direction. "It's nice to see you again."

"It's nice to be here. I can't wait until Grayson and I can move back."

"End of summer will be here before you know it," Meredith said.

But the realization sobered her. Because with the end of summer would also come the one-year anniversary of John's death. How could she miss him so much while also having these blossoming feelings for Sawyer?

"I made a casserole last night and stuck it in the fridge." Sawyer headed to the kitchen, loosening his tie. "Let me just preheat the oven and pop it in. Can we convince you to stay for dinner, Vanessa? It'll be ready in just about an hour."

"That sounds nice," Vanessa said. A buzz echoed through the room—the dryer. "Oops, there's the last load. Let me grab it so it doesn't wrinkle."

"I'll help you fold," Meredith said as Vanessa hurried away.

Sawyer raised an eyebrow, his eyes wide. "She's doing our laundry?"

Meredith placed a hand over her mouth, stifling a giggle. "Don't worry, no one's folding your boxers or anything. She's helping me wash all the clothes for Savannah and Josie."

His shoulders relaxed. "Ah. That's kind of her."

Vanessa reappeared with a basket of laundry on one hip. "Want me to dump it on your bed again?"

"Yeah, that's great." Meredith glanced at Sawyer. "Do you need help with dinner, or—?"

"Go." He waved her away. "I've got dinner covered."

In the bedroom, Vanessa lowered her voice to a whisper. "Okay, I knew you and Sawyer were getting along well, but whoa."

Meredith eased onto the bed, reaching for a white onesie with blue anchors. "What do you mean?"

"I mean, Sawyer looks at you like you're the center of his universe," Vanessa said, her voice still a whisper.

"What? You're crazy." Meredith focused on the onesie, her cheeks warm and heart beating rapidly. Did Sawyer look at her like that? She had no doubt that he adored the babies and she thought he enjoyed her company, but beyond that? She wasn't sure. He'd dated a lot since moving to Sapphire Cove.

"I dunno." Vanessa lifted her hands in a dramatic shrug.

"Come on. You know what it's like between us."

"I know what you've told me, but now I'm wondering if you've left stuff out." She picked up a tiny pair of socks and rolled them together, looking thoughtful. "Or maybe you just don't see it."

"You're misinterpreting things. Sawyer doesn't . . ." She glanced quickly toward her open bedroom door. The oven beeped—probably Sawyer setting it to preheat—but she lowered her voice even more so he wouldn't overhear. "You know why we got married."

Vanessa nodded. "And I stand by what I said, but be gentle with Sawyer. He's a fantastic guy and I think his heart might be more involved than you realize."

Meredith winced, the memory of their fight coming back to her. Then there was the electricity she sometimes imagined between them, and the tender way he held her when she was upset.

Vanessa's eyes seemed to see through to her very soul. Meredith swallowed, the tiny pair of baby pajamas limp in her hand.

"It's not just him, you know," Vanessa said gently, her voice so quiet Meredith had to strain to hear. "He looks at you with more than friendship, but the same can be said for you. When his car pulled up, you couldn't get to the front door fast enough. Your entire face lit up."

Meredith traced the heart design on the infant sleeper she held, emotion building in her throat. For weeks now, she'd felt like she might burst from confusion. But it wasn't like she could talk to Zach or Cheyenne—or, heaven forbid, Sawyer—about this.

"I don't know what's happening," she admitted, scooting closer to Vanessa and dropping her voice another notch. "He's just so kind and caring. So easy to spend time with. And I'm lonely."

She winced at the admission—such a weak thing to say. Less than a year, and already she was betraying John with her thoughts. He'd been on deployments that lasted longer than this, although they'd at least been able to video chat.

"Hey." Vanessa pushed aside some of the unfolded clothes and wrapped an arm around her. "It's okay to be happy, you know. It took me a long time to figure that out. And what's more, John would *want* you to be happy."

Meredith leaned her head on Vanessa's shoulder, fighting back the tears that always seemed so close. "Even if it's with his best friend?"

Vanessa's arm tightened around her shoulder. "You don't have to make any decisions now. When you're pregnant, your hormones go wild, and everything gets confusing. It's a bad time to make life-changing decisions."

Meredith lifted her head, giving Vanessa an eye roll. "Oh, you mean like getting married?"

Vanessa laughed. "That was different, and you know it. Just be gentle with Sawyer, okay? Sensitive."

She picked up a tiny pair of leggings and folded them. Sensitive. She could do that.

Hiding her feelings from Sawyer? That might be harder. But the guilt from sharing her feelings might eat her alive.

Vanessa was right—she was just lonely, with pregnancy hormones raging through her body. Once the babies were born, things would settle down and she and Sawyer could establish their new normal.

"What about you?" she asked, raising an eyebrow. "Do you ever think about dating again?"

Vanessa sighed. "Sometimes. But between Grayson and school, I just don't have time to find a new relationship."

Meredith understood that, but Vanessa had been alone for so much longer than her. "You deserve to be happy, too."

"I am," Vanessa said quickly. "Grayson is my entire world. That's enough for me, at least for now."

At dinner, Sawyer was an excellent host and Vanessa declared the casserole exceptionally tasty. After dessert, she left to put Grayson to bed. Sawyer shooed Meredith out of the kitchen, insisting he could handle the cleanup.

"Go relax," he insisted. "I've got this."

She rolled her eyes, but obediently left the kitchen. Her back ached a lot today, but she could at least tidy up the living room before heading to bed. Grayson had pushed all the throw pillows to the floor and left a blanket crumpled on the couch after his movie.

She bent down without thinking, reaching for a pillow. For a moment, she didn't realize anything was wrong. But then a sharp tug made spots dance across her vision, followed by a warm gush.

Blood.

"Sawyer!" Meredith screamed, reaching for the couch to steady herself as she swayed.

Something dropped to the floor with a crash. Sawyer rushed into the living room, surveying the scene with eyes that missed nothing. They lingered on the blood spotting the plush white rug they'd bought just last month.

When the water broke, that was clear, right? Not bright red, like what was soaking through her pants. Her breathing came in sharp gasps as her stomach contracted painfully.

"Let's go," he said, his voice calm and steady. One arm was around her waist as he ushered her toward the front door. "What happened? The doctor will want to know."

She blinked, trying to clear the dark spots from her vision. Her knees trembled, and she leaned on him heavily as he grabbed both of their coats and the keys to the minivan.

"I bent down to pick up a pillow, and then there was this sharp pain." When she rubbed her eyes, her fingers came away wet. When had she started crying? "I'm bleeding."

"I know." His voice was still eerily calm, a stark contrast to his quick movements as he helped her into the van and reached across her to buckle the seatbelt. "We're going to the hospital."

"It's too soon." She wrapped her arms around her stomach, gasping as a heavy cramp overtook her. "The babies—"

"Thirty-five weeks is excellent for twins. Dr. Mike will know what to do." He pressed the van's start button with a hand she thought she saw tremble, but then another contraction made her double over.

"Hurry," she gasped.

The plea hadn't been necessary. He was already racing down the road.

CHAPTER
Thirty-Two

Sawyer had been in a lot of combat situations where he wasn't sure if he—or his friends—would make it out alive. Enemies wielding guns had backed him into corners in abandoned buildings. He'd fought the pull of a ship's propellers as he swam away underwater after sabotaging the engine, and dropped onto rooftops in the dead of night from a helicopter.

That terror had been nothing compared to seeing the woman he loved dripping blood and knowing it meant her life—and the lives of their daughters—were in danger.

Meredith inhaled sharply, hunching forward so that the seatbelt strained across her. A glimpse of bright crimson blood on her pants had his entire body going numb.

He pressed the gas pedal, urging the minivan to go faster. If there had ever been a time to be calm and focused, this was it. He kept his eyes glued to the road as he sped through town, breaking more than one traffic law along the way. At least it was still the off season, which meant the streets were relatively empty.

Meredith gave a low hiss, sending him into another spiral.

"What is it?" he demanded.

Two minutes. She just needed to hold on for two more minutes, then they'd be at the hospital. The pinched look on her face cracked his heart in two. Witnessing her pain was so much harder than bearing his own.

"Contraction, I think." Her face was white, but she waved a hand to the road. "I'm okay. Just get us to the hospital."

She wasn't okay. She was pale and trembling, her pants stained with blood.

"How are the babies?"

"Still kicking." Her voice was tight with fear. "That's a good sign, right?"

He certainly hoped so.

Sawyer peeled into the hospital parking lot, ignoring the emergency entrance, and illegally parked on the curb outside the main doors just like Dr. Mike had instructed them to if they ever had an issue. They needed an obstetrician, not an emergency room doctor.

"Wait here," Sawer demanded, then ran into the hospital for a wheelchair.

At the registration desk, a woman rose from her seat when Sawyer burst through the door.

"Sir, you can't park—"

"My wife is eight months pregnant with twins and bleeding heavily," Sawyer interrupted. "Where's a wheelchair? I'll move the van later."

The woman's expression changed. She pointed to a wall with one hand while picking up the phone on her desk with the other. "Wheelchairs are over there. I'll notify maternity that you're on your way."

In moments he was back outside, helping Meredith into the wheelchair. An orderly with kind eyes and a firm tone met him at the sliding doors.

"I've got it from here," he said, taking the wheelchair from Sawyer. "You park the car while I take her up to maternity. She's in expert hands, sir."

Meredith stared at Sawyer with eyes full of fear and pain. She clutched her stomach, breath coming in sharp gasps.

"Go," she managed. "And hurry."

He wanted to curse at the orderly and tell him he didn't care about the minivan, even thought about handing him the keys and telling him to take care of it himself. But that would lead to arguing, which would delay getting Meredith to the doctors who could help her and the babies.

"I'll be right there," he promised, giving her a rough kiss on the cheek.

Sawyer parked the minivan and rushed back inside, not bothering to wait for the elevator and instead running up the stairs to the third-floor maternity wing.

He couldn't fall apart. Right now, his mission was to make sure both Meredith and the babies were healthy and safe. Once that was accomplished, he could go to pieces.

The doors to the maternity wing were locked, and he frantically pushed the button for admittance. A loud buzzing filled the small entryway, and he shoved the double doors open.

"My wife just came in," he said to the nurse at the desk. "Maybe five minutes ago."

"Sawyer!"

He looked around frantically, locating Meredith down the hall. She was still in the wheelchair and a nurse, not the orderly he'd left her with, was pushing it down the hall.

He ran to her side, his shoes squeaking against the tiled floor. Meredith reached for his hand, and he gave it to her, squeezing gently. Her skin felt cold and clammy, but it was the ghostly white of her face that worried him most. "What's happening?"

"We're headed to ultrasound," the nurse said. "Dr. Mike has been paged and should be there any moment. He's on call tonight and just finished up a delivery."

Sawyer sent up a silent prayer of thanks. He didn't trust any other doctor to handle this situation.

"The babies—" he began.

"Still moving." Meredith glanced behind her at the nurse. "That's good, right?"

"That's good," the nurse agreed.

But she was wheeling Meredith swiftly down the hallway, which had Sawyer's stomach clenching with nerves. The bright florescent lights of the hallway made his head pulse uncomfortably, and the sharp smell of antiseptic burned his nose.

What if she lost the babies?

What if he lost her?

Meredith hunched over again, grunting. "I'm pretty sure I'm having contractions."

"I'll get you hooked up to a monitor as soon as you change into a gown," the nurse said.

"Do you have any idea what could be wrong?" Sawyer asked the nurse.

Her lips pressed together in a thin line. Sawyer knew she was worried, even if she wouldn't say it.

"Dr. Mike will be in soon and can answer your questions," the nurse said finally, pulling the wheelchair to a stop inside an exam room. "Here's a hospital gown, honey. I'll let your husband help you change and be right back to hook up the monitors."

Sawyer helped Meredith stand from the wheelchair as the nurse shut the door behind them.

"Turn around so I can change," Meredith said, wincing.

"Don't be ridiculous," Sawyer said, picking up the hospital gown and unfolding it. "I'm not about to let you pass out because of modesty."

She didn't argue. That worried him more than anything else so far.

He held up the gown as a sort of curtain as she stripped off her shirt, tossing it onto a chair. He caught a glimpse of her bra, but it barely even registered.

There was so much blood. Traces of it had streaked the leather passenger seat in the minivan, not that he'd taken the time to clean it up. Meredith slipped her arms into the hospital gown, then dropped her pants to the floor once she was mostly covered by the gown. The dark bloodstains on the gray fabric made it hard to keep his composure.

"It's going to be okay," he whispered, as he tied the straps of her hospital gown shut with hands that shook.

He couldn't lose Meredith. Couldn't lose the babies.

Help them, John, Sawyer prayed silently as he settled Meredith on the hospital bed. If there was such a thing as guardian angels, he knew John was hers.

He'd barely covered Meredith with a thin blanket when Dr. Mike walked in, his expression grim. He went straight to the small sink and began washing his hands.

"What happened?" he asked.

"I bent over to pick up a pillow." Meredith's voice was thick with tears. "There was a lot of pain and then the blood."

Sawyer pressed a fist to his mouth. *Not yet,* he commanded himself. *You cannot fall apart right now. Hold it together for a while longer.*

"Let's take a look," Dr. Mike said.

The babies were moving. Meredith said the babies were moving.

Sawyer fixated on the small ultrasound screen, Meredith's hand gripped tightly in his. She let out a cry of relief as movement appeared on the screen. The babies were hard to differentiate between on the wavy image, but there was definitely movement.

"They're alive," Meredith breathed.

Sawyer kissed her hand. But he was no longer focused on the ultrasound screen. He focused on Dr. Mike. The furrow hadn't dissipated from his brow.

"Both babies' heart rates are a little lower than I'd like them to be." Dr. Mike pointed to the screen. "Your placenta has partially torn away from the uterine wall. That's what's causing the blood."

A fist had grabbed hold of his lungs and wouldn't let go.

"That's really bad," Meredith said, her voice rising.

Sawyer smoothed back her hair. He needed to stay calm so he could keep her calm. They were in a hospital, with a qualified doctor.

Everything had to be okay.

"It's not great," Dr. Mike agreed, setting aside the ultrasound wand. He set his hands on his knees, staring at both of them intently. "Right now, the safest decision for you and the babies is to do an emergency c-section. I'm going to have a nurse come and get you prepped for surgery."

"Today?" Meredith's grip on Sawyer's hand tightened. "But it's too early."

"Thirty-five weeks is an excellent gestational age for identical twins." Dr. Mike patted her knee and rose. "You did a great job, Meredith. Now it's time for me to do mine."

Sawyer brushed Meredith's hair out of her face and kissed her temple. "It's going to be okay. We get to meet the girls today."

He didn't know if he was reassuring her or himself.

A nurse walked in, pushing a cart of supplies. "I'm here to place your IV and get you prepped for surgery," she said with a bright smile.

Surgery. Sawyer felt like his entire world was crashing around him. He hadn't really registered what Dr. Mike said until this moment. Soon, she'd be lying on a table while a doctor cut into her stomach.

He squeezed his eyes tightly shut, forcing himself to take slow, even breaths.

"Sawyer can come with me, can't he?" Meredith asked the nurse, glancing up at him. "I want him in the room, if possible."

"Sure, dad's welcome to join the party," the nurse said cheerfully. "Once I get you prepped, we'll have him put on a surgical gown and hairnet."

"Good. Then you can go to the nursery with Savannah and Josie." Meredith was babbling, her words tumbling over each other. "I don't want them to be alone."

Sawyer didn't want that, either. But going with the babies would mean leaving Meredith behind. He pressed his forehead to their clasped hands, struggling to keep his emotions in check. "Don't worry. I'll stay with the girls the entire time."

She nodded. "And if something happens to me—"

"No." The word ripped from Sawyer like a curse.

Life without Meredith was unthinkable. Unimaginable.

"Sawyer, listen to me." She grabbed his face, her hands pressing into his cheeks. "If I die, you have to take care of Jo and Savvy. They have no one else in the world. Promise me!"

He squeezed his eyes shut, pushing out a single tear. "I promise," he whispered. "Of course I'll take care of them. They're my daughters."

Her hands slipped from his face. "Good."

Sawyer stood against one wall, his arms folded. He nervously flicked one thumbnail against his teeth as he watched one nurse hook up two fetal heart monitors while the other started an IV. Then, when the nurse pulled out a razor to finish the surgery preparations, he turned his back to give Meredith some privacy and sent a quick text to Zach and Cheyenne explaining the situation.

"I'm taking her to the OR now so the anesthesiologist can give her a spinal block." The nurse handed him a sealed package with his sterile garb. "Put everything in this package on. A nurse will be by shortly to take you down."

"Thank you." Sawyer pressed one last quick, fierce kiss to Meredith's forehead. He hated that they'd be separated for even a few minutes. "I'll see you in there."

He pulled something that resembled a jumpsuit out of the package and slipped it on, forcing himself to move carefully so he wouldn't rip the thin fabric. He zipped up the jumpsuit and put the shoe covers over his feet, then quickly put on the hairnet and surgical mask.

Where was that nurse? He opened the door and glanced into the hallway, his entire body buzzing with nervous energy. Meredith was alone and scared in that operating room right now, and he was desperate to once again hold her hand.

A nurse walked into the room. "Are you ready, Mr. Grey?"

"Ready," he agreed grimly.

His footsteps echoed in the deserted hallway, and they made their way through a series of locked double doors. He knew when they'd entered the operating room because of the powerful smell of antiseptic. Meredith was already on a table in the center of the room, her nose and mouth covered with an oxygen mask and a sterile drape hung just above her stomach.

Her entire face crumpled in relief at the sight of him, but the oxygen mask muffled her voice. "Sawyer."

He rushed to her side, the chill of the room barely registering. Her arms were splayed straight out from her in a T, but she didn't seem to notice when he touched her hand. "I'm here now. How are those babies doing?"

"I don't know." Her voice was thin, her eyes a little unfocused. "Everything's numb now. I can't feel a thing."

"That's what I like to hear," Dr. Mike said as he slipped his hands into a pair of surgical gloves the nurse held out for him. "Are you ready to meet your daughters, Meredith?"

She looked up at Sawyer, but even that movement seemed slow and weak. Had they given her something to slow her reflexes and keep her calm? He hoped that was why she seemed so lethargic and not because of the blood loss.

He brushed his fingers lightly over her cheek, then pressed a soft kiss there. "I'll be right here the entire time. I'm not going anywhere."

She smiled faintly. "Good. We're ready, Dr. Mike."

He beamed. "Then let's get these babies delivered."

CHAPTER

Thirty-Three

The bag of saline dripping into her vein was like ice. Meredith felt like she was in a dream—aware of what was happening, but distant from it all.

She was really having her babies today.

She tried to pull her arms under the blanket covering her, but couldn't seem to move them. Her teeth chattered, whether from adrenaline or cold, she wasn't sure. There was an odd deadness encompassing most of her body, unlike anything she'd ever experienced. The anesthesiologist had told her she'd feel tugging sensations as they performed the c-section, but no pain.

Sawyer bent down, his lips close to her ear. "You're shivering. Are you cold or just nervous?"

She tried to still her chattering teeth, but couldn't. "Both. Have they started?"

Sawyer glanced over the sterile drape and shook his head. "Not yet. Can we get a blanket for her? She's freezing."

"Certainly," a nurse said.

Moments later, a warm blanket that felt fresh out of the dryer engulfed her top half. She closed her eyes, relishing the heat. "Thank you," she whispered. She wasn't sure whether she was speaking to the nurse or Sawyer.

"I'm just going to do a quick test to make sure you're numb, then we'll start the c-section," Dr. Mike said. "Do you feel that?"

Meredith held her breath, tightening her grip on Sawyer's hand. She didn't care what she felt if it meant saving her babies.

"I don't feel anything," Meredith said. "Are the babies still okay?"

"We're monitoring their heartbeats closely and they're doing just fine," Dr. Mike said, his tone calm and reassuring. "I'm going to start now. Feeling pressure and tugging is normal, but if you feel any pain, let me know immediately."

She felt it then—the odd, tugging pressure that they'd warned her about. She stared up at Sawyer, her voice muffled through the oxygen mask. "What's happening?"

His face looked pale and drawn, but he gave a forced smile and tenderly caressed her cheek again. "They're just, uh, opening you up."

Some distant part of her knew that should freak her out, but all she could think about were the twins. Was John in the room right now, watching over them? She hoped so. "The babies?"

"They're not out yet," Sawyer said. "How are you doing, Mer?"

Why did he keep asking her that? Fear had her throat feeling tight, and she was suddenly grateful for the oxygen mask placed over her. "I just want Savvy and Jo to be okay."

"They will be." Sawyer kissed her forehead.

"Almost there, Meredith," Dr. Mike said. "You're doing great."

Almost there. Her babies were almost here.

Sawyer's face transformed, a look of total awe making him almost glow. She couldn't see his smile beneath the surgical mask, but it was obvious in his eyes. A moment later, there was a faint, mewling cry.

Meredith's eyes immediately flooded with tears as relief overwhelmed her.

"Baby A is here," Sawyer said, giving Meredith a look full of wonder. "She's beautiful, Mer."

"Savannah," Meredith croaked. "That's Savannah."

Another sound filled the room, this cry stronger than the first. Meredith let out a sob.

"Josie's here, too," Sawyer said. "Oh, Mer. They're perfect."

"Are they okay?" She couldn't see anything over the drape hiding her view of the surgery.

"They're in excellent hands," Dr. Mike said. "The neonatal intensive care unit team is assessing them right now."

The cries were getting louder, which Meredith knew was a good sign, as the nurses and doctors called out various readings and numbers.

"Go with them," she told Sawyer. "Please."

Sawyer nodded, his phone in one hand with the camera already pulled up.

"Baby A is five pounds three ounces," one of the nurses said. "Eighteen inches long."

"Wow, they really are identical," another nurse said with a laugh. "Baby B is the exact same size and length."

"They're so beautiful, Mer," Sawyer said, and she could hear the emotion in his voice. "So much dark hair. They've got John's chin and your long fingers."

Meredith held back a sob. Her babies were here.

She was a mother.

"And they're okay?" she demanded again. "Everything's fine?"

"So far so good, Mama," an unfamiliar female voice said— the pediatrician, maybe. "Both babies are breathing room air on their own, which is great, and their chests sound clear."

Medical professionals continued to call out numbers and words that meant nothing to Meredith. Sawyer kept saying things like, "She's so beautiful," and "Wow, you've really got a set of lungs, don't you, sweetie?"

Tears streamed into Meredith's hairline. She could feel a faint tug on her stomach—Dr. Mike sewing her closed, she assumed—but she was too attuned to her babies to care. Each of their cries was the most beautiful sound in the world. She hoped Sawyer was taking lots of pictures and videos.

The babies were here. They were safe. She'd done it.

A nurse appeared at her side, a tiny bundle in her arms. Meredith's entire world zeroed in on the baby while everything else faded away.

"Here's baby A," the nurse said. "Savannah, right?"

"Yes." Savannah's face was red from crying, her face screwed up in stress. It took all of Meredith's concentration, but she lifted her arm that felt like a concrete block and rested it gently on the baby's chest.

The crying calmed, then stopped entirely.

"She knows her mommy," the nurse said with a chuckle. "Isn't that sweet?"

Another nurse arrived, holding Josie. Her face was less red, her cries already settling. Meredith brushed a finger across the baby's soft cheek.

Two babies. She couldn't believe it.

"Want to hold them, Daddy?" the nurse asked, motioning to Sawyer's phone with her head. "We can take a quick family picture before whisking these beauties off to the nursery to assess them better."

Sawyer accepted the babies as though they were grenades who might explode if he moved too fast. The tenderness was evident in his eyes, even through the mask. Meredith longed to hold the babies herself. Soon, she hoped. Once she wasn't worried about dropping them.

"They're beautiful, Mer," Sawyer said. "They're perfect."

He crouched down by her, a baby in each arm. From this angle, she could see the blood and mucus matting their hair. Their skin was splotchy from the trauma of birth, too.

She'd never seen anything more perfect.

"Smile," the nurse said, and there was a click as she took a photo with Sawyer's phone. "Sorry, Mama, but it's time to get these babies to the nursery. You'll see them again soon enough."

A nurse took each baby, and Meredith felt an immediate sense of panic.

"You have to go with Savannah and Josie," Meredith said quickly. "Promise me you'll stay with them?"

Sawyer's brow furrowed. Was he going to protest? They'd talked about this. She needed him to be with the babies. She would be just fine on her own.

"You'll be okay?" he asked finally.

Meredith nodded, her eyes brimming with tears. "I'm fine. Go with the girls."

Sawyer bent down, pressing a firm kiss to her cheek. "I'll come check on you as soon as I can and bring you more pictures."

And then Savannah, Josie, Sawyer, and the team of medical professionals were gone, pushing the wheeled bassinet out of the room.

Meredith closed her eyes, letting the tears flow freely.

"You did great." A nurse in pink scrubs, mostly hidden by her yellow surgical gown, had taken Sawyer's place at her side.

"They're really okay?" Meredith asked.

The nurse patted her hand, her tone cheerful. "They were doing great when they left. You did fantastic today, Mama. Congratulations."

Mama. Every time someone said that word, it sent a thrill through Meredith.

"We'll be done here in another thirty minutes or so and get you to recovery," Dr. Mike said. "Just relax and try to get some rest. The hard part is over."

Meredith closed her eyes, the adrenaline wearing off now that she knew her babies were here and safe. The hard part? No, that would be the next eighteen years, when she had to raise two baby girls into women.

But it would also be the amazing part. The part that made life worth living.

She let the rhythmic tugging on her stomach as they stitched her closed lull her into an almost dream-like state. Images played in her mind, making her heart swell with love.

Sawyer playing peek-a-boo while the babies giggled. Chasing excited toddlers around the front yard while they shrieked with happiness. Teaching them how to ride a bike. Cheering on teenagers at their dance competition. Walking women in beautiful white dresses down the aisle.

She felt their absence like a physical ache. All she wanted was Savannah and Josie in her arms, with Sawyer by her side.

"How are you doing, Meredith?" the nurse asked quietly.

"Great," she said.

Sawyer had been so calm with the trauma of the day. Steady and reliable, just like she'd known he'd be. For the first time, she wondered how John would have reacted if he'd be the one with her.

I'm sorry you weren't here, she told him silently. *I'm sorry you won't get to raise our daughters. But they're in good hands. Sawyer already loves them like his own.*

She'd thought giving birth to the girls would bring with it a cacophony of painful *what if*s. Had expected to be inundated with memories of John. But her focus had been entirely on Sawyer and their babies. It still was.

An ache filled her chest as she finally accepted the truth. John wasn't the man she'd shared the most important moment of her life with. Not anymore.

Giving birth to Josie and Savannah had been, without a doubt, the most defining moment of her existence so far. And Sawyer was the man who had been by her side for every moment.

Meredith squeezed her eyes tightly shut, making little stars dance before them. *I'm so sorry, John,* she silently told him. *I wish you could have been here. But you aren't.*

She felt it then—John's arms wrapped around her, like they had so many times before. She didn't open her eyes, afraid of shattering the illusion, and let herself relish in his imagined embrace.

She didn't hear words from beyond the grave, but suddenly she knew what John would say if she could speak to him. *It's okay. I love you. Sawyer is a great guy. I want you and our girls to be happy.*

She loved John. That would never change.

But maybe it was okay to love Sawyer, too.

CHAPTER
Thirty-Four

"We're all done here, Meredith. You did fantastic."

She gave Dr. Mike a weak smile as he pulled up the rails on the side of her bed. "You're the one who did fantastic. You saved my babies' lives today. Thank you." Her voice choked on the word. Things could have ended so differently. The placenta could have torn away completely instead of partially, depriving her babies of all oxygen. She could have hemorrhaged after delivery. This could have happened a month earlier, when their lungs weren't yet developed enough to be out in the world.

But it hadn't. John had watched over them, and everything had turned out just fine.

Dr. Mike's hand covered hers briefly, then he and a nurse began pushing her from the operating room. "It was an honor, Meredith. Truly."

"Have you gotten an update on Savannah and Josie?"

"No, but no news usually means good news. They might have to spend a few days to a couple of weeks in the hospital since they're preterm, but that's not so much in the grand scheme of things. They'll be home before you know it."

"When can I see them?" Her arms were feeling less numb now, and she longed to hold her babies. To smell the sweet downy scent of their skin, to kiss the soft fuzz of their hair.

At least Sawyer was with them, taking pictures.

"We need to take you to a recovery room and monitor you for an hour or so, but then we'll see what we can arrange."

Dr. Mike wheeled Meredith into a curtained-off room, locking the wheels on her bed. "Someone will be by soon to take you upstairs to the mother and baby wing. Press the call button if you need a nurse."

It was the first time she'd been alone since this crazy evening began. She longed for Sawyer's steadying presence, but was glad he was with the girls. They needed him more right now, and she didn't mind sharing.

"Knock knock."

Meredith looked up in surprise. Vanessa pulled aside the curtain, giving her a big smile.

"Oh my gosh, Mer." She came to her side, leaning down to give her a hug.

"What are you doing here?" Meredith asked, returning the hug.

"Sawyer called me and said you'd had the babies. He was worried about you being all alone when you got out of the OR, so of course I rushed over."

Meredith blinked back the tears that unexpectedly filled her eyes.

"He's always looking out for me," Meredith whispered.

"He's a great guy," Vanessa agreed. "He didn't have time to tell me what happened, though—just that you and the babies were doing good. What happened after I left?"

So Meredith told Vanessa the entire story.

"I don't know what I would have done if Sawyer hadn't been there." Her voice grew tight at the thought of a different outcome. What if she'd been home alone tonight? She didn't even want to think about that.

"He's so good to you." Vanessa gave Meredith's hand a squeeze. "I'm so glad you two found each other."

A nurse arrived then and asked brightly, "How are you feeling?"

"Good," Meredith said. "I mean, I still can't feel my legs or anything."

"It can take a while for the spinal block to wear off," the nurse said, unlocking the wheels on her bed. "I'm here to get you moved to a room on the mother and baby floor. Ready to go?"

"Sure," Meredith said, struggling to sit up a little straighter in the bed. At least the head was raised so she could see okay. "When can I see my babies?"

The nurse gave Meredith a conspiratorial smile. "Well, I'm not supposed to do this, but it's pretty late at night and your little girls are the only ones in the nursery, so I think we can swing by and let you see them."

Nothing sounded more wonderful. But she still had no feeling in her body, and didn't think she could transfer to the wheelchair. "Like through the window?"

"No, I'll just wheel your entire bed into the nursery," the nurse said. "You can stay put and just let us push you around like the queen you are today."

Outside the nursery, Meredith tried to sit up in bed so she could see through the glass windows, but the lower half of her body was still too asleep. But she could see Sawyer in there, still wearing his yellow surgical gown, the mask hanging around his neck and hairnet still in place. She heard a faint, mewling cry and knew immediately it must be Savannah or Josie. How long would it be until she could tell the two apart?

"I can wheel you into the nursery if you'd like," the nurse said.

"Yes, please," she said eagerly.

The nurse nodded. "I'll let your nurse on the mother and baby floor know where you are, and she can come down and take your vitals. They're just getting your little girls ready for the level two nursery. They were struggling a bit on room air so they're giving them some oxygen so they won't tire themselves out trying to breathe, but that's really normal for thirty-five week preemies."

Vanessa held open the door, and the nurse wheeled Meredith's bed into the nursery.

Sawyer looked over, his entire face transforming with relief. He was at her side in an instant, his hand clasping hers.

"How are you feeling?" he asked.

"Fine." It was true. She felt wide awake, no doubt from the adrenaline, and still couldn't feel the pain she knew would come soon from the surgery. "How are Josie and Savannah?"

The love on his face was obvious. "Perfect. They just put them on oxygen, but the nurses assure me that's nothing to worry about." He looked over at Vanessa. "Thank you so much for coming."

"Of course." She patted Meredith on the shoulder. "There's nowhere else I'd rather be right now."

"Where are they?" Meredith asked, craning her neck.

"Right over here."

The nurse pushed Meredith's bed right over to the warmer where Savannah and Josie lay together, clothed only in a diaper, their eyes squeezed tightly shut with the vitamin E salve all over their eyelids. Tiny oxygen cannulas rested in their noses, the tubing held onto their cheeks by small, round stickers.

"Oh." Meredith breathed. She had only caught the barest glimpses of Savannah and Josie in the OR, and they'd still been covered in afterbirth.

"Aren't they beautiful?" Sawyer's entire face glowed with happiness. "They have your nose and John's chin, and they look pretty darn identical. All of that dark hair definitely comes from John, but that hint of curl is all you."

Meredith clutched Sawyer's hand, her heart so full she worried she'd start spontaneously crying. She was aware of Vanessa hanging back, of the nurses tending to Savannah and Josie, but the moment still felt incredibly intimate and private.

"I was just getting ready to give them a bath," the nurse said. "Would you like to stay and watch?"

"Yes," Meredith whispered. "Yes, I want to stay."

She watched in awe as the nurse grabbed a plastic container and filled it with warm water. She bathed the babies together. Josie's cry was soft and mewling, but Savannah's was a full-lunged yell. They all laughed at the difference in the babies' responses, but they both settled down as the nurse gently dribbled warm water over their entire body with a washrag.

"Can you believe they're really here?" Meredith asked Sawyer.

He shook his head, and she caught the moisture in his eyes. "No. You did so good, Mer. I'm so proud of you."

She squeezed his hand. "Thanks for being here."

"Thank you for allow me to be part of this." He kissed her forehead, and her entire body trembled.

Soon Josie and Savannah were both bundled tightly in a blanket, a blue-and-pink striped hat with a bow almost as large as their faces on each of their heads.

"We need to take them to the NICU soon, and you need to get to your room," the nurse said. "But would you like to hold them first?"

Meredith nodded, holding out her arms. The nurse gently placed Savannah in one arm and Josie in the other, and Meredith was amazed at how light five pounds, three ounces really was.

"Hey, baby girls," Meredith crooned, making sure to support their heads. Luckily, the hospital bed did most of the work for her. She leaned down, inhaling the fresh baby scent before placing a kiss on top of each of their heads.

Sawyer hovered over the three of them, his expression happier than she'd ever seen it. He reached out, his index finger gently caressing each baby's cheek.

"Thank you," Sawyer whispered. "Thank you for this, Mer."

"No," Meredith said, gazing up into his eyes. "Thank you."

She'd woken up this morning as a pregnant widow, but tonight she would go to sleep as a mother of two. They were a family—an unconventional one, but a family, nonetheless.

For now, that was enough.

CHAPTER
Thirty-Five

The sterile white walls of the hospital's level two nursery stood in sharp contrast to the bright pink of the twins' car seats. Sawyer leaned forward on his uncomfortable hospital chair, pressing his fingers together as he stared at Savannah and Josie. They looked so impossibly small in their car seats, their feet scrunched up nearly to the buckle and their heads leaning against the pillow to support their necks. Wires trailed from their bodies to monitors that tracked their vital signs and a blood pressure cuff no bigger than his thumb was strapped to each of their left feet. An IV trailed from Savannah's left hand and Josie's right, the backs of which were discolored and bruised. Leads snaked out of the top of their pajamas, and a heart monitor beeped out the rhythm.

Beside him, Meredith sat in the small room's only recliner, her face pinched in concern as her eyes stayed glued to the babies.

"I want them to pass so badly," she said, her hands clutched tightly together.

Sawyer massaged the back of her neck, his own hope nearly strangling him. "Me too. But if they have to stay in the hospital a few more days, that's okay, too."

Meredith sighed, rubbing her eyes. "I know. I just don't want to go home without them."

It had been five days since the girls were born. Today, Meredith would be discharged from the hospital. She could have gone home yesterday, but the babies were doing so well that Dr. Mike had kept her another day in the hopes she and the babies could go home together.

The car seat test was their last hurdle. Savannah and Josie had to sit buckled into their infant car seats for ninety minutes without having their oxygen or heart levels drop below a normal range.

"Five more minutes," the nurse said, glancing at the read-outs on the monitors. "They're doing great."

Meredith reached for Sawyer's hand, squeezing it. "I just want us all to go home. I'll sleep so much better once we're all in our own beds."

Sawyer chuckled, his love for her and the babies—his girls—making his heart nearly explode. "Even with waking up to feed them every three hours?"

Meredith gave him a comical glare. "I've already been waking up every three hours to, well, you know." Her cheeks blushed scarlet. She'd been trying her best to breastfeed the babies and had been waking up at night to pump. The lactation consultant said it would increase her milk supply, whatever that meant. Sawyer was just glad Vanessa had been here for the first couple of days to help, and that Cheyenne was still around to answer any feminine questions Meredith might have.

"Fair enough," Sawyer said, scratching the back of his neck.

"At least when I'm up, I'll be with the girls instead of a machine."

Sawyer had no idea how they would manage feeding at home. He helped where he could, but Meredith was doing her best to do something called "tandem nursing" where she breastfed both babies at the same time. Since neither of them felt comfortable with him being in the room for that, all he could really do was change their messy diapers.

John would have been able to do more. Meredith wouldn't have felt uncomfortable with him in the room while she nursed the babies. But Sawyer tried not to dwell on the platonic nature of their relationship. He was just so grateful that the girls were here safely, and that Meredith was okay.

"Sixty seconds," the nurse said cheerfully. "Look at them, sleeping through this whole thing. They are such dolls."

"Couldn't agree more." Sawyer gazed at Meredith, his heart flipping. "They look just like their mother."

Meredith's cheeks pinked, but she looked pleased. "I think they have a lot of John in them, too."

Sawyer saw the shadow of his best friend in the babies, too—in their rather square jaw and full cheekbones. He was grateful every day for the reminders. John had lived and loved and helped bring two children into this world. He might be gone, but he'd left an indelible mark behind.

And then he'd left it all in Sawyer's hands. The weight of that responsibility sat on his shoulders like a full military pack. He hoped he was making his best friend proud. That he could be the kind of father and husband he knew John would have been.

Savannah squirmed in her car seat, her bare feet kicking as her face scrunched up in concentration, growing red.

"Is she okay?" Meredith asked anxiously.

Sawyer held his breath. Whatever he'd told Meredith, it would be heartbreaking if they had to leave the hospital tonight without the girls. He glanced at Josie. What if they had to leave only one baby behind? He hadn't considered that they might not get to bring both girls home together.

The nurse examined the monitors. "Everything still looks good. She's just stretching."

A loud, wet sound filled the air, followed by a strong odor. Savannah's face relaxed as she let out a contented sigh.

Meredith put a hand over her mouth, laughing. "I think someone needs a diaper change."

"That means Josie will need one any minute, too," Sawyer said. Over the past five days, they'd learned just what *identical* meant. The girls seemed to eat at the same time, sleep at the same time, and poop at the same time, too.

"Yup, I think someone made a mess in their pants," the nurse said. "You can take her out of the car seat and change her. Congratulations! They've both officially passed the car seat test. We can start processing their discharge forms and get you guys out of here tonight."

Sawyer carefully pulled Meredith to her feet and gave her a gentle hug. She was still recovering from her c-section and wouldn't be able to drive or lift anything heavier than one baby at a time for at least another five weeks. He was gladder than ever they were married. What would she have done if she had to take the babies home alone?

"We can take them home," she whispered into his chest, clutching him tightly. Sawyer was all too aware of how different she felt in his arms now—how much closer he could hold her without her pregnant belly between them.

"I can't wait," he said.

He unstrapped Josie from her car seat and handed her to Meredith, being careful of the various wires and monitors, then unstrapped Savannah. She nestled against his chest, and he felt the same awe he had the first time he'd held the girls.

Something foul reached his nose again, and he chuckled. "Yeah, she's definitely made a mess."

A loud noise filled the room, and Josie grunted.

"And there goes the other one." Meredith grabbed a diaper and handed it to him, then picked up one of her own.

The next two hours were a whirlwind of going over discharge instructions and signing paperwork for both Meredith and the twins. As the nurse disconnected the final monitor, he felt a surge of panic.

This was it. They really were letting them take two tiny, helpless babies home. Even after all the training they'd received while the girls were in the level two nursery, everything from how to bathe them to how to perform CPR, he felt inadequate for the task.

"Will you grab the diaper bag?" Meredith asked. "Their going home outfits should be in there."

"Sure." Sawyer lifted the bag onto the tray near the crib the babies shared. He hadn't realized Meredith had bought specific outfits for this occasion.

She rifled through the diaper bag, pulling out a pair of gray-and-pink striped leggings with an attached sheer skirt that looked like something a ballerina would wear. The leggings even had feet designed to look like ballet slippers.

But it was the shirt that caught Sawyer's attention—a onesie with the design from King Trident's Scuba, an anchor with *refuse to sink* across it in swirly font.

Meredith held up the onesie, giving Sawyer a watery smile. "What do you think?"

He put an arm around her and pressed a soft kiss to her temple. "It's perfect."

A nurse wheeled Meredith to the entrance of the hospital, a baby in each arm. Sawyer triple checked that the car seats were installed correctly on the base before carefully strapping the babies inside. Then they waved goodbye to the nurse and were making the short drive home, which took almost twice as long as normal because he drove so cautiously.

Meredith let out a surprised gasp as he pulled into the front yard. A cheerful pink flag banner hung in the living room window, and large letters staked in the yard spelled out "welcome home!"

"Cheyenne and Zach set it up," Sawyer said with a grin. "Do you like it?"

"I love it."

He shut off the car engine and turned toward her. "You ready for this, Mommy?"

She laughed, placing her hand in his outstretched one. "I guess we're about to find out."

They had a wonderful evening cuddling together on the couch, a baby in each of their arms. He helped Meredith give each of the twins a bath, then worked on his laptop in the kitchen while Meredith nursed them in the living room. He wanted to stay close by in case she needed help.

"You can come back in," Meredith said, her voice so quiet he had to strain to hear. "I think they're asleep. I'm going to head to bed, too."

"The bassinet's already in your room." Sawyer leaned down, carefully picking up Savannah—no, Josie—no, wait, Savannah. The girls looked so much alike, but he was confident they'd learn to tell them apart easier soon. For now, they had colored bracelets on their ankles to make sure they didn't mix them up.

Meredith followed him into her room, Josie resting on her shoulder. Sawyer rarely stepped foot in here, but he had a feeling that would change now that the babies were home. Carefully, he placed Savannah in the bassinet, her arms tightly bound to her sides by the swaddling blanket. She barely stirred, her bottom lip quivering as she sucked on it. He took Josie from Meredith and laid her down next, the girls' faces automatically turning toward each other.

"They're so perfect," Meredith whispered, looking down at the sleeping girls.

Sawyer wrapped an arm around Meredith's shoulders, tucking her into his side. "The most beautiful babies I've ever seen, hands down."

Meredith nodded in agreement. Her arm dropped to her waist and the air between them became suddenly charged.

"I don't know if I can ever thank you for all you've done for us," Meredith said, her voice husky. "If you hadn't been here these past few months . . ."

She leaned into him, their bodies pressed close without the barrier of her pregnant stomach between them.

It was hard to breathe.

"When I was alone in the delivery room after you'd gone to the nursery with the twins, I realized how much you mean to me." Her soft words made the hairs on the back of his neck prickle.

"It's been my pleasure."

He placed his hands low on her back—not urging her closer, but not pushing her away, either. She bit her lip, drawing his eyes to her mouth.

The stress of the last week had his emotions frayed, his self-control unraveling. Her eyes were filled with emotions he couldn't decipher. All he knew for sure was that she wasn't pulling away.

Did she know how he felt about her? Could she perhaps one day feel the same way about him?

It was too much to hope for, but he couldn't stop himself from wishing for it, anyway.

"I care about you deeply, Sawyer. I think I even . . ." She pulled her bottom lip between her teeth again.

Sawyer stared, mesmerized by the motion. How many times had he dreamed about kissing her? A million?

"You think you even what?" he whispered.

Her hands drifted up his back and came to rest at the back of his neck. She rose on her tiptoes, lifting her face to his as she urged his head down.

Their lips met with a quiet hesitance. He longed to deepen the kiss, to crush her against him and devour her mouth. But he held back, letting her take the lead.

Her hands trailed fire from the back of his neck down his back. She pressed herself more tightly against him, parting her lips in invitation.

Heaven couldn't be better than this. His hands tangled in her hair as he took control of the kiss, drinking her in. He gently gripped her chin, angling her head for a better kiss.

He had the entire world in his hands. And now that he'd tasted it, he wasn't about to let it go.

Sawyer pressed his forehead against Meredith's, breathing heavily. "You have no idea how long I've wanted to do that."

Meredith bit her lip again, nearly driving him crazy. "Really?"

"Really." He closed his eyes, trying to reorient his thoughts. "But are you sure about this? I don't want to take advantage of you or do anything that could hurt our marriage."

A tiny furrow appeared between her brow that he longed to kiss smooth.

"And kissing is hurting it?"

"No. Maybe." He sighed, resting his hand on the back of her neck. The urge to kiss her again was almost overpowering. "It hasn't even been a week since you had the twins. You're still recovering from surgery, and your emotions are everywhere—"

She put a finger to his lips, silencing him instantly. It took all of his self-control not to give that finger a playful nibble.

"I know the timing doesn't make sense, but I feel like I'm finally seeing things clearly for the first time." She inhaled slowly, and the exhalation of her warm breath on his face had him unraveling all over again. "A marriage of convenience isn't enough for me anymore. I want more for me, for us, for the babies."

Those words—the mere possibility of a future with Meredith—made him want to fall to his knees in gratitude.

"Are you sure?" he whispered.

She nodded, her eyes luminescent in the dim light of the bedroom. "Yes. But I want us to take things slow. We have the twins to think about now, and I told you divorce wasn't an option for me. I don't want to screw this up."

He tightened his grip on her, his heart feeling like it might explode. "I won't let us."

One day, he'd tell her about how long he'd loved her. There would be days and weeks and years to figure out how their relationship fit in with both of their relationships with John. Later tonight, when he laid alone in his bed, the guilt would probably hit for kissing his best friend's wife.

But kissing Meredith hadn't felt like betraying John. It felt like coming home.

A baby squirmed in the bassinet, her tiny, mewling cry interrupting the moment. But Sawyer didn't care.

He'd just been given the entire world.

CHAPTER

Thirty-Six

*M*eredith hadn't known it was possible to be so exhausted, so emotional, and yet so blissfully happy all at once.

The next few weeks passed in a rosy haze. Josie and Savannah were relatively easy babies with sweet dispositions, but caring for two infants was more difficult than Meredith could have imagined. When one started crying, it wasn't long before the entire house rang with their displeasure. Nursing was difficult and time-consuming, especially since it was the one thing Sawyer couldn't help her with, but after three frustrating appointments with the lactation specialist, the twins got the hang of things.

They fell into an easy routine, so different from the one she'd had during her marriage with John, but infinitely more rewarding. Admitting that even to herself still felt like a betrayal at times, but it was the truth. She and John had shared a deep, passionate love and had built a beautiful life together.

But Josie and Savannah hadn't been part of that life. Late at night, when she fed the babies in the dim light of her bedroom, she'd whisper stories about John and mourn for a life where they got to raise the babies together. But when she woke up in the morning to find Sawyer in the living room with the girls in one arm while he pecked away on his work laptop with one hand, she was so grateful to experience this second chapter with him.

It was confusing and at times unsettling, but it was as though admitting her feelings aloud to Sawyer had allowed them to firmly take root and grow.

For his part, Sawyer was an attentive father who wasn't afraid to change a blow-out diaper or scrub spit-up out of the bassinet. Soon he could burp the babies better than her, and Savannah and Josie always slept better when he was the one to swaddle them.

But four weeks had passed since the girls were born, and Sawyer hadn't kissed her again even once—not a proper kiss, at least. They'd spent plenty of evenings snuggled together on the couch with the girls while they watched television or read a book, and they'd held hands while on short walks. Hugs had become longer and more tender, and she savored every forehead kiss and brush of his lips against her cheeks.

What she didn't understand was why he was holding back. Had he changed his mind about their relationship?

"Are you sure you three will be okay today?" Sawyer asked, his brow knit with worry as he hefted his computer bag onto one shoulder. He had a meeting in Portland today. It would be the first time Meredith and the twins had been alone for an extended amount of time.

"We'll be fine," Meredith said, cradling a cooing Josie in one arm. She could just see Savannah out of the corner of her eye, legs kicking wildly from her place on the living room floor as she gurgled at the ceiling fan. "We're just going to stay home and hang out. You'll be back in no time."

"I know." Sawyer's hands hovered over her shoulders before he shoved them in his pockets. "I'll keep my phone nearby if you need anything. I can be home in an hour, and Cheyenne and Zach are only ten minutes away."

"We'll be fine." She rested her hand on his chest, a thrill of electricity sparking at the rapid beating of his heart.

He liked her. Maybe even loved her. She knew he did. So why wouldn't he kiss her?

"I'd better go." Sawyer leaned down, his lips brushing her forehead so lightly that she had to wonder whether she was imagining things.

He kissed Josie's head too, and then he was out the door.

Meredith watched out the front window as Sawyer drove away, Josie kicking happily in her arms.

"There goes Daddy." She kissed Josie's cheek, then set her down on the blanket next to Savannah. They both kicked their feet, their tiny fists flailing. Meredith carefully sat down beside them, wincing at the pull in her midsection. She was recovering well from the c-section, but still wasn't back to one hundred percent. "Yeah, I miss him, too. But he'll be home tonight."

If only he'd let his walls down and allow them to be a real family, with a real marriage. She knew he felt something for her too—no one could kiss like that without having their heart involved. And yeah, they'd agreed to take things slow. But she hadn't thought that meant never kissing.

He was giving her space and time. Knowing Sawyer, he probably thought hormones had brought on her change of heart. But she wouldn't change her mind.

Having the babies—and nearly losing them—had shown her that life was too short to spend it sad. She wanted to be happy again. To be one half of a whole.

She wanted Sawyer.

Her cell phone rang, Vanessa's name flashing across the screen.

"How did the test go?" Meredith asked immediately. Vanessa had finished up her last class of the semester, but she'd had a tough class and had been stressing for weeks about the final.

"I feel really good about it," Vanessa said. "It was every bit as hard as everyone said it would be, but I felt as prepared as possible and I think I passed."

"Of course you passed." Meredith grabbed a pacifier off the coffee table and put it in Savannah's mouth, then found another one for Josie. They were getting restless, and she'd need to feed them soon. "And you're coming back to Sapphire Cove for the summer?"

"Yeah, I need a break before diving into my last year of school."

"I can't wait to have you here permanently." She loved Cheyenne like a sister, but she'd known Vanessa since they were kids. It would be wonderful to spend time together again. "I've missed you so much."

"I've missed you, too. How are those sweet babies?"

"Getting hungry." She smiled at the babies. Savannah had spit out her pacifier and was sucking on Josie's fist.

"Yeah, they do that a lot," Vanessa said, chuckling. "And how are things with Sawyer?"

Meredith sighed, thinking of that less-than-satisfying forehead kiss he'd passed off as a proper goodbye. "Sawyer is Sawyer."

"What do you mean?"

She bit her lip. Vanessa didn't know about the kiss. She'd almost told her a few days ago, but chickened out at the last moment.

John had only been gone seven months. In those seven months, she'd gotten remarried and had twins. Falling in love with her new husband felt like a step too far.

Maybe Sawyer was right, and they should take things slower.

"So, um, Sawyer and I kind of kissed on the night we came home from the hospital."

"What?" Vanessa shrieked. "Uh, way to bury the lead. Tell me everything."

Vanessa listened quietly while Meredith explained the way things had changed between them in the three weeks since she'd come home from the hospital.

"Am I insane?" Meredith asked, pushing a hand through her hair. "I know John hasn't been gone very long—"

"Stop," Vanessa interrupted. "No one gets to tell you how to grieve, Mer."

She inhaled shakily, the words hitting her straight in the chest. Josie squirmed, her legs pulled up to her chest as the pacifier popped out of her mouth, and Meredith put it back in.

"Can I still grieve for John while wanting to be with Sawyer?" She brushed away a tear. "Because I *do* still miss John terribly. But I'm so tired of being alone, and Sawyer makes me so happy."

"Then go for it," Vanessa said. "He misses John, too. Sawyer's a good guy and he'll understand. If you love Sawyer, then why wait to be with him just because you still love John, too? That's never going to change."

She pressed her fingers to her mouth, blinking rapidly. "No, it won't. John was my soul mate."

"Maybe Sawyer's your soul mate, too. Who made the rule that you only get one?"

Savannah was squirming more than ever. Meredith knew she didn't have much time left before the girls demanded to be fed, but she couldn't stop herself from saying, "What if he doesn't think I'm his soul mate? What if, after thinking about it, Sawyer has decided he doesn't want our relationship to change and isn't sure how to tell me?"

Vanessa's laugh startled her so much she nearly dropped the phone.

"That's a good one," Vanessa said, still chuckling. "Trust me, Sawyer wants more from you than an occasional hug."

She thought again of the brief forehead kiss goodbye less than an hour ago. That hadn't exactly screamed *come hither, babe*.

"How do you know?" Meredith asked.

"Uh, because I have eyes?" Vanessa laughed again. "It makes sense that he's hesitant, though. Think of it from his point of view. There's probably a lot of guilt associated with falling for his best friend's wife."

Guilt. Meredith had fought her own feelings after marrying Sawyer for the same reason, but after having the twins, something had shifted. Some days, she still felt guilty. But she knew John would want her, Sawyer, and the twins to be a real family.

"I know it's weird, but it's not like we had an affair and he stole me away from John."

"No, but it might feel like that to Sawyer."

Meredith sighed. She picked up the girls one at a time and placed them over her knees, patting their backs rhythmically to try to buy a few more minutes before feeding them. "That's silly. It's not like he's done anything to dishonor John's memory."

"Exactly."

Meredith paused, confused. Josie squirmed, letting out a small grunt, and she resumed patting their backs. "What do you mean?"

"I mean, he won't do anything until he's sure he isn't taking advantage of you."

Meredith cocked her head to one side, considering. "Explain."

"When you kissed him, you were not even a week postpartum. If Sawyer had tried to push your relationship forward at that point, with your hormones all crazy and stuff, he would've been a total jerk. My guess is he isn't sure if that kiss was actually from you, or if it was just a result of the trauma of the past week."

Sometimes she caught Sawyer looking at her in a way that she wasn't sure how to interpret. It wasn't that he hadn't been affectionate. There had been hugs that seemed to go on forever, gentle brushes of his fingers along her cheek that made her shiver.

Was Vanessa right?

"How do I show him it's not just the hormones?" Meredith asked carefully.

"I don't know, Mer. But I do know that the ball is in your court, so take a shot."

For the next few days, Meredith paid closer attention to the signals that Sawyer gave her and saw the internal struggle she'd been oblivious to before. It was there in his quick intake of breath when she touched him, in the way his eyes followed her around the room and sometimes traced the curves of her body.

He didn't look at her like his best friend's widow. He looked at her like she was the woman he loved.

But Vanessa was right. She'd have to be the one to take the next step.

Over the next week, she carefully planned how to prove to Sawyer she was ready to move on.

On Friday, Sawyer had to go into the office again. Meredith spent the day making his favorite meal—potato casserole and meatloaf, with homemade rolls and carrot cake for dessert. It took all day to prep everything since she had to keep stopping to feed the girls, but she didn't mind. Earlier that week, Dr. Mike had cleared her to resume normal activities, and it felt great to do things for herself again without asking for help.

By the time six o'clock rolled around, the scent of dinner filled the home. She'd set the table and even spent an hour on her hair and makeup. The girls were content in their swings, Savannah cooing contentedly while Josie's eyes fluttered closed.

Her stomach swarmed with butterflies when she heard the front door open.

"I'm home," Sawyer called out. There was a clunk as he set his bag on the floor. "Something smells delicious."

She closed her eyes, gathering her courage. It was go time.

Sawyer's jaw dropped when she walked into the living room, champagne glasses of sparkling cider in hand. His eyes raked her figure before resting on her face, his eyebrows raised in question.

"Hey," he said, taking a careful step forward. "Did I forget someone's birthday?"

She laughed nervously and shook her head. His fingers brushed against hers as he took the glass, sending heat racing up her spine. The urge to kiss him was overwhelming, but she couldn't lose her head. This wasn't about loneliness, or hormones, or anything else.

This was about a future with Sawyer—a real future, filled with all the love and happiness they both deserved.

"What is it, then?" Sawyer took a sip of his sparkling cider, his eyes not leaving hers. "Is everything okay?"

"Everything's great. I just thought tonight might be a good time to talk."

His eyebrows rose even higher. "About what?"

Meredith took a deep breath, then plunged. "About how I've fallen in love with you."

CHAPTER

Thirty-Seven

$\mathcal{S}$awyer nearly dropped his champagne flute. Had he heard her right?

"I love you, Sawyer," she repeated. "I love you like a wife loves a husband."

It was hard to breathe. He set the glass on the coffee table so he wouldn't drop it. How many years had he spent dreaming of hearing her say those words?

"You love me," he repeated.

She nodded, setting her own glass down. Her hair fell about her shoulders in soft waves, the makeup on her eyes making them look even wider than usual. But it was the black cocktail dress that was stealing most of his attention. It emphasized her new curves in a way he hadn't seen, and it took all of his restraint not to pull her into his arms and kiss her senseless.

Nothing had tested his self-control like the last month. Tasting Meredith and not going back for seconds felt like diving without a regulator—painful and stupid.

But as wonderful as that kiss had been, he'd known he couldn't take it at face value. Not when she was only five days out from major surgery and had just gotten out of the hospital.

"Mer." He took her hands gently in his, hoping she wouldn't notice how they trembled. "We're married and live together, and now we have the twins . . . I'm sure it's playing mind games—"

"Is it playing mind games with you?" she asked, her eyes sparkling with a fire he hadn't seen in months.

He'd missed that fire so much.

Maybe a better man would lie to her—say that he felt nothing more than friendship. Wait a year or two, so she had more time to get over John.

But that wasn't fair to either of them. And it wasn't what John would want.

"No," he said, letting his fingers gently caress her cheek. "No mind games here. I've been sure of my feelings for years."

When Meredith had seen him only as a friend, he'd been able to put his feelings aside and convince himself the chemistry between them was one-sided. But not anymore. Not when she was standing before him, admitting she loved him.

"Sawyer, do you get what I'm saying? I love you. I'm *in* love with you. I want to be your wife in every sense of the word. Maybe not today, or next week, or even next month. But I want a romantic relationship with you."

It was that first gulp of real air after surfacing from a dive—the rainbow at the end of a terrible storm. He knew Meredith's heart still belonged to John. It always would.

But it belonged to him, too. And he was more than willing to share.

He took her hand gently in his, reeling her in.

"Please say something," Meredith whispered, her voice trembling.

"Okay, I will." He cupped her cheek with one hand, fingers threading through the hair behind her ear. "Here are three words for you I mean with all of my heart: I love you. I've loved you since the day we met, and I've never stopped."

Her mouth fell open, goosebumps appearing on her neck and collarbone. He bent down, pressing his lips to the hollow of her throat.

She gasped, arching toward him. That was all the invitation he needed. He trailed kisses up her neck and across the line of her jaw before finally claiming her lips.

Meredith sank into him, wrapping her arms around the back of his neck and rising on tiptoes to better meet his kiss. He felt the contact in every nerve in his body, but forced himself to take it slow. They might be married, but he intended to date her like a proper gentleman.

The kiss was long and sweet and absolutely perfect. She leaned her head back, letting him trail more kisses across her neck before urging his lips to hers once more.

A loud grunt from one of the babies broke them apart. Sawyer glanced over at the girls, but they were perfectly content in their swings.

Meredith leaned her head against his shoulder with a ragged sigh. "Sawyer?" she asked, her voice husky.

He placed a tender kiss behind one ear, his hands resting on her hips and dragging her closer. "Yeah?"

She tilted her chin up a notch and didn't break eye contact. "You said you'd loved me since you met me. What did you mean?"

He rested his forehead against hers, the pain of those years without Meredith mixing with the hole in his life once filled with John's daily texts and weekly hangouts. "I mean I loved you even when it was wrong. I tried so hard to change how I felt, but it didn't matter how many women I dated. None of them could measure up to you."

From her wide eyes and stunned expression, he knew she'd never suspected a thing. He prayed John hadn't, either.

"But . . ." She blinked, her hands tightening around his neck. "Oh, Sawyer."

"I hope you know I never would have acted on those feelings." He brushed a strand of hair behind her ear. "Betraying John like that . . . I never even considered it."

"I believe you." She placed a hand on his cheek, her eyes filled with a love and respect that made him feel cherished in a way he never had before. "Even if John had known, he would never have felt threatened. You are one of the most honorable men I've ever met, and your actions through the years speak louder than any words ever could. I can't believe I didn't know."

He grinned, loving the way her hand on his cheek moved with the motion. "That was kind of the idea."

She shook her head, blinking quickly. "I don't know how to describe it. I love John so much, and never would have wished for this to happen. But I also can't imagine never getting to fall in love with you."

He tightened his hold on her hips, his heart swelling with love. "I feel the same way."

It was several long minutes before they once again surfaced for air, but the sound of a diaper being dirtied brought him back to reality.

Meredith laughed, pressed her hands flat against his chest. "I guess we better get used to interruptions."

"I wouldn't have it any other way."

"Me either." She tapped his chest. "I better go figure out which one of them needs to be changed."

He pressed a kiss gently to her forehead. "No, let me."

"Okay. I'd better check on dinner."

Both of the girls ended up needing diaper changes, so it was several minutes before he returned to the kitchen. When he did, he was surprised to find a manila envelope on the table with his name written across it in Meredith's familiar, loopy handwriting.

"What's this?" he asked, picking it up.

She set the pan of rolls she'd just pulled out of the oven on the top of the stove and leaned against the counter with one hand. "Open it."

He raised an eyebrow, trying to guess what was inside but coming up with nothing. He carefully undid the clasp on the envelope and pulled out the thick paper inside, flipping it over.

"The birth certificates," he said in surprise. While important, it made little sense why Meredith was being so mysterious. "I'm glad they finally came."

Her eyes sparkled. "Look closer."

"Okay." He read over the document, wondering if there was a typo. Had Savannah's name been changed to Sadie? Josie's to Jolene? But no, both of their names were spelled correctly, first and middle.

His eyes landed on the spot that said *father*.

Sawyer Grey.

He pressed a fist to his mouth, his eyes stinging with emotion. "You put my name on their birth certificates as the father."

She nodded, coming around the counter. "I didn't know that I could, but the lady at the hospital said since we're married, it would be legal to list you as the dad."

He set aside the birth certificates and crushed her to him. "This means everything to me," he whispered into her hair.

"*You* mean everything to us." She tightened her grip on him. "Me and the girls are so lucky to have you in our lives. I never want you or them to doubt that you are their father in every sense of the word."

"And John, too," Sawyer reminded her.

"Yes. John, too. If he'd known he wouldn't get to raise them himself, I know beyond any doubt that you would have been his first choice to replace him. For the girls and for me."

He pulled away, staring down at her. "You're amazing, you know that?"

"You're pretty amazing yourself."

A flash of silver caught Sawyer's eye at the hollow of her throat—her necklace. But something was different. A new charm rested next to the anchor with *refuse to sink* written on it.

"What's this?" He gingerly picked up the pendant, turning it over in his hand. It was a seagull with its wings open wide in flight. In its feet it held a banner. Sawyer squinted at the cursive writing.

Time to soar.

Tears sprang to his eyes, and this time, he couldn't hold them back. He leaned his head against her shoulder, emotion making him weak.

"I'm done simply trying not to sink," Meredith whispered, her hands threading through his hair. "With you by my side, I'm ready to soar."

SIX MONTHS LATER

"Savannah, stop pulling your sister's hair. That's not very nice." Meredith bent down in front of the stroller, swiftly pulling off her gloves so that she could save Josie from Savannah's iron grip. The girls were nearly eight months old now, and lately, pulling each other's hair seemed like their favorite hobby. The pediatrician assured her it was a sign that their hand-eye coordination was improving. She wasn't so sure.

Josie let out one last howl as Meredith freed her hair.

"Aw," she said with a chuckle, wiping away Josie's tears. "Here. Let's put your hat on so you two can stop tormenting each other."

She snuggly pulled the knit hats over both girls' ears, hoping that would do the trick.

Nearly eight months old. She couldn't believe it. They'd been exhausting, wonderful, stressful, amazing months of learning and growing with Sawyer.

Three months ago, she'd moved from the bedroom she shared with John into the new owner's suite with Sawyer. Eventually, she'd move the girls into the room she'd shared with their first father, but for now they'd converted it into a small photography studio. She'd mostly taken photos of the girls, but she'd gotten a few requests for studio photos from residents in town and had agreed to put them on her calendar. Sawyer said it was good for the girls to see their mother pursuing her passions, and Meredith had to agree. She didn't want to go back to working nearly as much as she had before closing the studio, but a few sessions a week gave her a creative outlet she desperately needed.

Sawyer jogged out of the old scuba shop, a flower arrangement Meredith had ordered in his hands. She'd been thrilled when a florist opened a store there. It was nice to know that someone else was living out their dream in the same place where John had lived out his.

"It looks great," Meredith said, admiring the arrangement. It was a large wreath of colorful autumn blooms, with a banner across the middle that read *refuse to sink*. A seashell anchor nestled behind it.

"Yeah, it turned out really nice," Sawyer agreed, setting the wreath carefully on the handlebars of the stroller. "We'll have to come by on Halloween—she's hosting a pumpkin carving contest."

"Sounds fun." Meredith placed a few yogurt bites on the girls' trays so they wouldn't get restless. "Ready?"

"Ready," Sawyer agreed.

Meredith tucked her arm into his as he pushed the stroller toward the cemetery. It was an unusually warm day for mid-October, and the brightly shining sun made it feel even warmer.

John would have loved having this kind of weather on his birthday—a rarity since moving to Oregon. She probably would have packed up the babies and headed to the beach, where she and Cheyenne would have kept the kids entertained while the men did a dive.

The memories of the past and alternate versions of the future were growing less painful to think about. She still had days when the grief took her breath away, but Sawyer was always there to hold together the pieces while she fell apart. Part of her had worried loving Sawyer would mean giving up John, but the opposite had been true. She and Sawyer talked more openly about their grief than ever before and worked through it together.

"You doing okay?" Sawyer asked quietly, glancing over at her.

The simple question threw her back over a year ago to when the world had come crumbling down around her. When she'd sobbed into Sawyer's shoulder at the hospital, her husband dead in the next room, she hadn't been sure if she'd ever be okay again.

She'd been drowning in a whirlpool, one hand reaching toward a sky she wasn't sure she'd ever see again. But Sawyer had grabbed her hand and pulled her into the sun once more.

"I'm okay," Meredith said, giving his arm a squeeze. "How are you doing?"

Sawyer sighed, his chest rising and falling. "I still miss him so much."

"Me too."

It was confusing to want John back so much, while knowing she could never give up Sawyer. She loved them both so much, just in different but equally powerful ways.

"I was just thinking about how he'd have been begging to go for a dive today, since the weather's so nice," Meredith said.

Sawyer laughed. "Oh yeah, he definitely would've dragged me and Zach into the freezing ocean."

"And after the dive, we all would have gone back to our house for cake and ice cream."

"We're still doing that," Sawyer pointed out. "What time did you say Zach, Cheyenne, and Bailey were stopping by?"

"Five-thirty." Cheyenne was pregnant again, and Meredith couldn't wait to find out what she was having in another few weeks. It would be nice to add a little boy to their group.

They entered the tall iron gates of the cemetery, the girls babbling incoherently as they gummed the yogurt bites on their stroller trays. Sawyer pushed the stroller up the small hill to where John's grave rested underneath a tall maple tree.

"Ready to say hi to Daddy?" Meredith asked the girls, leaning down to unbuckle them from the stroller.

She and Sawyer both took a baby, wrapped tightly in a blanket, and sat on the bench overlooking the headstone.

"Should we sing happy birthday?" Sawyer asked.

Meredith smiled, instantly warming to the idea. "Yeah, let's do it."

The two of their voices joined in a very off-tune rendition of the song, and by the end, they were both laughing and wiping away tears.

"That was awful," Meredith said, grabbing Savannah's fingers before they could tug at her necklace.

Sawyer shrugged, grinning. "Well, John knows we aren't rock stars."

"Here, hold her so I can place the wreath."

The bright yellow of the sunflowers and deep orange of the roses and mums stood out starkly against the black granite stone. She crouched down, pressing her fingers to her lips before touching his name.

Things felt different today. Part of her ached at the unexpected shift her future was about to take once more. She had loved John fiercely and deeply, and part of her always would.

But she also had learned to move forward with Sawyer.

Meredith pressed a hand unconsciously to her stomach. They'd planned to wait a year or so before trying for another baby, but last week she'd started feeling nauseous and taken a test.

The positive result had come as a major shock, and at first she'd been terrified to have another baby so soon after the twins. But with Sawyer by her side, she knew they'd weather this latest change just fine.

She'd ordered shirts online for the girls that said *Big Sis*. They'd be here by the weekend, and she couldn't wait to see the look on Sawyer's face when he learned the news.

She rose, taking Savannah from Sawyer. He shifted Josie into his other arm and wrapped an arm around Meredith's waist.

"I was thinking," he said. "The girls are going to be crawling soon."

Meredith laughed. "Yeah, and we'll have to childproof every inch of the house."

"That's not what I was talking about." Sawyer rolled his eyes, then pointed to John's grave. "I was thinking I should build a small sandbox to put over John's final resting place. That way, when we come to visit, the girls can play with their daddy. I've seen some plans online that look really nice, and I already spoke to the cemetery sexton and got his okay for the project."

Every day, she thought she couldn't possibly fall more in love with Sawyer.

Every day, he proved her wrong.

"That's a great idea," Meredith said, leaning into him. She rose on her tiptoes, giving him a brief kiss. "John would love that, and so will the girls."

"I don't want any of you to ever feel like I'm replacing John." He tightened his hold on her. "He deserves to be remembered."

"He will be." She tightened her hold on Savannah, who squirmed to get down. Both babies were rolling all over the house now and by Christmas she knew they'd be crawling everywhere.

She could already imagine what this spot would look like next summer—Sawyer and the girls playing with matchbox cars in the sandbox while she sat on the bench with her brand-new baby in her arms.

A cool breeze swept through the cemetery. She pulled the blanket more tightly around Savannah and adjusted Josie's blanket, then leaned into Sawyer with a shiver.

Sawyer didn't suggest they leave because it was getting cold. He just held her silently, allowing her the space to feel.

I miss you, John, she whispered. *But I'm happy. I'm okay. We all are.*

The breeze stirred her hair again, and she could almost imagine it was John running his fingers through her curls.

"I love you," Sawyer murmured, kissing her temple.

She looked up at him, smiling. "I love you, too. Let's go home."

"You sure?"

She nodded, pressing her cheek against Savannah's warm one. "Yeah. I think it's time we gave these girls a tiny taste of carrot cake. Don't you?"

Vanessa set the last can of food in the box and paused, puffing out an exaggerated breath so that the strand of hair stuck to her sweaty forehead moved out of her eyes.

Her small kitchen apartment was nearly empty now, save for the boxes stacked along one wall. Just that morning, she'd taken her nursing boards, and while the test had been challenging, she was confident she'd passed. Well, ninety percent sure, at least.

She could hear the faint rumblings of a video game from where Grayson played in his room. He'd helped her pack for a little while, but eventually grown bored and asked if he could go play instead. She hadn't minded.

Four years of school as a single mom. It hadn't been easy to move states away from any family support and do school, work, and parenting alone. But she'd done it.

The phone rang, and she smiled when she saw Meredith's number scroll across it.

"Hey," she said. "Still pregnant?"

"I feel like a whale," Meredith groaned. "If I haven't had him by next week, Dr. Mike said he'd induce me."

"He's just waiting for his Aunt Vanessa to come before arriving." She reached for another box—time to pack their small stack of plates and bowls. She had a few paper ones they could use for dinner tonight and breakfast in the morning.

"Hurry up, then. I'm so done being pregnant. Chasing after the twins with a bowling ball stuck to your stomach is no joke."

Grayson let out a yell of frustration from his bedroom—he'd probably lost a life in the game or something. A twinge of regret made her heart ache. Grayson was seven now, and she hadn't really dated anyone since Andrew's death other than the odd meetup for coffee with one of the guys from school. Her son would never know what it was like to have a sibling close in age.

But she'd grown up an only child and turned out just fine. Sure, it had been lonely, but she'd also gotten her parents' undivided attention. That wasn't a bad thing.

"Oops, got to go," Meredith said. "Sounds like the girls are waking up from their nap. If I don't go in there soon, they'll have smeared poop all over the walls again."

Vanessa winced. "Did you try putting their pajamas on backwards?"

"Yes, and they still got out of them somehow." Meredith sighed, but Vanessa heard the happiness behind the exhaustion.

"Go," Vanessa said. "No one wants a poop portrait."

"Ain't that the truth. Drive safely tomorrow, okay? Text me updates, so I know you aren't stranded on the side of the road in Idaho or something."

Vanessa laughed. She'd grown pretty independent over the past few years and the thought of making the forty-three hour drive towing a moving trailer with only Grayson for company didn't bother her. She and Grayson would be just fine.

They always were.

"Can't wait to see you," Meredith said. "We'll catch up for real once you get settled in at your parents."

"Will do," Vanessa said, then hung up.

She resumed packing the last of the kitchen, her mind wandering back to the unlikely romance that had blossomed between Meredith and Sawyer. Vanessa had wondered if something like that might happen when she'd encouraged Meredith to accept Sawyer's proposal over a year ago, but she'd been surprised at how quickly things had progressed. Not that she'd felt any misgivings. Sawyer and Meredith were so great together.

Vanessa rose on tiptoes, grabbing the last two glasses from the back of the cabinet. Her hands closed around stemware and she paused, instantly knowing what she held.

Not glasses. Champagne flutes.

Slowly, she pulled them out of the cabinet. One glass said *bride* while the other said *groom*, with the date of their wedding below two interlocked hearts.

They would have been married almost ten years now. Would his hair have started thinning yet? Would his stomach have developed a little paunch?

Would she have discovered his secrets or still been in the dark?

Vanessa took a deep breath, then carefully wrapped the glasses in newspaper.

She and Grayson were starting a new chapter of their lives in Sapphire Cove. Grayson had never spent more than a few weeks there during break, but Vanessa was confident he'd love being a permanent resident. It had been a great place to grow up, and Grayson would love it just as much as she had.

Maybe it was time for her to start a new chapter, too—not just career-wise or location-wise, but relationship-wise. She wouldn't have the demands of school anymore, and her parents would be close by and more than eager to babysit whenever asked.

Maybe it was time to put herself out there again. To go on more than a casual date once every six months.

She thought again of Meredith and Sawyer's happiness together. Vanessa wanted that for herself. And this time, it wouldn't be an illusion.

Slowly she taped the box holding her wedding champagne flutes closed, then took a deep, cleansing breath.

She made herself a promise—to finally be open to love again.

In Sapphire Cove.

Vanessa's ready to risk her heart once more... But is she ready for the doctor who wants to win it?

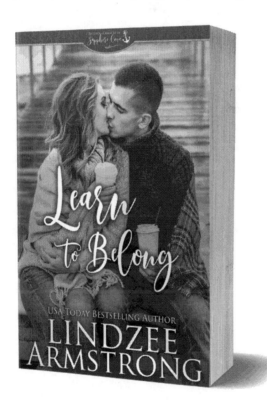

ABOUT THE

LINDZEE ARMSTRONG is the *USA Today* bestselling author of more than twenty romances. She met her true love while at college, where she graduated with a bachelor's in history education. They are now happily married and raising twin boys in the Rocky Mountains. Like any true romantic, Lindzee loves chick flicks, ice cream, and chocolate. She believes in sigh-worthy kisses and happily ever afters, and loves expressing that through her writing.

To find out about future releases and to join Lindzee's newsletter, visit her website at www.LindzeeArmstrong.com.

If you enjoyed this book, please take a few minutes and leave a review. This is the best way you can say thank you to an author! It really helps other readers discover books they might enjoy. Thank you!